OUR SATYR PRINCE

Our Satyr Prince

Myth Shifters · Book One

Dylan Drakes

UNRELIABLE NARRATORS

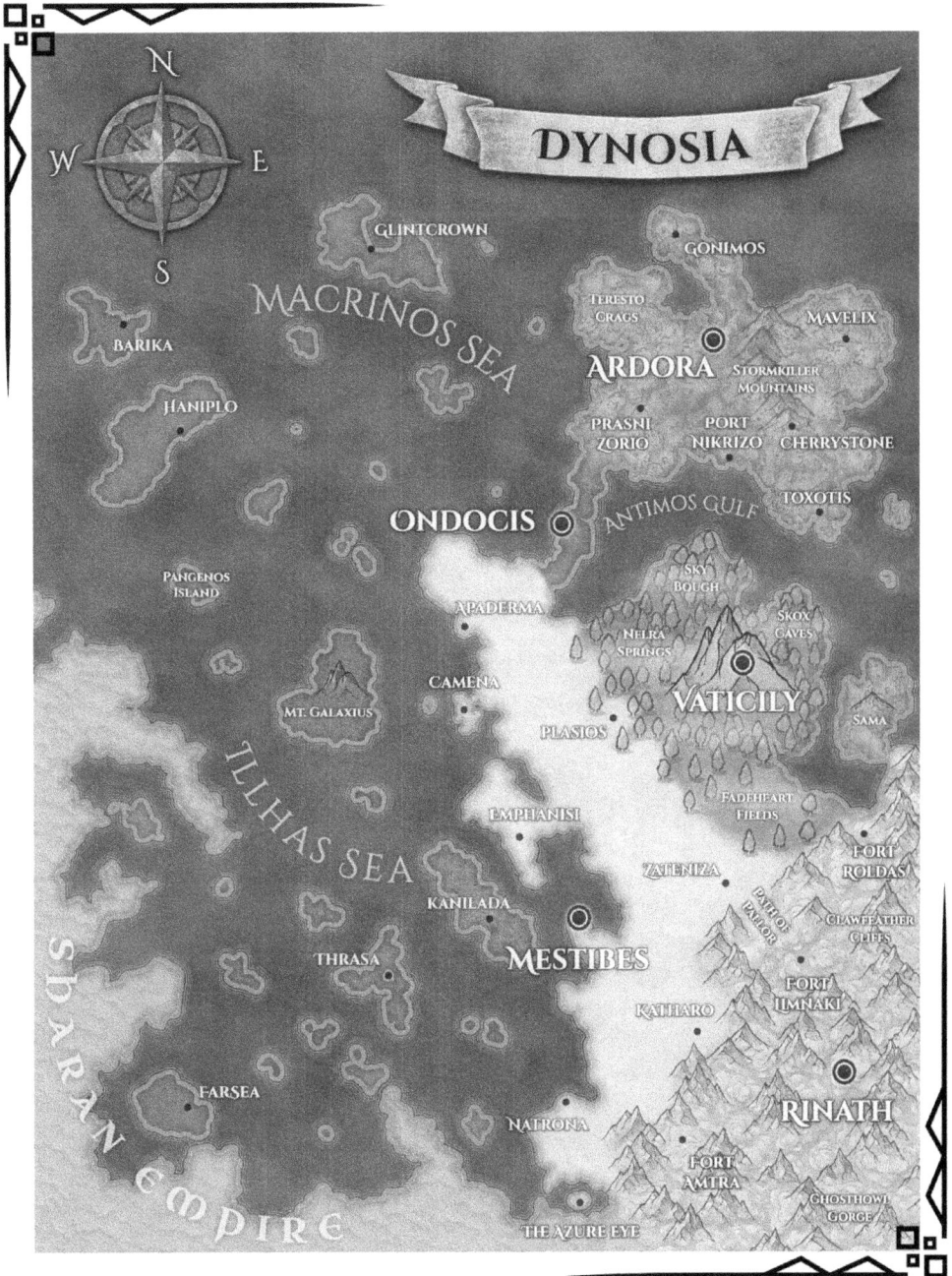

MAP

DYNOSIA

MACRINOS SEA

ANTIMOS GULF

ILLHAS SEA

SBARAN EMPIRE

N
W   E
S

GLINTCROWN

GONIMOS

TERESTO CRAGS

MAVELIX

BARIKA

ARDORA

STORMKILLER MOUNTAINS

HANIPLO

PRASNI ZORIO

PORT NIKRIZO

CHERRYSTONE

TOXOTIS

ONDOCIS

PANGENOS ISLAND

APADERMA

SKY BOUGH

SKOX CAVES

NELRA SPRINGS

CAMENA

VATICILY

SAMA

MT. GALAXIUS

PLASIOS

FADEHEART FIELDS

EMPHANISI

ZATENIZA

FORT ROLDAS

PATH OF PALLOR

CLAWFEATHER CLIFFS

KANILADA

THRASA

MESTIBES

FORT IIMNAKI

KATIARO

FARSEA

RINATH

NATRONA

FORT AMTRA

GHOSTHOWL GORGE

THE AZURE EYE

CONTENT WARNING

Some readers prefer forewarning about potentially confronting content. If you are not one of these readers, *beware some spoilers ahead*. This section is not required reading, and you will not miss anything by skipping it.

This book is intended for an adult audience. Although this story takes place in an original fantasy world, violence and prejudice are handled in a manner typical during Classical Antiquity (the era of the Ancient Greeks and Ancient Romans).

The following content is most likely to be of concern to some readers:

Racial and Religious

- Prejudicial language against fictional races and nationalities.

Queer

- Bi-erasure.
- Homophobia.

Mental Health

- PTSD / reliving trauma.

Sexual Content

- Explicit sex.

Violence (inc. sexual violence) and Death

- Death of a parent.
- Domestic violence (nonsexual).
- Gore.
- Sexual harm.

A more detailed content warning, including information about which chapters this content occurs in (where feasible), <u>is located at the very back of the book.</u>

The above content warning <u>is not an exhaustive list</u>. It is my best attempt at identifying content most likely to be of concern to the greatest number of readers.

Each reader has different content concerns, thresholds, and tolerances. If you have any specific content concerns that might prevent you from enjoying this story, please reach out to me at <u>www. dylandrakes.com</u> (or @thedylandrakes on socials). I will do my best to advise whether that content is present.

To my precious pixies.

I couldn't have done this without you.

Children born between a mortal and one of the Five High Gods are sometimes treated as a blessing. Some even dare to call them "demi-gods."

But nothing could be further from the truth.

Satyrs? Phoenixes? Sirens? Eidolons? Gorgons?

These five wretched creatures are "therians"—twisted children of the divine, thirsting for a godly power that they will never manage to quench. And on nights of the sable moon, when all is darkest, they reveal their true nature.

– from Gods, Myths and Beasts by Lapiso

UROSINA

MIDNIGHT WHIPPED THROUGH HER CLOAK. HOOVES POUNDED AGAINST the long-dry ravine, rendered ink-black under the moonless sky.

"Faster, Burascus!" screamed Urosina Savair, Herald of Mestibes, to the steaming white pegasus beneath her. His left wing had been badly broken in the ambush, but he somehow found a new burst of speed.

Her breath slapped off the high, ice-crested rocks in a mix of determination and panic. For all her thirty-seven years, she had trusted the warnings about riding at night through the Path of Pallor, the lifeless strip that separated the polities of Mestibes and Rinath. Legends said that an incautious rider could fall victim to a hideous keres—particularly now, on the dark night of the sable moon, when the protections of the goddess were at their weakest.

And on any other night, Urosina would have heeded those warnings. But no bat-winged beast could be worse than what was pursuing her.

If it even *was* pursuing her.

She didn't know.

She didn't dare look around.

All she could do was ride.

This whole situation was madness. The herald of Mestibes was supposed to be untouchable. To attack them was an act of war!

But this information?

This secret?

It was worth killing for.

Ahead, the ravine opened to the long bridge over the Synoro River, the true border between their territories. She pushed Burascus forward, willing every last glimmer from his fading physique. When they finally neared the stone, she allowed herself a desperate glance behind. Her stomach twisted, anticipating the horrors in pursuit.

But there was nothing. The only thing in her wake was the cloud of fine dust, expanding to fill the vast hollow.

She slowed her oldest friend, first to a canter, then to a trot. His own exhales rasped in the cold night. It would still be two days ride at full pace to the city proper, and she didn't want to risk laming him any further.

Not after all he had been through.

Not now they were finally safe.

Safe . . .

She clapped him affectionately on the neck. They were *safe*! Mother Mesti, they had done it! They'd escaped with the information the archon had demanded. The information that would save them all!

Far below, the rushing waters forged a path through the lands ahead—a path that would lead to their destination: *Mestibes*, the city of diplomacy, philosophy, art, and finest crafts. The most rational and reasonable of the five high polities of Dynosia. The one that had kept the balance of peace these last twenty-two years.

The sweat along her neck cooled in the frost-heavy night. Then, just as the slow clack of hooves hit the bridge, Urosina caught an orange glow in her periphery, lighting the dust as if a midnight dawn.

She turned, mouth agape.

The entire ravine was now a wall of flame.

A wall that was flying right toward her.

She gripped Burascus's leads, making to crack him back to a gallop, but her chest tightened. Before she knew what was happening, she'd crashed to the stone, her whole body shaking. And as she struggled to regain control of herself, she was overcome with a feeling she had never experienced before.

Terror.

Not fear. Not apprehension. But an utter and total terror. A terror so strong that she couldn't breathe, she couldn't think, she couldn't move.

And in that hideous moment, as the flames bore down, she knew she was about to die.

Her whole life had been worthless. She was just a sad, useless woman. She *knew* this, more clearly than she had ever known anything before. There was no use fighting it. All she could do was lay down and—

No! she screamed internally, rising up against the foreign thoughts. With the flames just seconds away, she remembered all that was at stake.

Sister! You have to know the danger that is coming!

"Go!" she yelled to Burascus, who squealed in protest. He would never knowingly leave her in peril, but a hard slap to his rump convinced him to flee.

She drew her kopis knife as the flames screeched across her. The pain was immeasurable. She could feel her hair melting and the fire being sucked into her lungs with each cursed breath.

But compared to that deathly heat, the blade tip that cut through the bubbling flesh of her forearm, carving out what little message she could muster, barely even registered.

She . . . has . . . to . . . know . . .

With the last of her strength, she rolled from the bridge.

There came the sensation of falling, the world tumbling around her.

Within the fire above, a figure seemed to form—a great set of incandescent wings, rising in furious, feminine glory.

Goddess, I thought the therians were just a myth . . .

Then came the smack of the water, the roil of the river, and the cold, soothing darkness of death.

1

AURELIUS

The conflict in Nihal's face was intoxicating.

At first, the low priest's eyes bulged with the sheer force of his orgasm, quaking so hard across Aurelius's tongue that he feared the twenty-one-year-old might buckle back against the old marble. Then, as the ecstasy subsided, Nihal's face swept with a medley of other emotions—guilt, residual bliss, and the knowledge that he'd once again fallen to sin.

Aurelius Savair, eldest child of the archon of Mestibes, could see all these emotions bashing through his oldest friend's face. And there was nothing in all Dynosia that was better than that look.

He'd known Nihal since they were children, being just one month apart in age. And he knew exactly what the only son of the high priestess of Mesti would be thinking. He'd be flogging himself with some sanctimonious rot about this not being *proper* behavior.

Not for someone who had devoted their life to the goddess of reason.

Not for someone who was supposed to be chaste to all "irrational" pleasures.

Nihal slumped back, his heavy white toga grouped around his

groin. Stone crunched underfoot from the unswept floor as he steadied his shaking legs. His brow was slicked with sweat, despite the high spring breeze that caressed the abandoned peak of the old Libercropolis, shrouding them in silence, and granting an infinite panorama over the otherwise bustling city.

Aurelius's private residence would have been far more comfortable for the occasion, rather than the long derelict library—it being his beautiful refuge of golds and silks and fragrant oils, creating a sensuous cloud of carnal delight in which he often indulged.

But that wouldn't do for Nihal, would it?

Aurelius rose, coming nose to nose with the boy whose gaze was diverted onto the shrubby grass between the yellow-flecked marble of the library and the dull gray limestone of the cliff. He waited, just like he always did, until Nihal looked back into his ice-blue eyes, framed by his permanently tousled shag of blond.

Only then did he swallow.

Heavily.

Extravagantly.

Making sure there was no way Nihal could deny it. Making his face once again wash with all that delicious conflict.

Oh yes. There is nothing better than this!

"We . . . we can't keep doing this, Aurie," Nihal panted.

Aurelius gave him an innocent smile. "Really, Hal? Like this wasn't your idea? *A chance to get away from it all? To climb to the ruins and forget about this terrible turn of events?*"

"And I meant it! I didn't . . ." The shame washed strong on his still-red cheeks. "I wasn't trying to take advantage of your grief."

Aurelius placed his friend's hand beneath his tunic—a sumptuous, saffron-yellow silk, damasked in gold with motifs of musical instruments, craftsmen's tools, and great scrolls of learning. "Does it feel like I was being taken advantage of?" he said, running the fingers against his hardness.

He delighted in the faint grip and ungrip against his bulge. Nihal wanted it. He'd been cooped up for months in the priesthood, running through all the little rituals and restraints that came with his holy training. Now, all he needed was one last push into temptation.

"And if you *really* wanted to take my mind off the grief, I know something that might help," he whispered.

With a groan like a wounded animal, Nihal eased himself from the gap between man and marble. "I'm serious, Aurie! This has got to be the last time. For Mesti's sake, I'm getting initiated as a mid priest next month. Mother would *literally* kill me if she knew this was still going on!"

Aurelius shrugged and lifted his tunic, revealing skin the color of milky mountain tea. His stiff cock bounced up to greet the cloudless sky.

Nihal failed to avert his gaze. "What are you doing?"

"Hal, I completely respect your decisions. I have been wicked to tempt you so. You just run back down to the Pentheon, like a good boy." Aurelius's eyes twinkled as he tended to himself. "But I saved up for three whole days. I know that's how you like it. And if you don't want it, I can't have it burning a hole through my balls during the service!"

Nihal's hands shook. Aurelius could practically taste the war between lust and light. And as the pleasure tingled through him, he knew it was time for a final act of wickedness.

He flexed his diaphragm, causing a single drop of dew to leak from his long stem.

And Nihal lost the battle.

The boy dove to the white dirt, swallowing him whole. Aurelius groaned at his force, sending waves of relief up his spine. Nihal was ravenous, choking himself on the length then pulling back, only to take it all again.

As he was devoured, Aurelius ran fingers through his lover's chestnut hair. The tension built with every swipe, a torrent yearning for liberation. Nihal was an expert. After so many years at play, he knew the meaning of every shudder and every sigh. With his free hand, the boy reached up and pinned Aurelius back against the column. Aurelius grabbed his wrist, willing even more force into his chest. Just like the force that was rising all through him!

The poison exploded in waves of ecstasy, causing his whole body to spasm.

When the shocks at last subsided, Aurelius looked down at Nihal's beautiful face. There was no conflict there anymore. No guilt as he brought himself up, eye to eye, and swallowed with the same enthusiasm that Aurelius himself had done.

Aurelius knew what was coming next, and turned just in time to dodge the kiss, sending Hal's lips to his smooth neck instead, where they took up a grateful nuzzle.

As they both caught their breath, and the thrill of the moment faded to the familiar desire for space, Aurelius wondered why Hal so insisted on ruining these rare moments.

They both knew what their relationship was. They knew what they could have, and what they couldn't.

And *kissing*? That wasn't part of it.

Not for the last six years.

Not since Hal had fucked it all up.

He was relieved when a sound from far below broke the moment —the ureglias calling the mourners to the Pentheon, the temple to the Five High Gods of the Pentariat. From this height, he could track the build and sway of the song across the neatly laid-out polity. It started first as a single voice, down near the Senate—imposing and grand and orderly. It rose through the art galleries and music halls, the workshops and the sculptors' studios, past the Forum that held the monthly symposium of finest art and debate and music, through the newer, even grander Lapiso Library, all the way round to the plebian suburbs behind them, much less loved and much less lovely.

Nihal's face blanched. "Oh, Mesti! She'll kill me for this!"

"Relax. Half of the city will be in attendance. It will take them forever to file in."

"But I'm supposed to be at the front of the procession! And you! You can't be late for your own aunt's funeral."

Aurelius adjusted himself with a bitter laugh and no apparent haste. "Believe me, no one is expecting the fuck-up of House Savair to be arriving on time."

No, they'll be expecting a grand entrance.

And I intend to give them one.

2

TEIGRA

THE CLENCH OF HER JAW DID NOTHING TO STOP THE TEARS.

Teigra Cosmin repeated the mantras from childhood lectures. That restraint was piety. That reason was perfection. And that emotion and impulsivity—those most bestial of human traits—were an affront to the goddess of reason, artistry, and the night sky.

Here in the Pentheon, flanked on all sides by mourners and the enormous bronze statues of the Five, those mantras should have meant something. They should have given Teigra the strength to hold her pain back.

And yet, she couldn't. The drips collected along the strong lines of the eighteen-year-old's chin, to be wiped away cautiously with fingers rough from labor.

Stopping the flow was pointless. How could she *not* feel this way? How could she stop the rip in her chest, so sharp and so deep she could barely breathe?

How could she stop it when up there, upon a dais overseen by the high priestess herself, was *Aunty Urosina*.

Up there was the woman who had never cared about rank and precedent and the appropriateness of dealing with House Cosmin.

The woman who saw the blood of leaders that flowed through Teigra's veins, not just the blood of peasants that the rest of the ruling class saw. The woman who, for eighteen wonderful years, no matter how short her time back in Mestibes, would find the time to visit Teigra. To train her. To give her fair counsel. To share her vast and impressive wisdom from all over the country.

This was the woman who three pain-wracked years ago, as the rest of the city had whispered cruelty behind their hands, staring at Teigra like she was some kind of criminal, had publicly approached her. Only her and cousin Aurelius had dared.

And now . . . she was dead.

It was impossible.

It was tragic.

It was as numbing as winter sea spray, despite the thousands of citizens crowded around her.

It was—

"Gods girl, clean your face! We have work to do!" came an unemotive hiss at her back.

She clenched her fists as the figure pushed past, grabbing Teigra firmly by the arm and dragging her through the press. She didn't dare look up from the polished marble of the Pentheon floor, glimpsed through the rushing gaps between togas and stolas and sandals.

She didn't dare, because she *knew* what was coming. And her blood pulsed hot at the shame of it all.

The ceremony had only just ended. The former herald's burned skin had only just been anointed with the fragrant oils that would hasten her journey to the fields of Evdonia. Her hands had only just been closed around the golden axia coin, currency to pay Vakaris, ferryman of the dark river Telikos. The other women of her extended family, including Aunty Sabina, *the archon herself*, were still holding vigil over the body!

And Mother was already working the floor.

"Senator Viturin?" said Senator Beeta Cosmin, pulling up in front of a proud man with a receding hairline. His white toga was edged with two stripes as yellow as fennel flower—the mark of the patrician class, the pinnacle of Mestibian society. One with the high honor of having *two* members of his house in the senate.

Of course, Mother would speak to *him*. She wouldn't waste her time on anyone dressed like themselves, in the single-striped garments of the mercator class. Or worse, to one of the plebeians at the back, too far down the rope to have any stripes at all.

Normally, a man like Gius Viturin could have just waved her away. He was consul of the senate, after all. Second in charge of the citizen's chamber after the censor.

But he can't do that today, can he? Not at the funeral of her own sister.

The patrician gave Mother a weary look. "Yes, Senator Cosmin?"

"I do not believe you have met my son, Jaronas?"

On cue, a boy of sixteen stepped forward, gripping the patrician's hand before he could extend it. "Rejoice, Patrician!"

Viturin grimaced. "Rejoice, Mercator. My condolences."

The tart insincerity of the consul's voice clenched Teigra's jaw even tighter. He wasn't sorry to see the archon's personal messenger killed, and everyone knew it. Teigra had heard the muffled whispers and barely hidden opinions. Viturin would rather that the position of herald didn't exist. That the *archon* didn't exist. That the senate ran the city on its own!

Even here, at Urosina's *funeral*, the consul couldn't bring himself to put aside petty politics.

Her thoughts were broken by Jaronas thumping a fist to his well-built chest. "Gratitude! But the men of House Cosmin are as strong as our steeds! Neither we, nor the beasts we break, dwell on such things as loss!"

The patrician weighed him. "You are too young to recall, young mercator, but I had my own racing team managed by House Cosmin for many years. Before *the incident*, of course."

Teigra gasped involuntarily, caught unprepared.

The incident . . .

Her heart felt at once like it would burst and yet never beat again.

The room dulled around her—sound muffled. Her forehead prickled hot, and her stomach felt heavy and rotted, like it was full of rusted iron.

She clenched her eyes shut as the dizziness overtook her, trying to drown out the nightmares never far from reemergence.

No! Not here! Not in front of the consul! Don't you dare disgrace the family!

Not again . . .

After long and hideous moments, she forced the heat from across her ears, forced *the incident* from her mind, and the sound of the room returned.

She wasn't sure how much time had passed, but the consul was in high spirits, midstory.

". . . with my hippocamp churning through the water at such speed the others could never hope to catch us!"

Jaronas laughed. "But that shows your cunning, wise consul. Even though there are three stallions in each relay team, far too many people waste their coin on the most famous centaurs for the first lap. Housing them in luxury. Catering to their every extravagant whim. Or, they'll invest all their time in the spectacle of the pegasus for the final lap. But a good hippocamp can gain more time through the water of the second lap than a centaur through sand or a pegasus through air!"

Her brother leaned forward. But not before passing a glance to the dais. Teigra's stomach twisted once more. The sight of their fallen aunt didn't bring a look of sorrow to her brother's face.

It brought a *smirk*.

"After all," Jaronas continued. "Balance is what *really* matters. In all things. Don't you find?"

The consul grew a dark, self-satisfied look. "Wise words, young mercator. It is pleasing to know that even on a day such as this, House Cosmin remembers where its true loyalties lie."

Wise words?

True loyalties?

Teigra didn't need to see Mother's face to know it would be beaming. And as the woman placed a loving hand on Jaronas's shoulder, the smirks and snorts continuing, another piece of her heart shattered across the marble.

Time was that her younger brother would laugh at Mother's obsession with status and social climbing. Time was they would roll their eyes together as she'd insinuate their family on events above their station, flirting desperately and making outlandish claims about their steeds.

But now? Now he was standing beside her. Rabbiting *her* statements. Speaking in that ridiculous, overenthusiastic tone that *she'd* taught him.

"And this must be your son, Domenin?" said Mother to the boy at Viturin's side.

Teigra knew it was. The young senator was eighteen, but still possessed a toddler's entitlement. His two-striped toga hung heavily on his scrawny frame, like laundry draped across a leafless sapling.

"I don't believe you've met my daughter, Teigra?" Mother continued.

And just like that, Teigra was shoved forward, barely able to suppress her rising shame.

She had no desire to join this awful display. She'd rather have pushed through the crowds and kneeled beside the archon. To take the wise hands of Granny Varena. To show deserved respect to Aunty Ura!

But her personal wishes meant nothing. Teigra knew what her duty was.

She gulped, and a hidden pendant around her neck felt even heavier than its usual choking weight.

Mother had once told her that a noble house was like a fine cloth —it only took one loose thread to weaken the whole twill.

And she wouldn't be that loose thread upon House Cosmin.

Not again.

Never, ever again.

"Rejoice, Patrician," she said, making her voice as high and light as she could.

"Mmm," Domenin grunted, without looking at her. She followed his gaze to a beautiful young woman across the temple. Her own face flushed red, and she made no effort to regain his attention.

He was right to pay her no mind. Not in the presence of *that* maiden.

Where the maiden's hair was short and styled, glowing like sun-soaked saffron, her own hair was long and curly, like the mane of a Caravagi stallion. Where the maiden's skin was soft and light as goat's milk, hers was sun-browned, her hands betraying roughness from years of predawn starts in the stables. Where the maiden's body traced the soft curves of ideal womanhood, her own flesh bulged in all the wrong places—slender around the hips and breasts, with shoulders made strong from years of carrying feed, and legs taught from a childhood of unwomanly activities.

She almost jumped when Mother's nail pressed into her back. It served two purposes. First, to encourage her to keep going with this pathetic flirtation. And second, to push her meager assets forward, placing her body *in a more pleasing posture.*

"So," said Teigra, not letting the waxen smile drip from her face, "is it true your family prepared *all* of the marble in the Pentheon?"

The boy scoffed. "Of course, I thought everyone knew tha—"

For the first time, Domenin met her eyes. And his look made Teigra yearn once again for his disinterest.

You . . . It screamed, heavy with the weight of all she was unable to forget. *You're Teigra Cosmin! You're the freak who—*

"Domenin . . ." warned the elder Viturin.

"Ah, to be young again," said Mother. "Why don't you take Teigra on a tour while your father and I talk?"

The boy shot Teigra a disgusted glare, before receiving the nod from his father. "*Fine.*"

As they weaved through the mourners, Domenin rattled on half-heartedly about the history of the temple—of the meaning of the dome and of the lore of the Five High Gods and their myriad offspring of lesser deities that made up the divine and extended family that was the Galaxians.

At each step, he sought to increase his distance, pushing into those sections of the crowd far from the powerful and the proper.

He can't even bear to be seen with me. Even now, three years on.

As Teigra face burned hot with shame and the sharp spikes of memory, she searched the crowd for the one person who might be able to release her from this torture.

For Evdonia's sake, Aurelius! Where are you?

3

AURELIUS

Every eye in the temple fell on him, sweeping in amongst the funeral dirges to Telos Rina, God of Death. As he moved through the nobodies at the back of the crowd, past the plebeian scum and mercator wannabes, he could almost *taste* their condemnation.

Arriving late to his own aunt's funeral!

And what is he wearing? A golden cloak and tunic? Where is his toga?

Well, what do you expect? Everyone knows what sort of man he is.

A man? More like a beast. No better than the uncivilized hordes that did away with poor Ura.

Aurelius let the hate wash over him—giving him energy, giving him life. He knew they'd be talking about him anyway.

At least this way they'd be talking on *his* terms.

He cut through the masses until he found poor Teigra, having her ears chewed off by the Viturin boy. He was a nasty sort, whose charm was as thin as his limbs.

But still, he was not without his uses.

Teigra caught Aurelius's eyes through the crowd and started stroking her proud locks of auburn hair, running in a thick braid over her shoulder, the twists barely containing the curling desire within each strand. It was the sort of vibrant, healthy mass that the other girls must surely envy.

On seeing their code, he swooped in and kissed her on both cheeks. "Tiggy, darling, so lovely to see you. Do you mind if I borrow the good patrician for a moment?"

Teigra's face twisted into a disappointed expression before she melted gratefully back among the mourners.

"Goddess save me, Savair," said Domenin, once she had departed. "How many people saw me with that freak? After what she *did*? It will take weeks to wash out the stink of her residual scandal. And her mother? She must be the most colossal bore in the city. I don't know how you handle them."

"Come, Viturin. Surely no one could be bored in *your* presence."

He puffed his bony chest out. "I wouldn't have thought so."

Those at the back of the crowd, too distant from power to understand anything of worth, might have wondered why the young senator was speaking to *him*. After all, Aurelius was a known pervert. An affront to the goddess of reason! And Domenin was a rising power. A future censor of the senate if he rolled his dice right.

But what they didn't understand, but those who mattered most certainly did, was that Aurelius derived his power through *other* means. Even as he chatted away, moving forward into the better part of the crowd, half-a-dozen other young patricians circled in his near vicinity, all awaiting their own turn to talk.

The reason for his allure was simple: Aurelius made it his business to know things. And better still, he made it his business to ensure that everyone *knew* that he knew things.

Through careful planning, he had turned this into a self-fulfilling cycle—an ouroboros of gossip. Being seen at his side made one's rivals nervous of what naughty little secrets he was passing on. Nervous enough to share some gossip of their own.

And what scandals he couldn't learn of, he'd found pleasurable ways to create for himself.

And yet, despite all he had done to claw his way back from the shit heap of irrelevance, it still wasn't enough. This *impression* of power he had built for himself wasn't enough.

The barely worn toga in his bedroom bore two hollow stripes along its edge—indicating someone from a patrician family, but not themselves a senator.

And after six years of struggle, those stripes would soon be *filled*.

"Tragic business," said Aurelius. "The herald of Mestibes murdered? Washed ashore all the way out in Zateniza?"

"I hear that if not for the half-melted signet ring, they may never have identified her."

"What is Dynosia coming to when a crown's representative becomes fair game?"

"Well, what do you expect? The Rinathi wouldn't know honor if it sucked their cocks. What shocked me was that she was up there at all. The archon can send her sad little pet wherever she likes, but I thought Ura was still up in Ardora, groveling to those ungrateful goatfuckers."

"Indeed," said Aurelius, noncommittedly. Truthfully, he hadn't known of the herald's redeployment either. But it never paid to advertise one's ignorance.

"And so," said Domenin, with a knowing smirk, "all of Mestibes asks: who will the archon chose as her new representative to the backwards polities?"

"Don't play coy, Domi. I've barely seen a senator around town since the body was returned. I doubt you've been conferencing on the price of Ondocian silk."

"My, my. Can it really be? Aurelius Savair, out of the gossip loop?"

"Even I can't read minds."

"Well," said Domenin, smugly, "the subject of the new herald *may* have come up in our private conferencing, Aurie. Informally of course. But it would be most improper for a humble senator to speculate on such things *here*—it being entirely a decision for the archon. I wouldn't dream on stepping on the crown's toes, just as she wouldn't dream of stepping on the senate's."

Up to the dais, a younger and infinitely less handsome version of Aurelius, with the gall to have two solid stripes on his toga, slithered among the powerful. "Of course, Domi. Or course. But should the new herald come from within your own ranks—*Benedict*, for example —you would surely have heard the whispers. After all, it would be the senate that elects his replacement for House Savair."

"On nomination by the head of the vacancy's house, Aurie."

"Indeed."

Domenin snorted. "After all that has happened, you can't possibly think your mother would nominate *you* as your brother's replacement in the senate?"

Aurelius smiled. Six years ago, when the archon had dealt him the ultimate betrayal, she probably thought that way too—despite him being her eldest child, with the position as one of the two senators of House Savair, alongside Grandmother Varena, *rightfully* being his.

But now?

No, he was far too powerful now.

He knew too many secrets of too many people for her to deny his return. Six years of scraping and scheming and screwing had ensured that. And bitch that she was, his mother was no fool.

The balance between the senate and the archon, a barely contained war of ideas and morals and good old-fashioned power, even at the best of times, was more perilous now than ever before. She could either keep him as an enemy on the outside, or she could bring him back into the family fold, installing him into the senate in the hopes his influence might help tame those power-hungry sods.

"Oh yes," said Aurelius with a chuckle. "I am quite certain she will."

"Well, I admire your confidence. But of course, if she chooses your uncle as the new herald, it will all be moot. The city would lose a respected philosopher, but your brother would remain with us. There'd be no senate vacancy. No place for little Aurie to slip into."

"Please. Uncle Balser is a fool."

"Perhaps your mother would prefer a loyal fool in her name, rather than a disloyal child in her senate?"

"You speak with confidence, Domi?"

The boy looked to the bronze faces overhead, towering ten times their own height. "My lips are sealed."

Aurelius smiled. He always appreciated someone who understood the value of a proper transaction. It was a rare trait in this city—particularly from a senator, with their stiff upper lips and obsession with piety toward the goddess.

"Very well," said Aurelius, waving his hand expansively, sweeping his arm high and slow for all the watching eyes. "Take your pick."

Domenin leaned in. "What have you heard . . . about *Erato*?"

"Erato?" said Aurelius, sneaking a glance to the curly-haired mercator a few rows behind them. The big-nosed idiot was too thick to even notice he was the subject of attention.

"What of it?"

"I'd have thought you'd select Scipio? She will be your toughest competitor for censor when the time comes. Erato is a nobody! A mercator from some third-rate house of scribes!"

The thin boy flushed red and shot the briefest of looks toward a young woman across the crowd. At first, Aurelius didn't recognize her, but then recollection crept in.

Dorina? Eldest daughter of House Mattic?

Had it really been five years since she was posted as low envoy to Ardora? And yet, the evidence of the passage of time was all over her body. Even Aurelius, no expert on the female figure, could see that she had blossomed during her time in the land of fertility and passion. And he had heard the none-too-subtle whispers that she'd declined the customary five-year extension usually given to low envoys, instead returning home in search of a mate.

"Oh, Domi!" he said, licking his lips. "That is your play? You get one chance to borrow from my well of intrigue, and you select a *love rival*?"

"There is more to life than power and infamy, Aurelius. There is such a thing as love. As actually making a connection with someone."

Aurelius scoffed. "With an attitude like that, you may well avoid both. You know as well as I do that power and infamy are all that matter in this game."

"For you, perhaps. But that is my price. *Erato*. And I want something shocking—no two-drachmae rumor. Something a young lady of noble repute would find . . ."

"Discouraging?"

"*Exactly*."

Aurelius shrugged and leaned in closer, sharing a tasty morsel about the fifteen-year-old daughter of a plebeian parchment maker, whose house had recently come upon a new baby daughter with the most beautiful mass of curly black hair, and a magnificent nose that looked *nothing* like the rest of the brood.

Domi grinned widely. He moved right up to Aurelius's ear and whispered one word.

That one word was as sweet as summer honey. As welcome as a thick-bodied lover.

Benedict.

His heart soared.

Finally! Good gods, finally!

In just a few days, Benedict would be flung off to the far corners of Dynosia as the new herald, doing his mother's seedy bidding, and Aurelius would replace him in the senate.

And from there, it would only be a matter of time until he reclaimed the *real prize.*

The prize that was rightfully his.

The prize that his little brother had tried to snake for himself.

The prize that his bitch mother had tried to rip from his grasp!

I will be the next fucking archon!

4

TEIGRA

GUILT CRAWLED ACROSS TEIGRA AS AURELIUS BERATED THE HORRIBLE boy—leaning in close, no doubt chastising him for his wayward eye and coarse manner. Treating a fellow patrician like that would risk his own ambitions. But he was doing it anyway, stepping in to protect her, just like he always did.

Just like he had in this very spot, three years earlier, grabbing the youngest Malus boy by a fistful of toga when he'd heard what they'd all been calling her. Whispering some secret so dark into the boy's ear that Malus had turned as white as his garment. Giving the rest of them a look of such ferocious *"do you want some too?"* that the whispers had stopped completely.

At least for a few days.

But even that brief respite was more gift than she could ever repay. Without it, she wasn't sure she would have survived those first, crushing nights.

Teigra sighed as she watched Aurelius work. She didn't know how he did it.

Though they often complained about those in power, Aurelius never hid those complaints away. He would call the pompous,

pompous; the ignorant, ignorant. If someone slighted him, he would ruin them. If someone failed to pay him respect, he would sit away in his opulent apartment with his syrinx pipes, contemplating his revenge. He didn't just fantasize about it. He didn't just keep it locked away in his head.

Unlike me...

"Don't worry," Aurelius said on his return, "he won't be treating you like that again."

"Thank you, Aurie. But you didn't have to—"

"Darling, please. Nothing is too good for my cousin. Now, what did I miss?"

"You mean apart from the entire ceremony? Only about a dozen dirges."

"How gloomy, invoking Telos at a time like this? You'd think this was a funeral or something."

"Shocking," said Teigra.

The flippancy of her own voice made her chest sink—heavy with the betrayal to her aunt's memory. But it didn't matter. Aurelius received more than enough judgment and mockery and sermons on piety from everyone else in this city.

He wouldn't receive that judgment from Teigra as well.

Aurelius had always been there for her. And she would always be there for him. Even if that meant going against her own wishes and instincts.

She forced a playful smile to her face. "It's almost as bad as Low Priest Nihal Sacredos missing the start of the procession and having to sneak in through a side door."

Aurelius appeared to ignore her, craning his neck past a few patrician minotaurs, dark fur the color of pinecones and with their thick togas scented of same. The giant creatures were casually chatting senate politics, one running his fingers through a loose tousle of wiry red hair, the other catching the firelight across her waxed horns with every tilt of her head. They talked of opportunities for exceptional students from the other polities to study music in the shaded woods of Plasios, or history and religion in the ancient halls of Zateniza, or pottery with the finest clay deposits down in Camena, or sculpture in the marble-rich workshops of Katharo, where most of the minotaurs originated.

Both of their snouts were pierced with thick rings of gold—the metalwork seemingly identical, but with each braid spinning a story of lineage and family and status for those who knew how to read them.

She'd read that other polities in Dynosia treated their nonhumans as inferior. Some, like the giants of Ardora, were apparently treated more like farm animals than true citizens.

Though the city hadn't always been kind to her, Teigra was proud that Mestibes wasn't like that. Here, minotaurs and even a few sphynx from the Azure Eye towered freely over the rest of the crowd. A few extremely well-dressed centaurs marched proudly through the press, fending off those shameful enough to try to use the occasion to get an inked hoofprint on parchment.

Aurelius was standing on tiptoes now, but it wasn't the minotaur's conversation that was engaging him. Instead, he was staring at an unusual patch of attendees up front near the dais—their strange dress only amplified by the sea of white togas around them.

"*Nihal Sacredos*?" Teigra repeated with a poke of her cousin's ribs. "I can't imagine what could have delayed him so!"

"Yes, yes. Hal is a big boy."

"Very big from what you've said."

"Exactly, cousin. A *very* big boy. And he is perfectly capable of making his own terrible decisions. Now lay off the guilt trip, you are starting to sound like your mother." Teigra gave him an exaggerated look of shock, which Aurelius returned. "Now, unless I am mistaken, we have some foreign dignitaries in?"

"Oh yes. From all across the country. It seems that Urosina kept many friends, despite your dislike for her."

Teigra caught the slight edge of bitterness in her voice, and hurriedly pushed it away.

Aurelius gave a throaty grumble. "It was she who disliked me, Tiggy."

"That isn't true! You know Aunty loved you. She just disapproved of some of your choices."

"It's the same thing. You saw the way she carried on whenever she was back in town—calling me a *confirmed bachelor* with her nose in the air. I don't need someone trying to change me. I possess the rare trait in this city of not actually hating myself."

Teigra nodded. It was truer than he knew. "Well, anyway, the ones in the white cloaks and bronze armor are some of the more powerful warlords from Rinath. The Commanders of Fort Amtra and Limnaki, I think."

"Really? They have some nerve showing up here."

"They're claiming no knowledge of the murder. They're blaming some breakaway faction up near the Clawfeather Cliffs. You know how it is—Rinath is barely a true polity, more a collection of warring tribes."

"Interesting," he said, unconvincingly.

"And the ones in the navy and silver silks sailed in from Ondocis yesterday. The Satrap of Torante and her retinue. And those three hooded figures must be some of the mid or low oracles of Vaticily!"

"They sent *lesser* priests?"

"Well, yes. They have to. Because the high oracles are . . . *you know.*"

"What?"

She cupped her hands. "*Gorgons.*"

Aurelius rolled his eyes, as he did whenever Teigra mentioned something even *slightly* divine or mythical. "Oh, please, Tiggy. You read far too many children's stories."

She said nothing in response, just smiling innocently and humming to herself.

"Really?" said Aurelius after a time. "So you'll tell me about warlords and soothsayers, but you won't tell me who the beardy square-jaw is?"

"Who?" she said, as if only noticing the most handsome man in the entire temple for the first time. "Oh, *him*? Come now, you surely must know who *he* is?"

"No. Why would I?"

That is so typical, Teigra thought, marveling not for the first time at the incredible contradiction that was her cousin. Aurelius was far better educated than her. Far better educated than almost anyone else in the city, in fact. While she'd been knee-deep in soiled hay, struggling to learn anything in predawn lamplight, he'd received the finest tuition on philosophy and mathematics and music and poetry; on the history of the Five and their heroes and monsters—even if he'd made it abundantly clear he didn't believe in half of those things; on famous beasts and even more famous battles. And it was true that he knew every noble house in Greater Mestibes—and probably all their secrets as well.

But of matters *outside* the polity? Of the movement of royal families across the hundreds of low and mid polities across Dynosia? Of trade deals and religious revelations and weather patterns and shifts in the political calculus? Of all the things a young Mestibian patrician *should* know about? Of that, he was blissfully unaware, as ignorant as the lowest pleb.

"Well, if you *insist*," she said, pausing for effect. "That . . . is the Crown Prince of Ardora."

"No!" said Aurelius, shoving aside some anonymous mercator. "*That* is Prince Calix Viralis? The Hero of Sama?"

Teigra nodded. The twenty-something man was what the scrolls might call, "formed by the Five"—square-jawed, square-shouldered, and a foot taller than anyone else around him. His raven-black hair fell to his shoulders, framing an imposing face and thick beard. Wrapped in a beautiful uniform of red wool and brown leather, he carried himself with the focused confidence of a proper military officer. The sort that Mestibes didn't really have anymore—with its commitment to diplomacy, pacifism, and its small domestic peace corps, far more used to fighting rogue wolves than other humans.

"Gods," said Aurelius, with a surprising grimace, "he looks *intolerable*. Stiff as an old sandal. Like he'd sooner piss himself than crack a smile."

"Yes," said Teigra quickly. "Just . . . just the worst, isn't he!"

She felt foolish. Though she'd only glanced briefly at him though the ceremony, she'd taken Prince Calix to be rather handsome, in a brooding sort of way. But Aurelius certainly had more experience with men than she did. Practically *everyone* had more experience with men than she did. "But still, you should have heard the girls titter over him. *Oh, he is so dreamy. Oh, he is so mysterious.*"

"I bet they did. Though I don't think there is much mystery there. A lifetime of six-word conversations and three-pump missionary, if I am any judge. And I assume Aunt Beeta is trying to throw you tits-first into his loincloth?"

"Not yet. Even Mother knows the patrician daughters get the first try," she said, her voice laced with undisguised acid at the flirtation her mother had forced on her. "Instead, she's thrusting me toward the jealous young men. Although, who knows. I expect her displays at the feast will be shameless. I don't suppose you'd like to try and grab the prince for yourself?"

"There is straight-acting, darling, and then there is *that*. I seriously doubt he and I would be saluting the same banner."

"Are you sure? It'd be quite the conquest."

"Tiggy, you may think I'm an outrageous flirt."

"I do, yes."

"But it may shock you to know that I prefer my men to *want* to fuck me. There is a big and rather important difference between a man who is charmingly coy, and a man who is actually unwilling. I trick my men into giving me their secrets. I don't trick them into giving me their cocks."

Teigra flinched at the frank language, remembered herself, and sighed.

Shameless displays it will have to be.

The congregation began to slowly circle toward the body, lining up to lay a hand on the shawl of the deceased, ensuring that Vakaris understood just how well-regarded she had been in life. Making sure he delivered her to the golden paradise of Evdonia, rather than the endless gray of Sriopi or the fiery torture of Dimethan.

Just as they were about to join the flow, something awful caught her eye. She shook Aurelius, who was still glancing over at the prince.

"Aurie! Quick!"

5

AURELIUS

"W<small>HAT IS IT</small>, B<small>ENI</small>?" <small>SAID</small> A<small>URELIUS WITH A SIGH</small>. H<small>E DIDN'T TURN</small>. There was only one person that made Teigra look like that.

"Mother is meeting with the simple folk," said the little toad. "And for some unfathomable reason, she wants *you* there as well."

Oh, but I do know why, baby brother. Even if you are too stupid to understand.

"Of course," he said with a warm smile that made Benedict flinch. "I serve at the pleasure of the archon."

Teigra started to move backward. She was probably hoping for a chance to get all boo-hooey over the dead bitch who loved nothing more than giving him piety lectures. The one who had always treated him like some kind of deranged pervert. "Well, it looks like you have some important business to attend to," she said. "So, I'll just—"

"Oh no you don't!" hissed Aurelius in departing. "Move one muscle from this spot and I'll get drunk and play personal matchmaker between you and Prince Boredom!"

The archon had moved to a little transept at the back of the temple, holding court with the lesser oracles of Vaticily, their hands held right to left, left to right. The lead oracle's face was shaded dark beyond the deep green of her cowl, but they were definitely human.

Gorgons? he thought with another roll of his eyes. *Poor Tiggy. She is obsessed with all that mythical monster rot. She really must spend less time in scrolls and more time in society.*

Around the edges of the space, dignitaries from two of the other polities moved through a ridiculous diplomatic dance—equidistant, eyes diverted, deliberately oblivious to each other's presence. One of the Rinathi was human, and the other was a great uniformed gryphon, a creature he had only heard about during long and boring days of tutelage.

On the Ondocian side, the Satrap was flanked by a small army of courtiers, including one woman with hair thick from sea salt, and a skirt that sparkled as if made of some blue metal, catching every flicker of light that filtered down through the oculus above.

The only outsider not participating in the dance was Prince Calix. Unlike the others, he had no fawning group of followers nor sharp-eyed guards. In fact, he wasn't even in the transept. Instead, he was out in the temple proper, kneeling in front of the great statue of Ardor. His huge body was still, although if Aurelius strained, he could just see movement from the prince's bearded jaw, whispering out some private prayer.

Benedict finally stopped a discreet distance behind the archon, alongside his grandmother Varena, who shot Aurelius a look of utter contempt.

Nice to see you again too, Granny.

The archon's brilliant yellow stola was brocaded in bronze, not just with the tools of Mesti, but with holy symbols to all the Five: the flaming heart of the war priests of Rinath; a deep-ink pearl from the farthest depths of the Illhas Sea; the albino opium snake of Mount Vaticily; and of course, the eternal rose of Ardora.

It was a shameless show for the senators and the more pious members of the public—who loved nothing more than Mestibes being the glue that held the rest of the country together. The archon he knew would slit the throat of any of these guests in a heartbeat if it furthered her own ambition.

"I give you my blessing, Archon," said the oracle, in a dreamlike voice. "I have warm memories of your sister's visits to the mountain. Brief though they were."

"It is my honor, Your Beatitude. My sister spoke fondly of the beauty and ferocity of your woods. Please let the high oracles know that as long as I sit on the Throne of Thought, Vaticily will have a friend in Mestibes."

"Gratitude, Majesty."

"Now, you will stay for the feast, won't you? I'd love to hear your recollections of my dear sister."

The oracle nodded warmly, bringing her crossed arms to her chest and giving a deep bow.

No sooner had she taken her leave than the Rinathi warlords clanked forward, shouldering each other uneasily for position—a contest easily won by the gryphon. They offered their profound horror at the death of the herald, which the archon accepted without so much as an argument.

And so, the process went on with pleasantry after excruciating pleasantry. Finally, they came to the last: Crown Prince Calix, who rose from the statue on cue and walked toward them.

No, not *walked*.

Prowled.

He moved like an apex predator, huge and confident. Up close, he was even bigger than Aurelius had realized, towering over him, and standing at least twice as broad.

But what surprised him most was not the man's size.

It was his *eyes*.

Aurelius had expected a deep brown, matching his imposing presence. Instead, the crown prince's irises were as golden as fresh honey.

The effect was disarming, giving a strange softness to his menace.

The prince bowed stiffly, standing further back than the others and making no effort toward physical contact. "Their Majesties send their condolences," he said, in a voice like smoke and mead.

"Thank you, Your Highness," said the archon. "And how fares your father? Please tell him that all Mestibes prays for his swift recovery."

"He bears his burden with strength. As he has done for all of these last five years."

"Well, I am glad to hear that. Now, you will stay for the feast, won't you? I would love to hear any recollections you have of my dear—"

Prince Calix raised his hand abruptly. "I cannot."

The air chilled. For the first time since Aurelius joined the conversation, his mother appeared surprised. All the other dignitaries had accepted the invitation. Even Aurelius, no adherent to protocol, knew it was the deepest offense to refuse.

"Yes," said Calix, without any hint of remorse. "The tides withdraw, and I have already stayed longer than I intended."

"Yes, yes of course," said the archon, regathering. "May Ondo grant you safe passage on the voyage, and may Ardor welcome you back into her embrace."

The prince gave a final, slight bow and turned to leave.

And then Calix's honeyed eyes caught his own. It was just for a moment, no more than a glance, but it seemed to last for an eternity.

At once, Aurelius's body roared. Heat crawled across his flesh. A sense of urgent lust, more immediate than any he'd ever felt, flooded through him. It was otherworldly. Like his skin wasn't his own. Like the prince had possessed it. Like the prince could do whatever he fucking wanted with it! Right here! Right now! In front of everyone!

Now!

As quickly as it had come, the feeling vanished.

Aurelius reeled, adjusting his tunic over his suddenly hard groin. He turned with a snap to the departing figure, who walked with renewed purpose through the crowd.

When he was halfway gone, Prince Calix shot a quick glance over his shoulder.

His expression chilled Aurelius to the bone. It was the sort of look he'd never expected to see on such a big, strong soldier.

Terror. Absolute, petrified *terror.*

What in Dimethan was that!? he thought once the prince had finally vanished from view.

"Well, *that* doesn't bode well," said Beni. "He's probably still mad about Sama, Mummy. And insulted that you saw him last."

"There are rules for these things, boy," said Grandmother Varena. "Those who arrive first are greeted first. And those who sail in an hour before the ceremony are seen when they are seen."

"He was traveling from the far north of the country, Granny. And besides, two-to-one odds are that his old man snuffs it before the year's out. It's a miracle he's lasted this long since the Rinathi's assassination attempt. Then, that prince will be the next *king of Ardora.* Responsible for over half of our food and wine, two-thirds of our horses, and almost all of our timbe—"

"Precedent cares not for expediency!" snapped his grandmother.

Beni was about to respond when the archon interjected. "A conversation for a more discreet location, perhaps? Now get off to the feast. Tell your father I will be along soon."

They both bowed, shooting daggers at each other. After a discreet pause, Aurelius made to follow them.

"Aurelius," said the archon.

He froze, a strange feeling running through him. It was the first time he had heard the woman say his name in six years.

"Yes, Your Majesty," he said, forcing down the sickening sensation of childhood subservience.

"Come to the palace tomorrow morning. I have something I wish to discuss."

Aurelius grinned internally and gave the deepest bow he could manage. "Of course, *Your Majesty.*"

6

~

Prince Calix slammed the cabin door, bolting it shut with trembling fingers. From above deck drifted the muffled laugh of Ondocian sailors, carting crates of apples and clanking amphorae of wine. Beneath the hobnails of his caligae boots, the ship groaned against the jagged shoreline.

But that was not the dominant sound. In the dark room, fast as a marching drum, came the thump of his heart and the stutter of his breath.

His face was drenched in cold sweat as he sank into the corner of the stately cabin. As if wishing to retreat as far as he could from any other soul.

"Control yourself! Control yourself!" he hissed through clenched teeth, his hand quivering so hard that it would have spilled a mug of water in seconds.

Ardora protect me.

So alive . . .

So powerful . . .

I've never felt . . .

Not since . . .

He tried not to think about it.

He tried not to think about *him*.

It was some time before the prince moved again, only rising later that night, once the ship was well underway, staggering to the shutters that covered the window.

The wooden slats carved his face between light and dark. With desperate movements, he threw them open, allowing the thin, silvery light of the half-moon to soak into his dark olive skin.

Only then did the shakes cease.

7

TEIGRA

D<small>AWN BROKE OVER THE RED-CLAY ROOFS THAT SURROUNDED THE</small> L<small>APISO</small> Library. The warm light blended with Teigra's lamp, illuminating a lamb-leather scroll.

She sighed. It was just getting to the good bit too, where the great Mestibian hero, Harophonies Savair, had rallied the forces of Vaticily, Ondocis, and Ardora against the bronze-armored might of Rinath at the end of the Third Dynosian War.

Stifling a yawn, she returned the scroll to its hive and made her way toward the exit. "Good night, Senator Vivlios," she said to the old sphynx behind the counter.

"Good *morning*, Miss Cosmin," he said, his tail swaying languidly behind him like a river reed, the crook of his wings resting gently against strong shoulders. "More stories on the therians, was it?"

"No, I was just reading about Snow Sands again."

"Ah. Your grandfather was a great archon indeed. Good that he is being remembered." The sandy-furred sphynx turned a codex page of his own and popped a piece of goat's cheese past his fangs. "Until tomorrow."

Teigra stepped into the late spring air of the agora, only now filling with merchants. The stars and half-moon retreated as she exchanged a handful of drachmae for a basket of fresh sprat, still wet with brine. The shores around Mestibes were rocky and steep—bad for seafarers, but good for the predawn fishers who clung to the cliffs with their long poles and longer lines.

Teigra loved this time of day more than any other: wandering the quiet streets as the sun roused the free citizens of Mestibes. Breathing in the leafy aniseed aroma of olive blossom and the inviting pear-and-walnut waft of hot tiganite cakes. Hearing those first few knaps of the sculptors, or the drifting notes of musicians tuning their instruments.

And as she walked the winding streets, she would think about what she'd read. And she always read something.

Just like *he* had taught her.

While she took care to read a selection of everything, even those scrolls and codices that made little sense to her, she loved the stories on history most—those tales with strange beasts and gods-chosen heroes, all fighting in grand battles between good and evil. And most of all, of the strange and unusual creatures born of the gods, like her absolute favorite stories: *the therians.*

Gorgons and sirens and eidolons and phoenixes and satyrs!

Children born of one of the Five and a mortal, just walking around among everyone else, totally unaware of the power within them. Until they ate something they shouldn't, or touched something they shouldn't and *bam*, they awoke! Cursed to wander the earth, changing into a beast each sable moon. Or worse! Sometimes they would be permanently changed! Creating terror or passion or mischief wherever they went.

Their stories appeared in tons of scrolls, and even more so in plays and music. And Teigra could see why. The idea that such creatures could be right here in the city. Just over there. Just over *anywhere*! Behind any of these doors and windows. Walking among the regular citizens. Living otherwise normal lives, without even knowing what they were? Without even knowing what they could be.

That thought made the familiar streets and familiar doorways just a little bit more exciting. The idea that behind every portal was potentially a touch of the divine!

Aurelius might not believe in them. Lots of people didn't in Mestibes, treating those tales as mere bedtime stories to scare obedience into children. But *Teigra* believed them. Not having seen a therian was no reason to believe they didn't exist. After all, she hadn't seen a gryphon until yesterday. Or their homeland of Rinath either. Or Ondocis. Or Ardora. Or Vaticily. Or even another polity within Greater Mestibes. She had never even left the city—not more than a few miles anyway. But she still knew that all those places existed.

Just like she knew the therians existed.

Just like she knew the gods existed.

Eventually, her daydreaming brought her to her destination: the Alogo Machy, the greatest hippodrome in all Dynosia. Home of the famous Mestibian relay.

The place where a different kind of hero is made.

And a different kind of beast.

The high, oval-shaped stands were silent now, the only sound the low chatter of some white-tailed kites in the distance. And yet, Teigra could practically feel the hum of the place.

By midday, the white marble seats, worn smooth by centuries of backsides, would be echoing with the chaos of the relay, one of the few times the staid citizens of Mestibes allowed themselves to reach full voice. There would be the grunts of the centaur superstars pounding along their oval track for the first lap; the splash of the hippocamps, weaving through their chicane of narrow canals dug all up the center of the stadium on the second lap; and finally, the great *thwump* of pegasus wings streaking through the air on the third and final lap, all played to the deafening roar of five thousand spectators, abandoning their usual stoicism for the thrill of the race.

Pale yellow sand filled her sandals as she passed the stables of other horse-rearing families, all nestled in the foundations of the stands: House Samari, House Chalin, and House Anavoleas.

She gave a little smile toward their sleeping steeds, absent any attendants. Even though it was a race day, they'd probably still be sleeping off the feast, rather than heading to bed at a reasonable hour and rising early, as she'd done.

As she *always* did.

And that was why House Cosmin was so dominant. This wasn't a *hobby* to them. This was their life. This was their blood.

Father used to tell stories of the two dozen stables that were here when he first took over the family business, all owned by different houses and all competing to train the best steeds and sign contracts with the snootiest centaurs. It had been his greatest pride that he'd managed to buy out so many of them—from that first victory on a risk-it-all bet, to now, where the Cosmin name was synonymous with the noblest of sports.

Long-gone words played across her memory: *Two Cosmins in the senate and one house in the Alogo.*

Don't worry, Da, thought Teigra with a deep sigh, as she was embraced by the comforting smell of hay. *I won't let you down.*

Not again.

"Morning everyone!" she said to a chorus of whickers from the pens and excited splashes from the pools of salt water. The Cosmin stables were vast, taking up almost half of the sub-stands, housing a half-dozen racing teams and almost fifty nonracing billets. The centaurs, of course, were nowhere to be seen. They had their own accommodations on the outskirts of town—on the premier cliff-edge plots that overlooked the sea.

Teigra treated the centaur superstars with the minimum level of respect required to not put them, or their wealthy contract holders, offside. But she had never been in *awe* of them. How could she be? She'd seen them at work, after all.

Today, those centaurs wouldn't wander down to the track until the very last minute, still cracking their necks and working the kinks out of their withers. Stretching just long enough to not risk injury from their sprint. Then, after two minutes of effort, they'd spend the rest of the day drinking and feasting and being fawned over. All while the real steeds, and the real riders, did the real hard work.

She threw the fish to the hippocamps and laid fresh barley for the pegasi, reserving the best bushel for Astrapi, a stunning Zante mare with hair of blood bay and wings that glinted gold in the filtered light.

"And how are you feeling today, lovely? Are you going to drag Jaronas to a first-place finish he could never get without you? Yes, you will! I think you just might!"

Astrapi nickered at her touch, grateful for the attention of the girl who had raised her from a foal. An ache formed in Teigra's chest as the mare guided the scratches along her neck, seeming to ask the same question she always did: What had she done to drive her master away? To make Teigra stop riding?

Nothing, girl. There is nothing else you could have done.

"Come on," she said, pulling herself back to the present. "We can't have you cooped up all day!"

She bridled and saddled Astrapi, leading her out into the morning. It was shaping as a beautiful day, and the growing warmth gave a kick to their speed. Soon Teigra was jogging down the centaur track, with Astrapi keeping pace.

Her beauty wanted to go faster still—to fly into the air, weaving and darting as only she could. She was a chained warrior, built for speed, caged away all night, and anything less than full pace was a mockery of her talents.

But rather than speed up, as they rounded the first corner Teigra slowed, bringing the mare to a complete stop.

Ahead was a sight that always took her breath away: the great straight—well-trodden sand below, with narrow white columns stretching into the sky, marking the much more winding track of the pegasi.

Half a mile of possibility.

Half a mile that had once been *Teigra's*.

Astrapi whinnied, extending her strong wings, her feather tips pointed to the azure. *What are you waiting for*, she seemed to say. *No one will ever know.*

In the deathly silence, her mind wandered to Aunty Urosina laying on the dais. One minute alive and breathing, and the next . . . gone.

Just . . . just like that.

A memory returned of a morning far cooler than this, with the stands just as silent and the scent of low spring bellflowers rich in the air. Of Aunty Ura appearing at the stable door, surprising her after almost a full year away! Of the hugs and tour of the stables, with Teigra yammering on about the foals Ura had seen a year prior, now strong and hungry for the race.

And then, of the wise woman taking Teigra by the shoulders, just as she always had in moments of sincerity. Of her looking into Teigra's suddenly downcast eyes and whispering what no one else saw. Whispering what no one else would tell her.

Tig, please. It pains me to see you torturing yourself like this. You love this too much to never return to the saddle!

Her aunt's warm voice hung in the rising light of the morning. The voice that felt like gazing up at the stars from a quiet hill. The voice that tasted like honey and herbs.

All Aunty wanted was for me to ride again . . .

After a long moment of aching indecision, Teigra sprang into the saddle. She relished the immense power beneath her. It was a power she had not felt between her strong thighs for three long years. A power she had missed with every inch of her being. It met her like an old friend, ungreeted for many moons, but with none of the familiarity drained.

But as she took hold of the reins, worn leather hot against her thumbs, the other memories flooded back—the ones she tried so desperately to suppress. Of the wind whipping wet through her hair. Of the smell of churned sand and fresh rain. Of the salt dripping cold from the bronze baton. Of the ground rushing past with each weightless turn of flight. Of the pulse of the nearby riders, getting closer! *Closer!*

And of not caring about any of that, because all she could hear was the roar of the crowd, punctuated by each brutal clap of thunder. All she could feel was the rippling mass of muscle beneath her legs, surging with the strain, summoning bursts of power toward the finish line.

And in Teigra's head came another familiar voice, making a familiar refrain: *Stick to the path, kiddo. Even if it terrifies you.*

She . . . she could hear it all now—all those roars, which had long since fallen silent. All of them calling her name. Her family's name. The name her father had built from nothing, into something that deserved those cheers!

Then those cheers twisted into *panic*.

It came from everywhere and nowhere all at once. It choked her down, punching the breath from her lungs.

And it was punctuated with a final, bloodcurdling scream.

Tears streamed down Teigra's face. One hand reached to a pendant at her neck as her other hand shook against the reins.

The pendant was a beautiful thing. The black hair was cut from the mane of Seraki, the first champion that House Cosmin had ever reared, almost a hundred and fifty years ago. It was held in place by a bronze, hipposandal-shaped clip at the tip, clumsily carved by a little girl she had long let pass into memory—made to replace the old clasp, which had finally worn away with the passage of time.

And it was hung on a silver chain. Silver which had been added by her late father, Andrin Cosmin. Silver that had been clipped from the first medallion he'd won as a jockey when he was just twelve years old.

Tears cascaded down her face now.

The pendant of the man I killed!

Her breaths were wrenching now, barely able to gather herself. She gripped the saddle hard with her free hand, feeling the stands twist around her.

All it would take was one crack of that leather and she could feel it all again. The good. The bad. The lost and the regained. All of it.

Perhaps the rush of air past her cheeks might dry the tears.

Perhaps it might do so forever.

But she just couldn't do it.

"I'm . . . so sorry," she whispered, turning Astrapi around and making the slow walk back to the stables.

Her blood chilled as a familiar voice echoed through the stadium.

"Teigra! Get down from there this instant!"

8

AURELIUS

Dawn hit Aurelius like sizzling skewers to the face, rousing him from the bliss of strong arms and honeyed eyes.

If he could've remembered the name of the servant shaking him awake, he would have told him to fuck right off. As it was, he just grunted a feeble objection, his hand flopping to the floor.

Without even opening his eyes, he knew the hangover would be bad. His mouth had the texture of sun-cured leather, with the ghost of a thousand grapes rotting over his tongue. His head pounded like merry dancers, smacking their feet here, clapping their hands there, spinning and spinning and—

He caught himself before his stomach turned, forcing down the bile and settling back into the lavender-scented mattress. As he drifted off, he thought of the funeral: of the face that had transfixed him all night. Of that moment when every single hair had stood on end. Of that instant where it felt like he might never—

Another shake wrenched him from the precipice of pleasure. "Fner?" he grunted, opening one crusty eye, and staring at the cowering figure.

"My humblest apologies, despota, but you wished to be woken at dawn?"

"Why in Vatic's cock would I have said that?" he said with a cough.

"You . . . you said you had an appointment? With the archon?"

Aurelius groaned in recollection, dragging his naked body from the bed with the weight of recollection. As he stumbled to the window, blinking through the fiery glare, his attention was drawn to the marble tablet on proud display nearby.

He had kept it there for six years, but this morning, it seemed particularly conspicuous. It was written in Voresoma, the language of the educated halls of Mestibes, and apparently in some of the more noble circles beyond, including Rinath in vulgar form, but certainly not in the markets or the hippodrome of Mestibes, or in the northern lands either, where Dynosian—the common language of the whole nation—was far more common.

The carefully chiseled script read:

Her Most Serene Majesty, Sabina IV, Archon of Mestibes, does on this day declare the removal of her eldest son, Aurelius, from prominence and succession of House Savair . . .

He ran his fingers over its creamy white face, listing the litany of his crimes. Perversion. Corruption of moral integrity. Bestial behavior.

Despite it all, Aurelius couldn't bring himself to hate her—not truly. She had sacrificed him on the bonfire of civic outrage to preserve her own position. Just like she always had. And in a twisted sort of way, he could respect that.

It was just like she had done with the Libercropolis, the city's crumbling crown, a year before he was born. Famously, she had risen to archon just before her nineteenth birthday, near the end of the Third Dynosian War—following the battle-death of Grandfather Harophonies, and when Mestibes was all but bankrupt. The other polities were already supporting them with blood and were in no mood to lend gold on top of it. Instead, the new archon had taken the unorthodox step of wooing an eccentric Ondocis noble, Satrap Antonio Meuccia of Farsea Island, a known collector of rare curios. She offered to sell him the whole Libercropolis, the literal and cultural pinnacle of the city—almost a thousand years of history and antiques, old religious text, and snippets of myth found nowhere else in Dynosia.

He accepted, of course. It was the ultimate prize for the ultimate collector. And when the war was won, and the time came to collect, the archon advised that he could take the marble any time he liked. For that was all their contract had stipulated—the *building*, with no explicit reference to its contents.

Aurelius gave a little smirk.

The senate had been appalled. Such trickery had no place in a civilized city like Mestibes—which was exactly the reason the Satrap hadn't checked the contract as closely as he might have done if it had been proposed by his own countrywomen. No one thought a Mestibian archon was capable of such deception.

The relationship between the senate and the new archon had never recovered. They considered her then, as they did now, as a moralless heathen who would do and say anything to get what she wanted.

And the archon hadn't cared. Why should she? She'd secured her position—winning favor with the regular people, who ultimately cared less about upholding high-minded religious ideals than having bread on their tables and a future for their children.

Yes, thought Aurelius, looking over the noble city he was soon to rejoin.

She does what it takes to survive.

And she will do so again today.

"What?" he snapped, to the sound of a gently clearing throat.

"What would you like to do about *him*?"

Aurelius turned to see a great lump on the other side of his bed.

One thick arm and one hairy leg were hanging from the blanket. A pillow concealed his identity and muffled the worst of the snores.

Ahhh.

He was no stranger to men in his bed—generally of the older, more powerful, and more desperate sort. The kind who would fawn over a young man with firm skin and loose morals. Others might cringe at that, but Aurelius had always found it a perfectly agreeable arrangement. Allow some old fool to clumsily fuck him for a few minutes, and in exchange, he would own their loyalty for years.

And while he couldn't *immediately* recall who he'd bedded, he had no doubt it was someone of suitable stature.

Aurelius lifted the pillow carefully, revealing...

He scowled.

The man was beautiful—bearded and tanned, with a strong body —but he couldn't recall ever seeing him before. He dragged his gaze around the well-appointed room, filled with frescos and statuettes from the finest artists in the polity. In the corner was a simple toga, twisted like a dead snake's skin.

And it was white. *All white!* There were no stripes of any kind— neither filled nor hollow.

The man wasn't a patrician. He wasn't even a mercator. He was *a plebeian!* One of the myriad drones that did the unlovely jobs that kept the city running.

What a waste of a fucking evening, he thought, dropping the pillow. The man beneath gave a slight grunt, then carried on snoring.

"Kick him out once I've left," he said, wandering off to handle his morning ablutions. The kiss of sunlight at the doorway brought him to a momentary pause. "But find out who he is first. I am sure we can find *some way* of using this against him."

9

TEIGRA

Mother stormed across the stadium, flanked by Jaronas, his face a painting of concern. Teigra had already dismounted by the stable door, but it was too late. Mother's eyes were pure fury.

"You were riding again! After everything you promised!"

"No! I swear I—"

The slap rang through the stands, striking across her cheek with such force it knocked her to the ground.

"Lies!" Mother placed a hand by Astrapi's resisting mouth. "Her breath is *hot!*"

From a gallop! Teigra screamed internally. Any fool could see that she hadn't been flying. But Mother was beneath even that, wasn't she?

For all Teigra's life, her mother had gladly taken the money from the business—the reputation, the social status—but even when Father had been here, she'd never bothered to learn the first thing about horsecraft. On race days, she was found in the stands, flirting and sleazing and building her sad alliances.

Teigra ran the fine sand of the racetrack through her fingers, the cascade of glassy grain was calming as the heat on her face cooled.

It didn't matter that she'd resisted the temptation she was now accused of. Mother had made up her mind. Fighting back? Pleading her innocence? All that would get was further punishment.

"You're right," she muttered. "We flew around the track. I'm sorry."

Mother paced back and forth. "What am I to do with you, girl? The only way this family will ever rise to patrician status is if everyone contributes! Your brother performed brilliantly at the feast—charming and spreading faith in House Cosmin. I had them all eating out of the palm of my hand. The censor is now seriously considering returning his team to our management. If he comes, others will also return. But you do *this*?"

"I know. I'm sorry."

"All I have ever asked is that you do your part. To keep the stable respectable. To marry a patrician boy of good repute. To knit our name deeper into the tapestry of the senate, guaranteeing the support we will need for elevation! You know how hard it is to graduate from mercator to patrician status. Just three families in a century have done it. Three! And you would risk it all? Right when we are so close?"

"I know. I'm sorry."

"Imagine if a potential suitor had seen you out there! Or the censor himself? We have tried for three years to erase the city's memory of *that* girl. The jockey. The savage. The beast who screamed and swore and played to the stands. Of all the tragedy you wrought on this family! Have you forgotten what you did? What you took from us!?"

Teigra's stomach twisted hard. "I know! I'm sorry!"

For a terrible moment, Mother went silent. Teigra didn't look up as she stormed into the stables. She didn't look up to see the flog of silver birch, wrapped in leather offcuts, which would surely be in her hands, just as it had been countless times before.

But she did look up when the strikes didn't come.

Mother wasn't standing over her.

Instead, she was a few feet back.

And she was offering the flog to *Jaronas*.

"Take it, boy."

Her brother looked horrified. "What? Why?"

"Because you are the man of House Cosmin. And you are now of age. It is your job to ensure its good order."

"But . . . Ma . . . No! Not like this."

Mother looked at him with a kindness she never spared for Teigra. "I know, my son. I know. Much that we do in this life we do not wish to. But if we succeed in our endeavor, then you will join me in the senate. And how can you take on the burden of a thousand houses, if you will not even take on the burden of our own?"

Conflict boiled behind the eyes of the boy she'd saved from bullies countless times in their youth, when they'd teased him for his softness and his fondness for his *mummy*. The sobbing kid she'd comforted beneath the pink-petaled almond tree the night their life was ripped apart, even as her own grief went untended. Even as the shock and sorrow had bored down into her very bones.

Her skin turned cold in the shade of the stands as she watched the moment unfold. She had never imagined she might lose two family members so quickly. Because to Teigra's immeasurable sadness, Jaronas took the flog.

He stepped forward, twisting the wicked implement between hesitant fingers.

"Just do it," she whispered, girding herself for familiar pain.

"Tiggy, I . . . I . . ."

"I'm not doing this for *her*," she hissed, quiet enough that only the two of them would hear it. "I'm doing this for *him*. For *his* vision. For *his* dreams for what this family could become."

The blows still didn't come. Jaronas was weeping.

"Just do it!" she screamed, unable to bear the anticipation any longer.

The first strike across her back tore the air from her lungs. Her thin fabric gave no resistance. Once started, Jaronas didn't hold back.

Mother knew well the proper sound of leather on flesh, and she would tolerate nothing less than full fury.

Teigra gritted her teeth with each crack, resisting the urge to scream, resisting the urge to cry.

She might shed a tear for her past. For the loss of the one thing which had given her joy. For Father—the one man who had loved her more than she'd ever deserved to be loved.

But she wouldn't shed tears for *Mother*.

Not one.

Not a single one.

10

AURELIUS

THE ARCHON GRINNED AS SHE STIRRED THE MINT MEAD IN HER GLASS cage cup. Each clink of the metal spoon cracked through Aurelius's head like a sculptor's hammer. "And how was your night, my little satyr?"

Satyr? A drunken and debauched creature of carnal desire and worldly decadence . . .

Aurelius would have snorted and shot back a response, but he could barely form the words to *think* the retort, let alone *speak* it. Instead, he slouched on the unconscionably firm couch, clutching at his head and dwelling on her remarkable talent for small evils.

The garden courtyard was filled with glass—trinkets and tableware, vases and cameos. Glasswear was the pride of Mestibes: a craft no other polity had mastered in almost a hundred years. And though beautiful, the cumulative effect was a glinting, white-hot river streaming directly into his eyes.

"If memories of Despota Mathain's tutelage are correct," he said, in a voice as rough as horseradish, "a satyr therian is created through the intimate congress of a mortal and the goddess of fertility. Is this your way of telling me that you were secretly shagged by Ardor twenty-one years ago, Mother?"

The archon sipped her spiced liquid. "No. Although I did manage to convince your father to dress as a satyr when I visited Ardora for their famous Black Night Festival. During my brief time as your grandfather's herald. He was quite a sight, you know, in full horns and hooves."

"Please, no," said Aurelius, holding a hand over his mouth. "And believe me, if I had been exposed to one of the five divine chrysalides and awoken as a demi-god, I'm pretty sure I would remember."

His skin prickled. It wasn't just the hangover that was throwing him off, this *whole situation* was wrong. They had not spoken for six fucking years. For more than a quarter of his life! He had expected some awkwardness in her interaction. Some combat? Some flare! But instead, his mother had greeted him with a warm embrace, chatting away and asking for little tidbits of gossip, just as she used to.

As if *nothing* had happened.

Aurelius did his best to recompose himself on the couch. If she thought he would simply forgive and forget, she was gravely mistaken.

But he could certainly *play along* until he got what he wanted.

And so, Aurelius spilled a respectable quantity of gossip. Oh, it was nothing too valuable, just a few of the more widely known affairs in the high society of Mestibes. The nobility might put on their public shows of wisdom and virtue, loving nothing more than posturing and posing their piety. But behind closed doors? In the privacy of their own impulses? There it was a medley of mischief. Each man and woman a creature of carnality.

At least I have the balls to conduct my affairs in the open.

"Well, well," said the archon. "It seems the good patricians of Mestibes have taken the lessons of the birds and the bees to heart this spring. And after they have the gall to judge me and my actions."

"And many people were keen to celebrate your sister's death in a rather loose-lipped way at the feast."

"Celebrate her *life*, my child."

"I know what I said."

Her show of happy families broke for the first time this morning. "We do not speak ill of the recently dead. Vakaris may still be listening and determining her final destination."

"And why not?" he snapped. "She spoke ill of me plenty enough. She thought me nothing more than a deviant!"

"She never called you that, Aurelius."

"No. She was like the rest of your high society, using their diplomatic speech instead. *Wayward*, I was. *Unconventional. Far from Mesti. A confirmed bachelor.* Or she'd accuse me of suffering from a divine illness—from *wandering vigor*."

"And you don't think she had a point?"

"Wandering vigor comes from the neglect of Mesti's virtues? It supposedly makes you act impulsively and without reason? Well, I am sorry to tell you, Majesty, but all my *deviant* behavior has been out of deliberate choice, not impulse."

The archon lowered her drink to the egg-shell-colored marble table between them. "She meant well, Aurelius. She loved you as much as her other nieces and nephews. But your actions were wont to undercut the power and prestige of all House Savair. As the second eldest child of a former archon, she was within her rights to preserve the family's name."

"Are we still talking about your bitch sister, *Mummy*?"

Aurelius took joy in her sudden shock. She had really thought he would come here sniveling, didn't she? Like a dog at the table, begging for a few scraps of prestige? But he was the one who held the power now. He was the one who had the influence and leverage.

And it was time she fucking realized that!

The archon was silent for a long time. At last, she turned to the olive trees overhead, their white flowers made clean and bright through dappled sunlight. "My, my. How the seasons progress," she said, quietly.

Aurelius glared. "Don't they just."

The archon sighed. "You know, my child, when I first came to power, I thought I knew exactly what my path would be. Your grandfather was a strong man. A *decisive* man. As a girl, it seemed to me that he woke each morning and bent the city to his will. And that was what I intended to do as archon, too. I thought that one person, one house, could make any decision they wanted. After all, that is what our laws say. Officially, the senate is just my advisory body. Officially, the plebeian class exists solely to be ruled."

A bee buzzed through the crocus flowers that ringed the courtyard, eventually coming to settle on the edge of her mead-sticky glass.

"You can imagine my shock when I learned that every change your grandfather made, every law he declared, had first been negotiated through the senate, and carefully crafted to win favor with the masses. For he knew it was the senate who would elect his successor. And he knew it was the long knives of the people, ultimately, who decided how soon that successor would be required."

The archon turned a ferocious look on Aurelius. Any defeat which had been there mere moments earlier was gone. Now her eyes glinted with calculated malice.

"That has been my greatest lesson as archon, Aurelius. That there is a terrible danger for those with power to presume to know the path ahead of them!"

Chills crawled over him. First of confusion. Then, and far worse, of hideous comprehension.

"No! No, you can't *possibly* mean . . ."

11

TEIGRA

"*HERALD*?" HISSED TEIGRA, RACING TO CLOSE HER BEDROOM DOOR. SHE cursed her volume at the smallest twitch of recognition from Tulla, their family's nosey old servant, out in the kitchen, shelling pea pods for dinner. "Aunt Sabina intends to nominate *you* as the new herald of Mestibes?"

"Shhh," said Aurelius, pulling a well-used pillow over his face, blocking the afternoon light. Though her family's house was above average for mercator society, it was far less grand than Aurelius's apartment—lacking the expensive silks and fashionable gifts from his many admirers. "The more you read the appointment scroll, Tiggy, the harder it is to pretend it doesn't exist."

She ran her finger over the supple leather. "Her Most Serene Majesty, Sabina IV, Archon of Mestibes, wishes it be known that Aurelius Savair is to serve as her herald and official voice to Dynosia, to be posted firstly to the Kingdom of Ardora."

Aurelius groaned from beneath the bundled straw.

"At least it isn't *Rinath*?" she said.

"Does that make it better? Ardora is a shithole in a vegetable field, a million miles from anything resembling civilization."

"Well, not a *million*. And I've read it's very beautiful up there. Apparently, they get so much rain that the grass is *green*."

"Oh, well let me pack my bags right now!"

"All right then, the people are also meant to be *stunning*. And it is also famous for its wine and its festivals and—"

"Tiggy, don't you understand? Even if it was my lifelong dream to go up there, it would only be temporary. As herald, she could ship me off anywhere she damn well wanted, whenever she damn well wanted. One day Ardora, the next *Rinath*. Just like she did to Urosina."

Teigra sat on the edge of the bed. "Oh . . . of course. And not even the five high cities, I suppose? She could send you to the mid towns and even the low villages as well?"

There was an uncomfortable pause. "*Thank you*, Tiggy. I hadn't even thought about that! But yes. It could be a big city, or it could be some three-pig village. That's the point: I would be entirely at her whim."

Teigra furrowed her brow. "I thought you said Benedict would be chosen as herald? And that she would nominate you to fill his spot in the senate?"

"I know."

"That would have made sense. Heralds are often future rulers. Aunty Sabina was herald to Grandfather Harophonies for just under a year, before she became archon, wasn't she?"

"I *know*."

"And Beni is still House Savair's designated heir, isn't he?"

Aurelius threw the pillow off and shot her a filthy look.

"Sorry," she said, soothingly. "I am sure you will be amazing! Mestibes will be lucky to have you as herald." His sullen silence at first confused and then shocked her. "Wait. You *are* intending to accept, aren't you?"

He curled into a ball. "She hasn't formally issued the parchment. That is just a draft. She has given me until tomorrow to decide."

"Why the urgency?"

"I don't know. I don't know about any of it. The urgency? Why she has chosen me? What I should do? Yes, it would be a wonderful opportunity to make Beni furious: me getting to act in the archon's name, rather than him? But what is the point of pissing him off if I won't be here to see it?"

Teigra shuffled gingerly onto the bed, her back still stinging from the morning's brutality. She ran her fingers along his arm. It wasn't like him to be so uncertain. "If it makes you feel any better, I'd miss you terribly. Life would be a lot more boring without you."

He sat upright. "Then come along!"

"What? How?"

"Dorina Mattic's low envoy position! You've heard that she turned down an extension once her five year posting was up? Apparently, she has come back to find a husband. And the senate hasn't voted on her replacement yet, have they?"

"I don't think so, but—"

"Don't you see, Tiggy? It is perfect! You would get to do all the envoy stuff with the senate, and I could do the mingle with nobility bit for the archon!"

"Like Calix, you mean?"

His face flushed, which also wasn't *at all* like him. "I wasn't thinking of him, darling! I was thinking about you and me. About us! Come on, admit it, it would be perfect!"

She stared into the middle-distance. The envoy–herald relationship was an ancient one, a compromise between the archon's right to absolute power, and the senate's desire for impartial decisions in the public interest. The senate appointed hundreds of envoys all over Dynosia, in practically every polity in the whole country, doing important technical work like making trade deals, ensuring the city had the best supplies of food and equipment, cultural exchange and legal representation and the like. By contrast, there was only one herald of the archon, speaking with royals and nobility, performing ceremonial tasks, and attending the fancy parties and weddings and funerals that only a ruler's family could muscle their way into.

Usually, it was a deeply fraught relationship.

But it won't be that way if we have the roles . . .

"You might even get to be a steed trader!" he said, alluringly.

A tiny spark fizzed up. "The best steeds do come from the Ardoran plains. Apart from the pegasi of course. They all come from the fountains near Emphanisi. Have I told you the story of how—"

"Exactly!" he said, smirking at her excitement. "See! And Aunt Beeta would love it, too! Having the senate declare House Cosmin worthy of civilizing the most backward of polities?"

As quickly as the excitement came, it faded at the mention of her mother's name. "No. She'd never allow it. She's obsessed with marrying me off right now."

"Don't worry. I can make her understand."

"But you know what she'll say. Ardora? The land of passion and fertility? Of brutes and wenches? Wrestling and drinking and dressing up like therians? She'll say it's *improper* for those aspiring to patrician status."

"Oh, come on, Tiggy. Stop making excuses! Your father would never have wanted you to live like this. He always—"

"You don't know what he would have wanted!" she snapped, surprising even herself. She dragged herself from the bed a little too fast, causing a stab in her back. "He . . . he wanted House Cosmin to advance! And that is what Mother is doing!"

"And you would go along with that? Even if it means being *beaten*?"

Her stomach clenched. How did he know about that? "I . . . that isn't . . ."

"For fuck's sake, Tiggy. There are blood stains on your tunic!"

The sudden heat of the exchange cooled in the silence that followed.

"Please, darling," said Aurelius, patting the bed. "Let's not quarrel.

Come with me to Ardora. You can start a whole new life there. Away from *them*. Away from all of this."

Teigra looked into her cousin's eyes—those big, ice-blue beacons of determination. He was so strong, so *competent*. He could march into any city he chose, without knowing a single soul, and by dinner, he would have the run of the place.

But me? Going to Ardora? As an envoy? Being entrusted with a position of power and influence by the senate? For five years?

The idea was ridiculous. Totally ridiculous.

She sighed, giving the most comforting smile she could muster. She already felt ashamed for raising her voice like that, after all he had done for her. "Thank you, Aurie. Really. It means a lot that you would think of me like that. But some of us must live the life we're told to." She smoothed the lines of her tunic, willing dry upon the drips of blood already running down the small of her back. "Whatever decision you make, you'll have to make it without me."

12

AURELIUS

ON A CLEAR DAY, AURELIUS COULD SEE FROM HIS MUSIC ROOM TO THE hazy, forested peak of Vaticily, far off in the distant northeast.

The faithful believed the mountain was where Vatic played games with the fates of men. Where people from Dynosia took pilgrimage, consuming strange medicines and conducting stranger rituals to induce guidance from the different ranks of oracles.

Aurelius didn't go in for prayer, and he could count on one hand the times he had visited the Pentheon since he came of age, beyond the social necessities of weddings and funerals. But as he blew a dark melody on his favorite syrinx pipes—not based on any song, but just letting his pink lips wander across the row of reeds—he could've used a little of that mountain insight right now.

The archon was more cunning than he had expected. Offering him the herald position was brilliant. In one move, she had all but made him the Libercropolis of the modern day—screwing him over while preserving her position.

If he accepted the role of herald, others would see her as merciful, using the tragic death of her sister to forgive her *wayward* son. And in return, she would control him for the rest of his damn life—and get

62

him out of the polity, where he couldn't cause any more local scandals.

And if he refused the honor? Well, she would still be viewed as gracious. And everyone would understand when she never offered him another title for the rest of his fucking life.

Oh, she hadn't said so explicitly. But he understood. This offer was all he would ever get from her.

Take it? Or leave it? Either way, she wins.

And yet, would she really go to such lengths just to neuter him? The herald wasn't some *honorary* position. It was an incredibly powerful role—one that was given to the ruler's most trusted confidant. A herald had to deliver declarations of war and surrender. To meet with kings and queens, warlords and rulers. To speak with the voice and authority of the archon in far-off lands. If the herald sneezed, Mestibes caught a cold.

After six years of hatred, would she really cede such trust, such power, just to keep me away from home and under her control?

The notes swayed out into a sky filled with brilliant stars. The moon was just as indecisive as he: caught halfway between bronze and sable.

Light or dark? Bronze or sable? Yes or no? Or just stuck on a distant mountain, waiting for guidance from some fickle god?

Aurelius sighed, swapping the pipes for an ornate oil lamp and wandering into the internal courtyard of his estate—richly scented with a rare bouquet of bear's foot flowers.

Only the richest and most powerful Mestibians could afford a private bathhouse, rather than the communal facilities interlaced throughout the city. And as he walked the cool night, he marveled, not for the first time, that his exile from House Savair had come at a substantial decrease in reputation, and yet a substantial *increase* in his wealth.

He mostly traded in kind, secret for secret. But he was not averse to having his silence or secrets purchased with riches from across Dynosia—fine silks and finer wine, gold jewelry, and objects of extravagance in glass and marble. All those lovely, decadent, *exclusive* goods that a wise Mestibian boy was supposed not to covet.

Candles flickered against the cream and umber marble as he entered the bathhouse. The servants had done their job and fucked off, just as they were supposed to. The little space was big enough to fit four, and swirled in the intoxicating aroma of lily of the valley.

Aurelius peeled away the layers of sumptuous fabrics and accessories: his yellow-and-black cloak, held with the golden fibula pin of a bee on an orchid; his zoster belt of luxurious kid leather and sandals of same, their straps twisting up his calves; and finally, a tunic of ruby red, embroidered with a golden motif of a celestial strix, the owl depicted on the arms of Mesti, and the abiding symbol of the senate.

This morning it had seemed a good joke.

As it turned out, the only one laughing was the archon.

He never wore the loincloth undergarments polite society considered proper. At first, it was an act of defiance—for if he was to be considered bestial by the masses, then he would gladly permit them glimpses of his beasthood. But now he had simply grown to enjoy the feeling of his fine tunics caressing his bare body with every step of the day.

The final piece of cloth fell to the floor, revealing his full nakedness. His body was lean and fair. His cock hung long below a patch of light pubic hair, with the pink tip peeking out from his foreskin. His ass was high and round, with surprisingly full thighs, both covered in a soft coat of blond fuzz.

The bath was *perfect*, giving the slightest sting on entry, before settling into a skin-penetrating warmth.

And as the water massaged the knots from his slim neck, the tension from his baby-soft feet, he thought of the decision before him.

He thought of *Ardora*.

And for the first time since it happened, his mind turned properly to that moment in the Pentheon with Prince Calix. That moment where every hair had stood on end as if lightning was arcing across his skin. That moment when it felt like he might never breathe again.

What in the gods' names was that?

Things had been so hectic since the funeral, first the feast and the night that followed, then his mother's offer, and then this blur of a day. He hadn't had the chance to consider that moment properly. But it had been . . . *unfathomable*. The heat, the immediacy, the realness of the sensation.

At that moment, he had felt the body heat. Tasted the sweat. Known the incredible yearning.

And in the eyes of Prince Calix, he had *felt* the terror.

Others might try to find a divine explanation for that. To see the meddling of the Five in mortal affairs or the influence of the therians who possessed a fraction of their sire's power—the satyrs of Ardor, the phoenixes of Rina, the gorgons of Vatic, the sirens of Ondo, and the eidolons of Mesti. After all, it was "well-known" that a satyr could drive people into fits of uncontrollable passion and delirious lust.

Perhaps that was the explanation?

Hardly.

Only fools believed that rubbish—magic and superstition, folklore and secret rituals.

The explanation was far more mundane. He was just horny. That was the only obvious explanation. Overwhelmed by the foreign man, so big and commanding and ferocious.

And the look of terror which crossed the prince's face? No doubt in his debauched thoughts, Aurelius had shot Calix a look of undisguised lust, and the poor soldier was disgusted. After all, Mestibes may look down upon Aurelius's *waywardness*, but that was as far as it went. However, the punishment in Ardora for such depravity was rumored to be far more severe.

Aurelius chuckled.

So, the big soldier can tolerate blood and mud and death, but not a lustful look from a cutie like me?

Aurelius sank deeper into the bath.

Yes, that was all it was. Some reaction to this stranger from strange lands, with his mysterious demeanor, his dark face, and his thick body.

The man truly had been a beast—bigger than any man he'd ever seen. So big and strong the prince could do whatever he wanted with him. So powerful he could throw him around, pin him down, force him to bend to his will.

Aurelius ran a hand down his narrow chest, trailing fingertips across his soft stomach until he arrived at his marble-hard cock. He rolled the foreskin back, sending tingles up his body. He let out little whimpers of relief for an urge he wasn't aware he'd been neglecting.

He moved his free hand down his slender waist, running the line between his thighs and smooth balls until he arrived at his pink entrance. His finger circled it as he gripped his cock, teasing the sensitive area, pressing gently with one finger, then two, all without letting them inside. His hips bucked against his touch—anticipating the sensation that nowhere else could give him.

With the gentlest of force, his fingers slid in, their passage assisted by the buttery warmth of the water.

The feeling of fullness was intoxicating. He paused for a moment, relishing the sensation. When he could stand it no longer, he grazed up against his magic spot.

The pulse was more intense than he'd expected, forcing shocked cries from his lips. His toes curled as he fluttered his fingertips, first gently, then forcefully against his most sensitive place.

Again and again, he rang his bell, until they weren't fingers inside him: they were Calix's big, dominant cock. They were the insatiable horn of that scary bull—grabbing him by the shoulders, biting at his neck, leaving him completely unable to move, unable to breathe, unable to think! Forcing him into submission! Using him. Taking what he wanted. Doing whatever he damn well wanted—too strong to resist.

Calix's enormous arms gripped his chest, pulling him back into his hard, hairy body. Rutting against him like a crazed beast, stinking of sweat and sex.

The dark prince didn't give a damn whether Aurelius was enjoying it or not. Whether he wanted it like this! He was taking whatever he needed. Taking what he *deserved*.

Deeper and harder the huge man fucked him.

Deeper and harder.

Deeper and harder!

Aurelius screamed as ropes shot from his cock, all up his chest and stomach. He shook hard as his whole body was wracked with pleasure.

Even after the shots subsided, the waves of rapture didn't, forcing him to keep slamming his fingers inside himself, until he was a shaking, whimpering little mess.

After what felt like hours, he collapsed back into the warm embrace of the water. Despite the remnants of vigor running milky into the bath, the memories lingered still. If anything, he felt barely satiated, the desire still shimmering in his blood—an itch beneath his skin that could only truly be scratched by the real thing.

Aurelius sighed. It seemed the decision had been made for him.

It seemed he would be going to Ardora.

13

TEIGRA

SOMETHING WAS UP.

In the days that followed, Mother was barely home. Even when she was, guests came banging on the door at all hours, sneaking off and exchanging hurried whispers in little side rooms. And unlike the usual pollen-sweet nature of Mother's socializing, this felt different. She would return humming a cheery tune, only for a visitor's news to send her into a fit of curses.

And all the while, Mother kept giving her these glances—like Teigra was a rug she was debating whether or not to buy.

The same thing was happening outside, too. One minute, Teigra would be tending the stables, only to glance up and find faces peering through the doorway, hurriedly departing when she noticed them. And not just any faces, but senators! The sort that only ever ventured below the stands to suck up to the centaur while they were getting their rubdowns.

At first, she dismissed it as paranoia. After all, why would anyone pay her special attention these days? But things only got worse once Aurelius was publicly proclaimed as herald. After that lavish ceremony in the Forum, it seemed everywhere she turned people were watching her. Noticing her. Judging her!

It was just like three years ago. Back when everyone was obsessed with the delicious tragedy of a daughter killing her own father.

On the fifth evening of this sickening strangeness, Mother dressed her and Jaronas in the finest clothing that had ever touched her skin—soft linen, so white and so clean it practically twinkled in the moonlight—with her hair tightly braided behind a band of golden owls.

It was a fitting symbol. For that night, they were to dine with *Flurin Scipio*, the Censor of the Senate. The most powerful person in the whole city, after the archon.

And while Mother brushed aside Teigra's curiosity, just telling her to be on her best behavior, House Cosmin had never had the privilege of dining in such grand company.

And the family certainly had no bachelor son to throw at her.

Is ... is it finally happening? What Father dreamed of for so long?

Was House Cosmin about to be elevated to patrician status?

She barely dared to hope. But, after all, what other reason could there possibly be?

The residence of House Scipio was beautiful, with manicured cypress pines and staggering white sculptures that bubbled water into crystal pools. She remained silent at the dinner of mint and pomegranate lamb—the meat prepared simply, but more tender than any she'd ever eaten.

Maintaining that silence became hard when the room filled with mockery of the archon and House Savair. Jaronas and Mother laughing at the *perversion* of her cousin and his obvious unsuitability as herald.

As their cackles clawed across her face, she ran her thumb slowly down her pendant, resisting the urge to defend her extended family.

Hold my tongue, Da. We are so close!

She was well versed in the tension between the archon and the senate, though she could never understand it. Surely, they all worked for the same cause? For the glory of Mesti and her people?

And yet, whenever Aunty Ura had spoken of the senate's envoys, she would first peer over her shoulder, as if one might be lurking in the shadows.

And even though Mother was the archon's youngest sister, and the youngest daughter of Grandfather Harophonies, she always went out of her way to deny her blood—sucking up to senators and patricians instead.

And as for Aurelius? Well, his behavior might not be the best service to the goddess, but there was a good person beneath his reputation. He had always been there for her. He hadn't chosen to be the way he was. And he deserved so much better than how people spoke of him.

"And so, *Teigra*, I hear you fancy your history?" said the censor, a tall man with deep wrinkles around his eyes.

She almost dropped her glass. The table fell silent, turning expectantly.

"*Me?*" she coughed.

Mother gave a warm laugh and jammed a fingernail into her back, grinding right near one of her half-healed scars. "Poor thing is just a little shy around her betters, Censor. An important trait these days."

"Indeed, Senator Cosmin. But there is no need to stand on ceremony, Teigra. I am also a history buff. Man cannot improve if he is ignorant of his past."

"No, Censor," said Teigra.

"And you spend a lot of your time in the Lapiso Library?" said the censor's daughter, Senator Chloe Scipio, a young woman barely older than she. Her ample assets jiggled as she tossed a piece of leftover meat to a keen-eyed celestial strix, the first Teigra had seen in real life —black as a sable sky, and with a scattering of iridescent indigo that made the bird's feathers twinkle like starlight. The woman had a noble bearing far beyond her family name, with eyes that made

Teigra's mouth go dry, and her heart beat a little quicker. "You visit there every morning before dawn, I'm told?"

"Yes . . . ?"

"How admirable," said the censor. "Reading the great history of our city while others are still sleeping. Please, enlighten us, what is your favorite work?"

She shot a confused look to Mother. She'd always said it was improper to discuss the education her father had started. She'd said that having too many thoughts and opinions would repulse the young men she needed to pursue.

"Come now, Teigra," said Mother, her smile bright below dark eyes. "We mustn't leave the censor in suspense."

"*A . . . A Nation United*," she muttered, blushing under the weight of the table's attention. "The complete history of the Third Dynosian War and the signing of the Compact of the Grove."

It wasn't entirely true. She loved that codex, yes, but *Gods Among Us* was her actual favorite. But frothy stories about therian mischief hardly seemed the right answer at *this* table.

The censor smiled. "Ah, a noble work. And which of its many stories do you favor?"

"The one about Grandfather Harophonies," she said, a little too quickly. "For the sacrifices he made as our last military general. And for the restraint he showed in not allowing the other polities to massacre the Rinathi into extinction."

As soon as the words left her mouth, she realized her mistake. By selecting that chapter, she was praising *House Savair* and the current line of archons!

You idiot! Why didn't you pick a hero from the senate? Or a tale of glory from House Scipio? Stupid! Stupid! Stupid!

To her surprise, the censor nodded. "Ahhh, now *there* was an archon who understood the proper balance of things. He didn't run off on whichever imprudent plan took his fancy. He understood that the city needed a chamber to instruct, and a leader to enact. An equality of authority. Sparing the Rinathi? Disbanding the Mestibian army? Those were *our* ideas. And he was wise enough to work alongside the senate to achieve them."

"Thank you, Censor," said Mother, with miles of carefully crafted humility. "My father was indeed a great man. And if I might say, proof that while the tree of House Savair may now be struck with twisted branches, some of its fruit still falls on productive soil."

The censor gave Teigra a long look. "Yes, Senator Cosmin. I think you might be right about that."

The evening continued without further explanation of the strange conversation. But one day later, all was revealed.

Mother had left early to attend a sudden senate vote. That evening, she burst into Teigra's room in triumph, wine on her breath. She sat on the edge of the bed, taking her by the hand, something she never did.

"It worked! We've won! They've elected you as the new low envoy to Ardora!"

Teigra's whole body went numb. It felt like she was watching herself from a distance.

She . . . can't be serious? Me? Leaving the city? Representing the senate? For five years!

And as the blood drained from her face, Mother's grip morphed, grabbing her so hard it felt like her knuckles could shatter. And in a voice of cold menace, she gave Teigra the three commandments that she was to abide by in her time abroad.

First, she was not to embarrass House Cosmin in any way.

Second, she was to do everything that the high envoy to Ardora asked of her.

And third, she was to find out why the archon had selected *Aurelius* as her herald.

14

AURELIUS

THE NEWLY APPOINTED HERALD OF MESTIBES FIDDLED WITH HIS SIGNET ring and sneered at the stuffy office. It was ghastly, just like the entire Administration of Dynosian Affairs—filled with statues and frescos so old he could practically taste the accumulated dust.

"Darling," he said with a wry glance, "I know we have always had strangely shared life experiences. And I will admit, it has played wonders for our bond. I get ostracized at fifteen; you get ostracized at fifteen. My little brother takes my place as head child; your little brother takes your place as head child. But really, becoming low envoy to Ardora? Just to remain close to me? You didn't need to do *that*."

Teigra was sitting bolt upright at the desk, looking as terrified as Calix had at the funeral. "It wasn't me!" she hissed. "It was Tulla! That . . . busybody! She must have heard your plan and passed it on to Mother! And Mother must have traded the information for my position! I didn't know any of this was happening!"

"Tiggy, please! There is no need for such invention. After all, imitation is the most sincere form of flattery."

"But it wasn't my idea!"

It was cruel to tease her so. Of course it wasn't her idea. Teigra? A million miles from home? For five long years? Surrounded by new people and new places?

It was a miracle she wasn't passed out in a pool of terrified vomit.

"And you aren't even supposed to be here," she said, grasping at the necklace she'd worn for as long as he could remember. "This training is just for envoys, not the herald."

"Well, if you really want to be left alone?"

He'd barely risen from his desk before she yanked him back down.

From outside the office came a crash, followed by a series of loud footsteps, like a minotaur was running laps in the hallway.

The door was swung open by . . . a minotaur running laps in the hallway.

The figure was a cameo of dishevelment—late twenties perhaps, although it was hard to tell with minotaurs, with a curly mess of cinnamon-brown fur, horns that weren't symmetrical in the slightest, and a toga so poorly wrapped it was running along the ground. The tail of the two-hollow-striped material trailed alongside his actual tail and the scrolls that tumbled from his arms.

A patrician, but not a senator.

"Hello there!" he said, in a voice of pure sunshine. "Sorry, I'm late. I swear I used to know my way around here perfectly. But you know how it is, a decade away and it all just disappears, doesn't it!"

The boy—and he was a boy, no matter his age—dumped the pile of scrolls on a side bench and held out a huge hand to Teigra. "Jaspar Accola, mid envoy to Ardora. And you must be Ms. Cosmin?" Teigra shook the hand, her faced stunned. "Amazing to meet you, Teigra! Can I call you Teigra, and you call me Jaspar? Technically I'll be your boss, but I don't go in for that *oh hello Mr. Accola* stuff. Moving to a new polity is supposed to be fun! Not all rules and regulations!"

Teigra blinked silently as the handshake kept going.

"And *I* am Aurelius Savair, the Herald of Mestibes," he said, in an imperious voice, hoping it might deflate the boy's unbearable happiness. "I know this training is not intended for me, but I simply demand that—"

Jaspar shook his hand vigorously, warm and soft with fur. "No, the more the merrier! You're coming to Ardora just the same as us. It wouldn't do to have you going in blind!"

"Well, yes," he said, rubbing feeling back into his fingers. "And a departure which is taking place *tomorrow morning*. The archon is certainly keen to send her new herald away."

It was a petulant complaint, and he knew it. The archon had originally wanted to arrange a steed for him, so he could go up to Ardora on his own terms, just like Urosina used to trot around on. Mother had even promised to procure a pegasus. But buggered if he was going to pick up that skill now, thank you very much. Nasty creatures. As liable to kick you in the balls as follow your commands.

"Alas, yes, Your Excellency," said Jaspar, with an apologetic pout. "Although I fear that might be more our doing than Her Majesty's. Ms. Securia was keen to have the low envoy position filled a month ago. Plus, tomorrow is the bronze moon, and the last day of high spring. Auspicious omens to begin a new journey, don't you think?"

Your Excellency . . .

Aurelius leaned back. The boy was the first to use his new title in casual conversation since he'd been proclaimed. He liked the sound of it, and he certainly didn't mind it coming from *his* lips.

He couldn't recall meeting him before, although that was unsurprising. House Accola famously had more of its brood posted abroad than they had lurking around Mestibes. They were probably the only patrician family for whom an appointment to senator, and being stuck in the city, would be considered a disappointment.

This particular Accola seemed just like the rest of them—perky and personable. Underneath the hyperactive energy, he was rather handsome, in a still-a-puppy-at-thirty sort of way. In all his conquests, Aurelius had never had the good fortune of bedding a minotaur. But their reputations for virility preceded them. And a quick look at this one's bulge, even nestled beneath the thick fabric of this toga, revealed a very promising—

"Ms. Securia?" said Teigra. "She's the high envoy, isn't sh—"

Aurelius sighed an interruption. "High Envoy Ramuna Securia. Third and youngest child of Tian and Tonia Securia. Sister of Senators Paula and Cornel Securia. Appointed low envoy to Ardora at nineteen, mid envoy at twenty-six, and rising to high envoy at just thirty."

He grinned at Jaspar, but the chipper expression didn't budge. The gold-braided ring in his nose twitched in interest. "*Thirty*? Wow! I knew she was young when she got the gig, but I didn't know it was *that* young!"

Jaspar passed each of them a wax tablet and a stylus, the dandelion-colored surface already tacky in the windowless room. "So, *Ardora*! The most important thing to know is that it is completely different from here. Throw away all your ideas about what 'normal' means. Mestibes is all about restraint and logic. But up there, the driving force is *passion*. In Ardora, a great poem wouldn't be judged on its perfect structure and its immaculate references, but on the power of its delivery. Take their famous Brotherhoods and Sisterhoods. They don't fight through careful formations or modern technologies, but as berserkers and outriders and little troops taking on whole hordes without any fear! Now, let's start with trade, probably our most important job down there —well, at least Teigra and mine's, Your Excellency! As you know Ardora is our main source of vegetables and wine, but did you know—"

And once the lesson started, it never seemed to fucking finish. The morning grew into the afternoon, which faded into pre-evening, until the intentional disobedience of his presence dimmed from delightful to hideously dull. Tiggy was no fun either, dutifully asking questions on trade and diplomatic protocol, jotting things down in progressively smaller letters, until her tablet was more lines than not.

Even he mouthed a thankful prayer when the tutorial finally ended. Teigra left with an armful of scrolls and spent the entire walk to his apartment vibrating with nervous energy, yammering on about the day's leanings.

Usually, he would have said a few words to calm her. But his mind was elsewhere—wondering the same question that had gnawed at him for days. A question that had only strengthened in the long hours of hearing about how important the relationship with Ardora was to the proper functioning of the city.

For food. For wine. For steeds. For wood.

For *everything!*

Why in Dimethan has she chosen me for this job? It can't just be a power move. It just can't!

He had expected to receive some kind of instruction from the archon after his confirmation. Some discreet little meeting that might shed light on why she had chosen him. But thus far, there had been nothing. No training. No secret briefing. No commands for his journey beyond, "Improve relations with the Ardoran nobility," and, "Make the meetings that Securia can't."

Nothing!

At least, nothing until that moment.

He arrived home to find a curious package on his gold-woven bedspread—wrapped in light-colored leather and yellow twine. Teigra didn't seem to notice, dumping her mound of scrolls by the pillows, still rattling off facts and nervous laughs.

A piece of parchment was tucked into the twine.

May you meet her standard.
   - S

Well, about bloody time!

He tore the twine apart. The wrapping folded away to reveal a sheath of parchment papers, held together by tied leather strips in the corner and wrapped with a beautiful dark-leather folio that bore the same symbol as his new ring—the holy shield of Mesti, crest of the archons. The pile smelled of age and occupancy, a lived-in sort of smell.

They were letters. Hundreds of them. All different colors of parchment and all different grades of ink. Some were dated almost twenty years back. And each was signed in the same way:

Your loving sister and loyal herald,
   - U

Urosina's cables home! A lifetime of reporting on her quests and travels! Documents of which there were only a single copy, all going directly to the archon.

And as he flicked through the neat handwriting, he was shocked to find not the boring reports he expected of the serious old bitch, but little snippets of *gossip*.

My Dearest Majesty, I bring news of much scandal in Ondocis . . .

Lady Morcel left Vaticily that evening in a frightful temper, and I must surmise that the low oracles did not give her the guidance that she sought . . .

I fear the glass lady has undersold the damage in the relationship. The crown would not meet with me during my entire time in Ardora . . .

He paused at that one, dated just three months prior. It ran through the things he would expect—movements in high society, updates on weather and expected prices for goods. But at the bottom was something wholly unexpected.

It was an extended and rather detailed passage about the Ardoran royal family: House Viralis, which like many of the oldest northern nobility had its family name drawn from Voresoma rather than Dynosian—an artefact of an age when Mestibian diplomacy and education held rather more sway in the land of fertility than it presently did.

The passage spoke of King Selkus III, wise and popular, still recovering from his poisoning at the hands of a Rinathi assassin five years prior, during the Sama invasion. Of Queen Dimitra, cold as an empty bed, but perhaps the real power behind the throne. Of their younger daughter, Zosime, just twenty-three but already the most impressive Sisterhood captain in the whole land. And finally, of Crown Prince Calix, strategos of all the Brothers and Sisters of Ardora. A distant man and committed bachelor, who despite being pursued by at least a dozen eligible . . .

Aurelius froze, re-reading the passage.

A committed bachelor . . .

"That fucking bitch!" he screamed to no one in particular.

Aurelius stormed from the apartment, making his way directly to the palace. Teigra jogged behind, asking questions he barely even heard.

So that was the archon's game all along! There *was* a secret reason she'd chosen him for the job of herald. And he had just been too blind to see it.

I got comfortable. I left myself open. Well, not again!

It hadn't occurred to him that she would use him for something like *that*. That even she could be this manipulative and hypocritical. But now, it was clear as the finest glass.

And after all she did six years ago? One day she throws me out of the family for who I am, and now she wants to use that part of me for her own goals?

The journey along familiar streets passed in a rush. Soon, Aurelius was deep in the palace, the building he'd been raised in— the marble columns a purer white and more finely sculptured than any other in the city.

He burst into the archon's private office, a small clutch of modestly dressed attendants scurrying in his wake.

"Did you think you could get away with this?" he barked, brandishing the folio like a shield.

The room was sparse in the way only real power could pull off—a deliberate display of well-fashioned restraint. The archon peered from her desk, the oil lamp flickering with the night breeze, carrying the smell of lemon blossom and betrayal.

"Apologies, Your Majesty," panted Kufan, his mother's ancient chief advisor, a man who had haunted the halls of the palace with his sharp eyes and sharper tongue throughout Aurelius's childhood. "We couldn't stop hi—"

The archon raised her hand, and the man retreated. There was a moment of silence before she spoke.

"Well, Herald. You clearly came to speak your mind?"

He marched to her desk and slapped the folio down, the offending page face up. "*Crown Prince Calix, strategos of all the Brothers and Sisters of Ardora. A distant man and committed bachelor, who despite being pursued by at least a dozen eligible noblewomen since his single-handed heroics in Sama, has not yet found a maiden that has captured his lasting attention. Instead, my extensive inquiries suggest that the fraternally minded prince is more interested in wrestling with the rough and ready menfolk from his own fighting days.*"

"And?" said the archon, stony-faced. "I gave you Urosina's cables to aid your work. I wouldn't have done so if I'd known it would upset you so."

"Don't play coy with me, Mother. Do you think I don't know Urosina's little codes? Do you think she didn't use them on me as well? *Committed bachelor*? *Fraternally minded*?"

"What are you implying?"

Aurelius leaned, his eyes narrowing. "Prince Calix is *gay!*"

15

AURELIUS

THE ARCHON GLARED. THE ONLY SOUND IN THE OFFICE WAS AURELIUS'S own agitated breaths.

"Yes," she said at last. "As far as I know, and as much as Urosina could uncover, Prince Calix is gay. Or at the very least, he is willing to entertain the advances of men as well as women."

Aurelius was incandescent with anger. "*That* is why you selected me? You abandoned me for this very thing. And now, you want to use it! Is this all I am to you? A convenience when you want me, and an inconvenience when you don't? Why shouldn't I walk out that door right now and let you send Beni in my place. Hmm!? See how well he does with whatever your sad little plan is?"

"Go ahead, my child. But you'll leave here without ever knowing the truth."

That gave him pause.

A secret? Well, I don't need you for that, Mother. Whatever it is, I can uncover it all on my own.

"Only Urosina and I know, Aurelius," she said, seemingly reading his mind. "Though you may take your chance with her corpse, if you'd prefer."

His fingernails dug up the beeswax polish of her desktop. He hated ceding her this power, but his curiosity was too piqued to walk away. He finally had half of an answer—she'd made him herald to seduce the prince. And now he wanted the other half.

He needed to know *why*.

He slumped into the hard chair opposite her desk, his arms crossed indignantly.

"I am afraid you must leave us," said the archon, peering over his shoulder.

Aurelius turned. Teigra was milling by the door.

"Of course, Your Majesty! Sorry! I'll just let myself—"

"She stays," said Aurelius.

"No, Herald. She *leaves*."

Before another staring contest broke out, Teigra decided for them. "Lovely to see you again, Your Majesty."

The archon said nothing as Teigra disappeared behind the near-slammed door.

Then they were alone.

The leader of Mestibes leaned back, weighing her son. Her hair was tied up and back in a braid, the lamp flickering gold across her smattering of gray and the sharpness of her eyes. "You know of the Battle of Sama, Herald?"

Aurelius rolled his eyes. Though his formal education had ceased in disgrace by that point, even he couldn't avoid news of a war. "Some squabble a few years back between the other four polities. Rinath stole some irrelevant rock from Ardora. Calix did some fighting things. Now his name is taught in schools as some kind of hero."

His mother sighed. "An island in the Antimos Gulf, just a few hundred yards from the Rinathi coast. It was handed to Ardora as battle spoils twenty-two years ago, after the Third and upon signing of the Compact of the Grove."

"The agreement you personally arranged? The one that completely gave up our military?"

She didn't so much as flinch at the accusation. "Your Grandfather had already reached that agreement with the senate before I took power. And the other polities were not rushing to disagree. It was a small price to pay for peace across the country."

You would say that, wouldn't you?

Outwardly, he said, "Fine. Sama. What does that have to do with anything?"

"Five years ago, Xiber Feron, the former commander of Rinath's northernmost stronghold, Fort Roldas, invaded the island. Though her forces were comparatively small, the effect was enormous. The Compact had been breached for the first time, and it was the duty of all the other polities to come to Ardora's aid. Ondocis answered the call with their ships. Even Vaticily sent a clutch of poison archers. But we, the initiators and supposed protectors of the Compact, did nothing."

"And who would we have sent? Some glassblowers? Some particularly ferocious stonemasons?"

"Our peace corps may be small, but they are modeled on the Brotherhoods and Sisterhoods of Ardora—small, tight-knit teams that punch stronger than an opponent would expect. They hunt all manner of beasts across the greater polity and have done so for over twenty years. They would have held their own in battle. Enough to meet our honor-bound commitment, at the very least."

"And instead you did nothing?"

"*I?* To preserve the Compact, *I* would have marched every sword-bearer we had to the island. But the senate was unmovable. They believed then, as they do now, that only through peaceful means do we honor the goddess of reason. Words, not war, they said at the time. So, I sent my herald, alongside a delegation from the senate, to negotiate a force of restraint from the other two commanders of Rinath. For them to intervene in Sama and stay their countrywoman's hand."

"You couldn't be bothered to send them to the capital and talk to the war king?"

"No Mestibian has set foot in Rinath proper since the Third,

Aurelius. The city is off limits to outsiders. Even the envoys only go as far as the forts."

She turned her face to the citrus-tinged breeze. The air seemed to flow with an acidic bite.

"But even that was too little. The war for Sama finished before we'd even commenced the negotiations," she continued, "and by that time, three hundred men had already died. Prince Calix was the sole survivor of his Brotherhood. The sole survivor of the *entire* Ardoran Brotherhood—most of the rest drowned in a storm on their approach to the island. At the time of the Third, their Brotherhoods were full of regular men. But after seventeen years of peace, at Sama, they were all first-born sons. Can you imagine such a thing, Aurelius? It would be like every patrician family in Mestibes losing their heir. All at once. All in a single night."

Her eyes turned sad.

"In the end and by some miracle, the anti-Rinath forces won. Even you must know the story of the prince who defeated an entire army. But it was a victory we should have been part of. It was a victory that we were honor bound to take part in!"

Aurelius shuffled uncomfortably. He had never seen his mother look so vulnerable or emotional before, and he didn't fully understand why this matter should hold such importance for her. "Urosina said in her cables that the royals refused to meet her? Even five years on?"

"And nor have they met with the envoys of the senate. Mestibes has been cut off. Our representation slashed. We are living off scraps of trade compared to what we used to get. Surpluses and leftovers. We have been fortunate for abundant harvests in recent years, but if Ardora were to have even one failed season, we would be the first polity cut off."

"And so *that* was the intention of choosing me? Send me down to use *unconventional methods* on the prince to win back their favor and improve our trade?"

She gave a long exhale. There was a deep weight over her posture. "Yes. But not for reasons of *trade*."

The archon opened a desk drawer, revealing an odd scroll of parchment—just a few inches wide and much longer than usual. She unrolled it, revealing a charcoal rubbing of strange symbols:

$$X \rightarrow \Lambda$$

"What is this?" said Aurelius.

"This impression was taken from Urosina's arm, wreathed in blood and scorch." The archon's voice turned brittle. "And it means that Xiber has returned."

Aurelius cocked his head. "She survived Sama?"

"Apparently so. If not for a Rinathi pilgrim to the monastery at Zateniza a few months back sharing a little too much when drunk, we may have remained blind to it."

Aurelius considered his wording carefully, not wishing to show his ignorance. "This information . . . is not yet well-known in Mestibes."

"No. It was ears loyal to me within the monastery that gave the information. And my herald who was sent to investigate." She paused, and Aurelius wondered if she was dwelling on her role in her sister's demise. "Her final message, which I am sure you didn't bother to read, told local gossip of Xiber's return, albeit in *extremely* coded language. She was thriving. Tucked away in one of the more indomitable valleys of the Clawfeather Cliffs. And she was rebuilding her forces. Biding her time."

And you ordered her to confirm those rumors, didn't you? You ordered your sister to march right into the mouth of the beast.

Out loud, he said, "How could she thrive? I thought defeat was the ultimate weakness to a Rinathi."

"Xiber is no fool. She has apparently turned her defeat into an advantage. *Look how pathetic we have become,* she tells the downtrodden tribes of northern Rinath. *We once conquered all Dynosia. Now we can't even conquer one little island.*"

"But Rinath didn't lose at Sama. *She* did."

"She wouldn't be the first leader to turn personal failure into patriotic grievance."

Aurelius studied her, one part of the conversation still not making sense. "But why do *you* care? Some washed up warlord is making a comeback on the ass end of Rinath? One whose only past goal was to reclaim some rock from Ardora, a thousand miles from here. A rock that is currently controlled by a polity that won't even meet with us. Why should you give a shit about any of this?"

The archon clicked her tongue softly. "Because she is different from the rest of them, Aurelius. For twenty-two years, Dynosia has been blessed with Rinathi warlords content to kill their own kind in some endless civil war. To keep their bloodshed to barren valleys and snowcapped peaks, while the rest of us could live. Could love. Could . . . leave dark thoughts in the past."

She looked down at the parchment in his hands. Aurelius took the cue and traced the dusty marks, the ones that had previously adorned his aunt's dead flesh.

There was something decidedly creepy about that.

"Xiber is . . . going to . . . ?"

He paused at the third symbol, appearing like a half-formed triangle.

"The Mountain," said the archon, darkly.

Xiber is going to the Mountain?

Realization crashed into him like waves in a storm. His blood ran cold.

As little piety as he held, even he knew the meaning of a warlord visiting *Vaticily*. It was a pilgrimage only taken before the most momentous of decisions.

"She plans for *war*?"

He searched his mother's face for some hint of levity. Instead, the archon nodded gravely.

86

"When?" he asked.

"Weeks? Months? Fates are only read on the bronze moon. And Urosina established lookouts in the border polities that lead to Vaticily. When Xiber makes her move, I will know about it." She took the parchment from him, passing a sisterly caress along the length of it. "But Ura sent this message with her dying body. I doubt that marks a fair omen."

"So Xiber intends to seek revenge against Ardora? To make another push for Sama?"

The archon gave him a haunted look. "Xiber did not visit Vaticily before that invasion. Not even to one of the low or mid oracles. If she intends to visit now, then she plans for something far bigger. Something worthy of the god of fate's attention."

No . . .

"Yes, Aurelius," she said, reading his face. "That was the rumor that Urosina uncovered. That Xiber intended to break the Compact entirely. To unite the tribes of Rinath and conquer all Dynosia again. And she would have to go through Mestibes to get to the others."

He shuddered beneath his golden tunic. "The other's polities wouldn't stand for that."

"You think Ardora would give us their children's blood, when they deny us a simple meeting?"

Aurelius rubbed his temples. It was all too much. The ground beneath him suddenly felt unsteady, like the floor could crumble. "I leave tomorrow, for the gods' sakes! What was the plan here? That I would just figure this all out?"

"*Yes,* Aurelius. Your grandmother told me how you looked at the prince. You are less subtle than you might think. I had every confidence you would place yourself in an *advantageous position* of your own accord. Ready for when I explained the situation in full."

"To what end? To fuck us all to safety?"

"No, Aurelius, to make a *real connection*. Prince Calix has devoted the last five years to rebuilding the Brotherhoods and Sisterhoods. Their numbers have risen to where they were during the Third. This makes Ardora the only polity with the military might to face Rinath. And he is their strategos, their most senior military commander. He is the one that must be won over. But Ardorans believe in *passion*. They can spot insincerity and contrivance a mile away. That was why you couldn't be told. Whatever bond you built with Calix, it had to be *genuine.* I needed you to charm him, to ingratiate yourself, to become his true confidant." She paused momentarily. "And when the time came, if he would still not come to our aid, then I needed you to purchase his cooperation through *other means*."

Aurelius scrunched his nose like the parchment still smelled of burned flesh. "*Blackmail*?"

"It is nothing you've not done before."

"Yes, but on my terms!"

A rigidity wrapped around the archon, a mix of stoicism and shame. In that moment, he saw just how much of a last resort he truly was to her. "Aurelius, you are the only one I can entrust this to. All our other efforts have failed. Mestibes needs Ardora. Mestibes needs *you*. And we need you *now*!"

He gripped hard at his own arms. She had tricked him! She had taken him for a fool! She planned to use him—for the very thing that she had disgraced him for.

She will pay for this!

And yet, a glimmer of calculation formed amidst his fury. He was not someone who lost his temper. Not without purpose. After all, he hadn't successfully recovered his shattered position through blind emption and impulsivity.

And she will pay . . .

"All right, mother," he said, breathing himself calm. "I'll play your game. But on one condition."

"Name it."

Aurelius's eyes sparkled in the lamplight—fire against ice. "If I do this, you will reinstate me as your chosen heir."

The archon's lips pinched. Her eyes narrowed. When she spoke, her voice bore palpable disbelief. "You would place your own position above your polity? Above the lives of tens of thousands of citizens?"

He stared long at her, finally snorting at her gall. "I still have your proclamation, you know. The one banishing me from House Savair. I suppose self-interest runs in our blood."

"Oh, for Mesti's sake, Aurelius. Nihal Sacredos is the son of the high priestess of all Greater Mestibes. If he can eventually purge himself of this scandal, he will one day be our high priest. The beacon of morality for all our people. He wasn't some plebian who could be secreted away once the truth came out! What would you have had me do?"

"I was fifteen, Mother. *Fifteen!* And you martyred me in front of the entire city, all to save yourself."

"I did it for House Savair! To protect the lines gone and the lines yet to come!"

"Bullshit! You did it for yourself! You screwed me then, and you'd have screwed me as herald, too! Keeping secrets. Bending me to your will. But no more! Here is what you will do. You will take the proclamation into the Forum, stand before your citizens, and you will smash it to the fucking ground!" He rose from his chair, palms slamming against her desk. "You will scream at the top of your lungs that Benedict is out and that I am your chosen successor once more. *That* is my price! Pay it, or I walk!"

And he meant it. He meant every fucking word of it.

Her face was heavy, her voice quiet. "The senate will never vote to confirm *you* when I die."

"That is *my* concern," he snarled. "Do we have a deal or not?"

She didn't move for a long time, staring up at him from her seat. "When the war is over, I will—"

"*No!* No delays. No tricks. You will do it tomorrow morning! Publicly! Before I leave!"

The fury built visibly in her throat. When she at last spoke, it was through gritted teeth. "You will deliver me a signed agreement from the royal family—a promise that they will come to Mestibes's aid if we are invaded. Give me that . . . and I will do as you ask."

A sick smirk grew on his face.

Finally, an ounce of reason.

With a curt nod, he plucked up the folio and made for the door.

"Tell no one of this matter, Aurelius," she shot in parting. "If the senate finds out, they will try to stop you."

He was about to disagree with her. To say something like, *Even they aren't so mad as to want war!*

But he stopped himself.

Of course they are.

He'd heard more than enough senators wank on about the Compact. About how superior it made Mestibes. About how only a truly civilized society could survive without an army. About how laying down arms and shifting to diplomacy had shown all the other polities to be backward, bloodthirsty savages. About how Mestibes's willingness to remain undefended was the highest form of prayer and trust they could give to *Mother Mesti*. About how it proved that Mesti was the greatest of all the Five.

He wasn't sure whether the senate would keep such nerve with an army burning down the city. But until that point, she was right. They were so set in their peace-loving ways that they probably *would* try to stop him.

Out loud, he said, "Even Teigra? You would keep this from your own niece?"

"She is their servant now," said the archon, giving him a final, weighty glare. "Just as you are *mine*."

Aurelius held her gaze, snorted, then exited the chamber.

Teigra was waiting in the corridor. "What happ—"

"Not here," he said, staring at a group of still-milling functionaries in the dark of the awaiting passages. He held his tongue until they were back on open streets, lit by nothing but stars, rendering the whole evening silver and navy. He looked over his shoulders to make sure that rat Kufan hadn't followed them.

The dreadful folio was heavy in his hands—packed with all the euphemisms and bigotry of the dead herald.

When he was sure they were alone, he studied Teigra's confused face.

She was the one member of his extended family who hadn't treated him as an outcast after he'd been disgraced. The only one who had stuck by him, despite the beatings her mother had given to try to keep her away.

There were only two people in all the city that he trusted unconditionally.

One was himself.

And the other was Teigra.

With his mother's warning still hot in his ears, he passed her the folio. "Burn it after you've read it, Tiggy. Pummel the ashes and scatter them to the wind. Our journey just became *a lot* more interesting."

16

TEIGRA

THE LAMP CARVED DEEP SHADOWS FROM HER BED—DAGGERS OF DARK that danced around the room with each flap of the heavy curtains. Those pools of black slid up her simple dresser and her simple mirror. They slunk over her simple chest of left-behind possessions and her simple scroll hive, full of biographical details of the Cosmin stables for over a hundred years.

The simple things of her simple life.

A life which was just hours from ending.

Teigra rubbed her knuckles into her eyes. It was not to stop herself from sleeping, for there was no chance of that happening, but rather to force some moisture back into them.

It must have been well past midnight now. She should have been in bed hours ago.

It was the wisdom that everyone had given her. Jaspar had said, *Get your head down early, Teigra, it will be a big one tomorrow!* Mother had nodded with something that almost resembled pride when she returned from her eventful evening with Aurelius, thick armfuls of scrolls clutched to her chest, telling her to turn in at once. Even Jaronas had rushed into her room after a hasty and simple dinner to help her pack her bag, making sure that she could get as much sleep as possible.

It was all good advice. Reserve her energies for the long journey by carriage to the other side of the country. To make sure that she was alert and able to cram in as much as possible on her short window on the road. To put herself in the best position to impress the high envoy, Ms. Ramuna Securia, by being well-read and well rested—rather than dry eyed and dull.

But . . . she couldn't.

Not now that she knew what she knew.

Not now that she had what she had.

Instead of sleep, she was scouring over the folio Aurelius had given her.

The folio of Aunty Urosina's cables . . .

For long hours, Teigra's fingertips ran over parchments and inks gathered from all across Dynosia. There were the simple and economical buffs that Apaderma supplied to the rest of Mestibes, crossed with well-performing but unfancy black swirls. Others were dark and thicker leather, sent from cities across Ardora and Rinath and Vaticily, more wide strokes than cursive flicks, and written with inks that tended toward browns and earth reds and even deep greens. And finally, there were the parchments so light and so thin and so white they could only be Kanilada Creams, the most expensive parchments in all the country. These were sent from Ondocis, of course, with pen strokes as thin as a needle and with inks that shifted as bright and purple as the dyes Aurelius had on some of his finest tunics.

And every line had been written by Urosina's hands.

The same hands that had clapped her shoulders in celebration after she'd won her first race at just thirteen years old. The same hands that had picked her up as a giggling child, on those rare occasions Ura had found herself back home in Mestibes, and thrown her up toward the sky. The same hands that had held her close when no one else dared, when the tears over her wicked mistake had been too sharp to suppress any longer.

These were the hands that had written more than twenty years of news back her master. Little triumphs and great frustrations. Short scandals and long explanations. The hands which had written down farming techniques and shipping patterns and page after page of laws passed in towns big and small. Twenty years of weddings and births and betrayals. Hands that had recorded a frontline glimpse into almost every coup and shift of power and important event in all Dynosia for over two decades!

And then there were the pages on Ardora itself. These were the hands that had provided a trove of insights into family names and petty squabbles and little tricks with individual personalities. Of leverage points to achieve the best results. Of lords and ladies and leaseholders. Of who could be set against who to get the most trade and most value for Mestibes.

Hands that had recorded it all . . .

And this was it. These pages were the *only copies* that existed.

With each turn of the page and each swirl of text, she could almost *hear* Ura again—those little turns of phrase that made her voice seem to carry with the flickering light. There were *unsavory sorts* in the courts and *complex individuals* in the chambers of power. There were *uncluttered minds* in the pubs, and *the women of high ambitions* in the bedrooms.

And then, as the pages already read started to vastly outnumber those that remained, the language shifted again. The messages became shorter and more urgent. The pen strokes wider and less delicate. Like the text was written with a faster and heavier hand.

As the stack dwindled, Teigra's shoulders pinched together, and her heart quickened. Each flip was a countdown toward an ending that she already knew.

The sun was threatening the sky when she at least reached the final page. And she finally uncovered the horror that Aurelius had wanted her to discover for herself.

No...

The secrecy of the archon and the coded whispers that Aurelius had given her in parting suddenly made hideous, breath-shortening sense.

When the sun finally broke through the dark, she gathered the pages, retying the thick leather of the outer folio.

And Teigra stared at it. Her heart was beating so hard she felt like she was swaying.

Burn it after you've read it, Tiggy. Pummel the ashes and scatter them to the wind.

She breathed as slowly as she could manage, knowing what she had been asked to do—what she *had to* do—but finding her crossed legs refusing to move.

Her household wouldn't rise until well into the morning. Even Tulla wouldn't start cleaning and preparing breakfast for another few hours.

There was still time to sneak into the kitchen and stoke the hearth. To gather the ashes and sprinkle them along her walk down to her departure point.

Of course that was what she had to do! Aurelius had taken a huge risk and shown enormous trust in giving her this folio. She was certain that Mother or Senators Scipio and Viturin would give *anything* to get their hands on this folio! All the secrets gathered by the archon and her herald for over twenty years?

It was the greatest of prizes. It might even be enough for them to grant House Cosmin's wish of elevation to patrician status right here and now. To finish the job started years earlier.

Perhaps, it might even be enough to keep her from having to go on this wretched journey—one that she was in no way qualified or prepared for.

But ... she couldn't do that.

She wouldn't!

Not to Aurelius.

Not after he had trusted her so.

Not with the mission that he had been set, and the awful outcomes if he failed!

And yet, her legs remained crossed and unmoving still, just as her fingers clenched tighter and tighter against the folio.

But . . . burn her words? Just like her body was burned by Xiber's soldiers?

This folio was it. All that was left of her. All that remained of her years of struggle and service.

No, she thought with a wretched, stuttering exhale. *I can't do that either. I just can't!*

But what then was the option? Hide it somewhere? Bury it or stash it away in some forgotten cellar? Hope that in the five years she would be gone no one would stumble across it?

She shuddered. The thought of five years in a new city already stripped her throat raw. She couldn't imagine how much longer it would feel if she had to spend every day worrying the folio might be found.

And what if they extend me? What if five years turns into ten? Or fifteen? There are plenty of envoys who have done the job longer than that!

It was almost too horrible to imagine.

Teigra looked around her room desperately. Finally, she came to settle on her bag—an old but good leather sack, tied with yellow ribbon.

Her grip lessened on the folio and her heart slowed. She scrambled across the bed.

Forgive me, Aurie, she thought as she retied the bag tightly, the folio now tucked safely between well-worn stolas and spare sandals.

17

AURELIUS

THE COBBLESTONES WERE CUNTS—SHIFTING UNDERFOOT IN A LAME attempt to trip him.

Nice try stone chunks, but you aren't gonna stop me! No one is gonna stop me! I'm on a mission. A mission you are too fucking stupid to understand. Cause you are just stone. And I'm Aurelius fucking Savair!

He was probably halfway home from the secret bar at the back of the Kostia's kithara school when the wine bottle between his fingers joined the cobblestones in their disobedience—leaping from his grip and smashing into a million stars.

"Ehhhh!" he shrieked at the pile of shards, mimicking their sudden spike of treble.

It was an annoyance, yes, but it didn't delay him much. After all, there was plenty more where that came from.

The dark streets stumbled by in a blur, a few faces swirling around in a burgundy haze. All the while, the warmth of the wine grew within him, stoking a familiar urge, made even more gnawing and uncomfortable than usual.

Eventually, he found himself somewhere altogether unexpected. He thought he'd been heading home. Not that he'd been thinking too much about it, really. But rather than his luxurious flat in the best part of town, he found himself at the base of the wide stone stairs that led to the *Penthenon*. Great, roaring sconces at the building's base made the column-wrapped edifice loom and glow against the dark.

It was a sight that cleaned away some of the wine haze, just as it also stoked the warmth beneath his skin.

Because round the back of the temple, down a little path and behind a little rocky outcrop, would be the priesthood buildings, all quiet and dark and silent. And through a first-floor window, easily reached by hopping a fence and climbing up a sturdy-branched pine, was a bedroom he knew all too well.

A bedroom where he could tend to his itching, aching warmth.

And yet, something stopped him before he could take his first step. It was the same thing that made him spit out onto the path—his saliva thick and laced with red-berry swirls.

It was the same thing that made him snort and turn on his heels, nose in the air.

He'd love that, wouldn't he. Spending my last night of freedom here, with him? Like I'm some baby bird, coming to him as my only option?

Well, fuck that.

Fuck that!

I've got options.

I've got plenty of them!

Of course, he did. Because Aurelius was a wolf—virile and ferocious and deserving of fear. He could take what he wanted. He could hunt whoever he wanted!

And there was plenty of other prey he could find.

As Aurelius finally reached his flat, the image of golden eyes and towering strength filled his mind, making his skin prickle and his cock twitch.

Yes, there is no fun in hunting scared little rabbits.

Not when I have a bear in my sights.

18

TEIGRA

THE AGORA BUSTLED WITH THE EARLY CROWDS OF SERVANTS AND OLD ladies, carefully inspecting the fragrant bundles of thyme and marjoram.

Teigra moved through the stalls in a sleep-deprived daze. Past the warm, honey-laden pastries which would usually tempt her senses. Past the mounds of pomegranates, a few torn open to display their ripeness—the thick, crimson juice dripping down onto the light gravel.

Just like freshly spilled blood . . .

They don't know, she thought, walking the streets with new eyes— eyes that now knew how temporary it could all be. The grand architecture, built with the ingenuity that was the envy of the entire nation. The great Forum, flanked by manicured cypresses, where great ideas could be debated, and great art performed. The Lapiso Library. The workshops. The great, squat prominence of the Senate. And more than anything else, the *people*.

All these people, committed to logic and diplomacy, learning and art, without a sword or a shield to protect themselves.

And none of them know what is coming . . .

The Pentheon was quiet when she arrived. She bought a five-stick bundle of incense from the attendant: four short, one long. Four were to show respect. One was to show devotion.

In Mestibes that would usually be reserved for Mesti.

Usually.

But not today.

Her footsteps echoed up the high marble of the sacred circle, with the five vast, bronze figures inspecting her from on high.

There were myriad lesser deities that made up the Galaxians, the family of gods and goddesses that governed every aspect of life in Dynosia. Those lesser deities could be called upon by those with specific needs—Evengis Vatic, God of the Noble Hunt; Selin Mesti, Goddess of the Moon; Krasi Ardor, Goddess of Wine; and countless others.

But these were just offspring and descendants. They were not the Five High—the Pentariat.

Teigra lit a short stick first to Ondo—God of Prosperity, Intrepidness, and the Oceans—a bag of gold in one hand and a deep-ink pearl in the other. She prayed that their journey to Ardora be safe and swift.

She lit a short stick second to Vatic—God of Fate, Vitality, and the Wilds—shears in one hand and a long-staff in the other, around which coiled a hissing albino opium snake. She prayed that the god twist his words of prophecy, dispelling Xiber from her bloodthirsty intent.

She lit a short stick third to Rina—Goddess of Discord, Bravery and Tempests—a spear in one hand, and the other holding a burning heart from one of her own war priests. She prayed that the goddess inflame the hatred of the other Rinathi warlords, leading to further civil war and division, rather than a united invasion.

And, after a moment of intense guilt, she lit her final short stick to Mesti—Goddess of Reason, Artistry, and the Night Sky—one hand holding a great shield, the other perched upon by a wide-winged celestial strix. She asked that the goddess give Aurelius the patience and insight to complete his dangerous mission.

Lastly, she came to the statue of Ardor—Goddess of Fertility, Passion, and the Sun—one hand raising a sprig of oak, the other holding an eternal rose to her bare bosom. Teigra twisted the long stick of incense in a nearby sconce, placing it at the goddess's feet.

It was only the second long stick placed there in recent times.

She kneeled, much in the same way that Prince Calix had done just over one week ago.

One week? Has it really been so short a time? And yet, so much has already changed ...

Words from long past scrolls rose with the earthy curls of pine-scented smoke. The incantation came to her in a twisting flow of Voresoma—the language that predated Mestibes itself, and one she was much better at reading than speaking. It drifted by the statues, up past the frescoed ceiling, through the oculus itself, all the way up to the skies beyond.

"Mother of Fertility, Mistress of Passion, sow seeds of affection within Calix's heart. May they grow under your holy sunshine into a verdant field of fervor for Aurelius, to be harvested in tribute to your divine vehemence."

Teigra stayed for the entire length of the burn, feeling every drawn-out second of the wait. Aunty Urosina's last letter, so coded that a casual reader wouldn't have understood its meaning, had been over a month ago. Just before she went on the mission that killed her. They didn't know when the attack might come. Weeks? Days? Perhaps Xiber had slipped by the scouts and was already making for the mountain.

They had to get going!

But favor with the Five was a two-way road. And the length of the incense was set for a reason.

And so, she stayed until the resin burned down to the wood. Only then did she make haste for the Administration.

When she arrived in the courtyard, with Jaspar preparing a

wooden carpentum, it all became hideously real. She was going to climb into that carriage and watch as the city faded from view. Away from her family. Away from the horses that she'd raised from foals. Off on the most important mission that she could ever complete. Just like the heroes of old.

Her breath grew heavy.

Hero?

Me?

It was the least funny joke that had ever been told.

Four centaurs passed as she entered the yards, three male and one female. They were not the muscle-bound sprinters from the Alogo, but taut and lean. Messengers, clearly. Off to tell the embassies of Ondocis and Vaticily and Rinath and most of all Ardora of the appointment of the herald, and perhaps of Teigra's own appointment.

The female centaur—her skin as deep and shimmering as obsidian, with hair down to her navel—gave her a curious wink as she passed, causing a little flutter in her stomach, over and above the existing nervousness. Then they all hit full pace, breaking off at the gate in four different directions, their saddlebags bouncing against their flanks.

There was no going back now. The word was out.

"Oh, no! Let me get that!" she said when she turned back to face Jaspar.

The minotaur was lifting the sack of possessions she'd left here at dawn. Part of her was worried that the folio might fall out and reveal itself. She hadn't told Aurelius that she'd kept it. She hadn't had the chance. But she would. Of course she would. When the time was right. When he'd settled into his mission.

But the other reason she was surprised that the minotaur was lifting her bag was simpler: it wasn't Jaspar's job to do that for *her*.

He just smiled and tucked the bag into something that resembled a fishing net, which hung from the four corners outside the carriage. "Morning, Teigra. Are you excited for the big day?"

"Of . . . of course!" she lied, jamming down her fears and giving what she hoped was a reassuring look. Her own nerves weren't something that he needed to take on.

Jaspar took the last bag—so dirty and scuffed it could only be his own—and pushed it under the footwell of the driver's seat.

"Wait. *You're* driving, Mr. Accola?"

"Please, Teigra, call me Jaspar. And of course."

"But shouldn't you be the one who gets to rest in the shade?"

He considered this. "I suppose so. But I much prefer being out in the free air than cooped up in the dark."

"That's unusual for a minotaur," she blurted, without thinking. She immediately turned red, cursing her nerves for making her to babble such an offensive stereotype. "I didn't . . . Of course, minotaurs can . . . It's just so many of them . . . of *you* . . . prefer to live in the mines and . . ."

"Relax, Teigra," he said, laying a big, soft hand on her shoulder. "Don't worry about it, or that I'll be driving. After all, I would be *very* impressed if you knew the way to Ardora."

Her cheeks blushed even hotter with her own stupidity. "Oh . . . of course."

He laughed. "Really, please. Don't worry, I'm not expecting you to wait on me hand and hoof. You'll have Ms. Securia for that."

She couldn't tell if he was joking and thought it better not to ask.

As he made the final adjustments to the net, the boy kept looking at her with his big, simple smile, making her blush grow even greater.

"Ah? What a beautiful scene," came an unexpected voice from the gate. It was Aurelius, his arms crossed and bearing a wicked grin. A servant behind him strained under the weight of several bags. Teigra didn't know the servant's name, but that was unsurprising—Aurelius seemed to go through a new one every month. "Imagine what your mother would say, finding you alone in the stable with a single minotaur of good breeding."

Her blush spread so far now that her whole face and hairline must have been as red as wine.

She helped Jaspar pack the final possessions and hitch the horses, thankful for the distraction. They were proud beasts, but just regular steeds, not pegasi. Winged horses were far too hard to catch, and even harder to train, to have them do manual labor. Outside of racing teams in Mestibes, and the famed springs at Emphanisi, about a day's ride north of here, they were basically unheard of.

But Ardora was famed for its regular steeds. So maybe that would help? Maybe she could use the one area of knowledge she had?

With a gasp, she realized that she'd been too distracted and shocked by last night's revelations to say goodbye to her darlings in the stables.

And now it was too late!

Oh, goddess, I'm sorry! I'll find time to come back and visit! And hopefully, you'll still be here when I . . .

She pushed that thought away, feeling that if she dwelled on it, she might break in two.

As they climbed into the cabin, Aurelius asked Jaspar for a boost, despite it only being a few feet from the ground. The minotaur obliged, doing a double take as Aurelius "tripped" on the way up, giving Jaspar a full view of his bare ass.

He extended the same offer to her, but she waved it away quickly.

She and Aurelius sat across from each other in the cabin, big enough to fit four at a squash. The interior smelled of freshly oiled pine.

The same smells as the incense? Perhaps it is a fair omen after all?

Then, without ceremony, they were off.

As the carriage clicked down roads she'd walked for as long as she could remember, Aurelius spoke excitedly of the journey ahead, bragging about how easy it would be to seduce the prince.

Teigra nodded along, but her eyes were fixed out the glassless windows.

The Alogo loomed in passing, then became small behind her. Then it was the city gates—at first dominant, then growing smaller and smaller, until the walls were completely concealed by the cloud of white dust kicked up by the carriage.

And then Mestibes was gone.

19

AURELIUS

Teigra was furious with him.

Oh, she hadn't *said* anything. That wasn't her style. But she positively glowered, hotter than the midday sun that the curtains were utterly failing to keep out of the carriage, itself clanking down the smooth ribbon of land between Ondocis and Ardora.

They had only been traveling for an hour today, the third day of their journey, which was far later than they'd intended to leave.

That was entirely his fault. Even he couldn't charm his way out of that little fact.

"Darling, can we please extinguish the glare," he muttered, feeling that his head might explode with each smack of the iron-clad wheels.

Her face morphed into a look of motherly disappointment. "Aurie, *you* were the one who said we should depart the embassy early."

"And I meant it! But I couldn't sleep with the sounds of the waves and the noises from the port. So, I thought a walk might help me drift off."

"Just a walk?"

"All right, yes, and maybe a quick drink somewhere. But just the one!"

"And how many did that turn into?"

"More than one?" he said, with a cheeky grin.

His charm bounced off her like a straw spear. "*Five hours* Jaspar and I had to wait for you this morning. Five hours of not knowing where you'd gone or if you were even alive! With a good run, we could have made Ardora proper by nightfall! Now we'll have to spend another night on the road."

"I know, I know," he said, raising his hands in supplication. She'd been in a bad mood ever since they'd left Mestibes, and his tardiness had not assisted that. "Please, just allow me to die in peace."

After a few moments of silent stewing, Teigra yanked his curtain open, exposing his face to the full force of the heat. "Was it worth it?"

It took all his remaining energy to stay impassive. *Gods yes, it was worth it!*

Aurelius had dreamed of seeing Ondocis since he was a boy—the city of gold and opulence. Of fine jewelry and beautiful fabrics, in dyes so vivid he almost fell to his knees and wept. Of strange spices and intoxicating perfumes from the Sharan Empire to the west. Of black magic boxes and crocodile-skinned codices from the mysterious Pharaohnate of Ptelik, across the northern Macrinos Sea. Of noble bitches and snooty bastards, flouncing around with pithy insults. Of the best food and the greatest wine that any mortal could taste.

And above all, of gossip, drama, and court intrigue at every turn! Every hall had been filled with a dark deal, a secret scandal, a whispered whim.

And for one magical night, he had shopped and bitched and schemed and drunk and fucked with the most fashionable young things in all of Dynosia. His only regret was knowing that he would have to spend the foreseeable future somewhere, *anywhere* else than that beautiful city.

Aurelius promised himself that once he was done with the

backwards polity of Ardora, he would have to trick his way into a long, *long* stay in the Kingdom of Isles.

Midafternoon, they finally left the narrow isthmus of Ondocis and crossed into Greater Ardora. He didn't need Jaspar to tell him that, or to see any kind of marker on the road. He could feel it with every punch into his spine.

If Ondocis's byways were paved with the riches of a thousand fully laden ships, then Ardora's paths were rutted with the meager returns of a thousand fly-swarmed ox carts. The road was *agony*—even Tiggy groaned as they banged their way along, holding their hands against either wall to brace themselves.

"Remind me again why we couldn't have just sailed?" he shouted over the clatter.

"The same reason we have centaurs deliver all of our diplomatic letters, rather than taking them by Ondocian ships!" said Teigra, her voice vibrating.

"Let me guess. Diplomatic protocol?"

"How did you know?"

Aurelius sneered, his mind filled with the process-obsessed old fools in the senate. "Just a hunch."

When Aurelius could take no more of the bone-shattering ride, he banged against the wood by Tiggy's head, which drew a muted "whoa" from the other side of the partition. Once stopped, Aurelius staggered outside, almost tripping.

"Are you all right, Your Excellency?" said Jaspar, his fur an even bigger, curlier mess than it had been when they'd set off.

"Mid Envoy," he said, grasping the carriage for purchase. "This simply *cannot* be the main road between Ondocis and Ardora."

"Bit of a change, isn't it?" he said with a chuckle, moving the fur out of his eyes. "It shocked me on my first trip down! There is a reason most travelers go by sea. All these paths are mostly used by local farmers with heavy wagons, not carriages."

"Aurie," said Teigra, stepping down from the carriage with considerably more finesse. "Didn't you listen during training? Ardora exports wine and meat and vegetables. They aren't poor, exactly, but things are a lot less developed here than back in Mestibes. The roads? The houses? Everything will be like this."

No, that simply won't do, thought Aurelius, wheezing his way up a nearby hill to get a better view.

His fury was momentarily tempered.

What hit him first was the *space*. You could barely throw a rock in Mestibes or even Ondocis without hitting a mountain or the sea or the other side of a valley, but here he could see for *miles*, the mountains replaced with gentle hills, expansive orchids, and fruit-heavy vineyards.

"Oh, Mesti," said Teigra, who had followed him up, albeit without the panting. "It's beautiful."

"What about up there?" he said, pointing to an overgrown fork a few hundred yards ahead.

Jaspar squinted. "I believe that's an old farming road. It runs by some outskirt towns whose soil went bad a few years back. If I remember right, everyone had to move to the more favorable fields around Prasni Zorio."

"Prasni Zorio?" said Teigra. "That's where we'll have to stop for the night, isn't it?"

"Oh, yes. We won't make Ardora proper at this pace."

Aurelius gestured. "And how much longer would that road take to get to Prasni."

Jaspar looked nervous. "Oh, I don't think we can do that, Your Excellency. That would be very bad luck. They say that the displeasure of Ardor has seeped right into the grass."

"It's the grass I'm looking at, Jaspar, rather than this dreaded potholed rubble! How long?"

Tiggy grimaced. "Aurie, I'm getting bumped around as well, but maybe we should listen to—"

"*How long?*"

Jaspar was exasperated. "It would probably add another hour or two. We would still get to Prasni before nightfall. But really, we shouldn't—"

"Good. Thank you, Mid Envoy. A few extra hours on grass sounds like a wonderful change."

"As you wish," said Jaspar, thumbing the reins.

And it was as he wished. The overgrown roads were bliss to the wheels, softening their path like a goat-wool mattress. As they traveled further down the disused byways, they even had the added benefit of overgrown orange trees by their flanks, blocking the harsh sun and filling the air with sweetness.

"We should have listened to Jaspar," said Teigra, peeking out at the abandoned towns—the buildings moldering and moss covered. "This place doesn't look well-favored at all."

"Oh, don't get all superstitious on me, Tiggy," he said, kissing his fingers in solemn devotion. "Oh Ardor, Mother of Fertility, Mistress of Passion, forgive us the sin for not wanting our heads rattled off by your hideous roads."

Just as he pressed his fingers to the thickly woven ceiling, there came an almighty shriek from the other side.

He yanked his hand back just in time to avoid three massive talons slashing through the cloth.

Overhead, framed by the brilliant sun, was a hideous female face, with layers of brown and ivory feathers where her skin should have been. The creature extended two great wings, as long as the carriage. A hideous smile stretched across its lipless mouth, revealing rows of razor-sharp teeth.

Harpy!

The beast swooped into the carriage, its talons bared.

Aurelius screamed, slamming his eyes shut and waiting for the sensation of tearing flesh.

20

TEIGRA

T<small>EIGRA LAUNCHED FORWARD JUST IN TIME TO YANK</small> A<small>URELIUS FROM THE</small> snapping jaw.

She twisted around in the confined space, kicking blindly and knocking great streams of drool from the harpy onto her feet and legs. To her relief, the beast didn't turn and bite her. Its wings were tangled in the roof, the hemp tearing with each thrash as it tried to break free.

"Go!" she yelled at Aurelius, grabbing his arm and diving out the door, the sharp teeth snapping at their heels.

She landed hard on the grass, knocking stars into her eyes. Despite her disorientation, she pushed Aurelius into the narrow space between the road and the carriage, making sure he was safely concealed before ducking underneath herself.

She looked around desperately for Jaspar, spotting him on the ground beside the bucking steeds. His huge body was still, but she couldn't see any obvious injury.

Then, with a sickening sensation, another harpy emerged into the clearing. Then another one, from the other side.

And both eyed Jaspar.

"What do we do? What do we do?" said Aurelius from by her elbow. "Do something, Tiggy!"

Teigra looked at her cousin. He was a noble of parties and decadence. He could outwit anyone she knew in the game of power. But she'd never seen him down in the dirt and mud. She'd never seen him throw a punch.

And in the horror of his eyes, she saw the mission—the reason Aurelius was coming to Ardora. He could save their homeland from invasion and ruin.

Only *he* could do that.

And right now, only *she* could save Jaspar.

She racked her mind as Aurelius whimpered beside her, trying to remember the stories. Harpies were beastly personifications of the storm winds, weren't they? Of the powerful squalls and gales that drenched Ardora?

Didn't Journius the Brave face a harpy when he was lost in the Illhas Sea? How did he fight them? Think!

The memories roiled just beyond recollection, hundreds of mornings in the predawn library blurring into one. The illuminated bestiary she'd so often read was glinting in the light. The little stories of their weaknesses were whispered just out of earshot.

It was all right there! *Come on!*

Then it snapped into place.

Fishing nets.

The beasts were savage and swift, but they were easily caught in nets or the rigging of sails, just like they'd become caught in the shreds of the roof.

And the carriage was *covered* in nets.

She gulped as the harpies closed in on Jaspar, her heart slamming against her ribs.

But there was no time left. She had to act!

"Hey! Over here!" she yelled, scrambling from beneath the carriage and grasping the nearest net, heavy with their possessions.

The ropes were already shredded and slightly loose from the initial attack by the harpy on the roof, threads fraying off here and there.

One beast turned from its path towards the minotaur. The one still tangled in the carriage roof snapped at her through the open door.

She yanked at the rope as hard as she could, a frantic, lurching tear. Arms that had spent a lifetime hoisting saddles and dragging feed tensed and strained. The already broken bonds started to tear further.

One bag tumbled out of the growing gap, then another. Then they came from all sides of the carriage as she wrenched with all her might—clothing and equipment strewn everywhere with each snap of rope.

They were snapping, but not giving way fully!

One beast was right beside her now.

It bared its teeth.

Its rancid breath was hot.

Teigra froze.

She was unsure if she should pull harder and hope that the final strands of the strong rope might snap, or if she should turn and run. Unsure if she should swing something at the beast or recoil in fear. Unsure if she should move or stay.

And as it stepped right up to her, she was left doing *neither*, stuck fast with indecision.

Just as the beast made to lunge toward her, a deep note resounded across the grove, followed by a swoop of air and the thunder of hooves.

And the nearest harpy turned just in time for a stampeding blur to slice its head clean off its body.

21

AURELIUS

THE FEATHERED HEAD HIT THE GROUND LIKE A MELON, ROLLING UNDER the carriage and coming to a stop by Aurelius's arm. He flinched in revulsion as its eyes flickered with a last moment of life, then stopped.

The bloodshed, however, did not.

He could only see to knee height from beneath the carriage, but it was enough. There was another blur of blood in the grove. Then a figure of red and leather leapt from a pegasus, hit the grass, rolled through the impact, and ran toward the carriage.

Tiggy dove out of their way, and the cabin bounced overhead as the swordsman leaped inside.

There was a monstrous shriek, the sound of splintering wood.

Then, silence.

Moments later, there came a torrent all around him—a rain of filthy blood dripping through the slats of the carriage floor.

The figure jumped down, dragging the harpy's corpse into a wet heap. Aurelius rolled out and scrambled to his feet, as much to escape the bloody shower as to see their savior.

He tried to steady himself in standing, but his legs felt like a sapling in a storm. The sight and smell of the monstrous corpses made the revelry of last night rise in his throat. Stars filled his eyes in shock and disbelief.

That shock came not just from the hideous signs of the slaughter. But also at the sight of the lead soldier.

It was a woman, six feet tall and dressed in a military uniform of blood-splattered leather, wrapped in a woolen cape the color of wine. Two other women, still mounted atop fine-looking pegasi and leading a fourth in tow, came around and joined her.

One of the women was wider and taller and far more muscular than any human he had ever seen, with a faint gray-blue tone to her skin; the other was far shorter, and sharp-featured, with darting little eyes that seemed to take in everything.

On the lead soldier, the plunging cheek plates of her helmet showed little but a set of intense, kohl-lined eyes, topped with the largest plume Aurelius had ever seen. She removed it, revealing a cascade of midnight-black hair, framing a face of high cheekbones and full, rosewood-colored lips.

She stood with easy, all-encompassing sensuality. She couldn't have been older than twenty-five.

"These roads are not safe for those unfamiliar with a sword, southerners," she said, her voice dark and resinous. "We will assist you to recover, but you must turn around and make for Prasni Zorio at once."

"Nnnf," came a voice, as Teigra shook Jaspar back to consciousness. "What happened? Oh, Mesti, did I crash again? Ms. Securia will kill me."

Aurelius made meager offers to help with the cleanup, his voice shaking and filled with nervous laughter. But thankfully the soldiers rebuffed him—whipping around and gathering possessions, retying shreds of mesh and packing the bags while he tried not to think about the filthy, reeking blood that covered him.

Or of the dead bodies just feet away that the blood had come from . . .

By the time Jaspar was back on his hooves, the women had already remounted their steeds, hitting the air with a swoop of wings, off in search of the monsters' nest.

And then they were alone, surrounded by bodies and blood.

And the smell.

Teigra hurriedly conducted her own inventory of their possessions.

"There is no . . . no need, darling," he said with a gulp, trying to block his nose and force the bile down from his throat. "They did it all for us. Rather a good welcome to Ardora, isn't it! Kill some monsters and help us clean up, too!"

He laughed again, hearing the manic tone in his voice but unable to stop it.

Teigra didn't smile. There was something equally manic in the way she went over the luggage, again and again. Eventually, he had to take her shaking hand and pull her up into the carriage—shushing her protests about Jaspar not being fit to drive yet. After all, the mid envoy assured them he was fine, and the sooner they got out of here, the better.

After just a few minutes, they were back underway.

"Goodbye Mestibes; hello Ardora, eh?" he said with a faint smile, using a spare bit of the shredded roof to clean the worst of the foul-smelling blood from his hair and ears. His beautiful cloak was ruined. Although, in this moment, with the pulse of fear still thumping through his blood, even he knew this was a less-than-pressing concern. "And did you see? They had pegasi. I thought you said they didn't have any of those up here?"

Teigra just gazed at him in remnant shock, her face as white as a freshly laundered toga.

22

TEIGRA

THE OIL LAMP CAST LONG SHADOWS THROUGH THE STABLE. IT SMELLED nothing like home. Back home, only the cheapest olive oil was used in lamps, still stinking of the vegetables or meat it had been carefully strained from after cooking. But the smoke here carried the scent of rich, green olives. Sweet and earthy.

Carrying so much promise.

A promise I've already wasted . . .

It was well past midnight now. Aurelius and Jaspar had already drifted off. She knew this because she'd stood at their doors for what felt like an age, her ear pressed against the splinters, waiting, *begging*, for the sounds of sleep.

But Teigra couldn't sleep. Not until she'd found *it*.

It will be in some weird part of the carriage, she reassured herself, tiptoeing around the corner of the stable yards, the unfamiliar softness of green grass underfoot.

She froze, ducking back behind the wall.

Their carriage was indeed in the stables, but it wasn't alone! From the yards came the sound of two people working. Their accents were the same sonorous tones *that woman*'d had.

She snuck a careful peek around the corner. One man was replacing the wooden frame of the roof, the other was scrubbing out the blood and remnants of the beasts from inside.

No! Stop it! I need to look there! Don't take anything away! Don't touch anything!

She stayed in that spot until the sun was just cresting over the tree-lined horizon and the workers had completed their tasks—with Teigra cursing every minute of their labor.

As soon as the men had returned to the inn, she dashed over, rummaging through the possessions that had been returned to the netting.

The first look revealed nothing, so she went over it again, turning over every box and bag, ducking to the ground in case it had somehow fallen out during the repairs. She'd already checked her own bag a dozen times in her room in the inn. Over and over, as if *it* might suddenly fall out of the folds of some tunic.

There was *still* nothing!

Desperately, she jumped into the carriage itself, running her hands into every nook and cranny of the newly polished pine.

And there was still nothing . . .

She slumped back into the cold wooden seat, staring blankly at the rising dawn across the tree line. Everything had survived the attack unscathed. Everything that was, except one thing.

The most important thing in the entire carriage.

The most important thing in the entire country!

Urosina's folio was gone.

Gods! She . . . she must have taken it!

Teigra's whole body shook. The culprit's face flashed before her—rivers of black hair and cruel eyes. A face that Teigra had seen described before.

"Mesti," she muttered under her breath. "I've ruined Aurelius's mission."

23

~

THE ROOM WAS WASHED WHITE, THE NEAR-CIRCULAR MOON JUST A FEW days past bronze. It was the time of the month the figure enjoyed most. The time of the month they felt most in control.

The room itself was grand, as befitted their immense stature in the kingdom of passion and fertility. Beyond the walls of the room were almost a hundred thousand people in the city, swirling with strengths and weaknesses, with passions and proclivities.

And the figure could *feel* them all, even now. To them, every person's gifts sparkled like distant stars, twinkling in desperate hopes of being noticed. Of being liberated. Of yearning for someone who *truly* deserved them.

And then, amongst all that delicious glint, right at the edge of recognition, came something entirely unexpected. Something that gleamed new and bright. Something that commanded the stage of the figure's observation.

And right at the core of that brilliance, hidden within the corona of its light, was another glimmer still. A tiny seed waiting to grow into the tallest of twisting trees.

The figure smiled, its teeth glinting in the celestial shine. When it spoke, its voice was as soft as the spring that had just passed. As warm as the summer that lay ahead.

"Welcome to Ardora, *Aurelius Savair*."

24

AURELIUS

Ardora was nothing like Mestibes.

In fact, there was only one word that came to mind as they entered the ramshackle city, nestled at the crown of an enormous, blue-twinkling bay.

Chaos.

Half-naked children chased after wild dogs and stray cats. At all angles, horses dug deeper grooves through the rich, red mud of the unpaved streets. Rough-skinned men in red uniforms and young women in dark green tunics elbowed each other around hissing charcoal grills, billowing smoke laced with lemon and lamb fat. On two separate occasions the carpentum was diverted into winding side streets to avoid a dispute between carts pulled by colossal, one-eyed giants, easily double his height and as broad as Aurelius was tall. Those massive creatures mulled around the carts, overladen with vegetables and freshly slaughtered meats, with their human owners dismounted in the middle of the road, hurling the vilest insults Aurelius had ever heard. And rather than trying to break up the uncivilized display, passersby were forming their own little mobs, arguing with extravagant gestures about which driver was *clearly* in the right.

It seemed that in every clanging, shouting, singing, cackling direction was a scene that would never occur in Mestibes.

And a smell that would never occur in Mestibes, he thought, ducking his nose beneath the hem of his tunic.

It was overwhelming. It was maddening.

Tiggy didn't seem to share his fascination, however. All morning, she had sat morosely in her seat, grunting perfunctory agreement when he'd pointed out the sights, trying to get her into the excitement of their new home.

The attack must have really messed her up.

He felt the smallest hint of regret for the part he played in that.

Just on midday, they finally clattered through the gates of the embassy compound—deep in the center of the city, beyond the parks full of green-tunicked families, the acres of grass and trees as big as whole suburbs of Mestibes, past extensive barracks where every man, woman, and steed seemed to be uniformed in blood-red.

He'd kept a lookout in those soldierly suburbs in case he caught a surreptitious glimpse of Calix. He was unsurprised, though a little disappointed, that he didn't.

The U-shaped, two-story embassy was large and unpainted, the raw, clay bricks on full display and supported with *wood* of all things. The courtyard it surrounded was as green as the countryside: edged with towering sword lilies, a grand pomegranate tree in the middle, and blanketed everywhere with fluffy grass.

Waiting outside the main doorway was someone who stood in contrast to all this easy vibrancy.

The name "High Envoy Ms. Ramuna Securia" might have conjured a certain image among people who had never met her. One of hunched malevolence and deep, life-worn grooves across her face. But Aurelius knew the Securia bloodline far too well to fall for that stereotype, and was not shocked to find someone entirely different.

She was older, yes, fifty perhaps, but as far from wizened as someone that age could be. Her bright-yellow stola hung confidently from slender shoulders, her back straight and her waist narrow. Her face bore the lightest wrinkles yet retained a firmness, and was set against long, straight hair of dark ash, swept back behind her ears and flecked with gray.

She was as stunning as she was striking. She could have walked into any training school for young priests or artists or philosophers and still turned heads and hardened groins. She had the sharp, aristocratic, and womanly bearing that probably made the baby-boy senators want to present their asses for a good smacking.

And her eyes had the menacing focus of a cat upon a wayward sparrow.

He had wrangled with the middle child of her house before— Cornel Securia, senator and chief designer at the family's famous glassworks. He was a coldhearted son of a bitch. The sort who, even in laughter, looked as if he were wishing some horrid curse.

Aurelius's eyes twinkled with mischief as the carriage came to a stop. The younger sister looked to have every bit of the family's famous fire.

This should be fun.

"Welcome to Ardora, Your Excellency," said Ms. Securia crisply, shaking his hand with a grip like a wolf's jaw. "I am—"

"—Ramuna, *darling*," he said, planting a kiss on each of her cheeks. "Simply *wonderful* to see you. Paula and Cornel send their love. They've been asking about you ever since they heard of my appointment!"

It was an obvious lie. House Securia was pious beyond belief and held him, and the entire Savair clan, in utter contempt. And someone like Ramuna would know all about his own scandals. She wouldn't let so trivial a thing as *distance* reduce her awareness of happenings back home.

Aurelius studied her while projecting utter innocence.

She was a worthy foe, parsing no flicker of confusion. "Indeed.

Well, you have had a long journey. Allow me to show you to your quarters."

Rather than taking him into the main building, Securia led him across the courtyard to an annex by the gate—the same height and style as the embassy proper, but around a tenth of the size. It was located next to the small stable, where the steeds were slurping gratefully at a copper trough. She opened the door to reveal . . .

Gods protect me!

The fashion in Mestibes was for the creamiest of marble, or at the very least, stone painted white with calcite or gypsum—"clean surfaces and a clean mind" was the oft-quoted aphorism.

And if that were true, then the minds of Ardora must be as rough as a farmer's balls.

It was *hideous*. Worse than the saddest plebeian hovel. The walls were unpainted brick, the room furnished in dark, barely worked wood—as if bits of a tree had been dragged inside and whacked into place. There were no frescos, no hanging silks, no decoration of note anywhere. The only fabric was the faded linen over the windows.

Linen which, to Aurelius's horror, was *flapping*.

"Welcome to your office, Your Excellency. Upstairs is your private quarters while you are staying with us."

"There is no glass in the windows?" he said, mouth agape.

"No, Your Excellency."

"Had I known you were this hard up, Ramuna, I would have asked the archon for an emergency stipend!"

"We want for nothing here but *demand*, Your Excellency. Ardorans do not live their lives caged up in their houses, keeping the sun and the rain at bay. They live out there, on the streets and in the parks, in the wondrous bounty that the goddess has gifted them."

"But . . . your family made its fortune in glass. Your great-grandfather *invented* the stuff. You must have at least tried to introduce it down here?"

She cocked her head, like an inquisitive crow. "To what end? Ondocis buys more glass than Mestibes can produce. The wait is six years on some of the finer pieces. What need is there to bring it here as well?"

"Well, for one thing, a bit of finery might stop the natives eating out of dried mud and bits of old tree," he said, noticing the drink tray —wooden cups around an awful earthenware jug.

"Your Excellency, your work is of course none of my business, just as mine is not yours—though I am sure we can work together productively to achieve mutually beneficial results for Mestibes. But whatever purpose the archon has seen fit to send you here for, I doubt it is some *civilizing* mission. In the very brief time you have been here, you may have judged Ardorans as backward and brutish, but they would consider us lazy and arrogant—too concerned with aesthetics to get our hands bloody or our feet dirty."

Aurelius turned to make a snide remark but found only space behind him. "Where is Teigra?"

"I am sure Mr. Accola is showing Ms. Cosmin to her office."

"Well, I am going to see—"

With the lightest of movements, the high envoy blocked the door. "Ms. Cosmin is *not* someone you need to concern yourself with during daylight hours, Your Excellency. She is my low envoy. Not yours."

"I am *going* to see her," he repeated.

"And I am sure she will make time for you this evening after all of her work has been completed."

Aurelius glared at her. Finally, he smiled, ceding ground.

So that is the game? Well, no need to play my hand right away. Let her have this sad little victory.

"On to matters of work," the high envoy continued. "I have arranged for you to be granted an audience at the palace on Friday morning to present your credentials."

"*Friday?* But that is four days from now!"

"Yes, Your Excellency. And considerably sooner than I had thought they'd meet you. On her last visit, your predecessor waited almost a month for a meeting which never eventuated."

"So, what? I just remain here waiting?"

"Yes. And until then, I recommend you don't leave the embassy compound."

He shot her a look as horrible as the decor. "You expect me to spend four days cooped up *here*?"

"Yes, Your Excellency. I do. For your own protection, of course. As is customary with diplomats across Dynosia, once your credentials have been accepted, you will have full protection—from arrest, from interference, from harm. But until that time, you are just another visitor in this polity. And you must understand that the Ardorans take a much less enlightened view of *certain activities* than we do in Mestibes. I am sure the archon wouldn't want you getting into any trouble, would she?"

He glared at her. "And which royal shall receive me? Calix?"

She gave the slightest flicker of distaste, and Aurelius wondered how much she knew of the prince's proclivities. Or of his own intentions in Ardora.

Urosina had seemingly only uncovered the information with considerable effort. But the high envoy had been here for almost thirty years. And it was her job to know things, after all.

"By convention," she said, "it should be their royal majesties the king and queen. You are the archon's voice in this land, after all. But given the current state of affairs? I suppose you could well be met by the crown prince."

He drummed his fingers on the rough table. "And there is absolutely nothing I can do until then?"

"Oh, I wouldn't worry about *that*," she said with a thin smile. "Your scroll hive is full of classical history about Ardora. Let me know when you have digested them, and I will have the next set brought to you."

25

TEIGRA

Teigra clutched the leather sack, the total of her worldly possessions, as Jaspar led her through the strange building—past the entrance hall, overlooked by a staircase to the second floor, along the long hall of offices that formed the western, ground-floor arm of the U.

Ms. Securia's office was located exactly where Mother would have put it, right at the head of the corridor, so that no one could come or go without her seeing everything from the desk that faced the open door. The high envoy's space was filled with codices along every wall and was also loomed over by one of the largest statues of Mesti she'd seen in a private space.

"They're all empty?" she said, as they passed office after neat office, the furniture perfectly positioned but absent any other life.

"Oh, yeah!" said Jaspar, as if only just noticing them. "Isn't that funny? They've been like that for so long now, I hardly even notice anymore."

"They weren't always this way?"

"Oh, gosh no. When I first got here every room was full! The corridor was so loud you couldn't hear yourself think. We had a contingent of thirteen, back then: one high envoy, two mid envoys, and ten low envoys. There was Ariti handling vegetables. Lykaois looking after wood. Pachis covering wine. Vivlios on grain. Samari on steeds. And . . ."

His voice trailed away.

Teigra gave him a sympathetic look. "What happened?"

"*Sama* happened. A lot of people here got mad when Mestibes didn't join the fight. I mean *really* mad. Like 'don't walk out into the streets' kind of mad. The royals even passed a decree that would have closed our embassy—and kicked out all the envoys across the greater polity. Ms. Securia managed to negotiate a minimal presence of just three positions with the king. But that's all they will let us have nowadays. The mid envoys we used to have in Cherrystone and Port Nikrizo and Gonimos and Mavelix—all gone! And that negotiation was also the last time Ms Securia was allowed to see anyone senior in the royal family. Or their officials."

Teigra juggled her bag and reached up to place a hand on his sagging shoulder. His fur was soft. "That must have been hard for you, to lose all your friends like that."

The shadow over Jaspar brightened, like a brief cloud over an otherwise sunny field. "Oh, it's all right. If anything, it helped! We used to only deal with the big players. But now that so many nobles won't talk to us, we make our contracts with the small farmers instead. It is a lot more work, but I've met more amazing people in the last five years than I did in the five before that!"

"So, does that mean you are here for another five years as well?"

"Yup. The same session that voted you in. And extended Ms. Securia's term as well."

"I'm sure there was a good deal less debate about your renewals than my appointment," she said, clutching her bag tighter.

"Maybe they just needed to make sure they got the right person for the job," he said. "And by the looks of it, they picked perfectly!"

Before she could respond, he threw open the door. "Welcome to your brand new—"

Teigra screamed and dropped her bag.

She was eye-level with a man's face.

Teigra stepped back and looked into the withering expression of a middle-aged centaur—black-gray coat peeking out from the most meticulously tied horse toga she'd ever seen. His chest muscles were as thick as his face was judgmental. His beard was a neat salt and pepper beneath a prominent brow and aquiline nose.

"Oh good," muttered the centaur, hoisting a coarse-bristled broom over his bare, muscular shoulders, exposed in a way they would never have been back home. *"Another one."*

"Good morning, Mr. Placi!" said Jaspar, as if nothing had happened.

Mr. Placi grunted. "The boss expected you back yesterday, lad. We've got more than a hundred condolence letters for the old herald, and she wants them done immediately."

The news of Ura's death has already reached down here? The position of herald is more well known that I thought.

"Oh, you know how it is," said Jaspar, pinching his shoulders in and tapping his fingertips nervously. "A harpy there. A delay here. But we're back now! And this is our new low envoy. Ms. Teigra Cosmin, may I introduce Mr. Frynod Placi."

"Cosmin?" the centaur squinted.

Teigra's heart raced at his glare. It was a look she'd seen so many times in the last three years. Did he know what she had done? She hadn't seen any hint of recognition from Jaspar, yet—or, if he did know, his diplomatic skills were such that he had no intention of bringing it up.

But surely even down here the news must have come? After all, tragedy has a traveling stamina that hope could never match.

Mr. Placi snorted. "Racing family, isn't it?"

She paused for more, but that was all that came. "Um . . . yes?" she whispered, running her thumb along her pendant. Her clothes were scattered across the floor around them.

"Well, a thousand apologies for scaring you, *my lady*," said Mr.

Placi. "I am sure this is the last place you'd expect to see a monster like me. But please, if you do see me on all fours scrubbing, just try to resist the urge to saddle me up."

Mr. Placi pushed past them and trudged away, muttering under his breath.

"I'm sorry!" called Teigra. "I didn't mean to . . . I was just surprised . . ."

The muttering got louder as her own voice faded.

She turned to Jaspar. "I really am sorry. It's not like that at all! Centaurs in the relays aren't slaves or anything. You know that! They are free citizens. And treated far better than most humans are!"

"Oh, don't worry," said Jaspar, helping her collect the scattered clothes. "He's like that with everyone. Being a housekeeper isn't exactly his dream job."

A housekeeper? The thought of a centaur doing manual labor seemed unfathomable. Every centaur she'd ever met was a superstar of the track. Barely able to walk the streets without crowds of children running up to shake their hand, or usually-hard-faced men dragging them into restaurants for free meals and company. Even the messengers that had departed Mestibes before them were doing an important job for the senate.

"Why does he do it then?"

Jaspar bit a fingernail in thought—quite a feat given the thickness of a minotaur's nails. "That is a *very* long story. And one for another time, I think."

Teigra nodded and took in the office. It was by far the smallest room in the corridor. A desk was pushed against the back wall, with the packed scroll hive so close that if she stood too quickly, she'd smack her head. The view from the window was not of the beautiful courtyard, but a close-up of the high wall that surrounded the compound.

She squashed the tiny thought that asked: *Why can't I have one of the bigger offices?* She'd spent enough time around senators and their hierarchies. This office was for the most junior low envoy in the embassy. It didn't matter that there were nicer offices that stood empty. This was the office for *her*.

"It might not look like much," said Jaspar. "But don't worry. Soon we'll get you out there, meeting with farmers and traders and the like. Once you are out of lockdown, of course."

"*Lockdown?*"

"Oh, it's nothing to worry about. You just can't leave the building until your credentials have been accepted. I'm sure Ms. Securia will get the herald to sort yours out whenever he heads to the palace. Until then, I'm afraid you are stuck here with me!"

"Oh," she said.

It was a conflicting development. On the one hand, being locked in the embassy meant there was no pressure to get out *there*, into the alien city she had just passed through—with its strange ways and stranger people.

But on the other hand, it meant being trapped inside with this awful guilt! With the gnawing worry about what she had done and what she had ruined!

"I'm sorry," he said, eyeing her expression. "It's stupid. The prince is probably just a dozen streets that way at the soldier's wrestling school, so the whole thing could get done in a few minutes. Still, it's good practice for moving to Ardora! Just because something is logical, doesn't mean it will happen!"

"You don't sound upset about that?"

"It keeps things interesting!" he said, leading her back through the embassy and up to the second floor. Her bedroom was directly over her office and just as small—barely big enough to fit the single bed pressed against the wall. "Why don't you settle in. I should crack on with those letters. The nobles might not like us, but we've clearly managed to win a lot of the small traders back! I'll come to see you in a bit, and maybe we can write a few together!"

He gave her another disarming smile.

And then she was left alone.

She unpacked what little she had brought into a cramped set of shelves, cursing her stupidity all the while. For making a fool of herself in front of Jaspar. For making poor Mr. Placi think that she was prejudiced against centaurs. But most of all, she cursed herself for the same thing that'd been gnawing at her all morning.

How could I have been so stupid? Aurelius trusted me, and I screwed him. Now he's in danger. And all Mestibes is doomed. Doomed! It is all my stupid fault. I am such a useless, pathetic—

"Mesti, save us. And I thought *my* room was bad," said a voice from behind her.

She turned with a jump. Aurelius was eyeing the room with disgust. "Oh, hello," she said, shaking the awful thoughts from her head. "I . . . thought you were with Ms. Securia?"

"I was. But she went off to meet someone in town," he said, flopping down onto her bed. "Which is lucky for *some.*"

"She told you about the lockdown?"

"Four days?" moaned Aurelius. "Can you believe that? Xiber could cross the border at any minute. I am in a race to seduce Crown Prince Grumpy Face. And we are stuck here for *four days* doing nothing. Doesn't she know we are on a time limit?"

"Literally, no? I'm not even supposed to know."

As she said it, she almost bit her tongue to stop the dark thoughts. *He trusted me. And I betrayed him! I brought the folio! And I lost it!*

"If only we knew where the prince was," he said, oblivious to her nerves. "Then we could bust out and just get on with it!"

Teigra's skin prickled, and a little hope bubbled up. The woman who had stolen the folio was far down south, near Prasni. And the prince was just a few streets away. Jaspar had said so.

If they moved quickly enough . . . maybe they could fix her screwup? Maybe there was a chance they could make it right? It wouldn't work forever. The woman was bound to return to the city at some point. But maybe Aurelius could start his mission. Maybe moving now could buy them some time—*any time!*

But, no. They'd been told they couldn't leave the embassy. And she'd promised Mother that she wouldn't embarrass House Cosmin in any way. She couldn't just break that promise. Not within half an hour of arriving! The destiny of her family was in Teigra's hands. If she followed the rules, then promotion to patrician status was all but guaranteed.

And yet, the alternative was surely worse? All of Mestibes's safety was at risk because of her stupidity. And who knew how long Ms. Securia might be gone? This might be their one opportunity in the next four days. If she did nothing, she was basically sabotaging Aurelius's chances. He could end up in grave danger!

Or perhaps . . . just a grave.

She shuddered.

The weight of the decision was awful. But that sealed it. She couldn't put him in danger like that.

"Actually," she said. "I think I know where the prince is."

26

AURELIUS

PALAESTRA XIPHOS, THE WRESTLING SCHOOL OF THE SWORD, WAS APTLY named.

Dirty sand filled the square, surrounded by roofed viewing stands —presently packed with a few hundred Ardorans of all ages, lazing and conversing and yelling encouragement. The half-dozen sparring pairs in the center were scattered around fifty or so other soldiers, training and flexing and eyeing each other off. And lining the edge of their earthen stage, separating the combatants from the crowd, was a fence of swords, stabbed into the earth in such a haphazard fashion, with different heights and spacing, they must surely have been staked by individual owners.

"Now *these* are some real men," said Aurelius, as they found an empty spot on the stone-slab benches, far less lovely than those of the Alogo.

The combatants were wearing nothing but loincloths, colored red, like the clothing of everyone else in the stands. These were not the diaper-looking things worn by some plebians back home, either, but perfectly fitted to their bodies, with flattering, sword-shaped strips running down between their legs at the front and back, adorned with various symbols that no doubt had special meanings to their owners.

He'd never seen wrestling before—Mestibes favored the nobility of the relay over anything so uncivilized as hard wet bodies slamming together.

It appeared he had been missing out. The men were *stunning*.

Muscles bulged as they crashed together like red deer stags. Sun beat off black hair and olive skin, several shades deeper than found in sun-fearing Mestibes. They glistened with the sweat of combat and the effort of their training. And all around the square came the sounds of exertion and triumph and fury.

The sound of men. *Real* men.

"Ardoran society divides all families into two: the Reds, which are the fighters; and the Greens, which are the farmers," said Teigra, reading from a scroll she'd hurriedly snatched before they'd snuck out. "Palaestra Xiphos, located in the soldierly quarter of Kastro Machiton, serves as a wrestling school and social hub for the Reds. It says here that there is another school on the outskirts of town for the farmers, called Palaestra Ampelos."

"School of the Vine? Do they wrestle drunk?"

"It . . . doesn't say."

Aurelius smirked. "Well, I may have to visit there as well to see for myself."

"Oh, look. There're *women* here as well," said Tiggy.

"Is that noteworthy, darling? I know plenty of women back home who'd pay good money to see strong, sweaty men beat the shit out of each other."

"No, not just in the stands. Women are *wrestling* each other."

She was right. Among the men was a pair of sparring women, surrounded by a tight circle of the same. One of the female combatants lunged forward, only to be flipped onto her back. The dominant woman then tried to jump on top, but the other one was up in a flash, immediately locking arms.

"They're really going for it, aren't they?" said Aurelius.

Teigra's face glowed for the first time since they'd arrived in Ardora. "I know! They're hitting just as hard as the men. It says here that the aim is to pin your opponent's shoulders to the ground for a count of three."

As Aurelius squinted to focus on the further-away group of female combatants, there came an odd stirring in the back of his mind. The strangest recollection that he had seen the dominant one before...

Tiggy gave a shocked intake of breath. "Over there!" she said, elbowing him in the ribs. "It's Prince Calix!"

Aurelius's heart fluttered at the sound of the name.

She was right.

Calix was on the far side of the square, surprisingly not in the most prominent position, as would be befitting his rank as prince and strategos. Instead, he was lifting a series of heavy rocks in a quiet corner, all on his own.

Teigra had said something about that on the walk through town. Despite being a very soldierly society, the royals of Ardora weren't shielded from the public in any way. They moved and mingled as might any other citizen. No guards. No entourage.

That certainly boded well for what Aurelius had planned.

He took the massive man in. Even though Aurelius had seen him before, it hadn't been like *this*—near naked and glistening, veins snaking across his enormous body.

The man was a god! Six and a half foot. Taller than everyone else in the square, with arms that looked like they could pull an ox cart and a hair-covered chest as big and solid as the rocks he hoisted overhead. His teeth were clenched, straining with the effort of each lift. But despite this, he was continuing long after others retreated for rest.

Aurelius felt a moment of absurdity.

Crown Prince Calix was *right there*. He was close enough now that Aurelius could practically smell the sweat on him. After all this time plotting about what he would do with this man, of traveling all this way just to be near to him, now he was *right there.*

"So," said a nearby old man to his equally elderly companion. "You putting a few drachmae on the prince to take down Kleio at the Ardoralia?"

"Hah. I ain't wasting my coin on *that* matchup."

"What? Calix's the reigning Paliad Games champion. Best wrestler in all Dynosia. And you saw him a few weeks back. Made short work of Minta. Damn near broke the boy's arm."

"Oh, Calix's got the skill, no question on that. And sure, after Sama he still seemed to have it in him—all that work he did rebuilding the Brotherhoods. I respect that. Course I do. But the last few years? Well, you've seen him. He just ain't got the heart no more! Everyone says he's come down with the ashen passion."

"What! Don't go saying that! That's a serious accusation, that is."

"So? All I'm saying is that *everyone else* is saying it!"

Aurelius rolled his eyes.

Ashen passion? For fuck's sake. Even a million miles from home, I can't escape the bigots and superstitious old fools.

Ashen passion was one of the five divine illnesses. It was to Ardor what wandering vigor was to Mesti. But looking down at the sweaty, determined man across the square, outlifting and outperforming all those around him, Aurelius certainly couldn't see any sign of the timidity and lack of motivation that supposedly accompanied the ashen illness.

And yet, even Aurelius had picked up the insinuation in Urosina's folio about Calix retreating from public life in the last year or so. And although he did not believe the rot about divine illnesses, he knew better than to *completely* ignore the chatter of a crowd.

He filed the information away in the back of his mind.

The battles played out for another hour, the crowd rising to their feet with a "*One... Two... Three!*" whenever someone was pinned.

All the while, Calix stayed on his own, barely noticing those around him.

Then, at last, he moved, lowering the rock for the last time, and making his way down a shaded path beneath the far stands.

Aurelius grinned and jumped to his feet. "Time to get to work!"

"Where are you going?" said Teigra, her eyes wide.

"Where do you think? I would bet all my money that tunnel leads to a bathhouse. And I didn't take a four-day journey just to *look* at him."

Teigra went bright red. "You don't mean you're going to try to . . . Right *here*? Right *there*?"

He chuckled at her delicate sexual constitution. "Oh, darling, this isn't like those dates your mother foists on you. Making boring small talk with even more boring men. Holding hands and doing little else? We do things a little differently in *my* world."

"But, no! You can't go back there! It's just for the soldiers."

He batted his eyelids. "I'm a *tourist*, Tiggy! Not even a diplomat yet. Just some posh fool looking to take my daily bath, as any citizen of Dynosia is permitted to. How was I to know the area was restricted?"

"Aurie, please, no! Stop! Don't do down there! You don't understand!"

He waved away her hysteria. Before she could say anything else to dissuade him, Aurelius blew her a kiss and sauntered away.

27

TEIGRA

CALIX KNOWS ABOUT THE MISSION!

Teigra wanted to scream the warning from the top of her lungs, but it fell silent on her lips. Instead, she watched in horror as Aurelius headed toward the bathhouse, filled with men that were trained to kill.

Her cousin was in grave danger! Anything could happen to him!

And it was all her fault. Because she'd thought that there was no way Calix could know about the mission. Because there was no way that the woman who'd stolen the folio could have given it to him yet.

But Teigra had been wrong.

Calix *did* know. He had to.

Because the person who stole the folio wasn't a day's ride south. She was *here*, standing in the center of the female wrestlers. Because the thief wasn't some lowly hoplite. Because the thief was someone important. Someone powerful. Someone whose unmistakable description was written into the very notes she'd stolen.

Because the thief is Princess Zosime Viralis!

Calix's sister.

The second in line to the throne of Ardora.

And she was standing right here, just fifty yards away.

With a chill far detached from the warmth of low summer, Teigra knew that Zosime would have already told Calix of Aurelius's intended trickery. The whole royal family probably knew by now!

Her fingers went numb.

Aurelius was halfway toward the tunnel now. She hadn't wanted to tell him about bringing the folio. And she'd certainly not wanted to tell him about losing it! The thought of what that betrayal might cost her filled her with such pain she couldn't dwell on the thought for long. Aurelius was the only family she had left anymore. The only one who cared about her. Who *trusted* her.

And after this, he might never trust her again. She might lose him as well, and she couldn't bear the thought of that!

But it was too late for that now. He was in grave danger. And she couldn't let him face it without knowing.

She would admit everything! No matter what it cost her. She had to! She had seen how her cousin had reacted at the death of the harpies. He was no fighter. But Calix was. One of the best in the land. And if the prince knew what Aurelius intended, then there was no telling what he might do.

Teigra stood with sudden purpose, pushing past the cheering spectators, and coming alongside the fence of stabbed steel. She couldn't just chase after him. Aurelius had gone around the edge, but he was too close to the tunnel now.

But she could catch him on the diagonal, if she ran across the wrestling grounds.

The sword wall glinted a cold warning—no higher than her waist, but as tall as city walls with menace.

Beyond here there is violence.

Beyond here there is combat.

She gulped, her whole body screaming for her to return to her seat. But it was too late. She couldn't allow Aurelius to be in that danger. She just couldn't!

She jumped over the swords and ran through the combatants,

eyes fixed on the tunnel that Aurelius was just moments from entering. The grains burned hot as they flowed through her sandals, but she kept going, weaving past goliaths of men slamming together. She ducked and darted on legs well-honed from years of exercise. She—

The body came out of nowhere. A man darted to one side, not out of malice to get her, merely a fighter trying to avoid getting hit. But it was enough.

The impact knocked her back hard across the sand with a great, sweaty smack to the side. Stars filled her eyes as she rolled to a stop and tried desperately to blink the daze out.

"Well done," came a bright and boisterous voice as she pulled herself up, unsure of which way she was even facing. "That's what we like to see. Got the snot knocked out of you without even a simper."

"Yes, Hoplite Afigi. Thank you, Hoplite Afigi."

"Good lass. Now, head back and grab a steam. Captain Megala 'as been looking for a girl like you to join her Sisterhood for years! Tomorrow, you'll head to the Stormkillers to join them. Life as a Sister starts today. For *you* at least."

The female speaker stood as tall as Calix above the circle of women that formed a ring. And she looked just as strong too, with skin that held a gray-blue undertone, like a paler shade of that possessed by some of the giants they'd passed in the street. Atop her rugged, square-featured face was a sweep of silver-black hair, trimmed almost to the skin at the sides.

"But look at the rest of them, Pikra!" the tall one continued. "Standing back with their knees a-shaking? Don't no one else want to challenge 'er Highness?"

There came sharp tutting from somewhere unseen, until Teigra caught a glimpse of a much shorter woman pacing the front row.

"Typical, Elexis. Just typical!" she sneered.

Unlike the tall one, this "Pikra" lacked the physical size to back up her directness. She was small and sinewy, with features that were sharp, although not unattractive. She had a narrow nose, full cheeks and lips, and a pair of defined eyebrows set in a mocking scowl. Despite barely coming up to breast height, the circle flinched more under her gaze than they had from Elexis. "You're an insult to Ardor, you lot! Where's your passion, eh?"

Amidst the dressing down, Princess Zosime stood radiant in the middle of the circle, looking as if she hadn't even noticed the other women, let alone felt threatened by them. Her muscular legs were sun-kissed as summer wheat, set astride in the stance of a warrior. Her shoulders were relaxed but strong. Even her hair, tied back in a loose ponytail, was black and sleek and *strong*.

Back in the orange grove, among the bodies of the harpies she'd sliced apart, Zosime had appeared powerful. But standing here, in little more than a light glisten of sweat and a few pieces of red linen, she seemed the most beautiful, the most powerful, the most commanding woman that Teigra had ever seen.

Teigra shook the last of the daze away and got fully to her feet, remembering why she was in the wrestling ground in the first place. She looked around desperately, finally falling on the tunnel where Aurelius—

Was already gone.

Her blood went cold.

And it only went colder with what came next.

"Well, well, well!" came a sneering voice from uncomfortably close.

Teigra's looked down . . . Right into Pikra's eyes.

She gasped and stumbled back, causing a laugh from the others.

"Look what we have here," said the little woman. "If it isn't a precious flower from Mestibes."

"Come 'ere to gawp at us *common folk*, 'ave you?" spat Elexis, her prior brightness darkening. "Not even been 'ere a day and already wanting to stare at the *silly northern folk and their funny little ways*?"

"N-no!" stammered Teigra, glancing back to the empty entrance tunnel to the bathhouse. "I was just . . . just . . ."

"Well, *Mestibes*," said the princess, her voice as dark and smooth as pomegranate molasses, "if you didn't come to observe, you must have come to participate?"

In the corner of Zosime's full, beautiful lips, crept a wicked smirk, confirming everything Teigra had suspected.

I could call her out! She's the thief. And from a diplomatic carriage no less! Breaking the diplomatic seal? That's tantamount to war! She is in the wrong here, not me! I could call her out! I could do it!

The princess's smirk spread even further, as if reading Teigra's mind.

After a beat, Teigra's shoulders sagged in defeat, and she mumbled her response—too shocked by the implication of Aurelius already being in the bathhouse to fight back. And worse, now that she'd been spotted, there was no way she'd be allowed to run *into* that bathhouse to warn him. She'd be held down and arrested if she even tried. And lead them all to Aurelius while she was at it.

"I just . . . wanted to thank you for what you did on the road," said Teigra, feeling detached from her own voice.

Zosime gave her a disgusted look. But no look could be worse than how Teigra felt.

"Look at that, ladies!" said the princess, raising her arms victoriously. "*That* is the civilized polities for you. You hurl insults at them, and they thank you for it. Is that all you are, huh? Are you sad little Mestibians? Or are you *Ardorans*? Are you delicate little flowers? Or are you roses with some fucking thorns?"

A cheer rose and another challenger rushed forward to face Zosime. The rest of the circle no longer looked intimidated but spurred on—all of them keen to show that they were nothing like Teigra.

As combat commenced, Teigra looked around for an option, *any option*, that might allow her to undo the damage she'd done.

She found none.

Instead, she walked numbly back from the circle, returning to the stands to sit in her silent shame.

28

AURELIUS

AURELIUS UNDRESSED TO FULL NUDITY AND WANDERED INTO THE bathhouse, breathing in the steam and scented oils—fragrant rosemary and invigorating grapefruit.

The maze of red-tiled rooms was mostly empty, occupied by a half-dozen vanquished wrestlers, too busy wallowing in their defeats to notice the arrival of a pale-skinned interloper.

As he walked through, his breath catching at each new doorway, Aurelius thought back to the Pentheon.

It seemed both an eon ago and like it had happened just yesterday. That inexplicable moment between the prince and himself had been seared onto his memory—the sudden feeling of heat and lust when they had locked eyes, a feeling he had revisited night after night in the privacy of locked doors.

And hanging heavy from that memory was the final image of Calix's honey-gold eyes.

And his look of terror.

That fear was a reminder of what Aurelius was dealing with. They weren't in Mestibes anymore—where a man of his own *proclivities* merely faced social exclusion. Ardora was the land of passion and fertility, where the man–woman breeding ideal was woven into the very fabric of society.

And that was just for *regular people*. But for a prince? And a crown prince at that? One with the responsibility of maintaining the honor, the status, and above all the bloodline of his entire house?

If Urosina was correct about Calix, then his desires wouldn't be some little annoyance for him. It would be his biggest, darkest, most terrifying secret. A secret that could bring down his whole bloodline, and their crown along with it. A secret that could even lead to his *execution*!

That meant Aurelius had to be cautious. A man like Calix would go to great lengths to protect such a secret.

Room after room passed by, filled with naught but steam and no sign of the prince. At last, the corridors ended, and he arrived at the last room.

His heart skipped a beat as he rounded the last doorway.

The prince was there.

Calix lay chest-deep in cloudy warmth just a few yards in front of him. Rivulets of water dripped from his trimmed beard onto his rough-haired chest, the muscles still swollen from exertion. His eyes were closed, his face impassive.

And he was alone.

Before Aurelius moved, before he even made a sound, Calix opened his eyes, as if sensing his presence.

The prince looked right at him.

And the terror returned.

Despite the heat of the room, that look chilled Aurelius to the bone. He was used to having many effects on people—lust, laughter, frivolity. But not *terror*.

Yet, even amongst the chill, that look told him one important thing.

He remembers me . . .

For a moment, he considered turning around, fearing he had

made a great miscalculation. But he wasn't one to back away from risks.

Besides, he was here now.

And this was what he did best.

"Afternoon!" he said in an overly chirpy voice, breaking eye contact and stepping into the heat of the bath. He moved in the lines he knew to be pleasing—swaying his hips to make sure his firm, perky ass was on full display.

His supple skin smarted at the temperature of the water, a good deal hotter than he was used to, but he resisted the urge to yelp. Once fully in the pool, he settled a discreet distance from Calix, looking around the small room as though he was barely aware of the prince.

Then, he licked his lips and started to whistle. The tune was "The Enchantment of the Eidolon," one of the five ballads composed by the famous poet and musician Nenia, each telling the story of a different therian. He didn't labor the choice. They were often played in the secret bars he visited back home. And for whatever reason, it seemed appropriate for this moment—not least because it contained several high notes that required his pink lips to purse together in a way he knew was alluring.

As the notes echoed, Calix's eyes closed, his face wincing as if in pain. The prince remained still, no longer looking at him.

Eventually, and with a grunt of effort, Calix stood up and walked toward the exit of the pool.

"Wait!" said Aurelius, more sharply than he'd intended.

Calix stopped, his muscle-bound back knotted tight.

"You trained well, Your Highness," he continued, refilling his voice with the high, delicate tones he knew older men liked in their conquests. "It seemed no man out there could keep up with you."

For the longest time, Calix did nothing.

Not speaking.

Not moving.

Then, slow as the tide, he turned, and Aurelius was looking once again into those luminous golden eyes. Calix's face gave no hint of emotion, but his voice was heavy with animal menace.

"Why are you here?" he growled.

"I thought it might be nice to see you before the official exchange of letters. Ruler's son to ruler's son? Before we are surrounded by all those attendants and hangers-on with their agendas and interruptions and formalities?"

Calix stepped closer. "And you thought to come *here*? To a place for those who have known battle?"

Calix didn't wait for his response, prowling forward through the stomach-high water, closing the gap between them. Aurelius stepped back, until he was pressed against the corner of the pool.

The man was right over him. He lay one giant hand on the edge tiles to his right, then another to his left, locking him into a triangular cage.

Calix was so close now that all Aurelius could see was his body. All he could smell was the remnant sweat in his thick chest hair.

Manly.

Enticing.

Terrifying.

Calix stared right into his eyes, two pools of golden fire. "Have you known battle, Your Excellency?"

"N-no," he whispered, lost for words for the first time he could remember.

Calix leaned in until their noses were just a few inches apart. "Do you wish to?"

A hot shard stabbed at his groin. It was like nothing he had ever felt, stronger even than back in the Pentheon. His heart stampeded, knocking the wind from his lungs.

Then came these *images*: sweaty, savage, but so vivid they felt like they were happening in real-time. There were blurred moments of the prince slamming him against a wall, grinding his huge, naked body into his. Of muscles like an ox wrapping around his chest and neck, pulling him close, blending the boundaries between their beings. Of his own nails, digging into a thrusting back as he screamed for more.

Aurelius could *feel* it. The pleasure, the absolute, unimaginable *rapture*. And he wanted it more than anything he'd ever wanted before!

Now!

Forever!

"No!" roared the voice by his ear. "Control yourself!"

The tremendous grip on his mind vanished, leaving Aurelius reeling.

He grabbed the tiles, dizzy and disoriented with lust. The room was spinning. He couldn't tell what was left or right, up or down. All he could see was a swirling figure, writhing and screaming to himself.

Aurelius barely noticed. His whole body swam now in the air of the bathhouse. The steam ran over his nipples like a hundred sensuous hands. The water lapped at his groin like a harem of hungry tongues.

He grabbed his cock on instinct and it was only a matter of seconds before his orgasm ripped through him, waves of pleasure shaking him so hard he thought he might break in half.

When he finally came to his senses, feeling like a wet cloth with every drop of moisture wrung from it, he looked around to see what had happened.

Calix was gone.

29

TEIGRA

TEIGRA SHUFFLED UNDER MS. SECURIA'S GAZE. THOUGH SHE AVOIDED looking directly at the high envoy, she could feel the glare on top of her head.

The high envoy's office was even colder and more intimidating on the inside. The ceiling-high shelves of codices closed in mockingly—whispering that the occupant had forgotten more than Teigra would even know. The statue of Mesti by the window glinted in the late afternoon light, beaming with judgment—whispering that the occupant had law and reason and the goddess on her side.

And all Teigra had was the same gnawing feeling that had plagued her all afternoon: that she had failed every person who had ever trusted her.

Yes, Aurelius had miraculously gotten out of the wrestling school unharmed.

But it was no thanks to me.

The desk creaked as Ms. Securia leaned forward, elbows perched. "Among the senatorial families of Mestibes, your mother has developed quite a reputation, Ms. Cosmin. The youngest sibling of the archon. A member of an excellent family—speaking in terms of their power, if not their *character*—who was nevertheless destined to a life of quiet service. She was to be comfortable, but unremarkable. It was of course unfathomable that *she* should enter the senate, though not unfathomable that she would marry a patrician senator. And with that duty complete, she would settle into a life of growing obscurity, drifting further from power with each blessed nephew and niece. That would have been the *proper* path. However, this was not the path she chose, was it?"

"No, Ms. Securia," whispered Teigra.

"No, it *wasn't*. Instead, your mother did something scandalous. She spurned her patrician suitors and married the son of a faded *mercator* family, House Cosmin—once well-regarded, but at that time so far down the pack it was at risk of being knocked from the senate entirely. Most thought the pairing a tragic mistake."

Ms. Securia leaned back, taking obvious relish in recounting the story that Teigra knew all too well.

"And yet, their union was not a mistake. Your father received ownership of the family business as a wedding gift, and in a little over a decade, they took House Cosmin from a laughingstock to a serious power player. From the twentieth-best stable in Mestibes to the only one that a self-respecting patrician would choose. And with the tragic passing of your father, she even secured his seat in the senate. Now, she has taken House Cosmin to the precipice of achieving what only three other houses have achieved in the last century—ascending from mercator class to *patrician*."

Teigra sat in silence. It was all true, although she was sure Mother deserved little of the credit.

"Do you agree that your mother is close to achieving this goal, Ms. Cosmin?"

Teigra stared at the floor, not wishing to dwell on Mother's naked ambition. But the woman in question had instructed her to show respect to the high envoy. And she was already in more than enough trouble to consider any further disobedience.

"Yes," she muttered.

Ms. Securia tented her fingers. "Then why would you seek to *ruin* all that your family has worked for?"

Her stomach clenched. "I didn't . . . I didn't mean to!"

"Are you saying you were not aware of your actions? That Mr. Accola was unclear in his instructions for you to remain in the embassy?"

"No! Please, he didn't do anything wrong. And neither did Aurelius. It was all my fault."

Ms. Securia rose, running a stick of incense through an oil lamp and placing it at the feet of the goddess. "Loyalty is an admirable quality, Ms. Cosmin. It does you well to show it. But you must decide *who* you are loyal to."

Curls of pine-heavy smoke rose across the bronze, wreathing Mesti in a dramatic haze.

"You love your family, Teigra. You just made a mistake today. But I have faith in your destiny. I have faith in your *family's* destiny. Just as you must put your faith in me."

The woman walked behind her, placing a hand on either shoulder.

Teigra shuddered under her strong touch.

"So tell me, why has the archon sent her herald to Ardora?"

Bile scalded Teigra's throat. Right now, all Ms. Securia knew was that they had snuck out of the embassy and gone into town. And that they had snuck back in a few hours later, right into her stiff-backed scowl. But she didn't know about the wrestling school. She didn't know about Aurelius meeting with Calix. And she didn't know about Aurelius's mission.

Aurelius had told Teigra all those secrets in confidence. A confidence she had already betrayed badly. And she couldn't betray it any further.

She just couldn't.

"I . . . I don't know," she said, her whole neck clenching.

The high envoy's hands were unmoving upon her skin, yet promised the potential of pressure. "Ms. Cosmin, your cousin will come and go from this place—traveling here and there, making the archon's grubby, transactional little deals. But you and I will work together for at least the next five years. Just as House Securia could work with House Cosmin for decades to come, as two proud *patrician* families."

Teigra shook under the woman's grip. She felt she was being torn into two.

Ms. Securia could make it happen. Her family was one of the oldest and most influential in the chamber. One letter of recommendation, one confirmation of her loyalty, and the deal would be done.

And all it would cost was the one person who had supported her unconditionally.

Tears tumbled down Teigra's cheek. She gripped her own hands in frustrated fury.

But she remained silent.

"So be it," said Ms. Securia with a sigh, releasing her grip. "Go to your office and await my instructions."

"And . . . and my family?"

Securia gave her a weary look. "If you will not tell me of the herald's plans, then you cannot proceed as you have. From this day forward, you will offer him no further assistance in whatever his mission may be. You will provide no aid, no advice, and no comfort of any kind. You are a servant of the senate now. You have no business with the Archon or her pet. And you will answer alone to *me*. Am I understood?"

Teigra nodded, her heart aching at what she was being asked to do—to avoid spending time with her only true family—but still thankful that there was *some* way out.

Ms. Securia narrowed her eyes. "Do this and perhaps I will not feel the need to inform the senate of your actions."

Teigra breathed a sigh of relief and made to leave, but Ms. Securia stopped her. "Is it true, Ms. Cosmin, that your father intended for you to join him in the senate when House Cosmin rose to patrician status? That he was training you in worldly affairs for that very purpose."

She stood still for a long time, eyes downcast and stomach twisting darkly. The future that never was flashed across her mind. It was the future that Teigra had ripped away from him. From House Cosmin. From herself.

"Yes," she whispered, leaving quickly before the tears could return.

30

AURELIUS

THE NOTES FROM AURELIUS'S PIPES FLUTTERED INTO THE HOT NIGHT— stickier than any he'd ever experienced back home.

He was remaining with the musical theme of the day, playing another of the Nenia therian ballads, this one the "Sonnet of the Siren," a cautionary tale about a young man who'd exchanged his youth for all the wealth and fame he desired, only to realize that the price he'd paid was worth more than the possessions he'd gained.

Perhaps there was something apt there.

Although, not *quite* yet.

His games with the prince had only just begun, after all.

A humid breeze kissed his naked body, laying upside down on his bed in the barely furnished insult that was his bedroom. He didn't care that Securia or Jaspar or even the rather handsome centaur might wander in. In Securia's case, it might be better that she did— give the old bitch a shock to the system.

At least she'd had the good sense to not try to discipline him. Instead, she had hauled Tiggy off, closing the main door with a filthy glare.

He'd thought of going after her, of telling the old cow to leave

Teigra alone. But his cousin had seemed resigned to her fate, just as she'd been when the archon told her to leave the room back in Mestibes.

And as sad as that was, he wouldn't always be there to save her. She had five years with the woman—or potentially even longer. Perhaps it was time for Teigra to make her own way.

The melody rose and swirled as Aurelius thought back to the bathhouse.

He had recounted the lurid details to Tiggy as they'd wandered back to the embassy, his blood still shimmering with excitement. He'd enjoyed her looks of shock when he'd described the sensations of the prince's presence. And he'd laughed off her concern, yammering about how there was surely some information in Ms. Securia's library that could help him.

That was so like her. Tell her you were the horniest you had ever been, and she'd rush to find a cure or make it about some myth or monster.

And he *had* laughed it off. Because it was all so laughable.

And yet . . .

He lowered the pipes and stared at the exposed-wood ceiling.

The first time he had felt the animal heat, back in the Pentheon, he'd thought it some twist of his internal sexual desire.

But the second time?

This second time had been even more *unnatural*. Even more *unhinged*. Even more *unrestrained*.

He reached down, his hard dick growing past his belly button at the thought of the prince pressing him back into the corner of the pool.

Just as he was about to give himself the attention his body demanded, he stopped, returning the pipes to his lips.

Most people thought that he was some uncontrolled bundle of debauchery, and he'd rarely sought to disprove that notion—it was far more useful that they underestimated him than know the truth.

Because the truth was that you didn't get to where he'd gotten by being impulsive and uncontrolled. All his decadence was not impulsivity, but a conscious choice. Calculated moves. Careful steps.

And so, it had to be with the prince, didn't it? This was not some frivolous romp. He hadn't come a million miles just to fuck some hunk. There were plenty of men in this city who could smooth that rough edge.

No, the prince served one purpose and one purpose alone: he was Aurelius's pathway back into the line of succession, to the status and future that was rightfully his.

And that meant he had to be smart about this. He had to be controlled. He had to be restrained.

And above all, it meant he had to be honest about what might be going on with his body—no matter how ridiculous and unbelievable it seemed.

31

TEIGRA

HER FOREARM ACHED AS SHE FINISHED YET ANOTHER LETTER.

Her eyes were as rough as a cat's tongue. Her hand was numb from gripping the reed pen. And worst of all, her stomach rumbled with the sheer agony of hunger. She'd been too worried to eat when they'd left Prasni Zorio. That meant it'd been a full day without food.

It must have been two or three in the morning now, and she'd only just reached the halfway point. Fifty letters were rolled in the basket beside her desk, wrapped in thin ribbons of yellow silk, with each to be signed by Ms. Securia.

She'd been very clear about that. It was her name that would go on the letters, and no one else's.

Every few hours, the high envoy had marched into Teigra's office to critique her work and ensure she hadn't drifted off, obviously not trusting that Jaspar would administer her punishment properly.

She was right to be suspicious—all throughout the evening, before both he and Ms. Securia had finally gone to bed, the mid envoy had popped his head in cautiously, whispering that he could take a few letters on the sly so that she could finish sooner.

When she'd refused, fearing even more trouble, he'd told her to keep her chin up, promising that he would show her around the city once her credentials had been accepted.

That was very sweet. *He* was very sweet, even though she had done nothing to deserve it.

And if there was one benefit to take away from this wretched day, it appeared that Calix did not actually know of Aurelius's mission. When her cousin had recounted his experience in the bathhouse, Calix had seemed genuinely shocked by Aurelius's presence.

That means Zosime hasn't told him.

But why not? It just ... it just doesn't make any sense.

The first option Teigra could think of was that Zosime hadn't read the folio yet. That seemed very unlikely. The princess surely hadn't just *stumbled* across their carriage—she must have been waiting for them at the border, assuming that the herald at least would be inbound. And anyone who'd steal a document like that would want to uncover all the secrets and bargaining chips within it right away.

The second option was that Zosime *had* read it but hadn't understood its significance. That seemed possible. After all, you had to read between the lines to understand the diplomatic codes and innuendos. The letters that detailed Urosina's final mission in particular were practically in a foreign language. There was certainly nothing that talked of oncoming war or that Aurelius would be sent to seduce Calix to secure a military agreement.

And yet, even that option held little hope. For even if Zosime didn't know the true worth of what she had, it was only a matter of time before she'd hand the folio over to some royal advisor who would.

And the third option, which confused her the most, was that Zosime *had* read the folio, and *had* understood it, but that she'd deliberately not told Calix?

Though it was frustrating the way Mother doted on Jaronas, of seeing him occupy the position and prominence that Father had long intended for her, she would never dream of *undermining* her brother.

Because that would only damage House Cosmin further. Her own flesh and blood and name.

But . . . that isn't how ruling families think, is it?

Aurelius so often spoke about Benedict in the cruelest terms. The same way Mother spoke about her siblings as well—Uncle Balser and the archon and Urosina when she'd been alive. It often seemed there was more jealousy there than love. Like they'd sooner ruin their own family than see their siblings surpass them.

And Urosina's papers had given no insight into the relationship between Zosime and Calix. Maybe it was cold? Maybe she knew of his sexuality, and feared the consequence for their whole line, just as Ura had feared about Aurelius? Maybe Zosime saw this whole situation as an opportunity to bring him down, and was making some kind of plans?

Teigra sighed. There was no way of knowing which reason it was. And regardless, it meant there was a little more time for Aurelius to work his magic.

As the hours passed and the evening grew into morning, her thoughts wandered into what Aurelius had described in the bathhouse. Not the explicit details he was always eager to share, knowing that it made her feel uncomfortable, but the strange sensations that he'd described—the unbearable heat and the feeling like he was losing control of his body.

Aurelius hadn't seemed worried about that. But she couldn't shake a growing pang of concern. After all, his mission was essential to all of them. And whole scrolls had been devoted to detailing the creatures that could cause such sensations!

But, no, that can't be right . . .

If that were true, that would mean Prince Calix is a . . .

Her pen lifted from the parchment, the swish of brown ink soaking into the fine valleys of the soft skin.

The final scroll was complete.

With a heave of relief, she shook herself back to the present and gathered the basket. Her legs were stiff from so long at the desk, aching when she kneeled to place the letters outside Ms. Securia's imposing office door, shut tight for the evening.

All she needed now was some food and water, then she could be done with this day.

And yet . . .

She looked around. She was the only one still down here. Even Mr. Placi had long since retired. Everything was still. Only her lamp gave any light.

And if she was right in her suspicion, then Aurelius was still in danger . . .

Her hand hovered over Ms. Securia's office door handle as her curiosity dug at her.

She was already in enough trouble. And Jaspar had made clear that this room was off-limits unless she invited you in.

But . . . if Aurelius was in trouble, then all Mestibes was in trouble as well. Would she really put all of those people at risk, just to protect herself? Because of her weakness? Because of her *cowardice*.

Just like she had done to Aurelius?

The sting of Zosime's mockery burned her ears like she was still standing among the fighters. All spurred on by looking at *her*. All desperate to prove they were nothing like *her*.

Are you a delicate little flower, Teigra? Or are you a rose with fucking thorns?

Teigra tried to steady the shake in her hand.

Then she opened the door.

Her lamp glowed along the cold bindings of the codices and the watching face of the goddess. With a catch in her throat, she closed the door quietly and scanned the shelves.

Eventually, she found what she was looking for, something she was certain the high envoy would have. It was the same codex she'd often read in the chilled air of prelight back in the Lapiso Library: *Gods, Myths and Beasts*, written by the same man for whom that library was named.

Teigra rested her lamp on one of the higher shelves and turned the pages, listening out nervously for any sound beyond the door. She flicked quickly past creatures she could only dream of seeing— the dryads of the twisted groves in Vaticily, the nerids encountered by Ondocian sailors in the Illhas and Macrinos Seas—until she came to the section she was looking for.

The title stared back at her from the top of the page, the single word bearing the cold reality of what she suspected Calix was.

Therians.

Her throat going dry, Teigra read:

Children born between a mortal and one of the Five High Gods are sometimes treated as a blessing. Some even dare to call them "demi-gods."

But nothing could be further from the truth.

Satyrs? Phoenixes? Sirens? Eidolons? Gorgons?

These five wretched creatures are "therians"—twisted children of the divine, thirsting for a godly power that they will never manage to quench. And on nights of the sable moon, when all is darkest, they reveal their true nature.

And what a wretched nature it is. As wretched as the creatures themselves. Because make no mistake, the therian is a monster, a beast of bronze, cursed with a taste of the divine power which sired it.

For why else would these beasts so often befall those known to have insulted the Five? To be birthed by heathens and betrayers, perverts and the corrupt?

The Five Therians

Phoenix—Born of Rina and taking the form of a winged human engulfed in fire. They thirst alone for terror and are empowered to strike fear and hopelessness. A phoenix's true chrysalis (the divine item that permanently awakens their power) is the consumption of a Rinathi war priest's heart.

Gorgon—Born of Vatic and taking the form of a human with serpentine attributes. They thirst alone for misfortune and are empowered to twist the fate of any mortal at a point of indecision. A gorgon's true chrysalis is being bitten by an albino opium snake.

Siren—Born of Ondo and taking the form of a winged human with attributes of a sea bird. They thirst alone for greed and are empowered to write contracts that grant wishes and wildest dreams, always at a terrible price. A siren's true chrysalis is wearing a deep-ink pearl from the darkest trenches of the Illhas Sea.

Eidolon—Born of Mesti and taking the form of shifting starlight. They thirst alone for jealousy and are empowered to take the form of any person they wish, copying their appearance and talents. An eidolon's true chrysalis is using a quill drawn from a celestial strix.

Teigra paused. Her eyes hovered over the final passage—the one which had brought her into the room in the first place.

Satyr—Born of Ardor and taking the form of a human with the attributes of a goat. They thirst alone for passion and can drive any creature into a fit of frenzy. A satyr's true chrysalis is being pricked by the thorn of an eternal ros—

Her spine seized. Footsteps were just outside the door.

Suddenly, all thought of sleep and hunger was gone.

The steps came closer.

The window of the office was just a few feet away. She made to dash for it, but before she could, the door opened!

A shadowy figure appeared in the frame. Then the figure darted toward her.

She screamed, but their hand clasped over her mouth!

"Darling," whispered a familiar voice. "Could you *not* wake the entire embassy?"

The hand released her. "Aurie!"

"So it would seem."

"But . . . what are you doing here?"

"The same thing as you, by the looks of it," he said, tapping the book. "Just getting a bit of light reading about hyrdas and hippogriffs, are we?"

"No, it's just . . . I was thinking about what you said. About how you felt when you were around Calix. And I know you'll just laugh it off, but I think that Calix might be . . . *a satyr*."

Aurelius crossed his arms and gave her a mocking smile. "Ah yes, for I distinctly recall his shapely horns. It is a wonder that more people don't notice them."

Teigra scowled. "You *know* that isn't what all therians are like! That's only the really bad ones, or the middle-stage ones around the sable moon. Look, it's all here—each of the five therians share three possible stages: dormant, metamorph, and imago."

She cleared her throat and continued to read the passage:

Contrary to legend, there is practically no difference between a dormant therian and a mortal human, save some persistent negative urges which speak to the creature's later forms. Indeed, most therians will remain in this dormant form for their entire lives, with neither themselves nor those around them having any awareness of their true nature.

However, this changes for any therian unlucky enough to be exposed to one of the five divine chrysalides.

Those therians fortunate enough to encounter one of their four 'false chrysalides'—the chrysalides of the gods that <u>didn't</u> sire them—will take on a 'metamorph' form, halfway between beast and human. Their latent powers will be awakened, alongside their primal thirst. They will have access to some skills of the beast and will be able to shift back and forth at will.

However, this 'will' is lost on the night of the sable moon, when they must transform into their beastly form, losing all sight of their humanity, and living alone to quench their sinful thirst.

Yet, even these tragic souls may consider themselves lucky compared to the beast's final form.

Those therians unfortunate enough to be exposed to their 'true chrysalis'—the chrysalis of the god that <u>did</u> sire them—turn instead into an imago. Their latent powers and latent thirsts are awakened in full. They are transformed permanently into their beastly form, regardless of the stage of the moon, losing all traces of their humanity forevermore and irreversibly, and falling to their darkest desires and darkest natures.

"Don't you see?" said Teigra, breathlessly. "Calix is a satyr! He's just in the metamorph form—neither human nor beast, but still with powers he can inflict on people. That's what happened to you at the bathhouse! He used his powers to drive you crazy!"

"Of course he did," said Aurelius, with a barely stifled laugh. "Just one small problem, love: 'save some persistent negative urges which speak to the creature's later forms'?"

"Yes?"

"That would mean Calix acts a bit like a satyr all the time, even when it isn't the sable moon?"

"Well, yes?"

"Have you *seen him*, Tiggy? All growly faced and gruff? Never even cracking a smile? Rather at odds with the image of a satyr, isn't it? All laughing and drinking and debauching under starlight?"

"I . . ." Teigra paused, looking down at the book. Aurelius was right. If Calix was a satyr, he should have some of those qualities all the time.

And he didn't.

"But, but," she stammered, "you said you came here for the same thing as me?"

Aurelius chuckled and ran his fingers over a higher shelf, bringing down a codex of his own: *Ailments, Maladies, and Curatives*, by Prolego, High Healer of Farmot Vatic, the Goddess of Medicine.

He flicked through the pages, before turning the book to face her.

"The five divine ailments?" she said. "*Ashen passion. Symptoms: A sudden loss in motivation and enjoyment of life, most common among citizens of Ardora—*"

"The bottom one, Tiggy."

"Oh," she said, in a voice of deep embarrassment, after reading the first few lines.

<u>*Wandering Vigor*</u>

Symptoms: Increased blood pulse, sudden and steeply rising body temperature, shortness of breath, dizziness and uncontrollable desire, heaviness of the abdomen and general impulsivity.

Cause: An overindulgence in the worldly gifts of the Pentariat—including excessive consumption of stupefying libations, persistent intemperate behavior, moral turpitude, and an overfascination with physical ecstasy. This ailment is most commonly found amongst the free citizens of Mestibes, no doubt indicative that Mesti holds her own citizens to a higher standard of worldly restraint than she does those of the other polities.

Remedy: Abstinence from all worldly pleasures until symptoms cease, and considerable restraint thereafter.

Teigra looked at the floor, her face burning hot. "I'm sorry, Aurie. I'm so stupid. I got all worked up over nothing, didn't I?"

He patted her shoulder. "I would have much preferred your explanation to mine."

The significance of his words snapped her from wallowing. "Wait. I thought you didn't believe in the divine ailments? You always hated when people said you had wandering vigor?"

Aurelius shrugged. "And yet, here we are? I can't say I fully believe this crap, but it would be foolish to deny that the symptoms are astoundingly similar."

"So, you are sick? Oh, Aurie. I'm so sorry! You have to take care of yourself. If this only happens around the prince, then you need to stay away from hi..."

Aurelius gave her a sympathetic smile as her voice trailed away. "Yes, darling. *Exactly.* I can't do that. Just as I can't avoid my mission."

"So, what will you do?"

He closed the book with a resolute snap, glaring up at the bronze face of the goddess, darkly shadowed in the flickering lamplight. "It appears that I must make the ultimate sacrifice."

32

AURELIUS

THE TAIL OF HIS TOGA DRAGGED ALONG THE WAX-POLISHED FLOOR, hanging as heavy as his fucking balls, sweating beneath the yards of unfamiliar wool.

The last three days had been *unbearable*. His cock screamed for attention. His tongue yearned for the sweet kiss of wine. And his entire body felt practically malnourished from the plebeian fabrics he'd been wearing—absent his usual jewelry or silks or finest brocades.

Despite this, he had stuck to the abstinence, just as the codex had instructed. There was simply too much at stake not to.

And besides, it would probably only be for a few days. A week or two at most, given the prince's obvious weaknesses.

However, the cumulative effect of all this restraint was that Aurelius was in the foulest mood of his life. He had even snapped at Tiggy this morning, as Aurelius had departed and she'd stayed behind, when she'd joked about how proud the archon would be to see him in the crocus-yellow toga, over top a piss-bleached tunic so white it practically glowed. For the gods' sakes, he had even combed his shag of blond hair, just to take his mind off the throb between his legs.

"You have memorized the protocol?" said Ms. Securia, quiet enough that she wouldn't be overheard by the pair of guards escorting them down the corridor—lined not with frescos or mosaics, as they would be back home, but with dark and heavy tapestries.

Through the glassless windows was a magnificent courtyard below, seemingly set in a permanent feasting configuration, with lounges for a hundred guests, surrounded by enormous amphorae and stands positively groaning with fresh fruit and bowls of nut-sprinkled yogurt. And beyond that, back at their elevated height, was a tholos—a grand, circular building overlooking the city, without walls, supported by three dozen columns as thick as tree trunks, all of which were covered with twisting wraps of green.

"Of course, I did!" he snapped, almost tripping on the toga. It was about the nineteenth time the bitch had asked. "Bow, present credentials, wait in silence, polite small talk, leave. I think even *I* can manage that, Ramuna."

He yanked the hateful cloth up over his shoulder, wondering firstly how anyone could routinely wear this damn garment, and secondly how much the old hag knew of his mission.

Teigra had seemingly been avoiding him these last few days, but in the brief moments he had grabbed with her this morning, she'd promised that she'd kept his secrets.

From the high envoy's demeanor, that appeared true. It seemed that as far as Securia was concerned, this would be the first time he had met the prince, and the archon had merely sent him down to improve relations with the noble classes. Nothing more.

That she didn't seem to know about the mission, or the coming invasion, was comforting. Things were complicated enough without her getting in the damn way.

The guards stopped at a pair of intricately carved doors. "She will see you now."

Aurelius and Ms. Securia turned to each other.

"*She?*" said Aurelius, glaring at the guards. "Where is the prince?"

A little pulse ran through him. It wasn't just the awful thought that he'd been a good boy for no damn reason. It was also that, after what had happened in the bathhouse, he had focused entirely on his own reactions, and hadn't given much thought to how it might have impacted Calix.

But the man had been in a frenzy, hadn't he? Fighting his obvious desire to bed Aurelius. What if, rather than a few days of confusion, the prince was now avoiding him too?

Or was it perhaps nothing? After all, Securia had only *suggested* he would be met by Calix—it was never a certainty. Perhaps with the death of Urosina, the royals were throwing him a social nicety and giving them a more senior audience with the queen?

Ms. Securia spoke under her breath. "The Brotherhoods and Sisterhoods of Ardora place a higher value on loyalty and passion than anything else, Your Excellency. They certainly won't be giving you information about the whereabouts of their masters."

The guards' faces betrayed a hint of pride.

"Fine then, *you* answer. You said we wouldn't be meeting with the actual rulers!"

"We will persevere," she said, through a false smile.

Aurelius grunted, dragging the heavy toga back into position. "Well, maybe this is a positive sign for you at least."

"Oh, I sincerely doubt that," she replied under her breath.

Her voice held a level of hostility he hadn't heard previously, and Aurelius got the distinct impression that she had much more to say about the queen.

But she didn't share it. Instead, she nodded her gratitude to the guards who opened the doors.

The throne room was opulent, in an Ardoran sort of way—cavernous and filled with extravagant wooden furniture. A red-woolen rug, so deep his sandal sank up to the skin, stretched to where two tall chairs loomed. In front of the thrones was a waist-high plinth, on which rested the most wicked crown he had ever seen—a bronze weave of three-inch thorns, each spike-tip glinting.

And standing next to it was a woman.

She was dressed in a flowing red himation, belted at the waist to highlight her dramatic curves. Black, wavy hair fell across her shoulders. She couldn't have been older than twenty-five, with lips the color of rosewood.

Aurelius stifled a gasp. *Her?* It was the woman who had saved them from the harpies.

What . . . what is this?

The moment of shock gave way to realization. The little snippets from his barely read briefings.

"Princess Zosime!" said Ms. Securia, bowing her head. "To what do we owe the pleasur—"

"Remove the hag," said Zosime, her voice as dark as fortified wine. "The herald and I need to talk. *Alone.*"

The two other fighters who had been with Zosime at the grove appeared out of nowhere and led Ms. Securia out.

Then his blood ran cold.

In the princess's hand was a leather-covered folio.

It was the same folio that had been given to him by his mother.

It was the same folio he had given Teigra, telling her to destroy it when she was done.

Urosina's notes? What? How in Dimethan did she have them?

The folio's content ran through his head.

The profiles.

The criticism.

The comments about weaknesses and *proclivities!*

She has them all! She must know about the mission.

The door clicked closed behind him, and he was alone with the princess—save her two cronies, taking up flank on either side of the exit.

Despite her saying they needed to talk, Zosime said nothing. Instead, her dark eyes fixed on him like an hungry raven.

Aurelius crackled with a combination of nerves and excitement. It was just how those wrestlers must feel as they circled a fresh opponent, both fearing the potential for injury, yet eager to test their skills.

And whether she knew it or not, the princess had already made her first move: showing off the folio, practically begging him to bring it up. She had wanted to shock him, to throw him off balance.

And he couldn't allow that.

"Thank you, *love*," he said with a good-natured smile, plonking himself down in one of the chairs that ringed the audience area. A rope was laid down in front of it, making what appeared to be a circular wrestling arena directly in front of the thrones, with the red rug in place of sand. "I have been trying to get that old woman off my back all week. Uppity commoners. You know the sort."

His nonchalance drew the response he'd hoped for—a barely-concealed mix of confusion and anger. It was quite a thing to see it on such a beautiful face, blemished only by a scar that ran down her left eyebrow, cutting the hair in two.

Poor thing. She probably had a whole speech ready and everything.

At last, she relented. "I know why you are here, *Herald*. You Mestibians think you're all so clever, don't you? With your fancy words and talk of diplomacy. You act like you are the mother of all Dynosia—helping the little children get along. But you are just the same as the rest of us. The Ondocians might screw us into a bad trade deal, but at least they do it to our face. But *this* is what Mestibes does."

"And what is that?" he said, glancing lightly at the folio she brandished.

Her eyes narrowed. "*Spying on us.* Taking trusted conversations and turning them into arrows."

Ahhh, he thought, his whole body relaxing. The poor thing is staring at a gold mine, and all she can see is a hole in the ground.

"My dear Princess, I have come to your land in a carriage bearing the crest of my polity. I am staying in the Mestibian embassy, right in the center of town. And I have arrived at your palace, by appointment, for your family to receive my credentials. If my goal is to hide, I am rather failing at it."

"You don't have to hide to be a spy."

"Actually, you do. A spy you can see is called a diplomat."

"Spy? Diplomat? What difference does it make!" she said, waving the folio emphatically, like some kind of club. "Either way, you have come here to twist and shape us, just like your aunt did before you. Just like that smarmy woman does. Trying to wipe clean your cowardice at Sama?"

"Of course."

The princess paused. "You . . . admit it?"

"Yes, Your Highness. I am representing the archon of Mestibes, who has made no secret that she wishes to normalize relations between our two polities. I am here to achieve that goal. And further, while I am here, I will meet with all manner of people. From those conversations, yes, I will write letters back to the archon, telling her of the progress of my work, and of any challenges that stand in the way. Including I might add, of *this* very discussion."

Zosime tensed. "You wouldn't."

"A meeting with a senior royal? Naturally, I will report on that." His eyes narrowed to Urosina's folio. "On *all* that has happened."

Her confidence unraveled, turning instead to anger. "No! I won't allow it!"

The two Sisters rushed from the door to Aurelius's side, their weapons drawn. Though his heart pounded, he did not divert his eyes from the princess as the steel was laid cold against his throat. He had diplomatic immunity, though he doubted this member of the royal family cared much for such traditions.

She was furious now. She was clearly used to people cowering before her. And if she had grabbed him in a dark alley, knife to his heart, he'd probably have already pissed himself.

But she was an utter novice at the subtler arts.

"Tell them to cut me down, Princess, if that is your intention," he said, his voice far more confident than he actually felt. "I am sure you have permission from your king to do so. Just as he surely gave you permission to follow us on arrival and defile the diplomatic seal? And just as your brother must surely be aware of all this, and is preparing his troops for the war that will follow my death?"

"Don't you dare talk to me about—" she hissed, eyes narrowing, before stopping herself.

Talking about Calix appears to have infuriated her. Interesting . . .

Impotent fury radiated from the princess. Her cheeks looked hot enough to roast lamb.

At last, she gave a dismissive flick of her hand, and the goons stepped back, resheathing their weapons.

Stifling a relieved exhale, Aurelius approached her, the air thick with her hatred.

He held out two scrolls—the credentials of himself and Teigra.

Zosime reached for them, but he pulled them back. "My folio?"

Her jaw clenched, and Aurelius knew that her darting eyes contained the admission that she hadn't even bothered to make copies, so confident had she been.

It took all his effort not to snort.

At last, she shoved the folio into his chest and yanked the scrolls away. "I'll be watching you, *Herald!*"

Aurelius gave a wink, drumming his fingers on the leather. "And I you, *Princess.*"

The doors opened, and he tucked the documents into his toga before Securia could see them. "Credentials accepted," he said, matter-of-factly, pushing down the racing of his heart and launching into a quick walk.

Securia's eyes darted to the side of his head as she met his pace. She wanted to know everything. Of course she did.

But she won't beg, even if the curiosity is killing her.

He was right, and the two of them marched in silence back down the corridor.

As they departed, Aurelius felt a strange urge to take one more glance out of the window overlooking the feasting grounds.

His pulse, only just quietened, pounded back to full rhythm as he did so.

Prince Calix was standing on the balcony opposite—his arms astride the balustrade, just as they'd been against him in the bathhouse.

His honeyed eyes stared right into him.

His gaze was as intense as the bronze moon itself.

33

TEIGRA

Teigra emerged into the sunlit courtyard. The morning air was warm and scented with the earthy aroma of crocus.

It was the morning after Aurelius and Ms. Securia had visited the palace. Apparently, their credentials had been accepted, although she hadn't yet had the chance to hear so directly from Aurelius. He hadn't returned with Ms. Securia, coming back instead well after dark—closer to dawn really, when she'd been awake in bed out of early morning habit.

She'd wanted to run down and ask him all that had happened. Whether his wandering vigor had acted up at the palace. Whether his three days of abstinence had paid off. To just sit on his bed and run through the events of the day, as they so often had.

But she hadn't. Just like she had only managed a few words in passing to him before he left for the palace.

Ms. Securia's words still burned in her ears. She'd already used enough chances and taken enough risks. It was a miracle that she hadn't been punished even more strictly! Now, there was no option for her. Now, she had to obey.

And besides, Teigra was sure that Aurelius would be fine without her. After all, seduction was his specialty. And he hardly needed *her* for that.

The only thing that had tempted her to find some secret moment with Aurelius was the folio. But she'd instead resolved that she would wait until everything had calmed down. When the heat had died and the risk of Ms. Securia's fury had lessened.

In a few days perhaps. Or maybe a week.

But she would do it. Definitely. He deserved to know. No matter the consequences.

Back in the courtyard, Jaspar had a skip in his step, which was quite a thing to see in a minotaur. "Are you excited to discover your new home?"

Five days ago, she might have mumbled a lie. And her heart did tremble at the sounds beyond the gates—laughter and hearty welcomes, passing workers singing, unbothered by who they disturbed. But after days locked away, her initial fear had dulled, replaced with an excitement to just get out there and see the city she'd be living in for the next five years.

And as painful as it was, if she was to avoid Aurelius, then she should commit to her new life. Do honor to her family name and make Ms. Securia confident in the loyalty of House Cosmin.

"I am," she said at last. "But . . . you promise you'll tell me if I do anything wrong? I don't want to just be another southerner, stomping around and not respecting customs."

He laughed. "Don't worry. People here go on about that 'southerner' stuff, but it's mostly just for fun." He gestured toward the gate. "You don't mind if we walk?"

"Not at all. I walked everywhere back home."

"You'll do well here then!" he said, clanking open the gates.

The street was chaos. They had to push past humming women carrying loaves of fragrant barley bread and circles of giggling children playing some game with ram knuckles.

Jaspar led her down one crammed and twisting street after another, before finally stopping at a strange building, marble-fronted and neatly columned, just like those back home, albeit worn to the color of a grandmother's hair. It stuck out badly compared to the surrounding buildings, with their red bricks and abundance of flowers.

"This part's a bit boring," he said, unlocking the creaking doors. "But Ms. Securia was insistent."

They entered the most curious place Teigra had ever seen. Inside was a concentrated mash-up of home. A statue of Mesti was up back, its bronze glinting in the morning light. However, that was the *only* part of the space that glinted—everywhere else was covered in a thick layer of dust.

The large floor was split into quarters: one appeared to be an oratory platform, elevated above the rest, just like the Forum; a second was set aside for stone carving and painting frescos, with little cups of color frozen in time; a third had racks of instruments—kitharas and lyres and aulos pipes, all stacked in forgotten silence; and the fourth housed the specialized equipment for glass-making and complex pottery, with strange bags of powders beside a kiln. Adding to the abandonment were the shelves and hives all along the walls, absolutely packed with codices and scrolls.

"What is this place?" she said, her voice echoing off the high ceiling.

"The Temple of Mesti in Ardora. Well, it used to be, before the royals shut it down," said Jaspar, turning an unsympathetic look to the space. "*Ghastly*, isn't it?"

Teigra wasn't sure about that. It was certainly in disrepair, but she could almost hear the ghostly clacking of hammers and the sounds of great speeches. There was something comforting in that—like if she closed her eyes, she could almost be back on her dawn walks to the Alogo, before any of this had happened.

"It's seen better days," she said, attempting diplomacy. "But why is a temple to Mesti on its own? Where is their Pentheon?"

"Oh, *whoops*, did that not come up in the scrolls yet? Ardorans don't really do that. Only Mestibians do. They believe in the Five up here, of course, but they don't worship them as equals. The temples to the rest of the Five are scattered around the city. But, to be honest, the shrines to the lesser gods of Ardor get way more visitors." Jaspar kicked a bit of marble along the floor. "If you ask me, this place is exactly what you said before: a bunch of southerners stomping around and not respecting customs. Trying to *civilize the savages* with our *cultured arts*."

Teigra ran her eyes along the walls. There were some very old documents—some that might be the only copy outside of the Lapiso Library. "Shouldn't these be returned for safekeeping?"

"The senate tried, but Ms. Securia won't let them."

"Really?' said Teigra, struggling to imagine the high envoy disobeying the senate. "Why?"

"She says that just because Ardora has abandoned Mestibes, it doesn't mean Mestibes should abandon Ardora. She thinks the royals will eventually let us open the place up again. And then all the people out there can learn our special little ways."

Teigra raised her eyebrows, surprised that the nasty woman would think something so profound. "Is she the one who's been polishing the statue?"

Jaspar nodded, leaning in with a sly smile. "She's super religious. She even observes the Sable Moon Sanctum!"

"Really?" said Teigra, with a positive lift that seemed to surprise him.

The Sable Moon Sanctum was an ancient ceremony, where adherents would lock themselves away in prayer on the night of the sable moon, when the sky was darkest, and the power of the Five was weakest. It was popular in the ancient Mestibian mid polity of Zateniza, a monastery town that was home to an even greater collection of history and manuscripts and religious texts than the Lapiso Library, as well as what was rumoured to be the most vivid and beautiful starscape in all the land. People from across Dynosia made pilgrimages to it, and some liked the Sanctum ritual so much, they brought it back with them on their return. "But that's a good thing, isn't it?"

"I suppose. But it's a bit old-fashioned, don't you think?"

"Didn't I read somewhere that Prince Calix also adheres to the Sanctum?"

Jaspar snorted. "Yeah, but he's just trying to impress people. People respect what he did at Sama, but they can see he isn't right these days. Leaning on the faith angle probably helps. And justifies why he has become such a recluse. But that's not why Ms. Securia does it. She says she spends twenty-nine nights a month with Ardor, so she wants to spend just one night a month with Mesti."

Jaspar laughed, and Teigra gave him a concerned look. "You don't think there is something beautiful in that? Of not wanting to let distance separate you from your homeland and culture?"

The mid envoy gave her an understanding smile. "Maybe. But I didn't come halfway across Dynosia to keep one foot stuck in Mestibes. The only way to survive as an envoy is to make *this* your home." He held out a hand, his face exuberant. "Come on. Let me show you!"

No sooner had she taken it than he was running, barely stopping to lock the doors. They flew through a flurry of street names and little stories until the air filled with the smell of salt.

Teigra's mouth fell open.

The agora was enormous—double, no, *triple* the size of back home. Stalls stretched as far as she could see, hugging the bay, with great ships bobbing against a background of crystal waters and distant green headlands.

But right here, in front of her, the only thing Teigra could see was *people*. There were thousands of them, all pushing and yelling and haggling. And not just humans either, but the looming shapes of other creatures—giants of all kinds hauling produce, and even a few little kobaloi gnomes, dressed in their tiny tunics, laughing and pinching individual grapes from people's baskets.

Now that she thought about it, *everyone* was dressed in tunics. Or even less, with not a toga nor a stola to be seen. This half-undress revealed manly chests and feminine thighs beneath thin, rose-red and deep-green fabrics.

"Isn't it *amazing*?" said Jaspar, his eyes going starry as he pulled her deeper into the madness.

The stalls were piled high with the lushest produce she'd ever seen. There were apples the size of fists, crisp cabbages and cucumbers, their stems still dripping, probably only hours from the field. Men sliced honeycombs as long as her arm, oozing the treasure into earthenware jugs.

At several points, Jaspar was greeted by traders, kissing him warmly on each cheek and giving him olives or grains, small pithoi of wine, or wrapped goat's cheeses. Upon seeing her, they did the same, welcoming her to the polity.

Their names came forward in a cascade, with many familiar from the pile of letters she'd written. Jaspar was right, he certainly seemed to have won over a lot of the smaller traders.

It was impressive but exhausting to see him work, inquiring about families and ailments, speaking fluently about the weather and the many upcoming festivals of the summer.

"You're very good at this," said Teigra, as he hauled away two baskets of sample goods.

"Oh, we have to be! Ondocis takes all the big players now. We have to be smart if we want to secure product. And besides, having Ardora as a patron goddess just brings it out in me. It makes everything here so . . ."

"Boisterous?" offered Teigra, looking up to a young man on top of a carriage, playing pipes to no one in particular. As they passed, he blew her an extravagant kiss, calling down a string of lurid compliments.

"Exactly!" laughed Jaspar, plucking the imaginary kiss from midair, and blowing it back to the musician, who almost fell off the carriage with laughter. "Oh! Quick, quick. There is someone you *have to* meet."

They pushed through the sweaty mass for another few minutes, before stopping.

Without having to be told, Teigra could tell that the owner of this shop was someone important—it was the largest stall in the whole agora, and located right in the center of the main roads, such that every shopper would have to cross it at one time or another.

The shop was circular, with dozens of baskets stacked high with flowers. There was wolf's bane and lygos, daffodil and hellebore, iris and hyacinth, and pile after pile that she'd never seen before, lending the air a thick and shifting sweetness.

And sitting amongst all of this, under a roof made of lambskins, was a creature she'd only read about in stories.

It was *centimane*—a giant fabled to have a hundred arms. Although, disappointingly, they appeared to only have six in real life.

Each of these limbs was ducking to and fro, pulling together dazzling bouquets at impossible speeds. Teigra hadn't seen enough giants yet to hazard her age, but guessed her to be young, with hair the color of wheat and skin like sunset copper.

"Gyges!" said Jaspar, ducking between baskets.

"Well, well! 'Ere I was thinking I might never see you again, lad!" said the giant, the bouquets still being made all around her.

"It was only a few weeks! I can't have missed that much."

The giant took a long sip of lemon water and shot him a mischievous grin. "Oh? Can't you?"

"*No!*"

"Oh, yes!"

"Don't tell me!"

"I'm telling you!"

"He *proposed*?" said Jaspar, practically vibrating with excitement.

The giant thrust out one of its many hands, the nails long and filed to rounded tips. On the middle finger was a ring of thick iron, inset with a giant onyx.

"Ohhh, that is so exciting! When is the ceremony?"

"Midsummer. We don't want to wait. And of course, you're invited, dear Jassie." There was a pause and a few arms pushed aside the baskets by Teigra's face. "Particularly when it looks like you might finally 'ave a date to bring?"

Teigra blushed fiercely as the two of them chatted for another half an hour. As they departed, Gyges reached into a hidden basket and gave a flower to Jaspar, humming innocently as though she couldn't hear his protests.

It was beautiful. A bead of dew ran down the petals, so deeply, impossibly red that they somehow glowed gold in the sunlight.

"Wait," said Teigra, her eyes widening. "That's not . . ."

Jaspar chuckled. "An eternal rose of Ardor? No, this one will wilt in a few days, not a hundred years. But they look pretty close! Gyges grows them. Some secret technique to get the coloration and that shine. Although she doesn't sell them *too* openly. Even up here, some people get a bit funny about knocking off holy symbols."

With a few clumsy flicks of his wrist, juggling overfilled baskets in his elbows, the big minotaur shortened the stem and removed the remaining thorns. "May I?" he asked, pointing toward her hair. "This is how all the fashionable young ladies wear them. If they are lucky enough to have a man to give them one, of course!"

"But . . . won't people think I'm taken?"

His eyes darted away, shyly. "Would that really be so bad?"

The blush returned.

Teigra hesitated. Her hair was much more liable to have hay stuck in it than beautiful flowers. But there was something in his eyes— kind and comforting, that made her give a slight nod of approval.

Jaspar pulled her hair gently into a loose plait, with the flower tucked into the top.

"It suits you," he said with a smile, before embracing a nearby olive trader.

All the while, Teigra's face flushed hot, and she said little else for the remainder of their tour.

34

TEIGRA

Teigra stared at the two wooden coins.

Every person entering the Ardoralia festival had received them, although no one had explained their purpose. Both shared a portrait of the king on one side and a rose and oak motif on the other, with one made of light wood, pink poplar perhaps, and the other dark, likely walnut.

"All those scrolls and they didn't tell you about the timber staters of the Ardoralia?" said Aurelius in passing.

"Not yet, no!" she said, the pleasure at having remembered the local wood varieties overwhelmed by the pleasure of her cousin *finally* speaking to her.

He'd barely said a word to her all week, coming and going from his residence at all hours—heading straight out and returning straight in.

At first, she'd thought that *she* was the one avoiding *him*. But after she'd crossed his path a few times in the embassy courtyard by accident, with him only grunting a few words to her greetings, she'd realized that the avoidance was now mutual.

Aurelius glanced at the oncoming figures. "Don't worry. I am sure your new friends will explain."

Teigra sighed as Aurelius walked away. This distance between them was unfamiliar and unwelcome, though no more than she deserved. After all, his words confirmed exactly why he was angry: she had put her new master ahead of her own blood. And now, he felt betrayed.

Worse, she still hadn't found the courage to tell him about the folio, meaning he had no idea that it even still existed, let alone that Princess Zosime had stolen it.

I'll do it when things are back to normal, she reassured herself. *I will!*

"A bit different from the temples back home?" asked Jaspar, bringing her back to the moment. Ms. Securia walked ahead without so much as a look in her direction.

"Is it?" she asked, looking around.

They were on the southern outskirts of the city, in an open meadow that stretched to the farmlands beyond. Dotted throughout the sunflower-speckled grass were black-fruiting olives and pink-flowered pears—without any logic to their placement. Some of the trees were bunched together in haphazard groups, creating shaded nooks where families and young couples were feasting. Elsewhere, spaces without trees left sun-drenched dells erupting with competition—men and women pulling on ropes or throwing flattened stones.

All humans, she noted, with not a giant or kobaloi to be seen. Jaspar might well have been the only nonhuman in the entire field.

Among all this, insects clicked in the grass and a medley of birds sang in the high trees. It was as beautiful as it was overwhelming. But the one thing it certainly wasn't, was a *temple*.

Jaspar had a look of amusement. "What?" she said.

"You're looking for a building, aren't you?"

"Yes?"

"I did the same thing when I first got here. It all makes sense once you stop thinking like a Mestibian."

It took several more minutes of wandering through green before she finally understood. "There is no building? This *meadow* is their temple?"

Jaspar nodded. "The Fields of Life, temple to the goddess Ardor."

"But, if this is a temple, then isn't all this sacrilegious? Running and screaming and fighting?"

"In Mestibes it would be. But what better way to celebrate the goddess of fertility and passion and the sun?"

"Yes, but—"

"Come on," he said, leading her toward a ring of apple trees in the middle of the meadow, so thick that it hid the space beyond. "I'll show you something that will convince you."

They pushed into the tree line, darting through the sweet smell of apple blossom, until they came to something which took her breath away.

It was a field, far wider than she'd expected. In the center was the most enormous oak tree she'd ever seen—its roots spread wide, like fists clutching the soil, its foliage so broad overhead that it formed its own meadow against the sky. Around the thick roots, Ardoran citizens were placing baskets of fruits and amphorae of wine. A man with an unclothed torso laid a fat lamb carcass, so freshly killed that the blood ran down his sweaty back.

And surrounding this mighty tree was a swaying sea of rose buds, a hundred yards deep and growing like grass rather than from a bush. They were all fully enclosed in their green shields, with not a single petal on display.

"The Great Grove! With the sacred Oak of Fertility and the Eternal Roses of Passion!" she said, stories from codices coming to life. "*This* is where couples come to test their love!"

And the roses are the true chrysalis of the satyrs, she thought. *The thing they cannot touch, or they'll permanently morph into their imago form.*

Teigra didn't say that last thought out loud. Talking about

therians and mystical beasts? Jaspar would probably mock her, just like Aurelius had.

"And of course, the rose is the true chrysalis of the satyrs," said Jaspar.

She smiled. "You believe in that as well? The therians? All the mythical beasts and legends?"

"Of course! I'm a *minotaur*. We were attacked by harpies on the way here! And every Ondocian sailor I've met will avoid certain seas in a storm, lest a massive cetus drag their ship under. If the Five can make creatures like that, like *me*, why not therians to punish those families that annoy them?"

There was a sudden commotion on the far side of the field, and Jaspar buzzed with excitement, just as he had on hearing of Gyges's engagement. "Oh, look! Look! He's going for it!"

A young man of perhaps twenty-one, with short hair and strong muscles stood sentinel at the edge of the field. Behind him was a girl of around the same age, with hair the color of saffron and eyes of sparkling green. She clutched her hands together, nervous but excited.

Teigra's eyes bulged. "He's . . . going to pick a rose?"

Jaspar nodded, his smile huge and expectant. "You've heard the stories?"

"If their love is true," said Teigra, "then Ardor will guide him to his one true rose, which will bloom at his touch, never to wilt or fade until both of them pass on."

"And if he chooses wrong, then the rose will wither, and he will be cursed to live a loveless life."

Teigra bit her lip. It was such a huge risk—one she could never imagine taking herself. Or, for that matter, that anyone would take for her.

Jaspar reached for her hand, eyes still fixed on the boy. His grip was warm and firm and soft.

The young man strode into the field, the stems parting at his knees.

The entire meadow held its breath as the boy stopped, kneeling without a second thought, and plucked a green, thorn-covered stem.

He held it up to the dappled light.

And it *bloomed*—green parting to reveal the of deepest reds.

"Yes!" said Jaspar, jumping on the spot, as the boy ran back to his partner, lifting her in a spinning embrace.

A pointed clearing of the throat behind them broke the moment. "If you are quite done, Mr. Accola, we have a *very* long list of people to meet with today."

Jaspar turned stiffly. "Of course, Ms. Securia. But I was just going to take Ms. Cosmin to the Garden of Plenty. I think it will help her adjust to her new home."

A strangely cruel smile spread across Ms. Securia's face as she led them back beyond the tree-line of the apple grove. "Yes, that might be just the thing to help her *adjust*. But best she goes alone. We have work."

"The Garden of Plenty?" asked Teigra. There had been nothing in the scrolls about that.

Jaspar gave her a comforting smile and pointed to the far side of the meadow, in the opposite direction they'd come in. There was a mazelike space down there, walled in yellow and green. "It's where you use those wooden coins. Just try your best to keep an open mind, all right?"

And then they were gone.

For a moment, Teigra felt lost, suddenly aware that she was alone in a city she didn't yet know. She did her best to shake that feeling, heading to where Jaspar had directed, her hands still bearing a little of his lingering warmth.

The entrance to the Garden of Plenty was walled with tall trellises, covered in twists of cucumber vines, with their long, full fruit and wide yellow flowers, so thick that she couldn't see the space beyond.

She scrunched her nose.

Try to keep an open mind? What could be behind those walls that would shock her so? And why would it need the two coins?

She stood there for a good while at the entrance, fighting an urge to turn away from the unexpected. Ms. Securia's nasty smile played in her head. Whatever lay beyond, the high envoy knew she wouldn't want to see it.

And that made her certain that she had to.

With a deep breath, Teigra entered.

She gasped.

No!

35

AURELIUS

THE CROWD BRAYED AT THE CRASH OF BODIES. ONE WAS A LARGE woman with ratty hair and a green loincloth, the other was smaller, dressed in red and with a more focused resolve.

There were thousands of people sitting up the gentle hillside of the Valley of Fury, cheering the violence in the wrestling circle at the base. After just one week of his mission, he had already met several of the nobility that now sat in the front rows, and had even started to gather a few of their naughtier secrets—although he doubted that tales of infidelity would have *quite* the same impact here as they would back home.

There had already been three matches so far, each closely fought. After buying a glass of wine for a rugged young man with agreeable eyes, he'd learned that the wrestling competition was held every Ardoralia, between the farmers and the fighters. Apparently, it was an even matchup, for while the fighters had the advantage of tactics, the farmers were flat-out stronger.

Just looking through the crowd he could see the accuracy of that. Those wearing red sat with the keen expressions of carnivores, with bodies that, although big, didn't immediately present their heft. By contrast, those wearing green were great mountains of barrel-chested stock and full-hipped fecundity, barking out their wine-soaked cheers.

The farmers were currently leading two to one, with only one match to come after this. The whole crowd winced with every strike and every throw. If the soldiers won this bout, it would all come down to the final match.

And Aurelius didn't need to flirt to know what *that* match was. It was the entire reason he had come.

The best wrestler of the farmers versus the best wrestler of the fighters.

Kleio Kormos versus Calix Viralis.

He strolled through the throngs—absorbing the little snippets of information that said more than a single conversation ever could. The crowd was excited. The crowd was anxious.

He scanned the masses but couldn't see Calix anywhere. But likewise, he hadn't seen Zosime or her two goons either.

That was welcome. The prince's reputation for distance and avoiding the crowds was already proving accurate, and Aurelius's precious few opportunities to meet with Calix were not being helped by his meddling sister. The princess had already proved infuriating, blocking his entry two days earlier to a private garden party he suspected the prince might attend.

Aurelius was sure that Zosime's interference was still just petty one-upmanship for outwitting her at the palace, and that she hadn't yet figured out his plans with Calix.

Despite the best efforts of Teigra to ruin it!

How could she have been so stupid? He had trusted her with the folio, given her something that the archon had explicitly said to keep away from those aligned with the senate. And how had she repaid him? By disobeying him. By bringing it here and almost ruining the whole damn mission!

And now she is avoiding me! Without even having the decency to tell me what she did?

That boiled his blood the most. He'd seen how she acted after the harpy attack—looking desperately through their bag. She'd known that the folio was missing all the way back then.

And she didn't yet know that Aurelius had gotten it back, either! As far as Teigra knew, Zosime still had it. The princess could be doing all sorts of wicked things with that information—and Teigra hadn't even told him.

Day after day goes by, and not one solitary word of warning!

He dwelled on that, sipping at a mug of unfermented grape juice —meant for children, but the best he could do while keeping his abstinence.

Perhaps he should maintain his own silent treatment toward her a little longer? Let her deal with that Securia bitch alone? That might teach her to appreciate him. To make sure she didn't do anything else to disrupt his plans over the coming months.

The coming months . . .

This wrestling match at the Ardoralia festival was just the first major event of the Ardoran summer season. Among numerous smaller gatherings were the other four major punctuation points— fighter battles in the Gipedo Thanatou, the "Stadium of Death"; a "Wax Crack" festival of wine; a grand "Rose Rain Ball" in the tholos at the palace; and all finished off with the most well-known of all Ardoran events, the Black Night Festival, where people paraded the streets dressed as therians.

He smiled as the female combatants beat the shit out of each other. It certainly wouldn't take *that long* to achieve his mission—no matter what Zosime or Teigra might try to do.

In the ring, the farmer ran full pelt at the smaller fighter. At the last second, the fighter ducked to the side, spinning around, and catching her ankle. Before the farmer could regather, the fighter leaped on top, pinning her shoulders to the dirty sand as the crowd barked the count.

Two matches apiece. It was all down to the final fight.

The chatter swelled around him.

Finally!

Here we go!

Mummy, Mummy, lift me up! I wanna see!

Can you believe it! This'd surely have been the championship match at the last Paliad, had Kleio not been injured. And we get to see it here!

Two-to-one odds on Viralis, come on, people, last chance!

Just as quickly, the crowd fell silent as the competitors emerged.

Kleio entered as a monster, barking and gesturing to the crowd, eliciting as many cheers as jeers. Calix entered with a more polite smattering of applause, staring ahead with a somber expression, making no effort to play to the crowd.

It wasn't just their demeanors that differed. Kleio was somehow even bigger than Calix. Not just taller—itself a feat—but with thicker muscles. His chest was less defined but impossibly broad, and his hairy shoulders looked strong enough to pull a pine from the ground. His stocky physique spoke of a man who ate and drank as hard as he worked.

By contrast, Calix's physique was tighter and leaner, with ripples of hard flesh pulsing over his rib cage and abdominals—showing off a sweat-glistening eight-pack and separated muscles along his thighs.

The two men circled each like stalking predators.

The bigger man stepped forward first. With hands as big as a lyre, he slapped his knee, sending a great *thwack* around the hillside.

The chatter rose sharply. People were suddenly amending bets.

"What happened?" asked Aurelius, to no one in particular.

"Kleio just made a challenge of pure strength," came a female voice from just behind. "No throws. No pins. Just brute force. The first one to take a knee loses."

"But won't that favor the farmer?"

"Of course. But there is a certain purity to the challenge that makes it hard to turn down in a crowd this size. And to defeat a farmer in a battle of pure strength? Why, the victory would be all the sweeter. The bragging rights even greater than winning at the Paliad."

Aurelius turned to face the speaker.

He almost pissed himself.

It was Zosime.

A dagger tip pressed into his back before he could move. "No, no, Your Excellency, I think we have the perfect view."

Aurelius did his best to remain cool. "Are you going to slaughter me in full sight of the crowd, Princess?"

The dagger cut through his fabric and pressed to his skin. "Should we find out?"

He held his breath. He was sure she wouldn't do it. A princess killing a herald with diplomatic immunity in broad daylight?

Impossible.

But as the cold metal scratched at his skin, just one slip from ending it all, he knew he didn't want to test that belief.

"Do you show all of your guests this level of attention?" he asked, flagging at the realization she had bested him.

"Only those who try to exploit my family."

"Oh, darling, you must be confused. I am only here to enjoy the charming customs of my new homelan—"

He gasped at the pinprick of pain, followed by the trickle of blood down his back. His whole face went pale. Stars appeared in his vision.

It was only a prick, but for one hideous moment, he thought it was all over.

"And yet, you seem to appear wherever my *brother* is," she hissed, right by his ear.

Aurelius gulped, cursing himself for underestimating her. She may not have understood the subtlety of the folio, but she was still a captain of Sisters. A stalker of beasts and a butcherer of bandits.

And he had been too cocky this week. Far too cocky! Asking questions about the prince to all his new noble friends. Assuming she was too dim to figure out what he was up to.

But she has! Or at least, she suspects!

"Your brother?" he said through dry lips, trying to sound as innocent as possible. "Why would I care about *him*?"

"Perhaps you don't. And if that's the case, why don't we make a deal? Once my brother has stomped that thick lout into the ground, you'll turn around and leave. You won't attempt to see or speak to Calix again. Any business you have with my family, you'll come to *me*. And if you disobey me, *Herald*, you'll find out just how much of your blood I'm willing to spill. Nod if you understand."

The blade tip twisted sharp against his flesh. Aurelius nodded vigorously.

"Good, now let's enjoy the match, shall we?"

Back in the ring, Kleio gave a bestial roar and offered his hands—one up over his head, the other by his ribs. After a long pause, Calix returned the knee slap and took the grip.

The crowd roared.

Challenge accepted.

The muscles on both men tensed with sheer effort—their thighs grouping, the veins on their arms slithering. There was no visible movement, but Aurelius could *feel* the exertion. Soon, the arms of both men started to shake, their heels digging into the sand for grip. Neither was giving an inch. Their eyes were locked with the same intensity. Their faces were screaming silent curses at each other.

As the battle raged on, minute after agonizing minute, the crowd amplified, yelling their encouragement, cheering the sheer determination of both men.

After long minutes, Kleio let out a guttural roar, looked up to the sky, as if invoking the goddess of the sun herself, and pushed forward with every ounce of his remaining strength.

Despite all his resistance, despite all his strength, the prince could no longer hold the brute back.

Calix fell to a knee.

The crowd rose as one, half screaming in joy, half wailing in despair. Kleio stomped around, feeding off both reactions. And in the middle of the circle, silent and alone, Prince Calix remained on one knee, staring darkly at the ground.

Suddenly the blade tip was pulled, and the princess ran through the crowd, all the way down to the ring, picking Calix up and leading him away.

Despite the trickle of blood down his back, despite her threat still warm in his ear, Aurelius was struck by a strange little thought. It was stupid. And yet, at this moment, when Calix looked so utterly defeated, being dragged through the crowd of fighters he had just failed, Aurelius couldn't think of anything more perfect.

Because unlike Teigra, he *did* know the meaning of the coins.

Aurelius took the dark wooden stater from his coin purse, aimed it as carefully as his limited skills for physical dexterity allowed, and flung it over the crowd's heads. He'd intended for it to land in the prince's path, but it pinged instead off the armor of a different fighter, a splinter of the wood flying off in some direction, before bouncing right onto Calix's sweaty chest.

The dark wood stuck to his sheen.

The prince stopped and drew it from his flesh. His face moved from despondency to confusion. His golden gaze scanned the crowd.

Finally, he turned in Aurelius's direction, somehow spotting him amongst the masses. Like he knew exactly where to look.

Aurelius gave Calix a little wave.

And in that single moment, just briefly, the anguish on the prince's face seemed to lessen.

36

TEIGRA

Teigra turned quickly, but the image was already burned into her eyes. The reason for the cucumbers and open flowers along the walls was now painfully obvious.

All around the Garden of Plenty, two dozen men and women were standing on stone plinths in dramatic poses.

And every single one of them was *completely naked*.

They were all the epitome of womanly beauty and masculine strength. The women had full breasts and perfectly sized nipples, their waists curving in before flowing into round hips and high bottoms. The men were bulls—their muscles bulging and tightly set, made even more fearsome by the poses they struck. And around their fronts, without any shame, were their fully exposed sex, on display for the hundreds of visitors.

The women were plucked of body hair, showing their . . . *passages of virtue* in full detail. And the men all had their . . . their . . . *things* out, large and thick, hanging like sleeping serpents, ready to leap up and strike.

The blush ran prickly from the top of her head.

It was awful! She felt embarrassed for the people on the plinths.

For the fully dressed spectators gawping and pointing and having *debates* about them, as they might do in front of a statue.

But most of all, she felt embarrassed for herself.

She was no stranger to *fertility*. She knew when a mare was in heat and had seen the incredible virility of the stallions—such that it put every man in the Garden to shame. She had paired steeds to mate. She had delivered countless foals. And she'd been completely overwhelmed with joy at the creation of new life.

But she had never seen such unabashed displays of nudity in people before.

And they knew, didn't they? Aurelius? Jaspar? Ms. Securia? They all knew I would react this way. Aurelius would be skipping in here like an excited child. Jaspar would be interested in the cultural customs. Even Ms. Securia would probably come in here with a scholarly outlook.

But not me.

Because I'm too weak to handle this.

And they were right. She couldn't handle this. She had to get out of here. Out of the Garden. Back to sanity!

"It can be a shock to the constitution, can't it, my dear?"

Teigra turned to face the richest-looking woman she'd ever seen. She wore a sea-green tunic, with a golden stola overtop. No, not a *stola*, which was the heavy, female counterpart to the toga favored in Mestibes. This was the lighter, form-fitting *himation* more common north of Apaderma.

But whatever it was called, the garment was impossibly detailed, and swept perfectly around her slender curves. Easy curls of blond were held back with a golden laurel band, encrusted with pearls. And around her emerald eyes was a smoky application of kohl-black, giving her a mysterious air.

Despite having the bearing of a matriarch, she couldn't have been older than thirty.

The woman held out a soft, ring-covered hand. "You must be the new girl Ramuna mentioned. Teigra, I believe?"

"Who . . . who are you?"

"Sophia Fabulosa, my dear. High envoy for the most prosperous and glorious polity of Ondocis."

"*Ondocis?*"

The woman gave a charming laugh, taking her by the arm before she could protest and leading her into the fray. "Of course! Mestibes isn't the only one with foreign dignitaries. Why there is scarcely a polity in all Dynosia where one of our officials aren't present. And with rather more resources that *your* envoys are provided with, I might say."

Naked flesh towered all around. Teigra did her best to avoid looking, but once or twice she saw someone's front, causing her whole body to clench.

"Did Ms. Securia send you to check on me?" asked Teigra.

"Ramuna? Oh, you are new, aren't you! Your high envoy wouldn't wish me anywhere near you! She and I have a little rivalry when it comes to matters of trade. Mestibes can charm and flatter all you wish, but in my experience, nothing speaks quite as loudly as gold. And my polity rather trumps yours in that regard."

"Then, why—"

"Did I come to your aid? Dear Teigra. I saw you standing in the entrance like a frightened little rabbit! Shaking in front of all the citizens you will soon have to bargain with. Consider me a sentimental fool, but if I am to be sparring with you in the battlefield of commerce, I would rather the odds were fair."

Despite her lingering disquiet, Teigra felt better for the woman's company. She seemed totally at ease with herself, radiating an impenetrable confidence.

"Ms. Securia said that coming here would help me adjust to life in Ardora."

"And how right she was! I know how difficult such things can be."

"You felt the same way? When you first saw this?"

"Oh dear, no. I meant I know how difficult it must be for *you*, coming from your more enlightened climbs. My polity does not share such sensitivities. In Ondocis, no noble of worth would be seen around court without both a powerful spouse and a beautiful lover. Of *either* gender."

There came the sound of wood clinking against clay. All around, people were placing their stater coins in little amphorae at each model's feet—light ones for the women, dark ones for the men.

"They're . . . *voting*?" said Teigra.

"Of course."

"But that's so . . ."

"*Crass*?"

"Yes!"

"First rule of surviving in Ardora, my dear. Throw off such notions of propriety. Does every animal not yearn to mate? Just as one of your poets might thank Mesti for their vocabulary, or one of my sea captains might thank Ondo for their navigational prowess, in Ardora, they thank the goddess for their big tits and thick cocks, for their strong muscles and childbearing hips! And they don't just give thanks, but *display* them—for why should they be ashamed of their divine gifts?"

Teigra ducked her head at the woman's volume, talking about *private areas* in full voice.

"Oh, you poor thing. Well, why don't we start easy? Best we stick with our own ilk before broaching the *male* form."

Fabulosa brought her to a stop in front of a woman that could only be described as radiant. Her skin was golden, with firm breasts and a particularly curvaceous backside.

"What about this fine specimen? Such full breasts and yet such a slender waist. A truly rare combination, don't you agree?"

Are you a delicate little flower, Teigra? Or are you a rose with fucking thorns?

Teigra breathed deeply, forcing herself to take the woman in, fighting the urge to look away. To her surprise, the beauty gave a smile at the compliment. Her mouth was alluring—her lips full and soft.

Her embarrassment faded a little. The woman didn't seem so

vulnerable now. If anything, she seemed *strong*. Confident. And utterly unashamed of her beauty.

"Yes," whispered Teigra. "Yes, I suppose that she . . . that *you* are."

The woman's smile broadened.

Teigra's stomach fluttered, as if a statue had come alive and noticed her.

"And don't you think she has the most magnificent cunt?"

Teigra spluttered. "What!?"

"Her *cunt*, Teigra," repeated Fabulosa, matter-of-factly. "We do not need euphemisms here. No *passage of pleasure*. No *hollow of hope*. It is her cunt. And I am asking if you think it is magnificent?"

"I . . . I . . ." stuttered Teigra, both looking and avoiding looking.

Fabulosa chuckled and turned to the model. "My dear, would you show us a little more of your *passion*?"

Without hesitation, the woman licked her finger and trailed it down her barley-colored stomach.

Teigra's heart thundered. Her whole body stiffened.

No . . .

Shamelessly, the beauty slid her finger between her sex, parting herself, revealing her most intimate place. The tip of her finger traced circles around her point of pleasure, drawing little whimpers from her lips.

Teigra's whole mouth went dry. She felt distant from her own body.

When the woman at last removed her fingers, she was glistening, her delicate folds swollen and pink. A trail of nectar followed on her fingertips, which she brought to her mouth, slowly swirling around her tongue.

Teigra's skin prickled as a heaviness came deep in her abdomen, uncomfortable and pressuring. The way the woman shook as she took her fingers away. Those little pants.

Teigra could *feel* the yearning.

"Beautiful," said Fabulosa. "I have a Satrap in Barika who would *love* to meet you, if you would be interested in such an arrangement?"

"What?" said Teigra, snapping back to the present. "You aren't seriously proposing to . . . *buy* her."

"There you go again, thinking like a Mestibian! Look around you, Teigra. Are these people desperate? Do they lack food or health? No, the only thing they lack is *excitement*. I do not propose to *enslave* her. I offer her a contract. Her body will be worshipped like the goddess she is. In exchange, she will receive sumptuous fabrics and the finest food, gifts, jewels, travel, and the attention of powerful people. I would think most here would prefer that to a lifetime holding a mud-covered hoe or a blood-covered spear."

Teigra looked around, hoping to find rebuttal. Instead, nearby models struck new and even more evocative poses, clearly hoping to catch the high envoy's attention.

Fabulosa raised a victorious eyebrow to the beauty. "My embassy is right on the bay, in the suburb of Chrysa Touvla. Come by if you would like to discuss the matter further."

The woman nodded enthusiastically and struck a new pose, her smile even brighter.

Fabulosa released Teigra's arm. There was no anger in her expression, but it was clear their time together had finished. "If you will excuse me, Teigra, I have many more beauties that I must meet."

Just as she was turning to leave, she gave Teigra a sly look. "You hold to the Pentariat, don't you? A good Mestibian girl such as yourself must pray to all the Five, not just your own patron?"

Teigra crossed her arms. "Of course."

"Then perhaps you might consider how best to show devotion to the assets Ardor has gifted you with."

37

~

ACROSS DYNOSIA, THERE WAS NO SHORTAGE OF SUPERSTITIONS AROUND the moon.

Never make an important decision on the night of the half-moon, believed the comparatively few humans that lived in Vaticily, as the choice will surely be fraught with indecision, potentially even opening oneself up to the incursion of a meddling gorgon—creatures that loved nothing more than leading men of uncertain will down dark and unfortunate paths.

Never trust an opportunity that arises on the sable moon, believed the rich and powerful of the Ondocian Islands, as the offer will surely appeal to your darkest inclinations, potentially even opening oneself up to the temptations of a wicked siren—creatures that loved nothing more than luring women of weak will toward gambles they could not afford to wager.

And in some of the more rural parts of Ardora, infertile men and women would wait until the night of the bronze moon before placing a mug of finest wine by an open window—hoping that it might lead a satyr to their premises, the brightness overhead restraining the worst of the creature's desires, and gifting them a little of their potent fecundity.

Others still held to myriad rules and rites around when to plant and when to harvest; when to make contracts and when to break them; when to marry and divorce and consummate and baptize. All marked out on charts and argued over in pubs, all while staring up at the sky each and every night to watch the swell and sleep of the moon.

The figure in the darkened room, however, needed no such chart.

Because they could *feel* it.

All day and all night.

During the temporary relief of bronze, and the soul-shredding rip of sable.

In their wake and in their sleep.

In the thirst that never, *ever* went away.

In the urge they could only barely suppress. In the urge that was difficult to control at the best of times. In the urge that had become almost impossible to contain these last few weeks. In the urge they needed to release!

All because of the *herald*.

And the power that lurked within him.

38

AURELIUS

Princess Zosime was fucking evil.

For two weeks the bitch had haunted his every move, seemingly hiding around every shrub at the Festival of the Summer Seed, and waiting behind every beer mug at the Feast of Barley and Boar. At each, no sooner had he started some charming conversation with a noble, garnering gossip and keeping a discreet outlook for his target, then *she* would appear.

Just standing there.

Just watching him.

Just making sure he remembered her threat.

And now there is this, he thought as he was jostled on all sides by a crowd of fucking *fighters*.

The one invitation she sends to me directly, and it is to this fucking event.

They'd passed the Gipedo Thanatou of Kastro Machiton—the stadium of death, right in the heart of the soldier's quarter—when they'd first entered the polity. However, the visage of low, undecorated stone had hidden the sheer press that lay beyond. Steep stands were packed with thousands of humid fighters, overlooking an oval of pink sand, twelve feet dropped from the crowd.

Pink, apparently, with the spillages of centuries of accumulated battle.

Everyone but him wore a uniform of dark hide with accents of metal, all underlaid by wine-red linen. And each man and woman—and it was only humans, with perhaps a few dozen half-blood giants in the mix—was rattling some implement of death. There were swords and daggers, spears and bidents and axes thrust in cheering hands, and spike-covered gloves slapped against shields.

And all the sweat-stinking mass were focused on one thing: Princess Zosime and her two goons.

And the chimera they were fighting in the ring.

The battle was ferocious—absent the tactics and soldierly discipline he'd expected. Instead, the three women's strikes were brutal and opportunistic. The little one distracted the spitting lion head to the front, while the big one wielded her double-headed axe behind. The hideous creature dodged a spear throw from the princess and rolled to a snarling stop, its drakon tail whipping in warning. Brimstone popped by its fangs, promising the full fury of flame. Despite the three-to-one advantage, the contest was surprisingly even, with neither side yet landing a blow.

Aurelius pushed through the steamy crowd, just as he had for the last twenty minutes. His destination was a balcony overlooking the stage. And the mass distraction was as much of an advantage as he could possibly hope for.

Because for all of the last two weeks, he had only managed to see Calix twice.

Once was at the Ardoralia.

And once, was *here*.

And he hadn't come here to watch some battle between a beast and a "Sisterhood," as they called their little female troops—although the thought of Zosime being gravely injured held a delicious appeal.

No, he'd come for one purpose alone.

It wasn't ideal. It was the fucking opposite of getting him *alone*. But he had to risk it.

Besides, what can she do from the middle of the arena?

When Aurelius finally reached his destination, he composed himself, mounting the platform and thanking the fact that royals in Ardora weren't under constant guard. He leaned against the railing, his arm brushing against the most lavishly dressed man in the whole stadium.

"I wouldn't have thought a chimera would be found in these lands, Your Highness?" he said in a high voice. "They exclusively roam the frozen valleys of Rinath, do they not?"

The prince's expression didn't shift, as if he wasn't surprised at Aurelius's arrival. His face peered out from a plumed helmet, the same design he had seen on Zosime back in the grove.

Calix stared long at him, as the crowd roared all around, before finally turning back to the fight. Despite his reaction, the prince did not move his arm away from the skin-to-skin contact.

"A great many things were lost in Sama, Your Excellency. But a great many things were gained as well. This beast was one of them. A pet of one of their *legates*."

One of the thousands of soldiers that you slaughtered, he thought with a slight shudder, remembering exactly who he was talking to. Out loud, he said, "You have kept it caged for over five years?"

"It has served as a useful sparring tool for initiates."

"Your sister is hardly an initiate."

"No," he said, his eyes affixed to the battle.

"Then—"

"Then today the beast dies."

Below, the creature swiped at Zosime, who backflipped out of its claws by inches.

"In my homeland, they would think that cruel," said Aurelius. "Keeping a beast, no matter its ferocity, in a cage for years and years, only letting it out to fight and eventually die."

Calix stared at the snapping creature. Despite the bright sun, his face remained dark beneath the helmet. "Some beasts deserved to be caged."

"And to die?"

"If they will not be tamed."

The creature pounced right towards the small one, causing a heave from the masses, only for the big one to tackle it out of the air at the last moment, rolling through and raining down strikes on its goat-haired body, like it was some bar fight, not a battle to the death.

"But surely caging it will only make its anger worse?" said Aurelius, taking in the prince's shadow-streaked face. "How can a beast be tamed if it is not shown some alternative?"

Calix was silent for a good while. "Some might consider it less cruel to cage a creature than to let it taste the freedom it will never be allowed."

Even at rest, Aurelius could sense the balled-up restraint of Calix's stance, the knotting of his words, and the strain in his knuckles against the wood.

That vicious tear between his desire and duty? It was familiar to Aurelius. In a boy he once loved.

It was . . . *heartbreaking.*

There was an almighty roar of celebration, accompanied by the clatter of a thousand implements of death.

Aurelius didn't need to look down. He already knew.

The beast was dead.

Calix pushed himself back from the edge and their forearms parted. "Farewell, Your Excellency," he said without facing him.

A sudden urge came over Aurelius to reach out and stop the prince. But he was already gone into the press of his people.

In the ring, among the gutted carcass, the victors soaked up the applause. And Zosime grinned *right at him*. It was a sick, mocking grin. The grin of someone who believed the beast had no option but to die.

His blood turned to fire.

To Dimethan with that!

Aurelius pushed through the crowd, going after Calix. Suddenly, his momentum stopped. A hand gripped his arm. Its owner's voice fluttered by his ear, warm and female.

"Perhaps not, Your Excellency."

He turned to see a halfway familiar face, one that had been at the periphery of every social event in the last few weeks, but which he hadn't formally met. She had the bearing of true nobility, and everything about her—from her confident posture, sumptuous fabrics, and glinting jewelry—screamed two words.

The first was Ondocian.

The second was *snake.*

"High Envoy Fabulosa, I believe? Charming to finally meet you, but perhaps another ti—"

Her grip tightened, surprisingly strong given her slender frame. When she next spoke, it was not in Dynosian, but in Voresoma, the ancient language of nobility and diplomacy. A language which practically no one else in the stadium would understand. "The Ardorans may not wrap their royals in a swaddling blanket, and I will confess that Calix may not be quite as popular as he was a few years ago, but do you really want to see what happens if they think their prince is under threat?"

Aurelius paused, allowing his anger cool. As rationality once again took hold, he stole another look at the princess. Her expression had changed. The grin had faded, replaced with annoyance.

That bitch!

She'd planned this. That was why she had sent him this invitation. She'd chosen a time and place where she would be indisposed, where she knew that Aurelius could sneak a moment with Calix without her intervention. Knowing that Aurelius would take it. Knowing that there was a whole crowd of loyal killers if his frustrations got the better of him.

"Perhaps we should talk? Beyond this wretched stadium?" said Fabulosa.

"Indeed," he said, suddenly wishing to be anywhere else but here.

They left the soldier's quarter quickly but cautiously, careful not to seem as though they were fleeing. When they were back in common streets, Fabulosa plucked a white rose from a passing archway, smelling it with a sigh. "An interesting man, isn't he," she said, returning to the common Dynosian tongue.

"Who?"

"Come now, Herald. Take it from one gossip merchant to another, you have hardly been masking your intentions at our little social gatherings."

"Should I consider it flattery that you have been watching me, High Envoy?"

"Oh, I didn't have to look too hard. What a pity you can't find some way to meet him alone."

They walked in silence through pretty streets, flowers blooming over eaves and along roofs of pubs and blacksmiths.

Aurelius weighed his options.

On the one hand, she was a snake. He couldn't explain how he knew. You didn't meet them very often, but when you did, you just *knew*. She was an untrustworthy, lying, conniving snake, and she would cross him as soon as it was convenient. Cornel Securia was like that. The archon was as well. The sort of person you never wished to be indebted to.

And yet . . . she was fundamentally an *Ondocian*. And a high envoy, no less. That meant she knew the value of a transaction. Of a contract. Of a *trade*.

"You know how to get the prince alone?" he said at last.

"One hears things."

"And what is the cost for you to say what you hear?"

She smiled. "My, my. So rare to find a Mestibian who knows how business works. But to let go of such information, I would need, oh, the full details of Mestibes's top three contracts this month."

"Impossible," he said with a hearty laugh, playing it off as though he was refusing, rather than the truth—that he didn't know that information.

"Ah, I can see you are no fool, Herald. Well then, perhaps you can tell me a little more of your *cousin* instead?"

"Teigra?" he said, cocking his head. "Why should you care about her?"

"Why should you care about meeting the prince?"

And a clever snake at that.

He considered protesting. But Teigra had hardly been loyal to him. Perhaps it was time to even the stakes.

And so he told her. It was nothing dramatic. Nothing that might be used *too badly* against poor little Tiggy. Just her interests and the like. Some general comments on her personality—such as it was. Things that Fabulosa could have find out herself, with a bit of effort.

Fabulosa stopped at a fork in the road. "You are new in town, Herald. You probably don't yet know where they serve the best drinks?"

"I do not," he said, with a knowing smile.

"If I were you, I would go out on a Tuesday evening and find the pub that serves the biggest drinkers in all of Ardora."

39

TEIGRA

THE SHOCK AT THE GARDEN OF PLENTY FADED IN THE WEEKS THAT followed, until Teigra was almost begging for something interesting to happen again. The work of a low envoy was basic and repetitive—writing out contracts and drafting responses to invitations, reading through page after page of family histories, and making little notes for meetings she wasn't allowed to attend.

Often, the gruff Mr. Placi was her sole company. Ms. Securia and Jaspar were barely in the embassy most days, heading out for lunches and dinners, for casual mugs of tangy posca at little farmhouses, or attending all number of ceremonies—weddings and promotions and good-natured contests over the quality of produce. Often, there seemed no purpose to the meetings at all, beyond simply *being there*, in the fray, making contacts and making friends.

And as the days passed, Teigra devoted herself to all these new friends in Ardora. After all, she couldn't devote herself to her one true friend.

She'd barely seen Aurelius for a month now. He always left the compound before the sun rose and didn't return until well after dark.

Once, when she'd been working especially late, she'd heard him limping through the midnight courtyard, grunting with each step. Unable to bear it any longer, she'd rushed outside to help him, clutching at his head, blood staining his tunic.

But he'd just brushed her aside.

She'd cried herself to sleep that night. But there was nothing more she could do. Ms. Securia was watching her. Those eyes saw everything. They bored into her like they could see her very soul.

And the future of House Cosmin lay in the high envoy's hands.

Days later, she'd been lying awake, homesick in her room, wondering what Mother and Jaronas and even the nosy Tulla would be doing, when she'd overheard her two masters returning from a dinner party.

She knew she should have covered her ears, but the words made her listen even more intently.

"The girl is useless, Mr. Accola. Utterly useless. If only we had Ms. Mattic back."

"Dorina returned to get married, Ms. Securia."

"Typical. All these girls, putting marriage before their polity! Well, at least we won't have to worry about that with *this* one."

"Ms. Cosmin is doing the best she can. She is in a brand-new city. You remember what that is like, don't you?"

"You are far too soft on her. Look at how uselessly she's handled the herald."

"*You* told her to avoid him."

"I did nothing of the sort! I merely said that she was not to help on whatever mission the archon has set for the boy. But I never said she couldn't *pretend* to remain in his good graces. That is what a true servant of the senate would have done—remaining close to the herald out of pretense, ensuring they knew what was happening, ensuring the archon's lapdog wasn't out there destroying the relationships we've spent decades cultivating. But she is clearly too stupid for such subtlety."

"And if she had done that, you wouldn't have punished her for disobeying your explicit orders?"

"I never said that," said Ms. Securia with a cruel chuckle. "She has the archon's blood in her veins. I doubt we will ever be able to trust her loyalty."

"Please, Ms. Securia, why don't we just give her a proper chance. She puts in the hours. She wants to help. I think if we let her get out there, into the fray, she could be a great asset."

"And if we do, you think she won't be passing on our secrets to the archon's little pet?"

"We have her for five years, Ramuna. We can't keep her trapped away that entire time."

"Well, on your head be it, Jaspar. On your head and your *reputation*."

Teigra lay still as the words cut, afraid that any movement would be heard.

It was kind of Jaspar to defend her so. He was always kind to her. And in the days that followed, she became increasingly thankful for his company.

The boy knew so much about Ardora, and always managed to keep his head up, despite Ms. Securia's micromanagement, or her insistence that *her* name appear on all contracts, even if he'd negotiated them. Ms. Securia was obviously jealous of his relationships around town, of his reputation, of his kindness, and never wished to give him even one sliver of credit.

After that overheard, late-night conversation, he started bringing her out on his trips to the surrounding farmlands, touring pear groves and vineyards. Despite the nerves of meeting so many new people, she was grateful for him nudging her to get involved in the conversations, throwing to her with a playful grin, making sure she couldn't just stand back and watch.

Once or twice, she'd even been able to use those little snippets of family history she'd read about to discuss the passion projects of a particular farmer, or to ask about the status of children and grandparents.

Afterward, Jaspar had praised her, talking about how well she was doing, and how much improvement she was making. Just as he praised her on the rare overnight visit they'd made to the small but well-heeled low polities of Caravagis and Zant, in the plains beyond the big city. They were home to two of the most famous and prestigious horse breeds: Caravagi stallions were beyond fearless, and few varieties could match a Zante for pure speed.

Over those two days, she hadn't needed to fake a single word, so excited was she to see and smell and touch that little bit of home.

Standing out in the field, surrounded by the familiar sounds and familiar smells, she could almost've been under the stands at the Alogo, next to a blood bay mare she never got the chance to farewell.

She must have talked more in those two days than she had in the weeks beforehand, running thumbs along withers to test spine stability. Pinching gaskins to assess the flexibility of the leg muscles. Laughing with rough old men in the common language of horse-rearing, to the point that Jaspar remained silent, head cocked and with a faint smile, completely out of his element.

And without even intending the outcome, ink had been laid on parchment, striking deals far bigger, and at far lower costs, than Jaspar had ever dreamed of. In just two days, they'd secured enough steeds to cover the needs of the entire Mestibian peace corps for a year!

On that night, back at their inn, Jaspar had hugged her outside their two rooms in giddy pride, holding her small in his arms, telling her how amazing she was.

He'd smelled of sweat and the citrus oil that smoothed his soft fur.

It had been . . . nice.

It had been . . . comforting.

She'd known he was just humoring her with all his kind words, as one might praise a child for their oratory skills after their very first symposium. But still, there were times—like when he looked at her with those big, friendly eyes or reached out innocently to brush a stray strand of hair from her face—when she almost believed him.

And on that night, with the steed deal freshly signed, as she'd lain back in the bed of the inn, she'd finally found herself heeding Fabulosa's advice.

She'd finally given praise to the gifts that Ardora had given her.

As their doors had closed, and she'd dwelled on the minotaur's smell, she'd found herself replicating, for the first time in her entire life, the sordid strokes of the maiden atop the plinth.

The amateur actions toward her own body had given her a sensation so intense, so wonderful, that she'd had to bite down on her pillow to stop her groans from escaping through the parchment-thin walls.

In the morning, she'd awoken feeling shamed and sinful, barely able to meet Jaspar's eyes. At that moment, she'd swore that she would never do the wicked action again.

And yet, in each evening that followed, she found herself a traitor to her own touch.

It was shameful and dirty and, above all, *strange*. For every time she began by thinking of Jaspar. Of his kind eyes and his warm touch. Of his big body—so soft but so strong. Of him laying a flower in her hair, but rather than pulling away, of him pressing forward against her back. Of him taking her around the waist and running a furry finger delicately against her breasts. Of him running that finger down her body, with him being the one giving her these sensations.

Of him kissing her.

Of him *wanting* her.

And of her wanting him in return.

And yet, each time, as the feelings built stronger, her mind wandered. For each time, the surging, shaking sensation finishing with the same strange flash—of the woman atop the plinth, licking the slick of pleasure from her fingers.

And with Teigra wondering, just for a moment, what that must have tasted like.

40

AURELIUS

"Oh, what a CHARMING story," hissed Aurelius, his knuckles straining against the clay mug of grape juice outside the Storming Stallion.

The ancient cow had been prattling on about the *old days* for an entire fucking hour—about predecessors of the king and long-gone relatives that no one could possibly care about. It was like she had an allergy to speaking about the *present* occupants of the palace. Of speaking about the prince—what his weaknesses were, where he went to be alone, whether there were any regular guests he had. Of giving him something, *anything* that might help him with this wretched game!

It had been over a month of this torture.

The wrestling school? The Ardoralia? They had been just the first sips of failure in the great deluge he would guzzle.

At every official engagement, it was the same story. For the most part, the prince wouldn't even be there. And on the rare occasions he was, the two of them would lock eyes, or steal a few moments to talk.

And there were sparks.

And there were butterflies.

And there was that most delicious conflict in his eyes!

But then he would break away, or Zosime and her goons would find Aurelius, dragging him away and showing him the rough justice he now expected from this stinking backwater.

He sipped the juice through pursed lips, cursing Securia. She had been right—the *help* here didn't talk. Aurelius had spent the last four weeks sleazing and flirting and trying to bribe every palace guard and domestic servant he could find, in every drink house and brothel across town. And *nothing* seemed to loosen their damn lips.

And that Fabulosa snake? With her stupid little riddles? He cursed her just as hard.

He had done the full rounds now, going to every one of the rough pubs in town on a Tuesday night—where one could logically find the heaviest drinkers. Places with fighters and farmers, where there was as much vomit on the ground as hay.

And the prince was nowhere to be seen.

I just have to find a way to get the prince alone! Away from his fighters. Away from his damn sister. And this . . . ? thought Aurelius, leaning against the crumbling wall of the rank wine den, *this time I am onto something. This old bag has worked at the palace since before King Selkus took the throne. She knows something useful. She has to! And before this night is out, I will get it from her.*

"You know," he said in a silken voice, "when I attended the Ardoralia, I just couldn't bring myself to give my light coin to any of the maidens there. For none was beautiful enough to warrant it."

"Oh yes?" the old cleaner croaked, swaying a little.

Aurelius clutched her free hand, placing the light wooden stater against her rough palm. "But I don't need to hold it anymore, Talia, for I have finally found the one woman in all of this polity who is worthy of my worship!"

She looked at it breathlessly, the ghost of long-faded romance haunting her face.

"But no!" he said, turning away dramatically. "I am a fool. For someone as lovely as you must surely have the eye of another. I am sure that even *Crown Prince Calix* can't keep his hands away from you."

"What? *Calix*?" she snorted. "Hardly. You didn't hear it from me, but I've heard that he's—"

Without warning, her face went as white as a midday cloud. She stumbled, dropping her cup and running away into the night.

Aurelius stared, dumbfounded, turning to see what had caused her reaction.

Princess Zosime was standing behind him.

"Oh, for fuck's sake!" he said, throwing his own cup down with a shatter of wet clay. The nearby patrons barely even glanced up. "Don't you have some fucking *princess* duties? Or are you going to spend your entire life following me?"

She folded her arms with an unexpected smirk. "I appear to have upset you, Your Excellency. And just when the conversation was getting interesting."

Aurelius caught his anger. There was something different in her stance. She moved with less immediate intimidation. Her goons were nowhere to be seen. And in her voice, there was something unfamiliar.

Playfulness?

"What do you want?" he asked, cautiously.

She shrugged. "I really must ask: what is it about my brother you find so intriguing? Oh, I accept he is attractive. Our family has always been graced with fine features. But a herald coming all this way just to bed a prince? That seems rather unlikely."

Aurelius sneered. "And who says I want to bed him?"

"Well, I doubt you are interested in his *personality*."

A little fizz hit him. That was an insult! A little sign that all was not perfect between the siblings. Just as she had seemed furious at him bringing up Calix's name in the throne room?

The knotted briar of the last few months opened in front of him, like sunlight through a storm. Was there a possibility, no matter how slim, that all of Zosime's shows of loyalty were just that: *shows*?

He gathered himself, oozing friendly energy. "You know, Your Highness, I must agree. Oh, Calix would go very well in Mestibes—all stoic and cerebral. But I have long wondered how such a man could serve as ruler here, in the land of passion?"

"Have you?"

"Well, up here people would be expecting a *different* kind of heir. One with passion and ferocity. Dedication and commitment. Not all detached and despondent. Not one they talk about having *ashen passion* behind his back."

She shrugged slightly. "And of course, some say that there are even deeper scandals than you know of. Ones that go to the very heart of his birthright."

The fizz grew. "Are there *really*?"

She gave a casual shrug. "So they say. Rumors can be so misleading, can't they?"

"Well, given all that, some might consider that Calix's ascension could pose great risks to your whole lineage. Amongst the *public*, of course. I am sure you harbor no such doubts."

"As your mother does of you, I'm sure. The archon of Mestibes does not send her herald for just any reason, after all. And if your mission was to simply improve relations, you would be focused on my parents. So, one must deduce that having my brother bed you somehow serves a grander strategy?"

Aurelius detected his own relaxation and tensed. Was this whole thing a ruse? A roundabout way of determining his intentions?

If so, she was good—only hinting at conflict between her and her brother, while allowing him to do the talking.

He pulled back. He needed to know that the conflict was real before he would tell her anything more. He needed to know that she was prepared to *betray* him.

"So, the rumors are true about Calix? He is—"

"Inclined the same way as you? Yes, Herald. Well, *partly* like you, though it is not widely known. Although, even if I were not standing in the way, achieving your goal would be near impossible. From what a little sister hears, he has been chaste since his return from battle."

"I have bested more challenging foes than him, Princess."

Her eyes twinkled. "Doubtless. But why climb a mountain when a smooth road leads to the same destination?"

A . . . pact? Really?

She was right though. Calix was just a means to an end. The goal was the military alliance. The goal was to become the successor to the archon once more!

And although she was not the strategos that Calix was, she seemed just as influential in military circles as he was. Perhaps even more so.

"And let me guess," he said. "You would be *thrilled* to help me. But you need to know what I want first?"

"How can I help you find something if I don't know what you seek?"

"And if I refuse?"

She gave another infuriating shrug. "Then you can see just how good you really are."

His lips twinged. Was this the same woman who had made his life miserable for the last month? And if he answered truthfully, would he be playing right into her hands?

After all, he was sure he could eventually win Calix's favor, even with her in the way. Of *course,* he could. This was what he did.

And yet, the thought of achieving his six-year goal hung sweetly in the air. And after all, she had just betrayed Calix's darkest secret, hadn't she? She had admitted his sexuality! That was something that could get him *killed*!

Aurelius turned to the gathering clouds, a cool change whistling through the alley. "Your storms come from the north, don't they, Your Highness?"

"They do."

"Well, in Mestibes, it seems some are preparing for a storm from the *south*."

She was quicker than he expected. "Ardor protect us. *Rinath*?"

"Indeed."

"And what you seek from my family is something your senate would not approve of?"

"*Indeed.*"

Zosime nodded, looking around cautiously for the first time. "Then meet me at the barracks in two evening's time. I will make inquiries. I am sure we will find ways to assist each other."

41

~

PRINCESS ZOSIME STROLLED THROUGH THE SUDDENLY COOL AIR.

It would rain before the night was out. And it wouldn't be the light misting so often received by the other polities—just enough to keep the olives in flower and the grapes on the vine. This would be a proper, Ardoran soaking.

It still amazed her the way the nights could go from poetically perfect to a howling gale, then back to the fire-coal warmth of sunrise, all in a few hours.

Fast changes. Just like the fortunes of those that live here.

An hour ago, she had been in the dark on the herald's intention, but now she understood perfectly. The archon had sent her brat to bypass the will of the senate, seeking a preemptive military alliance with Ardora.

It was a bolder move than she'd thought the woman capable of. Bold, yes, but also hideously heretical. Had the ruler of Mestibes so little faith in the goddess she was oath-bound to serve?

Zosime eyed a dark corner on a quiet street, distant from the drunken roars in all other directions.

It would have to do. She could wait no longer. Her skin already felt like scorpions were crawling beneath it.

She brushed her long hair beneath the cloak and took her place in the deepest part of the shadow, where even the half-moon could not reach. It was overly cautious. There was no one around. But it was better not to take the risk.

For the briefest of moments, the shadows were illumined in twinkles of purples and indigos, glinting with far-flung diamonds. The lights vanished as quickly as they had come, along with all that wretched metal and leather of the princess's uniform.

Now, a new figure lowered the hood.

They turned their face to capture as much of that pale moon glow as possible, willing it into their pores like the torrent which would soon bear down.

Their eyes and jaw were clenched, forcing back the urge to return to that prior appearance: to delve the full depths of that incredible potential for violence, for fury, for slaughter. Of all that magnificent prowess with a sword and bow and spear. Of all that untapped ability to command that even the princess didn't seem to know she possessed!

It was only a week until the sable moon, and the figure's throat was stripped raw—not for water, for that would not satiate.

They thirsted instead for all those talents, all those skills!

They thirsted to own them forever!

They thirsted for them to be in the hands of someone deserving!

After what felt like an eternity, the moon beat that longing back to its usual background hum. And the sensation related by a tremendous guilt.

After so long resisting the urge, they had finally succumbed to temptation . . .

They pushed those thoughts aside. It had been necessary. They needed to know the truth. And this had been the only way.

In the distance, a shard of lightning crashed beyond the headlands.

And to think, they thought, strolling on, *the boy doesn't yet know what lurks within him.*

42

TEIGRA

THE DRUMS POUNDED OFF THE JAGGED ROOF OF THE RANIOS GROTTO, joining the background rhythm of lapping waves and enormous clapping.

If Ardoran weddings were more raucous than those back home, then the weddings of Ardoran *giants* were about as far from Mestibian civility as you could get.

Giants of all shades were dressed in finest formalwear, which involved whole skins of livestock flowing over their shoulders, with the face and horns of the animals worn as something halfway between a mask and a helmet.

At first, the choice of skins seemed random, but it became clear once Jaspar had explained all the little patterns. Regular giants—or "byclopes" as she now knew them to be called—favored rams for men and sheep for women, with whites and browns and speckles separating family units as clearly as shield patterns might for humans.

By contrast, the larger and more intimidating cyclopes favored ox skins, with hide color less important than the length and shape of the horns.

And the two centimanes present—the bride, Gyges, and an older male at her side—wore skins of red deer stags, apparently a nod to the flighty independence of their subspecies.

In the lead-up to the event, she'd learned the deep twists and turns of giant society, which seemed a whole different world to the human nobility of the city. Apparently, the byclopes and cyclopes had a racial rivalry that extended back eons, long before humans had habited the land. While both subspecies lived and worked in similar fields, often quite literally, it was rare to find them both attending something as sacred as a wedding.

The reason they were all here now, as Jaspar had explained it, was purely because of the *centimanes*. The third giant subspecies were astoundingly rare and had long acted as a sort of intermediary and peacekeeper between the hostilities of the other two—a balancing force and quasi-leadership role that had allowed them to accrue power and influence, even if broader giant society was still treated several rungs lower than humans by the rest of Ardora.

So centimanes are sort of like the Mestibes of giant culture? she'd asked Jaspar, who'd laughed and nodded.

Back in the grotto, Jaspar spent the entire morning at Teigra's side in a rise and tumble of emotion. He whooped when the couple jumped into the sky-blue pool in the mouth of the cave, entering at opposite ends, but emerging together. He cried as Gyges's deer pelt was replaced with an umber-mottled sheep skin that matched the smitten giant holding two of her many hands. He spoke in full voice the prayers of the ceremony—not to the Five or any of the other Galaxians, but to the *Goliaths*, the ancient gods that the Galaxians vanquished millennia ago. And he swayed with the music during the festivities that followed, singing along in a strange tongue that made him sound like a slightly confused wolf.

Back home, such behavior would have been the height of incivility for a patrician boy—even for a minotaur. Praying to the Goliaths in particular, even if only doing so politely as part of another species' ceremony, would have been *unthinkable*.

And yet, as he wandered to the cauldrons of drink, shaking a dozen hands and giving a dozen hugs, she didn't feel that judgment. Even if he was a bit loud and a bit scattered, he genuinely cared about people. He took the time to learn about their hopes and interests and fears. And the strangest part was, he seemed to do it without trying. He didn't have to gird himself to talk to strangers or push through after a long day to attend yet another function.

He *liked* doing it.

"Drinks up!" he said on his return, thrusting an enormous cup of honeycomb mead at her. A waxen cube was stuck to the rim, scented as fresh and sprightly as the lemon blossoms they'd passed on the way out here, to the northeastern headland of the bay.

She held the drink awkwardly. "Ahhh . . ."

"Oh, sorry! I keep forgetting that you don't drink."

"Yeah. Sorry."

"No need to be sorry. It just means more for me!"

All around the grotto, giants were dancing and slapping each other on the back. Ms. Securia was engaged in conversation with a few cyclopes, wearing horns so large they had to be chiefs of some kind.

"Look at that," she said, pointing to a familiar figure roaring with laughter. "Even Mr. Placi is enjoying himself."

"Oh, he knows everyone in town. He used to be the mid envoy for nonhuman relations when I first started."

"*Mid envoy*? But . . . he's just the housekeeper?"

"He is now. But he was the longest-serving envoy here apart from Ms. Securia. So the royals made a special exemption for him—they didn't re-accept his credentials, but they didn't force him to leave either. He could stay, if he didn't do any official outreach."

"Well, that is something, isn't it?"

Jaspar gave an uncharacteristic scoff. "Maybe. Personally, I think it was their little joke. They knew we'd keep him on as a housekeeper. There were too few of us left with too much work on our plates to do any cleaning. And we couldn't risk locals rattling through our desks and overhearing things they shouldn't. Besides, what better way to insult Mestibes than making the former second-in-command dust and do dishes all day."

"That's so cruel! They can't do that."

"They can and they did," he said with a downcast expression. "And between you and me, I don't think it's an accident that our most senior *nonhuman* got that treatment."

Before they could wallow, the music kicked into a faster beat, accompanied by a *clap-clap-stomp* from the attendees.

Jaspar's eyed the dance floor, his expression lifting. "Come on! This is my favorite giant song!"

"Ohhh, no. Believe me, you don't want to see me dance."

"Come on, Teigra. How many giant weddings are you going to attend in your life?"

"But . . . I don't even know the steps. What if I insult everyone?"

"Giants don't care about that. They just care that you're having a go!"

Her pulse quickened. The thought of all those people—Ms. Securia and Mr. Placi and especially Jaspar—seeing her sad excuse for dancing was too much.

Jaspar gave a soft smile. "You're right. It is a bit silly."

"Oh, no, you can still go!"

"And leave you here on your own? That wouldn't be very gentlemanly of me!"

His face bore some disappointment, but no obvious resentment. If she wanted to stay at the side, he wouldn't force her or make her feel guilty about that. And nor would he leave her on her own.

And yet, the cold dampness of the cave suddenly felt colder. She thought back to how he'd praised her in the outskirt towns. How she was improving. How she was settling in.

With a sigh, and pushing down the intense embarrassment, she took his hand and joined the towering figures.

It was awful.

She was awful.

All through the dance, she looked around desperately, trying to pick up the steps.

And yet, when she turned to apologize to Jaspar, he was making the same mistakes she was—stomping on the wrong beat, moving left instead of right, twirling at the point they were supposed to stay still. So arhythmic was he, that his golden nose loop was flopping around like a lazy dog.

But, he said it's his favorite giant song? I know he's clumsy, but surely he knows the proper step—

The realization came with a flutter in her stomach.

He was doing them wrong on purpose. Just so she wouldn't feel bad.

Oh . . . Jaspar . . .

As he smiled at her—without judgment or critique—an unfamiliar warmth grew in her chest.

He really was rather sweet.

The party continued until well after midday before disbanding, with little groups wandering off at their own pace. The two of them took an hour to walk the semiwooded paths around the bay, the journey made quicker by Jaspar's vibrant chatter, aided by the huge mug of mead he'd taken from the wedding.

When they finally arrived back at the embassy, late in the afternoon, he was just about able to stand on his own.

"You're a good get, Teigra. You know that?" he said with a slur, as they reached the front door. "All the other girls from back home're so stuck up and stiff. Dorina pretty much refused to walk anywhere. Reckoned the sun and exercise brought on bad humors. Can you believe that? Coming to a place like this and not wanting to walk anywhere! But that's not you. You like getting out there. In the sun. Among the people. Among nature."

"Thank you, Jaspar," she said, her familiar blush taking hold. "I just hope I'm helping."

"You're certainly helping me," he said, laying a soft kiss on the back of her hand.

For a heart-fluttering moment, she wondered whether the big, kind minotaur might blush and stammer and ask whether she wanted to come up to his room. He had been nothing but a gentleman in the whole time they'd known each other, taking not one advantage of their close and often isolated proximity.

But now would be the perfect time, wouldn't it? With the inhibitions dulled by the drink, and the dancing still fresh in their feet, and the entire embassy all to themselves.

With a heaviness in her soul, Teigra waited. And as she did so, she wondered the whole time what she would say if he asked.

He was a good man, there was no doubt about that. And Mesti knew that he was handsome—in a boyish, messy-furred sort of way, which only seemed to make him an even more calming and attractive presence.

And she had thought about it dozens of times these last weeks.

And she was sure she could do much, *much* worse for her first time.

And she was sure he would be gentle.

And she was sure that behind that goofy smile was a creature who must have experienced a great deal of this world, and would relish the chance to show it to her, to teach her, to open her mind and body into the world of true adulthood.

And yet...

But the question didn't come. Instead, his smile broadened, and he gave an extravagant bow. "And now, fair maiden, I must depart. For the drinks were many! And the work is much."

He entered the building with a slight stumble, knocking a big shoulder into the door frame. She stifled a laugh, and a warmth beyond the summer breeze or long afternoon walk swelled beneath her stola. The air was sweet with pomegranate blossom.

She was about to stroll into town, going nowhere in particular, when her blood turned suddenly cold.

From across the courtyard rose the familiar sound of syrinx pipes, the notes haunting and unpredictable.

Aurelius was staring at her from his balcony.

And in his hand was something that she had all but forgotten about. Something that she had assumed still to be in the possession of a princess too foolish to understand its contents. Something she had meant to apologize for weeks ago.

Aurelius was holding Aunty Urosina's folio.

43

AURELIUS

AURELIUS GRIPPED THE HATEFUL DOCUMENTS AS THE PIPES SASHAYED across his lips.

He remained impassive at her horrified recognition. Not that keeping his face still took much effort. Even glancing down from his balcony made the mass of black swelling around his eye throb.

His cheek was scuffed with gravel burns, and over his eyebrow was the angry, half-healed contusion from a well-aimed sword pommel.

Now he would have a scar to match the princess's. He wondered if that had been intentional.

Aurelius had been a fool to trust Zosime, and even more so for underestimating her. The show she put on last night at the barracks was a thing of beauty. It was like she had no idea why he was there. Like the attack she inflicted on him was for his unannounced and unexpected trespass onto soldierly territory.

The princess was good. Far better than he had given her credit for.

But she'd had help, hadn't she?

She'd already received half the puzzle—the little details in the folio that had put her on alert in the first place, even if she hadn't understood them all.

Aurelius should have been furious with this whole situation. He had been betrayed by his cousin. The time was streaking by without result. Half the summer was almost gone. The Wax Crack, midpoint of the summer, was less than a week away! And everywhere he went, Zosime followed.

And yet, despite the ache in his face, despite the grinding frustration of his failures, Aurelius gave a tiny smirk.

Zosime might be good. But *he* was better. And in this game, he still had cards to play.

Because Calix wasn't the only one with *family*.

Teigra emerged from up the stairs and through his bedroom, panting. She turned a shocked look first to the folio, and then to his face. "Aurie? What . . . what happened?"

He turned the parchment pages slowly—letting each flick across his thumb. "You knew, didn't you, Teigra?"

"I . . . I . . ."

He turned, allowing the afternoon light to emphasize every wound across his battered visage. "Not only did you not destroy it. Not only did you bring it with you. Not only did you lose it. But you *knew* that Zosime had it. That is why you pushed me to go to the wrestling school on our first day here. You knew the danger I was in, the danger *you* caused, and you didn't even tell me."

She denied him his intended guilt trip by bursting into inconsolable tears, babbling out a list of excuses: of being ashamed of her mistake, of not wanting to see Aunt Urosina's work go up in flames, of the pressure that Securia had placed on her to tell Aurelius's secrets or ruin the name of House Cosmin.

As she collapsed before him, her tears staining his blue tunic a dark navy, he did feel a little sorry for her.

And yet, it didn't matter. The point remained the same.

She had put him in danger.
She had made his mission that much harder.
And now, she would repay that debt.

44

TEIGRA

TEIGRA TAPPED ON THE GOLDEN DOOR, HALF HOPING IT WOULDN'T BE answered.

She'd done everything else she could think of to find the information Aurelius had demanded: asking guarded questions to her contacts in the agora, hoping she wasn't being too obvious; walking around the Green Heart Park in the center of town as the nobles lounged and laughed, willing that she would somehow just *overhear* the crucial information.

That hadn't worked, of course. And now, with the Wax Crack just five days away, there was only one person who might know the answer she needed.

The door was opened by a posh-looking servant—impeccably dressed, with a face full of suspicion.

"Hello," she whispered. "I was . . . I was just wondering whether . . ."

"My dear! What an unexpected pleasure," said Fabulosa, rounding the corner inside the Ondocian embassy, wearing the most exquisite himation that Teigra had ever seen. The cut was sleeveless and shorter at the legs, made from a figure-hugging teal that was practically sheer, such that she could see the silhouette of the curves beneath. "To what do I owe the pleasure?"

"I . . . I wanted your advice on something," said Teigra, feeling the urge to look away.

Fabulosa cocked a knowing eyebrow and led her through the halls, past incredible vases and silks, until they arrived in a lavish drawing room.

The high envoy reclined into a sumptuous lounge—gold-leafed wood and sapphire velvet. She snapped her fingers and a young man entered, carrying two glasses of dark liquid. "I was thinking about you just the other day, my dear."

"You were?" she said, taking a seat on an adjacent lounge. She put the glass to her side.

"Yes. About your name. It means *tiger* in Voresoma."

It wasn't a question, and Teigra had no doubt that Fabulosa, like most senior Ondocians, could speak the language fluently. She nodded cautiously as the servant departed.

"A reflection of what your parents saw in you, I wonder? Or an aspiration? For I have not yet seen this little tiger roar."

The comment burned, but Fabulosa was right. She had no right to so powerful a name. All she had done in Ardora was simper and betray people. She hadn't even had the strength to tell Aurelius of the danger she'd put him in. After everything he'd done for her!

Teigra stayed that sinking feeling, remembering what Fabulosa had said in the Garden of Plenty. The woman wanted a sparring partner. And as unfamiliar as it was, this was no place or time for timidity.

"Well . . . what about you?" she forced herself to say, her mouth going dry. "*Fabulosa?* You can't have had a difficult childhood?"

"Why, of course I didn't! I was born the only child of one of Ondocis's most eccentric spice traders, making our family's fortune in flavors you would never have even heard of, let alone tasted. Tragically, they both died in a horrible storm when I was but a teenager, leaving the entire inheritance to me."

There was something odd in the way that she recounted the story —cold and factual, more an epitaph than a memory.

"Why do I feel that you aren't being truthful?"

Fabulosa's smiled. "Oh, Teigra, I paid far too much for my backstory to be telling you the truth."

"You . . . *bought* your family history?"

"Don't look so surprised! Did I not tell you that in Ondocis there is nothing that cannot be bought? In the streets of the Gilded Market, one may purchase anything one wishes—from an exotic animal beyond our seas to a gorgeous beast to share your bed. To purchase a new name, a new title, and new life? Why, it is but a trifle for those with the coin."

"And who am I addressing now? The real Fabulosa? Or the fiction?"

She smiled and supped the dark liquor. "You are addressing the one to whom you came with begging bowl in hand, little tiger. Which warrants the question, what do you wish that bowl be filled with?"

Teigra licked her dry lips. For a moment, she considered dancing around the subject, like she'd seen Aurelius do on so many occasions. Of picking up the glass and making polite small talk. Of having the conversation, without ever really *having* the conversation.

But she knew she'd just fail at that. She wasn't as clever or as charming as Aurelius.

And besides, she didn't need rumors and hints.

She needed *facts*.

"I . . . I want to know where Prince Calix may be found alone. Somewhere even his family doesn't know about."

The woman tutted. "Teigra, your high envoy has been here much longer than I. She would know the answer to that question."

"I don't . . . I don't wish to burden her with this."

The woman leaned back, revealing her smooth leg. "Keeping secrets from your master? And coming to the enemy for help? My, my. One can only wonder why this information is so important to you?"

Teigra did her best not to stare at the exposed skin. "My . . . my reasons are my own. Is it something that you can help with or not?"

Fabulosa swirled her glass. "I can. Although you surely know I will not give this information freely."

Teigra gave a tiny nod. She'd been afraid of this and had avoided thinking about what the woman might ask for.

"We are both reasonable women. So, I will make you a reasonable deal. You will return to your embassy and make a copy of Ramuna's social calendar for the next, shall we say, two months?"

Teigra's stomach twisted. Doing that would betray not just Ms. Securia, but the whole polity as well—putting all those hard-fought negotiations at risk. Ripping the food from the table of the people back home.

She made to stand. "This was a mistake."

Fabulosa swept to her side. "Good girl. I would have lost a great deal of respect if you had taken *that* deal. I can see you are a woman of integrity. You will not betray those who you serve so easily." She brushed a fingertip around Teigra's shoulders, causing a shudder. This close, Teigra could smell the woman's perfume, red rose and something that smelled the way gold glimmered. "Instead, I will request something which is yours to freely give."

"And . . . what is that?"

Fabulosa's eyes glowed in the candlelight. "A kiss."

"What?" she said. "Why . . . why do you want a kiss?"

The woman placed a fingernail on the nape of Teigra's neck. She ran it down the outside of her fabric, past her chest, down onto her stomach.

Teigra's breath stuttered.

"My reasons are my own. Is it something that you can help with or not, little tiger?"

Her whole body felt strangely hot. She had never kissed a woman before. She had never kissed *anyone* before. And she was sure that she didn't want to kiss *Fabulosa*! Quite sure! She wasn't like Aurelius, or as it seemed, like Fabulosa. She was good and goddess-fearing!

But she needed this information. She had to repay Aurelius for her betrayal. And she doubted that the woman would make a third offer.

"Just...one kiss?" she whispered, looking at her full, ruby lips.

"Just the one," said Fabulosa, pressing closer to her.

A hand came around Teigra's side, cradling the small of her back and arching her body toward Fabulosa. Teigra's fingertips grazed the soft, warm skin of Fabulosa's exposed thigh. It was unintentional, but the way she yielded under her touch made Teigra shudder.

Fabulosa leaned in.

Teigra's heart beat faster as she parted her lips, knowing it was wrong, but wanting the moment to happen. Just to be done with, she assured herself.

The woman's lips came soft as lambskin, giving way to her hot tongue. Teigra's body shook as a strange sensation came over her— the feeling of wanting to be *closer* to the woman. Closer than it was possible to be.

She wanted to touch the skin of her leg again, and trail her fingertips further into the folds of her fabric. To explore. To experience!

And then, it finished. The warmth of Fabulosa's mouth withdrew quicker than she'd expected, leaving a strange hollow in its wake.

"You are quite the surprise, Teigra," Fabulosa whispered, black-rimmed eyes staring into her own. "You are surely aware that your cousin asked me for this same information. I gave the poor boy a little riddle. If you are here, that means I overestimated him. I wonder if I will make the same mistake with you?"

"What information?" she said, her heart still racing. The woman's taste lingered on her tongue.

"I told him that the prince may be found every Tuesday night, at the place that serves the biggest drinkers in all of Ardora."

Teigra scrunched up her nose. Pubs? Some kind of rough pub with bad drunks? But surely Aurelius would have figured that out—

Her eyes bulged.

"Oh good," said Fabulosa, draining her glass.

Teigra left the Ondocian embassy quickly. Her mind raced as she ran through dark streets.

It can't be that simple, can it?

It's past ten. Will he still be up?

When she arrived at the embassy, she ran right past Aurelius's building, through the front door, and turned right, into the wing that housed the kitchen and dining room.

"What are you running for, girl!" said Mr. Placi, with his usual gruffness. He was in the larder, baking bread for their morning meal. "You'll wake the whole house with that racket!"

"Mr. Placi," she said, fighting for breath. "What pub do the *giants* drink at?"

45

AURELIUS

THE BEAUTIFUL BUNCH WAS MAYHEM.

The largest giant pub in Ardora was barely even a building—more a two-story pen of narrow corridors and shabby rooms to let, all surrounding a vast, open-air courtyard, packed tight with the largest drunks in town.

From the balconies above, dozens of oversized females in various states of undress posed and winked. On a platform in the corner, underneath one of those balconies, a band of kithara and aulos players filled the warm night with a pulsing beat.

In another corner was a ring, from which great thumps echoed. Giants were boxing. The bartender said they favored that over wrestling.

Over the last five weeks, Aurelius had spent scant little time with the other races of Ardora. The Ardoran nobility was exclusively human, and you never saw giants in polite company—save those garden parties where they might be off in the distance, tending to the orchids.

It appeared he had been missing out.

The Bunch was practically writhing with potential for mischief, a tinderbox awaiting a spark. Without knowing the full complexity of giant culture, even he could see the little factions and divisions among the tables. One piece of gossip, shared in the right ear, and the whole place would ignite—fists thrown and tables broken and hair yanked.

He mournfully sipped an enormous mug of unfermented grape juice.

The most infuriating part of his increasingly nontemporary abstinence was that it had damn well worked. At both the Ardoralia and the Gipedo Thanatou stadium, and in the little snippets since, he had been spared that animal loss of control when met with the prince.

He still didn't cede to the ridiculous idea of Mesti punishing him with *wandering vigor*, but the fact remained that the treatment was working.

And so, it had to be maintained. Particularly now that he'd finally caught his break.

And besides, even if *he* didn't believe in the five divine illnesses, those at the nearby table certainly did. For why else would five humans, all cloaked in hoods, come to a pub for giants?

It was all so obvious now. Once Teigra had got the name of the pub, the rest had cascaded out—the secret whispers at the edges of society, hinted at in shadows but never directly addressed.

Two days a week, The Bunch reserved a long table for humans: Thursdays for the farmers, Tuesdays for the fighters. There were no questions asked. No names taken. And you *absolutely* didn't say why you'd come. For every person there already knew. They came to drink. To fight. To fuck. To do anything and everything to coax a lick of heat from their gray souls.

For if the cure for wandering vigor was abstinence, then the cure for *ashen passion* was excess.

The crown prince sat with four other people, three men and one woman, at a table at the outer edge of the crowd, quite near the band.

Aurelius didn't need to see Calix's face to know which was him. He was the only one that might just have passed for a regular patron.

Aurelius breathed deeply.

Right here, right now, was the most consequential moment of the whole mission. Just as it was the most *dangerous* moment of the whole mission.

At the Ardoralia and the Gipedo Thanatou and the scant moments at parties, his interest in the prince could be explained away. Those were public events where people were supposed to mingle. It was perfectly reasonable that two children of rulers might find some time to talk, and that a herald of a hated polity might seek the company of a man influential enough to change that.

Even if Calix knew that Aurelius was trying to seduce him—and by now, Aurelius was certain that he did—it was still being done in the *open*, in such a way that observers would think nothing of it.

But *here*?

No, this was something else entirely.

Talking to the prince *here* would be an admission to Calix that seducing him was Aurelius's *main purpose* in Ardora. It would also show the extreme lengths that Aurelius would go to get the prince alone. It would show his willingness to pry into the darkest and most secretive corners of Calix's life.

To a soldier with a secret, that would move Aurelius from "annoyingly persistent" to "clear and present threat."

And if Zosime found out?

Aurelius shuddered to think.

But all that danger was necessary. Time was slipping by. Xiber could cross for Vaticily any day now. If he wanted to secure a military alliance, he had to make his move *now*. Because if he wanted the biggest of prize, he had to take the biggest of risk.

He scanned the room. He had options.

One was to innocently stumble into the prince when he went for more libations, parsing a cute comment about how *we simply have to stop running into each other like this.* It would be easy, if obvious. As subtle as a two-handed tit grope.

But he could do better than that.

The sound of the crowd faded as he focused in on the fighters. The biggest man at the table lifted his head, revealing his hooded face to the orange-flickering brazier in the center of the courtyard.

It was indeed Calix.

And he was . . . *smiling.*

It was a warm, hearty smile. And though it was laced with shyness, it seemed to make the gold of his eyes glint a little brighter.

Aurelius's palms went sweaty against the mug. He had seen the prince display many emotions—withheld frustration at being seen last at Urosina's funeral, the wrenching screams of self-fury in the bathhouse, and his default state of tightly wound stoicism.

But never happiness.

For the first time, and completely against his will, Aurelius saw the prince not just as the target of a mission, but as a man.

And the man was *beautiful* . . .

A sudden void broke the moment as the musicians ended their set. In the brief second before the din of several hundred voices merged into one indecipherable cacophony, he overheard a few snippets from a nearby table—some tasty little revelation about someone falling in love with their brother's wife.

Aurelius grinned. *I wonder what story the prince is smiling at?*

He weaved his way toward the soldier's table carefully. A beam near the stage provided cover, the closest point along the dark walkway before entering the courtyard proper.

Calix had his back to him, just a few yards away. Aurelius leaned out, straining his hearing. Though he could draw the outlines of words, he couldn't hear the actual conversation.

Just . . . a little . . . more!

Out of nowhere, a drunk cyclops bumbled by, knocking him hard in passing.

Aurelius tumbled into the courtyard, crashing across an empty chair.

He regathered and looked up—right into the eyes of Calix, now just a foot away.

At first, the prince was surprised. Then he settled into a weary glare. And finally, the edges of his lips curled into a wicked grin.

Calix rose and shoved him in the chest. It was forceful, but with just the right precision to avoid pain.

Aurelius stumbled back, coming to a stop in the middle of the now-empty stage.

"Well, well! Looks like we've got a new musician!" said the prince, in a slurred voice of uncharacteristic machismo. "And a Mestibian as well!"

"Oh, go on, give us a song then, *Mestibes*," said the woman at the table, equally drunk and making a kissy-face. "It's dead boring like this."

"Yeah," said another. "Isn't that all you do down there? Playing them *fancy* songs and sitting around crying about how pretty the stars are?"

The table laughed, and Calix gave him a weighty look.

Aurelius should have been rattled by the turn of events, as dozens of eyes started turning his way from across the courtyard. Instead, his pulse quickened in excitement. For the first time in weeks, he had the prince's attention.

And there was no way he was going to waste it.

"Very well," he said with a loud and gregarious laugh, as more and more of the crowd focused on him. He took one of the kitharas left behind by the musicians, tuning it expertly. "A great poet in my homeland once wrote a song for each of the five therians of the Pentariat. Seeing as I am a guest in your land, it would be my pleasure to sing the one he wrote for your fair polity."

There was a cheer from a few giants in the crowd, obviously used to working with humans of a little more education than the others. He brought the stringed instrument to shoulder height, smacking the back of the wooden frame with his knuckles to give a beat, and strummed.

Oh, merry on a Sunday morn,
  I was in ma' field adorned,
  Whistlin' songs of fun and play,
  Chasing all them crows away.

Then across the fields so green,
  What was that? A satyr seen!
  Skin like goats wit' hair like blooms,
  Weaving vines like flax on looms!

Get away, I tried to do,
  But she caught me round the shoe,
  Stumbled down, I couldn't run!
  'stead she said, "Let's have some fuuun!"

The notes came fast—far faster than they were supposed to. Back home, "The Satyr of the Seed" was played as a mockery of northern ribaldry. But Aurelius had long ago discovered that if you doubled the pace and sang the lyrics earnestly, it made a cracking drinking song.

Digging deep into her soil,
  Plunging tools with pounds and toil,
  Packed down hard'n twisted roots,
  Drippin' wet into me boots.

. . .

Digging deep into her dirt,
　　Goin' so fast it must'a hurt,
　　Her and me got what we need,
　　Coverin' earth with all our seed!

The crowd clapped along, picking up the chorus in full voice. Aurelius drank in the moment, the *attention*, strutting up and down the stage.

In too short a time, the final note echoed out. There came a moment of silence, then a roar of applause. He turned back to the table of soldiers in celebration.

His throat tensed.

The others were all on their feet, clapping.

But Prince Calix was gone.

46

TEIGRA

Teigra paced the embassy courtyard. Despite being well after midnight, the grass still carried the day's warmth. But that provided little comfort from the wrenching in her belly.

Everyone else had gone to bed hours ago. She'd tried herself, but just couldn't sleep—not while Aurelius was still out there. If what he'd said was right, then this was the most dangerous moment of the whole mission.

Teigra grasped her pegasus-hair pendant. Aurelius being out so late meant one of two things: either the evening was going very well, or it had taken a horrible turn. And as much as she knew that being out of bed like this might invite difficult questions, she had to make sure that he was all right.

Besides, she had listened by the bedroom doors before coming out. Everyone else was well and truly—

"Good evening, Ms. Cosmin," came a voice from the doorway.

Teigra shot around. "*Ms. Securia*, I thought that you were ..."

"Asleep? Safely tucked away so you could break the ultimatum I so gracious extended to you?"

"N-no," stammered Teigra. Suddenly it all came back. The

threats. Her family. The promise she'd made to not help Aurelius! "I just ... I just ..."

Ms. Securia came to her side. "Please, Ms. Cosmin. I have lived in this city for almost thirty years. Do you think I don't have my eyes and ears? How *could* you? Even after I gave you a second chance?"

"No! Please! I've been working so hard as an envoy! I have! And it was just one time! I only found him the venue because ..."

The woman's grin was pure malice. Realization stabbed like a sword.

You idiot!

The high envoy didn't know she'd helped Aurelius, otherwise she'd have said something days ago. All she'd done was see her in the courtyard after dark, obviously nervous, pacing around, and taken a stab.

And Teigra had walked right into the blade.

"Yes, child," the woman hissed. "Now, tell me *everything*."

The thought of disobedience came and went. She'd been given enough chances. There would be no more mercy.

With guilty fire in her heart, Teigra complied, sparing only two things: the first was her intimate moment with Fabulosa, which she'd anyway tried to shove to the back of her mind since it happened; and second was the true reason for Aurelius's mission.

"And why shouldn't I send you back to Mestibes this second?" said Ms. Securia, when she was done. "Why shouldn't I tell the senate exactly what kind of family House Cosmin is?"

Stick to the path, kiddo. Even if it terrifies you.

Teigra's whole body twisted. The images flashed in front of her. All of her father's work. All of his sacrifice. All destroyed because of her.

Mesti ...

Aurie ...

I'm so sorry.

Tears fell down her face as she offered up the last and biggest of

Aurelius's secrets. "If you let me stay . . . I will tell you why . . . why the herald is here . . ."

Ms. Securia scoffed. "Girl, I am aware of the archon's ridiculous fears about *Rinath*. Of your cousin's sinful attempt to remilitarize our homeland. Had you told me that a month ago, it might have earned you some mercy. But I have my own sources in the senate. And the archon has been a little too lax on who she is briefing. It appears she has been making some contingencies in case her son fails her."

"Then . . . what . . . what would you have me do?" Teigra sobbed.

Ms. Securia bared her teeth. "If you want to be with your cousin so badly, Ms. Cosmin, then you have your wish. Because now, you will work *against* him. You will delay and obstruct. You will do your service to the senate to make sure he never succeeds in his twisted mission!"

47

AURELIUS

AURELIUS KICKED SOME BROKEN CLAY ALONG THE OTHERWISE EMPTY street.

He'd fucked it.

After weeks of searching, he'd finally tracked his quarry. He'd found the perfect vantage point. He'd lined up his aim. He'd released the shot!

And he'd fucked it.

He gave the clinking shard another sandal-full.

It wasn't just that the evening had failed that upset him. It was also that this whole mission was taking him down unfamiliar paths—paths he was only now realizing he didn't feel comfortable walking.

He hadn't imposed many rules in his quest to claw back his rightful role of prominence in House Savair. He'd lied and cheated, ruined and wrecked. He'd tempted men who'd only previously slept with women on the promise of forbidden pleasures.

But that was only after obvious flirtation. Only when he was confident that the invitation would be welcomed.

He'd never, *ever* forced himself upon someone.

Oh, back home, with Hal, there was a certain allure in his

longtime lover's indecision. All that delicious lust held captive with weak twine, destined to snap with the gentlest pressure.

But that was with someone he'd known since childhood. Someone he knew unambiguously wanted to fuck him. Someone who, despite all that he'd done, he still cared deeply for.

But doing the same thing with Calix? Deceiving someone he barely knew? Someone with whom he shared undeniable attraction, or at least a certain *curiosity*, but who kept his lust captive with fist-width rope?

That was starting to feel . . . *icky*.

He curled the clay off the road into the outer tree line of Green Heart Park, the public garden at the center of the city. Oak and poplar trees rose higher than the surrounding buildings, all resting on a rug of lush green. Among the city's pervasive smell of sweat and horse shit, it presented the more neutral smell of vegetation. And while it was a good deal more ordered than the Fields of Life at the city's edge, it wasn't at all like the tortured promenades back home, where every tree was teased to conform to some perfect ideal.

Clouds shifted overhead, sending thin bands of light through the park. The moon was little more than a sliver now, only a few days from sable.

As he passed the park's entrance, his eyes were drawn to the fountain in the middle. Pale light glinted off a cloud of mist.

He stopped dead. A figure was sitting on the fountain's edge— their hood pulled back, their posture sharp as a sword.

Even from this distance, he could see that it was Calix.

A hundred thoughts raced through Aurelius's head. What was Calix doing there? Aurelius had been walking aimlessly for about half an hour. They weren't particularly close to the palace, nor particularly close to the Beautiful Bunch.

Although . . . this was the obvious path back to the embassy. Was the prince just wanting space to clear his head?

Or perhaps . . .

Perhaps things weren't so different from down in Mestibes, where he never needed to play the hunter? Where people knew exactly what he was offering, and would find some contrivance to make his company?

Aurelius's foot tapped the dirt, just a few feet from the grass.

He couldn't risk another failure, not in a single night. If he got it wrong, he would be seen as an absolute menace, scaring the prince off for good.

Yet, this was the first chance he would have to see Calix alone. And after all this time, after all this effort, there really wasn't a choice. It was too good an opportunity to turn down.

Aurelius entered the park, making his way toward the fountain.

Control yourself . . .

That was what Calix had screamed at the bathhouse, right at the point of falling to his lust. That was where the man's mind could go— one minute deeply engaged, the next desperate to escape.

He was afraid of losing control. He was afraid of what might happen if he gave in to his urges.

As Aurelius's footsteps swished across the vibrant grass—made silken monochrome by the moon—it was a mantra he repeated.

Control yourself, Aurelius. Don't scare him off.

The prince glanced up at his approach, the air around him cooled by the fountain. One hand was to each side of the stone lip, gripping it hard as if fearing he might fall. But there was no surprise in his dark face.

"Beautiful night for it," said Aurelius, sitting beside him—not so near as to frighten him, but not so far as to appear standoffish.

The prince looked around as if seeing the park for the first time. "Yes. It is."

"In Mestibes, people will be preparing for the sable moon. Visiting the Pentheon to pray their talents don't fail them. Many preparing to observe the Sanctum, clutching their instruments and tools all through the night, as if the dark might steal them away."

"Your whole city fears the sable moon?"

"Oh, it's just superstition. They just want to make sure they are prepared for the monthly Bronze Moon Symposium the fortnight after. Back home, people think that when the moon is bright, they'll be bright. And when the moon is dark, so too will they be."

The prince looked to the thin crescent overhead. "Perhaps that is why we Ardorans celebrate our festivals on the sable moon."

Aurelius laughed. "When all is darkest in the hearts of men?"

"Something like that. I'm sure you've heard of the Black Night Festival."

"The final party of the Ardoran summer? Everyone dressing up as therians? Getting up to all sorts of naughty mischief?"

The prince grunted. "Some men don't need a change of clothes to become animals, Your Excellency. Some *always* carry that instinct with them."

"And many men are not afraid of that beast, Your Highness. Did the great philosopher Sofos not say that there is a time for both the lion and the lamb?"

They were silent for a while.

Without warning, the prince's fingertips pressed against his own —little glides of warmth against the chill of the mist. "But some men need to hold back on those instincts, Aurelius. For some animals are far wilder than others."

Aurelius . . .

It's the first time he's said my name.

Calix looked up, his golden eyes glinting with a sudden hunger— the same hunger as at the bathhouse, albeit a paler shade of it. But unlike there, the feeling inside Aurelius was not some primal lack of control, but the usual anticipation of where that warm touch might wander next.

"And some prey," said Aurelius, "does not fear being bitten."

After a moment's hesitation, the prince leaned in, so close that Aurelius could smell the wine on his breath: sweet and dark.

Just like him. Underneath all that power. Underneath all that restraint. Sweet and dark.

"Are you afraid of me, *Aurelius Savair*?"

"No, *Calix Viralis*," he said, softly, pressing his fingertips back against the prince's.

Calix paused just a few inches away. His eyes clenched shut. His fingertips shook. The prince's pulse thumped through his skin.

Then the big man opened his eyes—two beacons of amber in the night.

"You should be," he whispered.

Calix leaned in for the kiss.

Just as their lips were about to touch, a shriek came from the trees. A crow swooped down, cawing off into the night.

When Aurelius turned back, the moment was gone.

The prince's jaw stiffened. His brow furrowed. "I have to go."

"What? But we were just about to . . ."

"I know *exactly* what we were about to do. It's what you've been trying to trick me into doing since you first arrived, isn't it?"

Trick you . . .

Fury rose inside Aurelius. He was used to this sort of bastardry. Of being blamed by all the "straight" men who sought him out for dark dalliances under the influence of drink, then cried deception when the daylight washed the wine away. It was nothing but cowardice from those who didn't have the balls to live their truth.

"Me?" he said. "You were the one who came to this park! Halfway between the pub and the embassy? Sitting in the moonlight, right in line with the entrance? Somewhere you knew I would pass?"

"So what. Maybe I did want to see you. Because maybe I wanted to tell you to leave me the fuck alone!"

"Bullshit!" he said, pointing hard at the still-visible bruise around his eye. "Your sister and her cronies have sent that message loud and clear already. You just wanted to see *me* again."

"Maybe," he growled. "And maybe after tonight I never want to see you again!"

Calix turned and marched away down the path.

"Is this how you want to live your life?" Aurelius yelled, throwing his words like a punch. "Denying who you are? Denying *what* you are?"

Aurelius caught up and grabbed at the prince's arm. Calix spun around, trying to free himself. Their eyes connected.

And it hit him. A lightning shot of desire sizzled inside Aurelius. Not just for sex, but for *everything*! The desire to do and taste and feel everything.

It was passion incarnate.

It was pleasure manifest.

The feeling vanished as the prince pulled his arm free. Calix's face was blanched white. Tears were forming in the corner of the big man's eyes.

He . . . felt it too?

"You have *no idea* what I am!" he roared, before disappearing back into the shadows.

The fine mist covered Aurelius's skin like icy fingernails.

He hadn't had a drink in a month.

He'd kept his pledge of abstinence.

And yet the feeling had returned.

This could be no *wandering vigor*.

There was only one thing remaining that could cause that effect.

As decades of sneering confidence were ripped from Aurelius, it suddenly all made sense. The hot and cold. The push and pull. Letting people think he had ashen passion, retreating from society, all to hide something even worse!

For his entire life, Aurelius had mocked those who believed in such ridiculous things. Those people who observed the Sable Moon Sanctum and kept statues to the Five in their homes. Superstitious young men who stored musical instruments and workman's tools in boxes painted with an apotropaic eye, warding off the hungry gaze of the skill-thirsty eidolon; or old women burning rosemary and sage as the nights grew darker, all to stop the temptatious songs of a trickster siren from crossing their doorstep.

And yet, they had not been the fools . . .

Aurelius's legs felt unsteady—as if the world was swaying beneath his feet. It was like the park was stretching away around him. Though he hadn't voluntarily attended the Pentheon since childhood, Aurelius said a silent prayer to Mesti.

Teigra had been right the first time.

The therians were real.

And Calix was a *satyr*.

48

AURELIUS

YELLOW-GREEN HILLS ROLLED AWAY FROM THE ROYAL VILLA—A NATURAL auditorium at the bay's northwest headland. Rows of grape vines filled the stands, each twist of green heaving with purple and gold, the early set of fruit that would, by autumn, be so plump it could burst.

Down on the stage, manicured gardens were teeming with the nobility of Ardora, laughing and wandering through brightly colored stalls that extended to the azure water, so clear you could see to the navy-green depths below.

Across the bay was the distant outline of Ardora proper—only a fifteen-minute journey by steed, but far enough to seem a distant memory.

Aurelius breathed deep the atmosphere of the Wax Crack, the festival that marked the debut of last year's wine vintage. Family banners waved in the warm breeze, soft with the sound of strings and sweet with the smell of rose—with red, pink, and white blooms climbing over every column and arch.

The air held the promise of gorging on roasted seafood and dancing in the sunset. Of sampling the wines held captive for a year, yearning to escape. Of stealing kisses in secret nooks and diving out from the cliffs that overlooked the sea.

It was fabulous.

Or at least, it *would have* been, if not for Tiggy.

"Where is he?" she said, darting her head around like a sunflower in a gale. "He isn't here, Aurie! He isn't here!"

Aurelius sighed. It had been a mistake to get her involved with the mission again. He'd only needed her for that one piece of information. But now, he couldn't seem to shake her off. She was probably getting off on the secrecy angle—waiting at his door before dawn, trying to insinuate herself upon the situation, only to duck inside as the rest of the embassy rose with the sun, appearing more dutiful than ever to her high envoy.

He might have suspected foul play there, if not for two things. One, Ms. Securia was continuing to shoot him nasty glances every time they spotted each other across the courtyard. And two, there was no way *Teigra* was clever enough for that kind of deception.

"Darling," he said, patting her arm, "we discussed this. We have to stay relaxed."

His words did nothing to calm her, and he did his best to push her manic energy out of mind.

Because now, things were different.

The mission had moved into a whole different stage. He wasn't just trying to *seduce* the prince anymore. Now he was moving into *confidant* territory.

Because he knew Calix's big secret.

Not that he liked men. Not that he had ashen passion—which he was now fairly sure was just a cover to explain away his withdrawal from society. A cover for the real reason he hid from others.

He knew that the prince was a therian.

A beast.

A *satyr*.

And best of all, the prince knew that he knew. He'd seen it at the fountain—that awful little spark of recognition. That meant Calix would be nervous. That meant he would want to talk, to clear up any "confusion." But there was no confusion. Aurelius knew the truth.

And now, Calix was at his mercy.

A movement at the villa's entrance silenced the crowd, as a party of four descended toward the rest of their nobility. Zosime headed them, and Aurelius was delighted to see that she looked *extremely* uncomfortable, dressed in a heavy white himation with gold and red trimming, a single pink flower in her plaited hair.

Aurelius snorted. Many traditions in Ardora were different from Mestibes, but even he knew what *this* costume meant.

She was being offered as a bachelorette.

Big scary Zosime, the warrior princess, was being trotted out just like any other young woman of eligible age—no better or different from Teigra.

Aurelius clicked his tongue in delight. It was a delicious turn of events.

Calix followed closely behind, wearing a red-purple himation with a laurel wreath in his thick hair. His victory trophy for winning the wrestling at the last Paliad Games, perhaps. He wasn't wearing a tunic beneath the shoulder-wrapped garment, revealing his magnificent, furry chest to all. He, too, looked nervous, eyes darting around like a scared little rabbit.

Excellent!

The siblings were followed by two older figures whom Aurelius had not yet made the acquaintance of. The woman, who he assumed to be Queen Dimitra, was *perfection*, her hair up in a coronet of bronze oak leaves, bejeweled with rubies and emeralds.

And beside her, in the crown covered in dagger-sharp bronze thorns that Aurelius had seen in the palace throne room, was—

Teigra hissed. "Is that *the king*? I knew he was sick, but I didn't know it was *that* bad."

There was no one else it could have been. The man at the back of the pack looked like a stunted tree. His limbs were thin. Like they could snap at any moment. His face was pock-marked and hardened, with a yellow tinge across it, like sickly bark.

And yet, despite this appearance, he wasn't wincing or panting. If anything, he seemed more alive than his children—sharing jokes and slapping backs as he entered the crowd, wielding the special hammers to crack the wax seals upon the amphorae, and having to be pulled away by the queen when he lingered too long at a single stall.

"Come on," said Aurelius, yanking Teigra through the throng.

The crowd near the royals was just thin enough that he had a clear view, but just thick enough that they hadn't yet been noticed.

"Honestly, Polimea, this vintage is even better than last season. How do you do it?" said the king, in a surprisingly strong voice.

"Family secrets, Your Majesty," winked a large woman with tits like wrinkly melons. "Of course, I could never give them away."

"And I suppose I'd be wasting my breath asking you once again to take responsibility for my vineyards? I am afraid my current vintner favors the more delicate varieties that the sea wolves buy. Not the proper ball kickers for an old soldier!"

"No breath from you is ever wasted, Majesty!"

The queen and Calix stood stoic-faced, but Zosime was already rolling her eyes. She clearly knew this routine well, and by the looks of it, they were settling in for another long conversation.

Aurelius looked around in annoyance. There were thirty more stalls around the grounds. At this rate, it would be dusk before they finished up.

I'll never get Calix alone at this pace!

Zosime crossed her arms and gave a loud sigh, gesturing for another refill. The red sloshed into her cup, a single drop skipping off the rim and onto the grass.

And Aurelius had a wicked little idea. Something involving the colors red and white . . .

"Tiggy, don't be nervous. I think you'll be *great* at this," he said.

She cocked her head. "Great at what?"

"This!"

Before the surprise even registered in her eyes, Aurelius pushed her through the crowd. Teigra crashed right into Zosime, causing the princess's cup to tumble over her himation—streaking the white cloth red.

Aurelius ducked. "Can you believe it?" he said, putting on his best Ardoran accent. "This Mestibian wench just said she could *outdrink* the princess!"

"Outdrink Her Highness?" scoffed someone nearby. "Bullshit!"

"Let her have it, Zos!" called an old woman, her cheeks the same color as the wine dripping down Zosime's furious face. "Show that uptight marble lounger how we do it in Ardora!"

"Yeah!"

"Go on, give it to her!"

Aurelius didn't wait to see the result. Instead, he scrambled out the back of the growing throng and slowed to a saunter. As people rushed by, he stretched himself out, extending his arms overhead, before running his hands down creamy legs, revealing a peek of buttock kissed by the summer breeze. Only then did he give a lazy glance over his shoulder.

Calix looked away hurriedly, a blush spreading fast across his cheeks.

Aurelius grinned. But instead of walking toward the prince, he strolled right on by, wandered up past the edge of the festival grounds, past the royal villa, all the way up the sun-drenched hills beyond.

And as he did so, he whistled a little tune—a familiar ditty about a satyr laying its seeds deep into fertile soil.

He waited until he was at the cliff-top before looking back.

Quite a way behind, far enough to have had a moment of indecision, Calix was following.

49

TEIGRA

Zosime's nostrils flared. Teigra hunted for Aurelius but couldn't see him over the sudden press of the crowd, now barracking for a drinking contest that *she* had supposedly called for.

"No! I didn't say anything about outdrinking you," she said, raising her hands.

The crowd laughed. All but the queen, who weighed Teigra's face. "I don't think this is a good idea," she whispered to the king.

"Nonsense!" he said, slapping both Zosime and Teigra on the backs with a force stronger than his withered frame. "If there is one thing we like in this polity, it's a bit of good clean competition!"

The crowd cheered, encircling the stall like a noose. Any escape pathway was gone.

Teigra gave Zosime a pleading expression. "I didn't . . . I wasn't . . ."

Without breaking eye contact, the princess grabbed two cups, filling them to the brim. "And yet, here we are."

She slammed her drink in a single gulp, giving an overdramatic *ahhh!* to the masses.

Teigra stared at her own blood-red liquid. She'd never drunk before. Not a drop.

She'd seen what it did to people: Aurelius after a big night, being a wreck the next day; respectable men at the hippodrome, turned into beasts after a few glasses; and worst of all, Mother's behavior at feasts and symposiums, cackling and flirting and making a total fool of herself.

In the distance, she caught a glimpse of Aurelius walking up the hillside, being followed by Calix. Her throat tightened as Ms. Securia's instruction rang in her head. She had to stop him, or else her whole family would be ruined!

Even if Ms. Securia didn't hear about Aurelius and Calix wandering off together—a big "if," given how many spies the woman surely had—she would definitely hear about the low envoy from Mestibes starting a drinking a contest with the princess, bringing in almost every single attendant at the festival! And Ms. Securia was smart enough to draw her own conclusions from that.

Teigra's apprehension was reflected back in the crimson mirror. She didn't want to drink it any more than she actually wanted to stop Aurelius. But she had no more warnings left with Ms. Securia. And the quicker she got this over with, the quicker she could try to undo what had been done.

She winced as the thick liquid hit her throat—the taste like rotten fruit, with a cloying sweetness and an unpleasant burn. She coughed reflexively, splashing the awful brew up her nose, but somehow forced the rest of it down.

Zosime watched her with a sick grin, leaning in close. "I've been meaning to thank you for what you did back at Palaestra Xiphos—coming over to my new potentials like that. Some people might have convinced themselves that their precious cargo had just been misplaced. But you *knew!*" Zosime licked her lips, relishing her dominance. "And do you know what would have happened if you'd called me out? Those papers would have turned up on your doorstep. Your cousin figured that out. He called my bluff. But you didn't do *shit*, did you?"

Zosime leaned back, smacked her cup against the table and downed it. "Your turn, *Tiggy*."

The mugs came and went. Each time, Teigra fought the urge to gag. The crowd was spinning now. She gripped the bench for a stability that wouldn't come.

At the sixth or seventh cup, Zosime leaned in again. Her breath stank red, even though she seemed in full control. "You know, you Mestibians think you're all so superior. That you know everything about everything? But I got some of my people to do a little digging on the two of *you*."

She snorted at Teigra's discomfort.

"Oh, your cousin was easy. He just tells people that he's a bent stick." Zosime waggled the wine cup with a tut. "But you? I heard the most interesting story about *you*. Perhaps you can tell me if it's true?"

The wine churned in her stomach.

There was only one story of her life worth telling.

One that she hoped to never hear again.

"Three years ago, there was an incredible race down in Mestibes —the final run of the relay season. A young prodigy had joined the Cosmin family team only a few years prior. Just fifteen years old, but already blitzing the field."

"Stop it," whispered Teigra.

"But then, race day comes. And it's raining! Raining like it never does down there. A proper monsoon—wind and hail and drops hammering down so hard you can't see a foot in front of you. The officials come to the riders and ask if they want to call the race off. There's some murmuring. But the little prodigy? Not a bar of it. *Let us race*, she said. And all the big men had to go along with that, didn't they? Couldn't be outdone by a little girl."

"Stop it," she repeated, clenching her eyes shut.

"And so they race. The centaurs around first, barely able to grip the sand. Then the hippocamps, doing their laps in channels so churned the riders almost drown. And then it comes to the pegasus jockeys to take it all home. The racing is hard and fast, the closest one of the season. The little prodigy is leading, but the others are close by. So she tries something crazy. She takes the final corner at full pace—so fast it would snap the wings of any other steed! No one thinks she can make it!"

"Stop it!" Teigra hissed, tears welling.

"And they were right. The steed can't hold it. So girl and beast go tumbling through the air. Round and round and round and round until *crack!*" Zosime slammed her cup down, the clay smashing across the bench. She grabbed a handful of the earthen shards, dripping as red as blood. "The steed sweeps a marking pillar, which collapses into a hail of stone, right into the crowd! And against all odds, it only takes out one person—the little rider's own fucking *father!*"

Tears streamed down Teigra's cheeks. The sound of the crowd faded to nothing but the roar of the gale and the scream that she could never unhear.

Teigra flung herself back—pushing through the onlookers, desperate to get away, desperate to be anywhere else but here!

The world was a blur of flags and flowers and people!

Then came the sensation of falling and a wet, cold crash.

50

AURELIUS

Aurelius sat at the crest of the headland, separated from the still-raucous festival by a thirty-foot dive into azure. Curving all around the northern side of the bay were the rolling vineyards and little villas that eventually joined the city proper.

He'd discovered the location of Calix's personal vineyard a few weeks back—though he hadn't yet visited it. The prince had been shaken enough by his presence at *public* events. He couldn't imagine that turning up at his private home, uninvited, would have played to his advantage.

Calix stopped when he reached the crest, gifted expansive views of the ocean beyond. He paused for a long while, just a few feet away, before eventually approaching.

Calix sat beside him on the soft grass. The muscles of his exposed thighs rippled with strength.

The silence persisted, with naught but the clicking of insects in the pleasant warmth.

"Can your cousin hold her liquor?" asked Calix, eventually.

"Tiggy? The only thing she can do with liquor is hold it. Drinking it would certainly be a mistake."

"Then I fear my sister will make short work of her. Few can outdrink her when she is in her element."

"I imagine there are few who could outdo her at *anything* when she is in her element," said Aurelius with a bitter laugh.

"Yes," said Calix, taking in his half-healed face, the bruises having begun to lighten. "She is a remarkable woman."

"Remarkable and persistent. I had to learn about your little social group at the pub just to see you."

"I am sure she is only trying to protect me," he said.

His tone was neutral, and Aurelius couldn't tell how much Calix knew of his battles with Zosime—or whether she was acting on his instructions.

Aurelius took a deep breath. He had waited for this moment for a month and a half. And now he had him. He knew his secret. Whether they fucked or not was irrelevant, though seeing him here, in the warm air, with this view, the thought was as tempting as ever.

But now he had something to trade: his silence in exchange for what he wanted—the military alliance that would get him the inheritance he so richly deserved.

And Calix knew that he knew. That was why he'd followed him up here.

But he won't raise it himself, will he? For a secret like this, he wants to know for certain.

"Do the others at the Beautiful Bunch know that your true affliction is different from theirs?" said Aurelius. "That the reason you appear so stiff in public is that you are trying to suppress an entirely different curse from the divine?"

Calix didn't flinch, but nor did he respond immediately. He just stared out at the white-tipped swell. "That song you whistled as you passed, it is the same one you sang at The Bunch?"

"'The *Satyr* of the Seed'?" he said, putting a slight emphasis on the relevant word.

Calix's face gave nothing away. "It is another of your Nenia songs, isn't it?"

"Another?"

"You whistled a different one when you followed me into the bathhouse at Palaestra Xiphos."

Aurelius thought back, the memory of a random song rather more faded than other events of that day. "So I did. 'The Enchantment of the Eidolon.'"

"Yes," said Calix. "A song about two young lovers, nearing their wedding day. If I recall, a jealous eidolon copies the man's image and tries to seduce his betrothed. The young man sings the song to convince her that he is the one she fell in love with."

"And what of it, Your Highness? You are rather avoiding my questi—"

"I would like you to sing it for me."

Aurelius laughed. "Why?"

"Do I need a reason?"

"So, you wish for another show? Well, I am afraid there isn't much of a crowd up here."

Calix looked at him, and the entire ocean seemed to swell across his face. "*I* am here."

After long consideration and still confused as to why the prince was asking, Aurelius relented.

He'd barely got through half a line before Calix stopped him. "No, not as you did in the pub. Not for entertainment. Perform the song as it is meant to be performed."

"Why does it matter—"

"*Please*," said Calix. His golden eyes were soft. The lines around his mouth betrayed a vulnerability. "Please just do it. For *me*."

Aurelius weighed the man's intentions. He didn't know what this had to do with revealing his secret. But it seemed important to the prince.

With a slow exhale, he did what was requested, singing the song as it was usually performed in the music schools of Mestibes—all soft and soppy and boring.

· · ·

You cannot doubt my feelings for you, sweet one.
  The love we share cannot be bought or sold.
  I love you so without a rhyme or reason.
  You'll be my one and only till we're old.

Don't listen to his mischief now, my darling.
  Don't listen to his grifting now, my dear.
  Don't listen to his tricks and all that snarling.
  You'll be my one and only through the years.

There's nothing he could say or do to break this.
  For we are so much stronger than his lies.
  Just take my hand, our lips will now embrace bliss.
  You'll be my one and only till we die.

It felt strange to sing the song earnestly, rather than with mockery. And despite the golden sun in the distance, Aurelius grew a little colder with each stanza.

The young couple were so in love.

So full of hope.

So devoted to each other . . .

When he was done, there was no celebration. The notes wandered down the hill and faded to silence.

That silence was broken not by applause, nor by whistles, or even by a, "thank you." Instead, it was broken by grinding in Calix's throat.

At first, Aurelius thought the prince must be crying.

But then, it became clear.

He was *laughing.*

Aurelius scowled, blushing a rare blush. "What's so funny?"

"Sorry," said the prince, holding up hands of placation. "It was beautiful. Really. It's just . . ."

"What!?"

"You really don't have the first clue about yourself, do you?"

"What is that supposed to mean?"

"You, *Mr. Savair*! You chase me down like a horny dog for over a month. On your first day in my city, you create a reason to find me naked and wet. Today is the first day you've not spoken to me in that ridiculous, high-pitched voice. The way you posture and pose like a model in the Garden of Plenty. You think that's the *real you*?"

"Unlike some, *Your Highness*, I am comfortable with who I am."

"And that is your true self, then? Someone who pursues what he wants at all costs? A heartless animal who just fucks without emotion? Without any connection or passion or need for something more?"

"Yes, what of it?"

Calix's eyes glowed with deepest sympathy. "Then why do you sing about true love with *such sadness*?"

All air left Aurelius.

Flashes shot through his memory.

The image of a familiar bedroom.

Of a boy he had known since childhood, their hands entwined. Of whispering the words he'd been so scared to say—the words he'd worked up the courage for weeks and months and years to finally fucking say! Because they had to be said! Because if they stayed trapped inside for even one second longer, he feared he might be torn in two!

And the final flash, seared across his memory like a cruel bolt of lightning, of the silence that followed.

Aurelius turned from the prince, hiding the shameful tear running down his cheek.

Calix grabbed at his hand. He jerked Aurelius around until they were eye to eye again, two beams of gold hunting inside him. "Who was the boy that made you hurt so?"

The images rose again.

No! I was a fool. I was weak! That kind of thing doesn't happen to people like me!

Aurelius tried to wrench free, but Calix held on, sending them both rolling down the vineyard side of the hill, coming to a stop beside the knotted trunk of a vine.

Aurelius was laying on his back, the sky hidden by the huge form of Calix overtop. The prince's eyes were flowing with tears now—frantic, desperate tears, which fell onto Aurelius like warm rain.

"Don't you see?" said Calix. "Don't you know that you deserve so much more than those faceless fucks. That there is *so much* more inside you! You hide it, but it is there! You deserve the *passion* you lock away!"

In his peripheral vision, as if growing directly out from the man's temples, he saw the shining, semitranslucent glow of two twisted horns. "And I can give it to you."

With the slowest of movements, Calix pressed his lips against his own.

And the world exploded.

A thousand sun's worth of heat burned at every point inside him. A million volcanoes erupted in blistered fury. His body felt like a living immolation, consumed with a fire he wanted to stoke. A fire he wished could burn hotter still. To never burn out! And in those blissful licks of flame, he felt it. He felt it!

Mesti!

Ardor!

Ondo!

Vatic!

Rina!

I FEEL IT!

Aurelius kissed back hard, spreading the man's lips with his tongue. He wanted him closer. His legs hooked around Calix's big hips, bringing him down, grinding his rock-hard crotch against his ass. He pulled aside Calix's fabric and licked all up his chest—sweaty and rough. The prince shoved him back and returned the gesture, tearing his tunic open, taking his pink nipples against his tongue without mercy.

Aurelius screamed in indescribable pleasure. He screamed for it to never, ever stop! He screamed so loud that all he could hear was the screaming, echoing around his head.

And then, in one awful moment, all that heat was torn from him.

There was a blur overhead as Calix rose, making straight for the edge of the rocks. Without stopping, he dove right down into the water!

Aurelius shuddered with a sudden chill.

The screams continued, but they were no longer his own.

Now, they were screams for help, coming from down in the villa.

51

TEIGRA

WHAT IS THIS?

It was strange.

The world was all twisty.

From far away came a sound like a scream, but stretched out and fuzzy.

Her whole body was surrounded by a swirling, cold roil.

Water?

Then it hit her like a punch to the gut.

I'm . . . drowning!

She searched for a way out, but all she could see was hair and fabric, choking her, surrounding her.

She tried to scream, but the air just bubbled out.

Her chest was empty!

A crash came from somewhere nearby.

There was force around her.

Then the feeling of sudden momentum.

Then air! *Sweet air.*

She gasped for it amongst a cascade of drenching salt. Water clogged her eyes and ears. She couldn't hear or see properly, but she could feel the crowd standing around. Sunlight beamed overhead, bright and hot, filling her blurry vision.

Then a cool shadow crossed the burn. A strong hand brushed the hair from her face.

"Are you alright?" asked a resiny voice, now blinking into focus.

It was . . . *Crown Prince Calix.*

Calix had saved her!

She was alive.

She was alive!

Teigra threw her arms around him and laid a big kiss on his lips. "Thank you! Praise Ardor, thank you!" she sobbed.

The crowd cheered and all the blurry, well-dressed people clapped in relief.

All of them, but one.

From the back row, panting and gripping a torn tunic, his face twisted in anger, stood Aurelius.

52

AURELIUS

THE DOCKS BUSTLED—BURLY MEN HEAVING HUGE CLAY AMPHORAE, birch-wielding old women whipping braying goats into pens. All the clangs and clacks of a morning bay front, hard at work.

To Aurelius, every sound was like rapturous applause, all for him. Because he'd done it. It had taken him far longer than he had thought, but he'd finally won Calix over.

Oh, Teigra throwing herself into the water for attention hadn't been part of his plan, and it had dragged the prince away just when they had been about to seal the deal. But he wasn't concerned. There would be plenty of time for that.

Because now, he was Calix's *confidant*—perhaps the only person in Dynosia that knew his wicked secret.

Aurelius could already hear the outpouring of pent-up emotion which would soon follow, feel the giddying closeness of *finally* having someone to speak to. He'd seen it all before, with countless "happily" married men. Once that seal was broken, all indecision melted away, as their life reoriented around the one person who *truly* understood them.

Soon the prince would be a puppy at his heels. Securing the

military agreement would be a matter of moments. And then, he'd have done it. After six long years, he was just weeks away from being reinstated as the anointed success of the archon, in a context where even the senate couldn't deny him his birthright. How could they? He was about to be beloved and powerful—the man who'd single-handedly saved Mestibes from invasion.

And as he strode through the streets, Aurelius couldn't help but dwell on the taste of the prince.

He wasn't the sort of man he normally pursued—so big, so quiet, so *mysterious*. Of course, it was all just a means to an end. And yet, the heat of his mouth lingered. The fire across his skin. The unbelievable power of the beast.

And that was just from a *kiss*. Aurelius shuddered at what would surely come, wondering how anyone could think it a negative to be a satyr.

When he arrived back at the embassy, a dozen young women were waiting outside, craning their necks—their voices all overlapping.

"Are you sure this is it?"

"Definitely! This is the Mestibian embassy. She has to be in there."

"Oh, I hope she's alright!"

"Did you hear how she challenged Zosime?"

"I didn't think Mestibian women had that sort of spunk."

"Well, I heard that Calix dived from the top of a cliff just to save her!"

"Really? I didn't know he had it in him!"

"Oh, it's all so romantic!"

"Look! Look! The curtain moved! Lady? Laaady? Are you alright?"

Aurelius suppressed a laugh. Why did women always try to project some great romantic fantasy onto banal things? Thinking that Calix might be interested in Teigra?

Teigra?

The poor confused things.

There was movement from the top of the street, which sent the gaggle into raptures. A figure rode a white steed at midpace toward them. Morning sun caressed his bare shoulder.

Aurelius grinned. Not even a day had passed and the prince was already coming to see him. Just stopping by for some light refreshments and polite conversation?

Yes, that is where it will start.

He squeezed past the throng, skipping to his building and striking a nonchalant pose in the doorway.

But when the prince also pushed through the adoring group, he didn't even pass a look in Aurelius's direction. Instead, he continued straight on to the front door of the embassy proper.

Aurelius glanced around before trotting up and hiding behind the pomegranate tree in the middle of the courtyard.

The centaur servant whose name he couldn't quite remember opened the door and bowed deeply. "Your Royal Highness. To what do we owe the honor?"

Calix spoke loud and clear. "I have come to see Ms. Teigra Cosmin."

53

TEIGRA

As she blinked herself awake, a silhouette formed against the burning blur. It was Jaspar, peering through the curtains of her bedroom. There seemed to be some commotion in the courtyard.

"What . . . what happened?" she rasped.

Her mouth felt like she'd swallowed a handful of dirt. And not the rich, black soil of Ardora either, but the white, gravel-clumped dust of back home. Her head pounded in a way she'd never felt before. Every movement, every *breath* made the blood thump against her temple like hooves on cobble.

Jaspar dropped the curtain. "Oh, hello sleepyhead! I was worried for a moment."

"Worried?" she said, moving her sweaty limbs beneath the sheets. "Why?"

Recollection smacked her in the face.

The Wax Crack. Aurelius pushing her into Zosime. The cup after cup of sickly wine. Almost drowning. Kissing the prince!

And then, worst of it all, the snippets of being back at the embassy. Of Ms. Securia's disgusted expression as Jaspar carried her up the stairs to bed.

The high envoy had been leaving for the Temple of Mesti and her monthly Sable Moon Sanctum—communing with the goddess of reason while Teigra spent the night sleeping off her shameful debauchery.

"Oh . . ." she said.

It was all she could say. Even among the hurt of the hangover, another pain came sharper and more abrasive in her chest.

It was over.

She'd ruined her family.

It didn't matter that she'd done everything she could to follow Ms. Securia's instructions. It didn't matter that Aurelius had forced her into the situation. It didn't matter that she hadn't knowingly helped him!

It'd still happened.

And now?

Now . . .

"Yes, *that!*" said Jaspar with a laugh. "I heard all about it at the market this morning. Don't worry. The embarrassment will wear off. The Ardorans like a bit of spunk. Truth be told, I was only two weeks into the job when I had my own . . ." His voice trailed away at the sounds of her crying—at first a muffled squeak, which morphed into sobs of desolation. "Teigra, what's the matter?"

She covered her face. "I'm ruined, Jaspar. Ms. Securia . . . Didn't she tell you?"

"No. What?"

"She . . . she set me an ultimatum. I had to watch Aurelius closely. To stop him on his mission. And under no circumstance was I to help him. If I did, she'd send me home with a black mark against my family's name. Meaning all of my family's work . . . all my father's dreams . . . all of it . . ."

Her words collapsed.

She couldn't breathe.

Memories of her father thumped through her aching head—him holding her on her shoulders so she could see the races, her little legs gripping his neck like a steed's flank; staying up till all hours of the night, thinking up strategies to beat the other stables; taking her to the library before dawn, teaching her the knowledge she'd need when they rose to patrician status and she joined him in the senate.

All that work.

All that effort.

Gone!

All because of me.

And in that moment, in a way she'd never fully realized before, Teigra understood the pain and purpose she'd kept for so long. All the effort that she'd gone through since that awful day, all the beatings and humiliations at the hands of Mother, all the horrible things that she'd been forced to do. She'd done it all to keep *his path* alive. To keep some small part of *him* alive.

Stick to the path, kiddo. Even if it terrifies you.

She'd failed that final instruction. The words he'd said while securing her into the harness, moments before the race that had ripped her life apart.

And now it was like she'd killed him all over again!

"No," said Jaspar, pulling her hands from her tear-soaked eyes. "I don't understand what is happening, but I won't let her do that. No letters have gone today. I'll talk to her. I'll—"

The door was thrown open. It was Mr. Placi. "You have to come downstairs, girl! Quickly!"

Teigra's heart dropped. It was to be like this, was it? Straight to the door. Straight to the carriage. Back to Mestibes at the earliest possible point. No time to even pack.

She pulled her broken body from the bed—all pain now numbed —and dressed in a thin yellow stola. Mr. Placi took the stairs more gracefully than she imagined a centaur could.

Ms. Securia was waiting at the bottom of those stairs. But her expression was not of fury? It was of . . . *restraint*?

Because standing in the doorway, lit by scorching sunlight, was the *crown prince.*

The muscles in Ms. Securia's neck visibly strained. "His Royal Highness has come to see you, Ms. Cosmin. Let us not keep him waiting."

The prince gave a forced-looking smile, no doubt mortified at the sight of her. She probably looked an even bigger mess now than yesterday, when she'd placed a drunken kiss on his beautiful face.

He stood like finest statuary, the sort Mother would slap her hands away from if she tried to touch—too nice for the likes of her. Tall and strong, with a square jaw overlaid with a thick and manly beard, and with cheeks that the young suitors of the senate could only dream of.

He gave her a stiff nod. "Ms. Cosmin, I've . . . I've come to check on you."

"Oh? Thank you," she muttered, blinking against the blinding blur. "For saving me and . . . you didn't have to come here or anything but thank you for that as well."

"It is such a shame that one of your first big experiences in Ardora was so regrettable," he said, his voice deep and loud through her hangover. "I must make it up to you."

"To *me*?"

"Yes. I was wondering if you would join my family for dinner tonight. At the palace?"

Teigra squinted in stunned silence.

It was all too much. Moments ago, she was to be driven home in shame, with her whole house ruined. And now the Crown Prince of Ardora was on the doorstep, asking her to come to the palace? To *make it up* to her?

As kind as the offer was, she obviously couldn't accept. She'd already embarrassed herself enough! The thought of attending a formal dinner—with all the people who watch her almost drown—was unimaginable.

But just as she was about to politely decline, she saw a face peeking from behind the pomegranate.

Aurelius.

He was shaking his head, even mouthing the words *no*, as if his thoughts might be unclear.

She clenched her fists. After everything he had done to her, he wanted her to say no, did he? He almost destroyed her family with his cruelty, and he wanted her to say *no*, did he?

Well . . . well, to Dimethan with that!

"Yes," she said, wincing a little at her own volume. "I would love to come to dinner at the palace."

54

AURELIUS

It was past midday when Aurelius arrived at Calix's vineyard, the air hot and dry under a cloudless sky.

He stomped past the surprisingly modest villa, looking down over thirty even rows of vines, housed in a funnel between hills that gave the property more seclusion than the others he'd passed.

His fury had sustained him on the hour-long walk from the city, running the morning's events over in his head.

What is Calix playing at?

He spotted the prince about halfway down the sun-drenched slope, his olive skin glistening. He was practically naked, save a wine-red loincloth, the front and back panels extending down past his bulging thighs like fabric swords, just like those worn at the wrestling grounds. He was swinging some double-headed farming tool, forming shallow trenches between the rows. Each swing caused the muscles on his back to ripple.

Despite Aurelius's residual anger, Calix's godlike figure remained captivating as he approached. After a little too long, Aurelius remembered himself. "What are you doing?"

Calix neither paused nor turned, once again unsurprised by his presence. For the first time Aurelius wondered if that was a satyr thing. If he had some way of *detecting* his arrival?

"Laying ruby clover," said Calix. "It will help the vines replenish over winter."

"No, I mean why are *you* doing it? I thought the fighters fought and the farmers farmed."

Now he turned. Beads of sweat glinted in his chest hair. "We rule for all Ardora. House Viralis might come from fighter stock, but we can't be blind to the challenges of the Greens. We must feel the pain of droughts and the joys of bountiful seasons, just as they do."

"Every other vineyard has a bunch of giants working it. Surely you could afford a whole army of them?"

"No one is too good for hard work. Not a prince. Not a king." He gave him a long glance, then tossed the tool, trailing a path of black dirt. "Not even a herald."

Aurelius surprised himself by catching it, though he held it like a rotting fish and had to steady himself against the unbalanced weight of the metal head. "You can't be serious?"

The prince was already kneeling back over the freshly dug trench, placing straw-colored seeds. "You came to talk?"

"Well, yes."

"Fine. But the rains are coming. So we talk and work."

Aurelius eyed the tool with suspicion, already resenting the brown-black smear of dirt across his palms. Eventually, he relented, struggling to copy Calix's swinging motions. "So, what was that about at the embassy? Asking Teigra to dinner?"

"*That* is your first question? After everything that happened at the Wax Crack?"

"Yes," he said, flinching at the accuracy of the barb.

"Your cousin had a bad experience. It was the proper thing to do."

"Well, that is very dashing, but there was no need. You fished her out of the sea. I'm sure she is best left to her duties."

"You sound jealous."

The bluntness was once again like a smack to his forehead.

"What? Hardly! You may do whatever you want with whomever you want. My only concern is that you left me high and dry—filling me with such delicious sensations, then stopping before completion!"

His flirtation had the opposite effect than intended. Calix scowled. "I'm so sorry about that. I should have controlled myself."

"Well, I'm glad you didn't. My only regret is that we didn't finish what we started."

Calix remained still for the longest time, running the rich soil slowly through his fingertips. "Why aren't you scared of me, Aurelius?" he whispered. "Now that you know what I am."

"I'm not sure," he admitted. "Maybe because you don't seem like some evil beast?"

"You don't know me very well."

"No, but I'd like to."

After another long pause, the prince returned to his work. "Fine."

Aurelius wiped his brow. "So, you really are a *satyr*?"

"You know the answer to that."

"Yes, but I want to hear you say it."

Calix gave a surreptitious glance around the otherwise empty vineyard before giving a single, curt nod.

"Cursed by the goddess of fertility for some grave offense of your parents?"

"So the legends say."

"And do you know what they did to earn such ire?"

The prince continued as though he hadn't heard the question, and Aurelius didn't push. "Well, you don't *look* like a satyr. So you are the middle form. A metamorph?"

"According to books."

"You don't know?"

"We don't get a tutor on the subject."

Another accurate barb. "So the divine chrysalis you encountered was not the eternal rose of Ardor? Otherwise, you would be in the final form. An imago. You'd permanently be a satyr."

"Not the rose, no."

"Which one was it then?"

Calix stared long into the black earth. "Rina."

Aurelius's stomach turned at the memories of teenage tutelage. "You consumed *black brave*? A soup made of a war priest's hear—"

"Yes."

"When fighting at Sama?"

Another pause, then another, tiny nod.

"Was it—"

"I have *no intention* of talking about my time in battle!"

Aurelius raised his hands. "All right. I was just asking."

They worked in silence for a while, with Aurelius doing his best to hide how puffed the digging was making him. After some consideration, he thought it best to ask about a different topic before returning to the one that really mattered.

"You don't have ashen passion, do you?"

"Not like the others at The Bunch, no."

"But you let some people think you do?"

"When I must."

"So that if someone wants to dig into why their prince has now taken to hiding himself away from his public, they will find a suitable explanation? Something bad, but better than the truth: that their prince both likes boys and is a satyr?"

No response came, but he hadn't expected one.

"Which of those truths is the bigger secret, I wonder," Aurelius continued. "The boys or the beast?"

Calix exhaled ruefully. "Either would taint my lineage and disqualify me from the throne."

Aurelius had expected no further response, but after a long while, Calix continued. "But the *boys*, I suppose. In the mid and low polities of Greater Ardora, you can find rural shrines to satyrs. They are revered and called upon by people who don't know any better. Infertile couples. Those with ashen passion. But no one, *anywhere*, gives sacrifice to men who fuck other men."

"Well, I can see why some people might worship the beasts!

Those powers you have are incredible. Can you do that to anyone? Just walk up and make someone hornier than they've ever been?"

"It isn't just for sex. It's for any passion. For family, for friends, for battle, for competition. Whatever it is, if a person already has some passion for it, I can take that feeling and enhance it to extreme levels. Sex is just . . . the most *visceral*. The most . . . *satiating*. For me. For . . . for the *beast*."

"You say it with bitterness? But what I experienced was wonderful."

"We don't do it as a *kindness*," spat the prince. "We *feed* on it. We are little better than flies and vultures. Believe me, if you'd experienced my full abilities, you wouldn't think it *wonderful*. You were fortunate we were interrupted before night fell. On the day before the sable moon? If not for your cousin, I don't think I'd have been able to stop myself."

Aurelius furrowed his brow. "The moon really matters that much?"

"It's more manageable closer to bronze. Much harder to use powers around that time. But I *always* feel it. Even on the brightest moon, it's still like having a thirst you cannot quench. A throat stripped dry and being surrounded by the clearest, coolest water, whispering for you to guzzle it."

"And on sable moons?"

Calix stilled. The sun did not falter. No cloud drifted across the sky. Yet, the air seemed to cool.

"I change."

"As in . . ."

"You are a prince, Aurelius. You've received the best education. *I change*."

"We don't technically have *princes* in Mestibes. Or kings and queens for that matter. It is more of a first among equals arrangement."

"This isn't a joke," he said. "On the night of the sable moon, I become . . . *that thing*. I'm not *me* anymore. I'm . . . *it*."

Aurelius turned to face the tiniest sliver of moon, faded aqua against a deep blue sky. "So last night, you grew goat horns?"

"Yes."

"And proper fur?"

"Yes."

Aurelius gestured to his crotch. "And your . . ."

Calix rolled his eyes and stood, dusting his hands. "What difference does that make?"

"Oh, please, Your Highness. Do you think we won't end up fucking?"

"We won't. *Ever.*"

Aurelius bit his bottom lip and placed a fingertip on Calix's furry chest—the heat radiating off him. He trailed the finger down to his rock-hard stomach, over the ridges and grooves, and down toward his loincloth. "Are you sure about that, Mr. Satyr? Will you not tell me where you locked yourself away last night, so I can come and visit next time?"

Calix snatched his wrist, so hard it felt like the skin had been punctured. His eyes were pure carnage.

"*Don't!*" he growled.

And it was a growl. A wolf threatening a lamb.

Aurelius looked up in shock. "I just thought . . ."

Calix's fingernails dug deeper. Aurelius gasped as blood dripped down his forearm.

"You want to know what I am, Aurelius? You want to know what I can do? With these *wonderful* powers, I can ruin lives. I can take the people I love the most, who trust me the most, and I can force them to act like animals. I can build the zeal inside them until they think they might explode. And then, at the peak of their passions, I can drain it all away! Hollow them out! Leaving them as broken, joyless husks!"

"I didn't . . ." said Aurelius, trying to step back.

Calix pulled him closer. "Don't you get it? I am a *beast*! I am a *monster*! And if I ever allow myself to lose control, I know that I can *kill*."

"I was just . . ."

Calix's face was beyond fury. "None of this is a *game*, Aurelius! None of this is *fun*! I do everything I can to lock this thirst away. I do everything I can to lock these powers away. And I will never, *ever* use them again!"

55

TEIGRA

Ms. Securia drew the bronze-tipped comb through Teigra's hair, making it, if not necessarily *neat*, at least closer to straight than usual.

Though only a few doors down from her own, she'd never been inside Ms. Securia's bedroom. It was sparser than she'd expected— little more than a bed and the dresser that Teigra sat at.

Through the window, dusk washed the surrounding roofs, confirming what she already knew: the hours were fast slipping away.

She thumbed her pendant as the comb rasped through knots. This morning it'd seemed the perfect way to punish Aurelius. And though it shamed her to admit it, it had felt good to see his shock. Not just for personal revenge, but also that he might learn a lesson about the hurt he inflicted on others.

But as the hours passed, that smugness had faded. Now, the situation had become mortifyingly real.

She was going to be the guest of honor at the *palace*. Around every member of Ardora's nobility.

The first blow came when she'd visited the baths for a particularly good scrub, with women she'd never met pointing and whispering and peering around corners. Next had been the awful, brittle smile that Jaspar had given her when wishing her luck "on her date."

And now there was *this*, being sat in terrifying silence before Ms. Securia's polished bronze mirror, waiting for the dreadful hour to come.

Across Dynosia, bronze was reserved for the holiest of objects. In Mestibes, that meant scroll handles and statue plinths and the like. In Ardora, that meant things like mirrors and combs.

But no amount of holiness could hide the vision of discomfort staring back at her from the pool of glowing orange.

I don't belong at the palace! I'll just embarrass myself again! In front of everyone. In front of all the people who are already laughing at me!

"Quite a turn of events," said Ms. Securia, without pausing the combing. "Me asking you to stick close to the herald, and you doing the opposite."

"Please, Ms. Securia," she said, relieved the silence had been broken, "I can explain! Aurelius forced me into that situation. He shoved me into the princess and—"

"He forced the wine down your throat? He forced the kiss you placed on the future king of this land?"

Her mouth gaped.

"Exactly. We must take responsibility for our actions, Teigra. That is what Mesti expects of us."

"And I do! But just . . . please know that I didn't do it to help Aurelius. I *promise*. I know the punishment for that."

Ms. Securia looked at Teigra's reflection, the swish of oiled metal the only sound. "Whether I believe you is not important. What matters now is your invitation. You might not be aware, Ms. Cosmin, but no member of our delegation has been invited to dine at the palace since before Sama."

Teigra gulped and sat up straight. So *that* was why she hadn't been sent home yet. It appeared she'd been given a final chance—if only by circumstance, rather than mercy.

Entirely unexpectedly, a dark thought crept forward, giving her the same feeling as she'd had this morning when she'd accepted Calix's invitation in front of Aurelius.

She's been waiting for over five years for this moment. Dorina couldn't get her this invitation. Nor could Urosina. Nor Jaspar. And she couldn't even get one herself!

But I have. She needs me. I can be . . . useful to her.

And I can turn this all to House Cosmin's advantage!

Teigra steadied herself, shocked at her thoughts. This wasn't like her. She didn't think *that* way—using situations and people to further her own goals.

But . . . but why not?

Was it not what Aurelius had been doing this whole summer? Was it not what Ms. Securia had done on countless occasions, exploiting Teigra's loyalties to increase her power? Was it not exactly what Mother would do, in this situation? What the head of her family would want her to do as well?

She placed her hands flat against her thighs, the sweat already starting to form. She did her best to speak calmly. "Then this is a great honor, Ms. Securia. For *all* of us. For even if we both consider the herald's actions shameful, good relations with Ardora are still essential."

"Indeed. It is the purpose of our mission here."

"Then there would be nothing sinful in improving those relations? Not transactionally, like the herald, but for the benefit of civilization across Dynosia?"

Ms. Securia glanced up with the faintest hint of approval. "No, Ms. Cosmin. That would be most proper."

She grinned internally. *It's working!*

"Then I must beg your guidance, Ms. Securia. So I can best serve Mestibes this evening."

Ms. Securia laid down the comb, her eyes twinkling. "My, my, Ms. Cosmin. What an agreeable idea."

56

TEIGRA

Teigra wasn't sure what she'd expected of a royal dinner, but this wasn't it.

During those relatively few times that House Cosmin had been entertained by patricians, the meals were appropriately restrained—a little roast lamb and vegetables, with some goat's milk yogurt and fresh fruit. Finest quality and perfectly prepared, but hardly decadent. A glass or two of watered-down wine would flow among the adults over discussions of the latest happenings in the senate. Then it would be handshakes and back home before midnight.

But this?

The word *dinner* didn't cut it.

This was an *orgy*.

Around a hundred people—and they were all people, with not a single nonhuman present—lay on soft lounges all around the internal courtyard of the palace. The warm night was perfumed by the roses that grew all up the walls. In the center, a band played drums and bagpipes.

And surrounding them was the most mouthwatering feast that Teigra had ever seen!

A dozen roast lambs, two dozen pigs, and three whole oxen were being torn apart by the guests, their brassy skin smelling of garlic and lemon, or basil and rosemary. Great trays were mounded with steaming barley, the same height as herself, drizzled in sesame and mint, alongside fresh radishes and cooked beans, rich cheeses, and crisp lettuces.

All around, in more bowls than she could count, were fruits and nuts she'd never even heard of—dried jujube and elderberry, green pistachio and desert dates. And amongst all of this, placed under three dozen roaring sconces, were *cauldrons* of ruby wine, into which guests were greedily dunking their wide, clay kylix cups.

"A little different from the embassy?" said Calix, reclining around a small circle with the other royals—King Selkus III and Queen Dimitra; the dowager queen, Kallipole; and of course, the glaring face of Princess Zosime.

The princess's two fellow Sisters, as the female fighters were known, Elexis and Pikra, were lurking around the feasting tables, watching her intensely.

"Yes, it is," she said, "but it is always wonderful to see new things!"

Teigra spoke louder than was comfortable, doing her best to follow Ms. Securia's instructions.

Chin up, girl, and hold yourself with pride. Remember, you are no one's kitten, and you won't win favors in that room through deference and good manners. You must speak loudly and with passion. If they insult you, you must come back just as hard. They won't respect you if you don't. And above all remember that you are the voice of the Mestibian senate. Mestibes may seek good relations with all, but we are supplicant to none. We have never apologized for not assisting at Sama. Not once. And we won't start tonight. It would have been sinful to take up arms then, just as it would be now!

"And what would dinner be in Mestibes?" said Zosime, lounging back in a pink himation, her full cleavage on alluring display. "A wafer of dried rye, a cup of water and a prayer?"

The king roared.

Teigra's first instinct was to recoil.

Come back at them. You can do this!

"No, Your Highness," she said, the words half choking against her instincts. "Just a small bowl of restraint and a glass of intelligent conversation. Though I doubt such a meal could be prepared in *this* room."

The king howled even louder, and the queen gave her offspring a teasing poke in the ribs. Even Calix gave a little chuckle as he popped an olive past his thick, black beard.

The only person who didn't laugh was Zosime, who bored hateful holes with her glare.

They all chatted away in the circle for a good while, with the king and queen adding texture to the lives of famous farming families she'd met. Despite her nerves, she was not only able to keep up with the conversation, but *contribute*, telling stories about some weak attempts to drive down prices, failed jokes and little cultural misunderstandings.

Now and then, she exchanged a few words with the prince, who mostly seemed content to listen.

It was strange. On passing glance, he looked like an utter brute— a drunken, dangerous thug of the worst kind. But up close, he was quiet and restrained. Even the way he sat on his couch was bunched up, as if he wished to inflict as little of himself on the world as possible.

"You aren't drinking your wine, Teigra?" said Zosime, during a lull.

"No, Your Highness. Contrary to recent events, I am not much for drink. I will defer to you in that regard."

Zosime didn't laugh as the others did. Yet, some flicker of mirth tweaked on her lips. "What a shame our contest wasn't held at *Sama*. Then you could have been a true Mestibian and avoided it altogether."

There was a collective *ohhh* from the others. All except Calix, who went even quieter.

Teigra hunted for a good comeback, but none came. "Your . . . your polity may seek to solve things through violence. But we work in different ways."

"Different? Like letting the Rinathi regain their strength after the Third? When every other polity wished to squash the vermin for good?"

Teigra recalled the lessons that Ms. Securia had given her. "All of the Five's children deserve to thrive, free from the burden of their parents' sins."

Zosime grinned. "Well then, I'm sure you'll be happy to see the Rinathi *thrive* all the way to the gates of Mestibes?"

Teigra's stomach churned.

No . . .

The queen rested a hand on Zosime's shoulder, giving her a *play nicely* expression.

"Oh, it's just a joke, Mama. Just a little rumor I've heard amongst the sailors. There are whispers in Mestibes that the Rinathi will soon invade. Our old friend Xiber has returned, it seems."

In her peripheral vision, Calix and the king both went rigid.

Zosime grinned. "But it's probably just a misunderstanding. I'm sure the envoy can clear it all up. Can't you, *Tiggy*?"

In the silence that followed, a question she'd wondered months ago—when she'd tried to confront Zosime at Palistrada Xiphos—was finally answered.

Who else in the royal family besides Zosime knows the truth? Of the coming invasion? Of the real reason for Aurelius's mission?

The answer was none of them. Not one.

All the rest of them had moved forward in their seats. Their eyes hung on her silence. And none more so than Calix, his expression practically pleading for her to deny it.

Teigra gulped. She *could* deny it. Of course, she could. It would be better for Aurelius that she did. It would allow him to keep whatever fiction he'd built with the prince.

But Ms. Securia's words came back to her. Here, Teigra was the voice of the senate. The institution that housed the destiny of House Cosmin. And the senate's position on this matter was clear.

She exhaled heavily.

And she confirmed the coming invasion.

The royals gasped. All except Calix, whose eyes turned as heavy as her own stomach.

A shard stabbed through her. She'd been angry at Aurelius for his carelessness. But was this too far?

"Oh, how *awful*," said Zosime, without sympathy. "But given what you've just said, you won't be seeking any military assistance from us? That would be ever so hypocritical. Trying to get Ardora to fight the very forces that Mestibes kept alive?"

"No, we won't!" she snapped, taking pleasure in the princess's surprise. She spoke next with the voice that Mother used when speaking to the plebian classes. "The Mestibian senate will not strike *any* alliances on this matter. We believe all combatants must be allowed to see the errors of their ways, even the Rinathi. And should the worst come, we are confident Mesti will bring aid to her children, filling all aggressors with her reason."

"Well said!" barked the king. An eavesdropping group nearby, dressed in green fabrics and including the most enormous man she'd ever seen, also nodded their approval. "We can't force you to be sorry for not showing up at Sama, but at least you aren't going to beg for help when you wouldn't do the same!"

"Yes," said Zosime, turning to Calix. "Thank Ardor we haven't had anyone from Mestibes trying to snake their influence onto us. Aren't you pleased to hear that, brother?"

Calix grunted, his eyes fixed on the floor.

"Hah," said the king, jumping unsteadily on withered legs. He wielded his walking stick like a sword—eliciting laughs from nearby sofas and a concerned look from the queen. "I'd like to see them try! You Mestibians are good with your silver words, but nothing can pierce the heart of an Ardoran! We fear no army! We fear no—"

It all happened so fast.

The king collapsed, his whole body shaking.

Blood poured from his nose and ears.

His thin limbs twisted up like a dying spider.

There was a sudden break in noise as the band stopped. The surrounding families rose, the green-clothed ones nearest showing some strange combination of shock and anticipation.

Calix moved quickly, taking his father's head, adjusting it to the side, reaching in and scooping out the vomit which had pooled in his cheeks.

"It's alright, Dada. Just hold on," he said, with a calm she couldn't fathom. "It will pass."

The king's eyes were terrified. His twisted hand grasped at his son's strong forearm, like a drowning man reaching for rescue.

After what felt like hours, but must have been no more than a minute, the shaking stopped, and the king was still.

With utmost grace, the queen helped her husband up, wiping away the worst of his mess. Loudly, and with a forced laugh, she said, "Oh dear, just like old times! Gorging yourself sick and getting all excited! Let's go change so you can tuck into *seconds*, eh!"

The crowd laughed with relief. The king waved to them, his strength seemingly returned. Zosime moved effortlessly through the crowd, bringing the conversation and laughter and music back to full volume.

In a matter of moments, it was like nothing had happened—if not for Prince Calix, kneeling in the red puddle of bile and blood and half-digested food.

"Are you all right?" she asked, placing a hand on his broad shoulders.

Tears welled in his eyes, and he turned away in shame. "I should take you home."

57

TEIGRA

CALIX WAS SILENT ON THE RIDE BACK—KEEPING HIS WHITE STALLION AT a gentle pace through the midnight city. She'd asked if the king would be all right, to which he'd muttered a few platitudes of, "It's just something that happens."

But as much as his words wished to dismiss the topic, his body told a different story. Even sitting behind him in the saddle, he bore a demeanor she'd seen before—one which had stared back at her for years in the wavering troughs of suddenly silent stables.

The prince was carrying great pain. He held it in the grip against the reins and in the stuttering of his breath.

Without thinking, she reached around and placed her hand on his forearm, right where the king had clutched him, feeling the cold tension beneath his skin. "I know you only asked me to dinner to be kind. And I know that I am just a low envoy from a whole different polity. But if you ever need to talk, I am here. I know what you must be going through."

"How could you understand this?" he said, without anger.

"My . . . father died when I was fifteen," she said, omitting the full truth of that tragedy.

His body untensed. "I'm sorry. That must have been awful."

"Yes, Your Highness," she said with a weak smile. "It was. And it still is."

They rode in silence. When he next spoke, his voice was barely audible. "How did you survive something so terrible?"

"I had to stay strong for my family," she said, giving his forearm another squeeze as they reached the embassy gate. "More than money, or fame or titles, duty and family are the only things that really matter. Don't you agree?"

As he helped her down, his eyes shone in golden resonance. "Yes, Ms. Cosmin. I agree. I agree *entirely*."

Then he disappeared back down the street, back toward the palace of wax smiles and comforting lies.

The poor man. He has to bear so much.

When she entered the embassy compound, Aurelius was waiting. "How did it go?" he asked, rushing to her side.

Her jaw clenched. There was something repulsive in his voice. *Desperation.* Wanting to know whether his *relationship* with the good and decent man he'd been tricking for months was still intact.

Would you have noticed his pain, Aurelius? Would you have cared that his father is dying? Or would you have cursed the king for ruining your moment? For messing with your mission?

"Oh, Aurie," she said, conjuring all the doe-eyed, bachelorette fascination she could. "It was simply *magical*."

It took all her willpower not to turn around and see his expression as she clicked the door closed.

58

AURELIUS

SIMPLY MAGICAL.

The words had knocked around his head for five fucking days. At first, he'd thought nothing of it. It was laughable to think of *Teigra* as a threat. To him? For the affection of a man?

And yet, with each passing day the gnawing worsened.

Things were not going as expected.

By now, the prince was supposed to be chasing him. He should have been groveling at his feet for how he reacted in the vineyard, with all that disgraceful yelling and grabbing of his wrist, the grip so hard it left bruises and little puncture marks in his soft skin. He was supposed to be scared, relieved, desperate to connect, and fearful that Aurelius would expose him!

Instead, Calix was *ignoring* him.

Just this morning, he'd visited Palaestra Xiphos, shooting Calix a dashing smile as he neared the bathhouse tunnel. And the prince had just walked right by. As though Aurelius was just another face in the crowd. As though he didn't have a huge dagger hanging over his head!

As though Aurelius was nothing . . .

He couldn't imagine *Teigra* was the cause of that. An evening with her had all the impact of being hit with a lettuce.

Oh, she was all right when she knew her place—being a rapturous audience to his tales of debauchery. But she had no right to sit at the high tables of power, where one was expected to dazzle and captivate, not just soak it all up like an old rag.

And yet, the rumors were *everywhere*. Every bachelorette in the city whispered some story of seeing them together. Of stolen kisses and fleeting touches.

And Teigra appeared to be spending longer away from the embassy during the day . . .

It was nonsense, of course! She was probably just out doing her pathetic little envoy role. And Calix was obviously gay—otherwise he would have found himself a wife years ago. It couldn't be the reason!

And yet . . .

Simply magical.

A few days later, while walking the same dockyard paths he'd strutted in triumph just a week earlier, he decided enough was enough. This wasn't who he was. He didn't stand back and worry. He made others worry. He didn't get outplayed. He outplayed others!

Calix was wrong to suggest that Aurelius might be *jealous* of her. The only reason he cared was that Teigra was messing up his carefully laid plans. Swooping in and damaging his long journey of redemption.

And he wouldn't stand for that.

When he arrived back at the embassy, closer to dawn than dusk, he marched straight past his building and towards the front door of the main residence, just as Calix had done when he'd invited Teigra to the palace.

He completely ignored the dark-skinned centaur that rode past him in the opposite direction, grabbing a pomegranate from the tree without stopping. The messenger from Mestibes came every week. It wasn't a special event, although this was very early in the day for a delivery.

He was going to set Teigra straight. Winning over the prince? Getting the military contract? Regaining his rightful position as heir to the archon? It was too important to be messed up by some selfish amateur.

He would tell her that. Family or not, she did not want to make an enemy out of him. She knew just what he did to his enem—

He'd expected a quiet building. But the others were all awake, standing in the entrance lobby—Teigra and Securia and Jaspar and even the grumpy centaur who tended the grounds and occasionally served him what passed as a meal.

The gathering had the air of a funeral, the attendants dressed in sleeping tunics and holding flickering oil lamps.

Ms. Securia's expression was even graver than usual. Teigra's face was drained of color.

"What is it?" he asked, glancing at the scroll in the high envoy's grip, the yellow ribbon and owl seal of the senate cracked open at the top.

Ms. Securia gave him a somber look, paused, then handed him the parchment. "Xiber Feron has crossed the Synoro River, Your Excellency. She makes for Vaticily."

59

TEIGRA

WAR . . .

Dawn crept into Ms. Securia's office. The high envoy's hands were tented across her face. Jaspar paced the small room, nearly tripping over his toga, rereading the message from Lucius Scipio, Censor of the Senate.

Teigra pressed her back against the shelves of codices, running her hands against the smooth, comforting goat skin.

It wasn't possible. Blood and death and fire and destruction? It just *couldn't* be possible!

"Five days ago," muttered Jaspar. "This warlord crossed the border five days ago."

"So it would seem," said Ms. Securia. "The senate is going on whispers. The key information appears to have gone directly to the archon."

"And the belief is that she will seek Vatic's favor to launch an invasion of Mestibes? To visit the oracles and everything?"

"Yes."

"Then we must act!"

Teigra nodded furiously. The bronze moon was a week away, and everyone knew that was when Vatic received requests for favor. Soon, Xiber would climb the mountain and commune with the god of fate! Soon she would receive his answer! Then she would be heading back to Rinath to commence her invasion.

It could happen any day. There's no time left!

"Calm yourselves," said Ms. Securia. "Obviously neither of you have made the holy pilgrimage."

They shook their heads. Teigra had never even *met* anyone who had.

It was famously the most brutal of journeys, particularly if you wished to see the high oracles at the summit, with the path full of tests and trials and twists. It was only undertaken by heroes and conquerors and those facing the most momentous decisions.

"A fortnight is not enough time to prepare for the ceremonies," Ms. Securia continued. "Not for the high oracles, anyhow. The rule of the wild applies in Vaticily. No beast may be put to burden in aid of a man. That means no steeds, no donkeys, no oxen, no horse of any kind. And no *tourists*, either—no supporting party to assist. Such sins weigh heavily on Vatic's favor. Xiber must trek alone through gnarled paths and forests that fight back against navigation. And even then, there are arcane rituals and sacred rites which must be completed at the summit. If she wants to meet with the high oracles, the children of the god himself, then it is a moment of a lifetime. It is *not* something one rushes."

"So, she is traveling for the *next* bronze moon?" said Teigra.

"Over a month? Just to climb a mountain and pray a bit?" said Jaspar.

"Only one who has not made the pilgrimage would be surprised at that, Mr. Accola."

"You speak as though you have done it before, Ms. Securia?" said Teigra.

The high envoy glanced briefly at them, before returning to her far-off stare.

"All right then," said Jaspar. "So, we have, what, *five weeks*? Then we have to plan. We should bang down the doors of the royals. Rally military aid before it's too late."

"We will do nothing of the sort!" snapped Ms. Securia.

"But we have to do something!" said Jaspar.

"Indeed we will. We must prepare for a *siege*. A long one. That is the only honorable path."

"A *siege*?" said Jaspar. "Just wait quietly and face the Rinathi on our own? But Ardora can help us, Ms. Securia. We have the time to sign a compact. To apologize for Sama. To buy weaponry. To lay traps! We must—"

"What we *must do* is pay honor to our goddess, Mr. Accola. That is what your senate has demanded. We must show faith that Mesti's reason will defeat Rina's discord. We must *suffer* for her. We must *endure* for her. We must show our devotion. And when we can take no more, when we have shown the purity of our commitment, then and *only* then, she will come to our aid. After all, we already have a ruler who has insulted the goddess, squirming her child into the seedy business of military pacts. We will not make it worse by joining him!"

Jaspar scrunched his nose. "*Aurelius*? Is that what he's been doing, here?"

Ms. Securia gave Jaspar nothing, and he turned instead to Teigra. She did her best to keep her face blank, but his betrayed expression showed that she'd failed.

"Oh ... I didn't know," he whispered. "About *any* of this."

Teigra turned away in shame.

She should have told him earlier. If Ms. Securia knew, then it was only right that he did as well. The high envoy already kept much from him and took all the credit for his work as well. And after all, he had been so good to her and had trusted her with so much.

And this is how I repay him?

"So ... what are we to do?" he asked, his voice cracking a little.

"Mr. Accola, advise our friends across the polity of the news. *All* of them. Every smallholder. Every market stall owner in the city and beyond. Our envoys may be gone from the rest of the greater polity, but we still have our old contacts. Send word to the fruit wholesalers in Cherrystone. The bird rearers in Port Nikrizo. There is no point keeping this a secret—the Ondocians will get wind and spread it around. They *always do*. We must impress the urgency of our plight, but without placing any undue pressure. Am I understood? We are *not* calling in favors. We are *not* twisting arms. We must rely on our efforts over many years to speak for themselves, and hope that our friends make the right decisions. Any assistance which may be freely offered would be welcome—early access to food or materials or additional supplies being granted in time to fill Mestibes's stores. Go! To work!"

Jaspar snapped to attention, clearly relieved to have direction.

"Remain here, Ms. Cosmin," said Ms. Securia, as Teigra went to follow Jaspar out, hoping to apologize for keeping him in the dark on the herald's actions. "And close the door."

She did so, more in confusion than concern. The two of them looked at each other in silence.

Without averting her gaze, Ms. Securia placed another scroll on her desk. It was beautiful: the creamiest-looking parchment Teigra had ever seen. Kanilada Cream, she was sure, with edges glinting with gold. The red wax seal over top had already been broken, but she could just make out the top half of a letter "C".

"This letter was handed to me yesterday morning by the royal courier," she said, her eyes narrowing. "It appears that His Royal Highness wishes you to attend the Rose Rain Ball as his guest of honor."

Teigra took a step back. There had to be some kind of mistake. The dinner they'd shared a week ago had given her a new perspective on the prince, but they hadn't spoken a word since. Now he wanted her to stand alongside him, the future ruler of the city, in front of everyone's gaze, at a *royal ball*?

"Me?" she spluttered.

"Yes."

"As his *date*?"

"So it would seem."

Teigra reached for her pendant. On the one hand, she couldn't think of anything worse than being there, with every other woman judging her for being with the most eligible bachelor in the city. And this was hardly the time. Not with the prospect of war still fresh in the air.

And yet, part of her also wished to see him again. There had been something there last time, hadn't there? Some kind of connection?

Is it possible that the prince isn't gay? Is it possible . . . that he actually likes me?

"And what is your decision?" Teigra asked. She knew that attending was not her own choice to make.

Ms. Securia took Teigra firmly by the wrist and dragged her to the statue of Mesti. The high envoy laid Teigra's palm against the cold, sanctified metal, right over the breast of the celestial strix.

"You are to answer truthfully, Ms. Cosmin. Under the gaze of your goddess, where a lie will incur a curse beyond any mortal punishment I could deliver. Do you understand?"

She nodded, her breath stuttering. "I do."

"Did you deliberately assist the herald at the Wax Crack?"

Her heartbeats slowed in the certainty of her honesty. "No."

Ms. Securia pressed her flesh more firmly. "Are you now party to any effort to trick or ensnare His Highness into granting a military pact to Mestibes?"

"No!"

"And do you care about him?"

The calm deepened still. "I do. He is a good man who carries a heavy burden."

Her skin didn't burst into flames against the metal. After a time, Ms. Securia closed her eyes and released Teigra's hand. "Then we must make sure you are dressed for the occasion."

60

AURELIUS

"War?"

The giantess hooker was a pro. She hissed the word at exactly the right volume to gather them in—just soft enough to be alluring, but just loud enough that everyone could hear.

It was a quiet night at the Beautiful Bunch. As few humans as the bar usually got, the appeal of the Rose Rain Ball, happening a mile or so to the east, had still sucked the gravity of merriment away from this part of town.

From the ringed balcony, Aurelius counted no more than ten drinkers below, holding their wine as close as their desperation.

"I'm afraid so, Hemlock," he said, leaning back precariously as the others gathered around—giants in skimpy pelts, a few humans in sheer fabrics, and even a kobaloi or two, one of which popped up right behind him, its tiny tits a-wagging, in a sad attempt to scare him into falling.

He paid her no mind, focusing instead on his third or eighth mug of wine.

Gods, it was good!

All these last three days had been good!

After two months of deprivation, he had almost forgotten the glory of the grape—that upfront explosion of flavor and the comforting warmth of the linger. And this vintage in particular was better than any of the watered-down swill from back home. You could practically taste the fucking sunshine in it . . .

His gaze rose to the crowd. There were expectant looks on faces of hugely variable size.

After a moment of haze, he remembered. "Oh, yeah, *war!*"

"It can't be true!" said one of the humans. "The Rinathi are going to invade?"

"Pfft," spat a giantess, hocking a fat gob onto a wooden bucket a few feet away. "Gonna invade *them*, not us. My da' fought in a Brotherhood during the Third—back when those fucking red-cloaks actually let us full bloods in. He said we 'ad the chance to kill all them Rinathi! But it was *your lot* that stopped us!"

She prodded a huge finger into his chest.

Aurelius grasped the single digit and shook it, as much to steady himself as for the companionship. "I couldn't agree more, Oleander. Kill 'em all I say! What does Rinath bring Dynosia? Nothing! Ardor brings wine and feasts. Vatic brings medicine. Ondo brings gold and luscious fabric—just like you're wearing tonight, Mousebane, don't think I haven't noticed!" He said this to an enormous figure at the back, with a half bolt of shit fabric tied around her broad shoulders. "But what does Rina bring, eh? Just steel and sand and snow and chimera piss."

They all laughed.

Or he assumed it was laughter.

Either that or the kobolai were making noises like spooky spirits.

Probably laughter.

"So, what you gonna do?"

"Now don't you worry your pretty little . . . ah . . . *enormous* face about it, Nightshade," he slurred to another of the giantesses, who didn't even have the decency to stay in focus. "I've got a plan. Got a man I've been working real good. Well, you whores know how it is.

Been getting him real invested. Inveshtad? Inverstid? Whatever. He can't keep his hands off me."

"Then why ain't you with him?" snickered one of the kobalos, bouncing from his left ear to his right. "Why you here like a sad old drunk? Pin dick sad old drunk!"

"Oh, you know. He likes me *so much* he's been staying away. Scared of his feelings."

Aurelius could tell from the looks of the humans up back—raising their eyebrows and shaking their heads—that they knew *exactly* what he was talking about. Course they did.

"But if he keeps staying away," he continued, "I got other plans! Cause I know his secrets!"

Oleander snorted. "Yeah? And you reckon you got a month till it all goes pussy up? Then what you waiting for? If I 'ad dirt that could save my people, I'd be out there making it 'appen!"

He waved his hands. "I'll do it. I'll do it. I'm just waiting for the right moment."

"When would that be, eh? After the first arrows've been fired?"

Poor Oleander, he thought, draining his mug. She didn't have his expert sense of timing. Of course he'd do it. There was no reason not to. Calix'd had his chances and used 'em all up! He'd been given all the space he could want. And he was still staying away? From *him*? From the fucking *herald of Mestibes*?

Well, that was what Mother said when she first gave him the mission, right? If you can't seduce him, blackmail him?

That was the next step.

And he would do it.

If Calix didn't yield, then he'd ruin him!

He didn't care if he harmed Calix. He didn't care if it got him *killed*! He was on a mission. That was all that mattered! This was his future at stake!

He would do it!!

Any second now he would do it!!

So do it, you pathetic fuck! What is wrong with you? Have you lost your touch?

His mouth washed with wave after wave of sweet crimson.

But ... he saw something in me ...

Better than all of this ...

He saw ... me.

"Oi, Mestibes?" came a voice from beyond.

Ahead were three giants, all dressed like the barman and all doing an amazing trick of synchronizing their movements a few feet from each other.

"Hmmm?" he said. The rest of the crowd was nowhere to be seen.

"I said, what can I get you?"

His forlorn mug was wrapped in a grip so tight the clay had carved grooves into his hand. "Can you get the old me back?"

"'Fraid that ain't on the menu, friend."

He wrestled with his tunic and pulled out his coin purse. Alongside it fell a folded parchment page, which fluttered onto the bar.

It had come to the embassy yesterday morning, addressed to him. It was closed with a fat wax seal. The deep valleys of glistening teal formed a "F".

On his third attempt, he scrunched the letter back into the crevasses of his clothing.

She can wait, he thought, dropping the purse with a golden clatter. "Keep the drinks coming until either the purse runs dry, or the cellar does."

61

TEIGRA

THE PETALS DID INDEED FALL LIKE RAIN, FLUTTERING ACROSS HER shoulders in warm-toned droplets.

The Floret Tholos was the most beautiful building she'd ever seen, with rose thickets climbing all up the walls and the slatted ceiling, forming a garden of blooms overhead, just as the finest frescos might be painted back home.

To the sound of lively music and the kiss of warm breezes, five-hundred couples drank and danced the night away. It was a joyful, disorganized display, kicking up the ankle-thick carpet, with not a single structured dance to be seen.

And all Teigra could think about was the children in the mid and lower polities of Greater Mestibes, without the benefit of the thick walls of the city proper.

The monastery at Zateniza.

The marble quarries at Katharo.

The parchment-making town of Apaderma.

The forested village of Plasios, famed for its musical instruments.

The clay works at Camena!

They would all be burned alive by the coming invasion, as swords cut and spears thrust and blood poured down the streets.

In some ways, they might be lucky to have it end so quickly. Unlike the citizens of Mestibes proper, who would face the drawn-out death of a *siege*.

She'd read about sieges. It seemed a horrible way to die. Starvation and thirst. Filth and infection. Families doing everything they could to survive, betraying every moral, one after the other, until even the best turned bad, murdering best friends over the last crusts of rotten bread.

And it could all be prevented . . .

She'd been fighting that thought for days now.

The senate believed it was the will of Mesti to not take up arms. They believed the goddess abhorred violence in any form. That she respected reason and peace and treaties instead.

And after all, those same senators were so much smarter than her. And they were so much wiser than her. And they were so much older and more respected and *better* than her!

And yet, didn't they know? The belief that Mesti demanded passivism . . . that had only existed for a few decades! Only since the signing of the Compact of the Grove at the end of the Third Dynosian War!

The Lapiso Library was *full* of stories of the brave champions throughout Mestibes's long history who'd invented brilliant military strategies to save their homeland. Her grandfather had been one of them—a proud ruler who'd given worship to Mesti not through inaction, not through standing around and hoping for divine intervention, but by finding the smart way to win. By using the tactics so clever and inventive that no other polity would even think of them.

But to just stay back and do *nothing*? To know that war was coming and not make military preparations? To not buy arms? To not make alliances? To not train the sculptors to fight? To not have the poets write inspirational battle verses? To not have the glaziers turn their strange and volatile powders into weapons that could scald and injure, poison and obscure?

It just didn't make *sense*!

"I'm sorry," said a deep voice by her side. "I fear I have been rather dull company this evening."

Prince Calix was dashing in his formal military uniform. Other men were dressed similarly—those of the upper nobility of the fighters at least. But none looked as fine or as commanding as their strategos.

His breastplate matched the curves of his enormous muscles. A full helmet covered much of his face, bearing the largest plume that Teigra had seen since Princess Zosime saved them from the harpies, all those months ago.

In comparison, she looked plebeian in her yellow and orange stola, borrowed from Ms. Securia—beautiful quality, but about thirty years out of fashion.

She gave him a guilty look. "Please don't apologize. I have just been . . . well, it isn't important. Your uniform looks wonderful."

"A necessary burden," he said. "When I was first initiated, we didn't have such things. The Brothers and Sisters wore whatever they liked." He sighed slowly. "More luck to all the Greens here, that they can get away with wearing whatever is in fashion."

Dashing though the uniform was, Calix had a point. The formal uniform of Ardora was very different to the ramshackle leathers and half-to-full nudity the old scrolls had described of the Brothers and Sisters. It was, if anything, closer to the description of the *Rinathi* uniform—all glinting metal and sweeping cloaks.

She wondered if that was intentional. Some kind of boast for beating them at Sama? For *him* beating them at Sama? Or maybe it was just something, *anything* to knit a society back together?

According to the scrolls, the Ardoran military had transformed into a smaller and more exclusive club in the seventeen years between the Third Dynosian War and the Battle of Sama. It was a luxury of peacetime. Eldest sons and daughters of noble Red families were made captains of small Brotherhoods and Sisterhoods, and were picky about who else they recruited. Whole armies worth of men and women who would previously have been blooded were turned away for not "meeting the captain's needs and expectations."

And in one fateful night, at the first test of war in almost two decades, that exclusive club had been wiped out. The fighter nobility had lost an entire generation of eldest sons at Sama. All in a single storm, before a single sword could clash.

Teigra couldn't imagine the grief and upheaval that must have caused. Not that she needed to *imagine*. Jaspar had told her all about the last five years. About how the internal power games between the Reds and the Greens had gone into overdrive. How, with the Reds in disarray, some in the Greens had come achingly close to launching their own bloody claim to the throne.

And they might have, too, if not for Calix returning as the glorious Hero of Sama. The man who had single-handedly defeated the invading forces. The man who would one day be their conquering king. How he had spent his first few years back home rebuilding the Brotherhoods from scratch, with Zosime doing the same for the Sisterhoods. And not just rebuilding, but expanding dramatically—back to the size they'd been during the Third.

A necessary burden?

Perhaps the uniforms were part of that rebuilding? Too many new and rough fighters to tolerate a lack of discipline? Too many impertinent ideas to allow the freedoms of old?

Teigra looked at his face, hard beneath the savage lines of his cheek plates.

She still hadn't asked him about his renowned victory on the island.

She wasn't sure why.

Perhaps because he didn't seem to revel in the fame and glory of that day. Perhaps because, without any obvious reason, Calix had famously started to withdraw in recent times, being seen less and less in public. Perhaps because, if she did ask him, she would be reminded that this was a famous champion, someone that she'd *read about* in codices.

And if she thought about *that*, it would make it even more difficult to breathe.

"Would you prefer to dance?" she said, changing the subject.

"I think not."

"Fancy balls not really your thing?"

"They used to be. Not anymore."

"Well, there are worse things than staying sober. *Believe* me."

Calix didn't laugh. Instead, he sighed again. "A future king of Ardora *should* be out there. Drinking and dancing and sneaking off into dark little corners. Being the life of the party. Setting an example. But nowadays these events are little more than a ghastly duty."

"And is that what *this* is, Your Highness? With me? Just another ghastly duty?"

She hadn't meant it to be an accusation. She hadn't meant to say it at all! Yes, the thought had been banging around her head ever since she'd received the invitation, but the words just slipped out before she could stop them.

Calix looked mortified. He rose with a snap. "Ardor, condemn me. I am so sorry, Teigra! I cannot put you through this!"

Her chest tightened. She'd known there must have been some kind of deception. There was no way that a man like him would willingly spend time with someone like *her*. But there had still been some little part of her that had hoped otherwise.

"It's all right," she said, forcing back the hurt. "Please, talk to me."

The prince lay his head in his hands, before finally coming up for air. "You are cousins with the herald. You must surely know that he has...that *I* am..."

"Gay?" whispered Teigra, with what she hoped was a comforting smile. "And that you suffer from ashen passion as well, if we are laying all the truths out. I assume that is why you started withdrawing from society? Some lingering pain from battle?"

The prince stared hard at her, as if expecting her to add something else.

When nothing was forthcoming, he nodded. "Yes. That. Although I don't think the term your cousin uses to describe his inclinations would fit me so well. I have been with my share of women, and found it perfectly enjoyable. But it is only towards men that I feel any . . . there is attraction certainly that I still feel for women . . . but that spark of something deeper than just the physical just . . . it just never seems to . . ."

She found no joy in his suffering, despite whatever trickery was happening. Instead, she had the same urge which always overtook her in these moments—to push down her own pain and soothe the wounds of others.

To heal.

To help.

To be *useful*. Even if no one noticed or thanked her for it.

She took his unresisting arm, ceasing his stuttering explanation, and led him out to the cooler air of the balcony.

As they left, dozens of other couples watched them intently, just as they had been all evening. It was just like the crowd of women who'd gathered at the embassy the morning after Calix had saved her. And every day since, growing in size and voice.

Then, something clicked.

"Your Highness," she said, slowly, "have I told you I'm a lover of stories?"

"No?"

"Well, I'd like to tell you one now. It's a new one. But I would love to hear your thoughts."

He gave a confused look, then nodded.

She put on a bright voice—summoned from her bedside on windy childhood nights. "Once upon a time, there was a prince called Calix. Not *you,* of course, this is someone else entirely. He was big and strong and had the hopes of the whole polity resting on his shoulders."

"Handsome as well?" said the prince, sneaking a tiny smile.

"Oh yes! So handsome that when he attended a funeral in a foreign land, every single eligible maiden, and quite a few who weren't, entirely forgot about the ceremony and spent the entire service talking about him."

"Oh, Ardor! I . . . *he* didn't cause that?"

"Shhh, Your Highness! You're interrupting my story! Now, as this prince grew older, he started spending time in the company of men—big, strong soldiers, just like himself. And he enjoyed it. Oh, he enjoyed the company of young women as well, and even broke a few hearts as he roamed the lands. But all the while, something was missing. Something indescribable. The flesh felt right. But the heart? Something just didn't feel as *good* as it should've."

Tension built in Calix's thick arm.

"Until, finally, circumstance came for him: perhaps one night when the drink was flowing and the "joking" with a close comrade went too far. When neither of them stopped the other. And suddenly, nothing had ever felt more right. All the words in the poems, all the feelings that had been missing for so long? Stomach twisting, heart fluttering, fire across the skin? All of it came at once! Not over a woman, but a man."

Calix's blush burned as red as his cloak.

It was unfair that she should know such things.

It was *Aurelius's* experiences she was borrowing, after all.

Her cousin had figured out his attractions at just twelve years old, and she could still recall the day he'd admitted his feelings about Nihal. It had been summer then, too, standing in the hot stables on a busy race day. He'd been so nervous, that gangly little kid, not yet grown into his slight features.

And how, just as he'd whispered those fateful words of admission, Teigra's father had walked in, obviously overhearing everything.

And as Aurelius's face had washed with a terror she'd never seen on him before—her father had dropped the saddle, thrown his big arms around Aurelius's tiny chest, and said: *my darling nephew, you are loved, you will always be loved, this changes nothing!*

"Have I upset you?" said Calix.

"No," she said with a warm smile, blinking back the tears. "Well, this realization sent a shiver through the prince. It couldn't be! He was to be king one day. Of the land of fertility and passion no less. Where the love between men and women was more celebrated than anything else. He couldn't be in love with a *man*! It would ruin his family. Disgrace his kingdom! And so, what did he do? He buried it. He buried himself. And not just his passion for love, but all of it, his passion for life, his passion for living. He blamed it on war. He fell to the ashen passion. And all the while he hoped that no one would realize the true reason."

Calix shook his head. "I am so sorry, Teigra. I should never have agreed to her plan."

Teigra scowled, picturing the mocking, raven-haired face. "Zosime did this?"

"*Zosime*? Ardor, no. If it was up to her, I would have shouted the truth from the rooftop years ago. She thinks I could rule even as I am. This was *Mother's* idea. She said that with Father the way he is, that the time had come to fulfill my duties. To return to my role as the champion. As the hero. And after the Wax Crack . . . after you kissed me . . ."

Teigra nodded. It was all so obvious.

"Of course. It was too good an opportunity to turn down. It couldn't have been one of the local girls. You'd been around them for decades without showing any romantic interest. Why now, they would say. A contrived courtship, all for the sake of duty?"

"The ultimate insult to Ardor."

"But a young woman from distant lands? Sweeping in suddenly with her strange ways? Showing you the joy you'd lost?"

Yes, people would believe that. They'd *want* to believe that. Princes aren't supposed to be miserable. That doesn't fit the story.

"And instead of saving me, I found a kind young woman to exploit."

She patted his arm. "You did what you had to do. For your people. For your family."

Calix stared with disbelief. "How can you be so forgiving?"

"How can I be angry at someone who puts the happiness of others before their own?"

They walked in silence along the balcony, the necks of every other attendee at the ball craning to see them wherever they went. Craning to be part of some magical story.

If only they knew.

"And so, what was to be the plan," she asked. "A whirlwind romance, marriage in record time, and then? Would people not ask about the matter of an heir?"

"That part would cause no challenge—it never has. But I have no intention of siring children. I know the punishment for bearing a child absent any passion for their existence," he said bitterly. "Zosime is strong and brave. Whatever offspring she sires will be worthy heirs for House Viralis."

"I thought princes would sooner see their polity perish than their siblings on the throne."

"Why? She would lead all the fighters of the land into battle in my name. She would die for me without a moment's thought. And she would make a far better monarch than me."

"You wouldn't just abdicate for her?"

"And disgrace my family name? Cause a civil war between Reds and Greens over who should rule? It may look calm, but there are six generations of resentment in this city, just waiting to be released. They would use an abdication to contest the throne. My people are relying on me to do my duty and keep things stable. My family is relying on me. Everyone is relying on me! And yet, I cannot do what they want! I cannot be what they want! And I cannot do that to *you*. To force you to live a lie, just to save my own faults? I won't allow it!"

Calix was resolute. His intentions were plain.

And in that moment, clear as the night, the paths were laid before her.

She could do nothing, as she was expected to do. She could comfort Calix and forgive his trickery. She could leave his side and return to the embassy, helping Ms. Securia prepare for a siege in which most of Mestibes would die.

Or...

Her hands shook.

Could she really be contemplating this?

It wasn't what Ms. Securia wanted.

It wasn't what the *senate* wanted. They wanted purity in Mesti's name—to seek friendship without asking anything in return.

But that isn't what friendship is! Friendship is helping each other in times of need!

Calix was a good man. He couldn't bring himself to exploit her.

But perhaps he could bring himself to help a friend?

Her heart felt as if it might explode. If she did this, her whole life would change. She'd be giving away all hope of genuine love, all hope of genuine happiness! All to save her polity.

The face of poor Jaspar swept through her mind. It wasn't like they were a couple. It wasn't like they'd even started courting. But the way he looked at her. The way he smiled. There was *something* there—something better and kinder than any of the awful boys before him. If she was destined to wed some patrician, she was certain she could make something beautiful with him.

A gust of wind swirled rose petals out into the night. As they fell, the faces came back to her, each one a drop of suffering.

And she knew.

How can I do this?

How can I not?

"Xiber Feron has crossed for Vaticily," she said, so quiet she wondered whether she'd even spoken.

Calix's expression made it clear that she had. And that he

understood the terms of what she was offering. "You . . . would do this? Knowing all that you know?"

A tear rolled down her cheek. "For my people? For my family? There is *nothing* I wouldn't give." Their fingers entwined. He was shaking just as hard as she was. "Don't you agree, Your Highness?"

A look of sorrow and thanks swept his beautiful face. "Yes, Teigra. I agree *entirely*."

"Well, then. Are they watching?"

"Every person here."

"Then kiss me," she whispered. "Kiss me as if the story was real."

He removed his helmet, taking her smallness into his arms and pressing his lips against hers. He kissed her as though she was someone he wished to never let go of. As if his lips could revive long-lost memories.

And she felt nothing.

When Calix withdrew, the cheer which greeted them was deafening—men pumping their arms and young women crying with joy. Teigra squeezed the prince's hand and forced the warmest smile she could manage.

He took the cue, drawing her closer and raising his helmet victoriously, just like a commanding warrior from a story, returning to his people in glory.

Just like a shadow stepping back into the light.

Mesti . . . thought Teigra, as the cheers rose and rose, causing a strange surge of self-satisfaction within her. *Is this how Aurelius feels all the time?*

62

AURELIUS

AURELIUS AWOKE TO GUTTURAL SNORING. THE OLD HAY OF THE mattress scratched half of his naked body. The other half was cocooned in a humid cave of fur-covered stock and the stink of unwashed man.

The tiny room was unfamiliar, and it took a few moments for the events of the last night to creep back—sticky and red, sweaty and rank.

He'd ventured to the southern outskirts, to where the polity-proper rolled into the dozens of mid and low polities beyond. A place of rowdy pubs and rowdy men. A place that housed Palaestra Ampelos, wrestling school for the farmers. A place full of men who were thick in *every* possible way.

There were closer piss joints and closer rooms, but those were near Kastro Machiton. And last night, that was the opposite of where he needed to be. Because last night, he'd heard the hideous news on the street, practically bellowed from every red-cloaked shithead.

Calix and Teigra had kissed at the Rose Rain Ball. And rather than spontaneously vomiting, the idiots of this city were cheering! *Cheering!*

Aurelius dragged himself from beneath the barely familiar, booze-laced lump on the bed. He dressed quickly—his head pounding—and staggered into the sun-streaked streets. It was already hot as balls, with a heaviness to the air that threatened a storm later in the day.

He patted the square of parchment beneath the folds of fabric. It had been almost a week since he'd received it, and he still hadn't responded.

But she could wait.

He could only imagine what she would offer him, and he was in no hurry to confirm it.

Not yet at least...

He blocked the worst of the sun and gathered his bearings. Just as he was about to start the long walk back to his own bed, he was confronted with the last person in the entire city he wanted to see.

Across the street, chatting amiably to an old man tending a stall stacked high with eggs, was Ramuna Securia. Their eyes met properly for the first time since she'd shared the news of Xiber crossing. Not that he'd needed her for that, as it transpired—the messenger centaur had also left a letter from the archon on his own doorstep with the same news.

Rather than shoot her usual glare, the high envoy bid farewell to the trader and walked over, the slightest hint of victory on her face. "My, my, Herald. I didn't expect to see you this far out," she said, pointedly glancing at the sign over the inn.

As prudish as she was, she had still been here for almost three decades. And she surely knew that the Swaying Stem was the sort of place you booked by the hour, not the night.

He didn't give her the satisfaction. "Here to gloat about your pet snagging a prince, are you? When it was me, it was an affront to Mesti! But when it is *her,* you are just going to sit back and allow it to happen?"

She gave him an infuriating smirk. "I have no opinion on the matter beyond that which might offend the goddess, Your Excellency. And in this case, I can find no reason to object."

"Prince Calix is *gay*!" he said, dragging her into a quiet alley between the inn and a stable. It was cooler and smelled of fresh hay. "Is that not reason enough?"

"I have been here long enough to know that the prince has been with both men and women. And unlike you, Ms. Cosmin has only pure intentions."

Aurelius scoffed. "No one is as innocent as you think, Ramuna."

"And few, Herald, are as wicked as you imagine."

"*Wicked*? You want to talk about wicked? Fine! For someone like you, I must be the fucking epitome of wickedness. I don't lock myself away every sable moon. I've got the urge for a drink and fuck now and then. And worst of all, I do it with other *men*! Isn't it disgusting? What a beast I am! Do you pray for me, Ramuna?" Aurelius grabbed the nearby wall, steadying himself. "Because I think it is far more wicked to knowingly condemn our homeland to a slow death through inaction, than it is to try and fuck a man to stop it all from happening!"

Her eyes narrowed. "Not long after I was first posted here, my nephew was found in bed with another boy."

"Of course you would say . . ." he started, before his ears caught up. "What?"

"Yes, shocking. A scandal upon House Securia. Cornel was appalled. In his panic, my brother wrote to me, asking what he should do. He intended to send the boy on patrol with the peace corps, slaying beasts and keeping compact with the outskirt towns." She had a faraway look in her eyes. "Would you like to know what advice I gave him, Herald?"

"That a bit of blood and brutality would turn the little sinner into a *real* man?" he spat.

"I said that he was a sweet child. That he was respectful of his mother and had a gift for poetry. I told him that if the boy was prepared to be more discreet with his activities, he should be accepted with understanding."

Aurelius scanned her face for deception but found none. "A nice story. But I am well acquainted with Cornel Securia. He has two adult daughters and no sons."

"Indeed," she said, her lips pursed.

The silence grew as realization bashed through his hangover.

He'd heard the stories from the few, terrified boys back home who shared his inclinations. Enlistment was a simple solution for such *waywardness*. Even the threat of it was enough to silence tongues and stay sinful hands.

Because it was a dangerous life in the Mestibian peace corps. Particularly for those boys more used to swallowing swords than swinging them.

It was a man's life. Danger and death. Beasts and bandits and broken bones.

And if the battles didn't finish the job, there were all those quiet roads and high hills that a feeble young boy from a scandal-averse family might *lose their footing on*.

Securia's face was fire now. "So believe me, *Herald*, any objection I have with your behavior has *nothing* to do with your sexuality."

"Then what?"

She sighed. "Mr. Savair, Mestibes has survived on the border of Rinath for over twenty years since the Compact, and for centuries before that. We have weathered three country-wide wars with our city intact. Our families sleep safely in their beds. And we have achieved this by laying down our arms and building peace. But if we strike a military deal, what message would that send? To Mesti? To the rest of Dynosia?"

"It would say that we are human, Ramuna. That we are prepared to do the rational thing and defend ourselves!"

"No, it would show that we are *cowards*. That we would abandon our values at the first sign of danger. Then the goddess would have no reason to protect us. We would be *dooming* ourselves."

He shook his head. "Some of us, Securia, care more about staying alive than posturing for a voice in the sky."

"And some of us, Savair, care more about what comes after this life than any pain that might occur within it."

Aurelius glared at her sanctimonious smugness. She was a fool for believing this nonsense. And an even bigger fool for believing that Teigra and the prince actually cared for each other.

It was so obvious. Teigra had found an opportunity to seize *his* glory for herself! Beeta Cosmin had always wanted more status, and a daughter as a princess was even better than elevation to patrician class. This had probably been Teigra's plan all along! And Calix? He was just using the opportunity to improve his popularity. To distract everyone from his shameful secrets!

There was no love there. No affection! There couldn't be!

Aurelius stormed off, barely registering the walk back to the embassy. On arrival, he barged into the main building, searching for his deceitful cousin. The centaur grunted that she was *out*.

Out? Out! Probably off with Calix. Probably pushing their ridiculous farce to the rest of the city!

Ignoring the housekeeper's protests, he grabbed a half amphora of wine, downing the lot before he'd even reached his door.

For the first time in months, he went downstairs in his building, to the space set out as his office. Dust had gathered over everything. Sweeping the worst of it off, he slapped the best parchment paper down, taking three stabs to get the pen into the ink.

You fuck with my family's mission, Tiggy? Then I'll fuck yours right back!

He wrote:

Her Most Serene Majesty, Sabina IV, Archon of Mestibes,

My darling Mother, I write to update you on my important work in Ardora. Over the last two months, my efforts have been tireless and ingenious, and significant progress has been made in our mission to win a military alliance from Prince Calix. I have no doubt that were more time available, I would certainly achieve the mission you set for me . . .

A sick grin grew on Aurelius's face as the ink soaked into the creamy leather.

However, given the time imperatives we now face, cousin Teigra and I have come upon an alternative plan. She will now be the one to win favor with the prince, with the ultimate intention of marrying him to secure the military alliance we so desperately seek.

In this endeavor, I have nothing but praise for my cousin, who has assisted willingly and at my personal direction. We are very fortunate that she, and all of House Cosmin, remain loyal to our cause.

Your son and herald,
- A

He sealed the letter with wax, then stumbled back through the main house.

Jaspar looked pleased with the sound of his arrival but reverted when he saw who it was. "Oh, Your Excellency. I thought it might have been . . ."

"I think her arrival would have been accompanied by the sound of the prince's hooves and cheers from the gaggle, don't you?"

"Yes, I suppose so," he muttered, staring out the window at the crowd beyond the gate, now swollen to such an extent it all but blocked the street.

The boy looked drawn, like he hadn't slept in weeks.

Lots of effort preparing for Ramuna's siege, probably. Honestly, the woman's madness knows no end!

"Is there anything I can help you with, Your Excellency?

"I'll likely be out when the messenger comes. Can you include a letter in the next run to Mestibes?"

"Of course," he said, taking the sealed but unaddressed envelope. "To the archon?"

"Oh no," he said, his eyes glinting. "Please direct this letter to the censor of the senate. I wish to thank him for Ms. Securia showing the censor's advice on Xiber's crossing as soon as it came. I also received the news separately, but the high envoy's gesture is still very appreciated."

"Oh, well that's good!" he said, brightening. "I always hated the tension between your predecessor and the envoys. I'm glad we are all working together on this."

"Yes," he said, grinning. "Like one little ship in a storm."

63

TEIGRA

TEIGRA DODGED THE WHIP OF FOLIAGE. THE BRANCHES WERE NO thicker than her pinky, yet were impossibly strong, scratching every inch of her exposed skin.

"Is this what all of Vaticily is like?" she asked, ducking through the tangle.

"No, it is far worse," came the voice of Ms. Securia, walking ahead with considerably less bother. "This is entirely the wrong climate for fate brush. On the path to the holy summit, it grows so thick you can't see the sun. And snakes lurk in the undergrowth, with venom powerful enough to kill a man in seconds. Not to mention the gorgons and the drakons that stalk the forest. And the dryads getting snippy at you for messing with nature."

"Goddess. It sounds awful."

"That is rather the point of the pilgrimage, Ms. Cosmin."

Well, let's hope Xiber faces every one of those challenges.

Their path was on the northeastern side of the bay, around halfway between the city and the Ranios Grotto. It wasn't a popular track. If not for Ms. Securia, she'd never have known it was here.

The branches soon gave way to a hollow among the brush.

Morning light filtered over a strange sight—a floor of gray-white granite among the leaves and grass, upon which was formed a perfect spiral groove, starting from where they stood, wrapping around and around, until it came to the exact point in the middle.

It was so flawless it looked as if it must have been carved; and yet, it was so naturally worn, it was impossible to imagine that it had been.

"There's no statue?" said Teigra.

"Do you think the god of the wild would want a *statue* in his temple?" said Ms. Securia, less unkindly than usual.

"No, I suppose not," she said with a soft laugh.

This temple was the fourth they'd visited this morning—taking the mini-pilgrimage that Ms. Securia did once a week. Teigra had been shocked when the high envoy had invited her, and even more shocked by how different all the temples were.

In Mestibes, all the gods were worshipped in one place. But here, the temples were either the grand grounds where the Ardoralia had been held, or little unloved nooks, barely visited by the locals.

Rina's "temple" was little more than a fireplace up back of a blacksmith. Ondo's was a shack by the harbor, bustling with sailors dropping a single gold coin into a bronze chalice of salt water.

"Do they think we're odd? Praying to the Five as equals?"

"Quaint, perhaps. People down here are more likely to pray to Ardor's dozens of children than another High God. Krasi Ardor, the Goddess of Wine. Lagnos Ardor, the God of Lust. Elfoti Ardor, the God of Fraternity. Honestly, even now, after all these years, I am still uncovering little shrines and lesser gods I didn't know existed."

Teigra traced the spiral with her gaze. "I don't suppose we should ask Vatic to give Xiber the wrong answer?"

"If it would bring you comfort, go ahead. But in my experience, Vatic favors boldness. I would expect the warlord will be viewed favorably."

In her experience ...

Teigra still hadn't summoned the nerve to directly ask Ms.

Securia again if she'd done the pilgrimage to Vaticily. And she didn't intend to push the matter here. Not now that they were finally getting along.

Teigra said a small prayer, even though she knew her chances were slight. After a respectful amount of time, they departed, making their way through the tangled path and back toward the city.

"And how fares His Highness?" asked Ms. Securia when they were back on the bayside path.

"He fares well. He is a very good man."

"Well, that is good, isn't it," she said, in a strange voice. It wasn't genuinely happy. But nor did it carry her usual stiffness.

If anything, it had an air of *sorrow*.

An unusual boldness came over Teigra. "Ms. Securia. Have you ever been in love?"

The woman stopped dead. "What a thing to ask!"

"Sorry. This is all new to me. I . . . I was just curious about your own experience."

After a long narrowing of their eyes, they continued walking. "I was, yes."

"*Really?*"

"You must stop sounding so surprised, girl. But, well, I will admit it was *rather* a long time ago."

"What happened?"

"The usual, I suppose," she said, looking wistfully over the gently lapping brine. "Not long after I moved here, I fell for a young Ardoran."

"Was he a good man?"

"Better than he knew," she said, with a faint softening of her eyes. "That was part of his appeal. The whole thing was a whirlwind, of course. But you'd know all about that?"

She gave a demure look. The lying was becoming easier with each passing day. She hardly even needed to remember to act like a young lover anymore—to blush at the sight of Calix and steal kisses in full view, acting like she hoped no one had seen them.

334

She was quite certain that Ms. Securia suspected nothing about her intentions with Calix. She was quite certain that *no one* suspected anything.

"So what happened?" Teigra asked as the grass-lined path gave way to the horse-print pocketed streets of the city.

"What always happens: *circumstance*. He was from a good family. And though he and I were terribly fond of each other, the Third Dynosian War broke out just a few months into our secret courtship. The whole place suddenly became far more parochial. Mestibes was a friendly nation during the Third, but still, those few that knew of our interactions began asking why the boy would choose a foreigner over his own countrywoman."

"But you loved each other?"

"We did."

"I'd have thought that here, of all places, that would count for something?"

Securia gave a hollow laugh. "Something you will learn, Ms. Cosmin, is that the higher in society you travel, the more one talks about beliefs, and the less one actually lives them. I did absolutely everything I could. But it wasn't enough. He was forced to start courting a local girl as well. And in the end, she prevailed."

"*Absolutely everything*?" asked Teigra, her eyes bulging. "Surely you don't mean . . . you visited the Great Grove?"

Ms. Securia gave a long look to a hanging arbor of white roses, only a few streets from the Temple of Mesti now. "I did."

"And you picked an eternal rose?"

Another pause, the longest one yet. "I did."

Teigra suppressed her gasp. "What . . . what happened?"

They came to a stop just outside the temple. Muffled by the closed door, there came the unexpected sound of hammering. "It matters not what the outcome was, Teigra. The important thing is that I paid my devotion to the Five as best I could. That is what Mestibes has always done. And what we must continue to do."

Ms. Securia entered the temple before she could ask any further questions. But Teigra didn't need to hear her say it out loud. She already knew the answer.

It suddenly made so much sense.

Why she seemed so cold all the time.

Her rose had *withered*. Ms. Securia had put herself on the line. Plucked the rose to show her love. And it had withered, all because of the man's indecision. And since that time, she'd been cursed to never know true love again.

After a moment's reflection, she followed her inside.

Securia was at the back of the hall now, thumbing a codex from the large shelves, all the while cocking an eyebrow toward the stonemason's station. There, a figure sat in front of a mangled block of marble that vaguely resembled a face. A hammer and chisel were held inexpertly in their hands. They were so covered in stone dust, it took a second to realize who it was.

"*Jaspar?*"

"Oh, hello!" he said, bright enough to light the gloom. "Fancy seeing you here!"

"I know! We're never at the embassy at the same time these days."

"Well, we have both had a lot on."

There was no venom to his voice. But still, Teigra felt the sting.

She didn't know if the two of them had been heading somewhere. She'd never had so easy a relationship with a male before, apart from Aurelius, back before all this started.

And she'd enjoyed his company. She'd enjoyed *him*. He'd been a good friend when she didn't have any others. And she was sure that some part of him had felt similar toward her.

And she'd betrayed him. She'd kept him in the dark.

She gave a heavy breath. "I've been meaning to talk to you. I just wanted to say—"

"Are you happy?" he said, his face as open as the evening sky. Little lumps of marble in his fur only accentuated his relaxed air.

"I am."

She wasn't sure if her answer was true. But it was the truth she needed to believe in this moment.

"Then I'm happy for you," he said, giving her the most tragic smile she'd ever seen.

With a suppressed sigh, he brought his chisel up to the nose of the marble bust. He lined the angle up, weighed the force, and swung.

He completely missed the base of the tool, instead smacking the statue right where the nostril would be.

With mocking slowness, the crack spread up and around, encircling the appendage, before it slid to the floor in a shatter of white.

"Oh . . . *bugger*," he said. "I thought we minotaurs were supposed to be good at this!"

"Is there any way to fix it?" she said, stifling a laugh.

"I don't think so. Although I could claim it's a new sculptural style?"

"A face without a nose? I don't think it'll catch on."

"Well fine," he said, dragging a thick block onto the stand without any apparent effort. His face bore a familiar playfulness. "Shall we start over?"

"Yes," she said, taking a seat beside him. "Let's start over."

64

AURELIUS

"A fascinating time to be the herald of Mestibes!" said High Envoy Sophia Fabulosa, as the sunset turned all beneath it to fire. "And how unfortunate that Vatic has fated the duty for you at this time."

Aurelius sipped his third glass of wine, drawn from her personal cellars. The rooftop of the Ondocian Embassy was replete with libations and exotic foods. It was lined with fragrant lavender and bay plants in large terracotta pots, giving way to the best view in all Ardora—the harbor below, the bay beyond that, and an all-around view into the bedrooms and private studies of the rich and powerful houses of Chrysa Touvla, the suburb where most of the city's nobles lived. If one was so inclined, there was no limit to the little secrets one could uncover while partaking of an evening drink.

"I expect you will serve as your mother's chief negotiator during the war? That is traditionally one of the herald's functions, is it not?"

"Who can say?" he said with forced laughter. "There are many back home who believe Vatic will deliver bad news to the tyrant."

"Well, may that indeed be the case. And may the rumors of what

Rinath does to messengers who bring unfavorable terms be nothing but old myths!"

She flicked a strand of blond behind her silk-lined shoulders. It may have looked casual, but Aurelius was certain that every movement of her body, every tone in her voice was a calculated ploy. It was just like the opulence of the hospitality, all designed to show the power of her polity.

"To happier news," she said, thumbing a lavender stem. "I had the good fortune of attending the Rose Rain Ball a few nights back. A shame you couldn't make it. A most enchanting evening."

"So I've heard."

"Ahhh, the herald does keep his secrets close! Will you really not tell me the latest news of the courtship? The whole city speaks of little else. A great heir, lost to sorrow, awakened by the care of a mysterious woman from afar? They say that a grand engagement must surely be imminent?"

He smiled through clenched teeth.

Teigra had barely returned to the embassy since the ball. Too busy being out and about, if the bar chatter was to be believed. Strolling through the agora, hand in hand with the prince. Him plucking flowers and laying them in her hair. Her stealing kisses when she thought no one was looking. Of the whirlwind of it all— from not knowing each other to everyone asking when the *wedding* would be, all in just a few short weeks.

His cheeks hurt from the strain of not screaming. "I really couldn't say."

He stayed for three more glasses before leaving Fabulosa behind —until the sun had set fully, the bronze moon turning the whole bay a ghostly gold.

Their conversation had been a delicate dance, but he'd gathered enough of Fabulosa's intentions. It was just as he'd expected, though that hardly made it better.

She could find somewhere for him to reside during the war, with enough coin and wine to ensure he forgot all about the death he'd leave behind.

And in return?

She was smart enough to leave that unaddressed—*for now*. But it would surely be some humiliating betrayal. Stealing contracts, perhaps? Helping her polity find ways to profit from the coming conflict? Maybe even serving in the court of king Psari, like some house-trained curio?

Whatever her price, his name would be worthless back home. He would be a traitor. The herald who ran at the first clang of steel.

Just a few weeks ago, it would have been absurd to accept such a proposition. He had been on the up. Finally seeing fruit to all his harvests!

But now?

Now Calix was ignoring him entirely in favor of this ludicrous "relationship" with Teigra. And if he returned home, he *would* have to do the things Fabulosa mentioned—liaising with the enemy. Riding into harm's way as some hapless messenger. All while Mestibes was sure to burn to the ground regardless.

And even if by some miracle the polity were to survive, *Teigra* would get the credit. News would already have reached home by now. Securia would have made sure of that. House Cosmin would be the talk of all Mestibes, not him!

Why the fuck wouldn't I take Fabulosa's deal?

Aurelius sighed. It was definitely time to go somewhere rowdy and make sure his half buzz didn't fade any further.

He turned from the gentle bay, then stopped.

A figure stood in front of him, their face lit with the yellow-brown light of the full moon.

It was Calix.

He experienced a disgusting moment of joy, accompanied by an inexplicable desire to run past the coils of salt-crusted rope and embrace him.

He stamped down that urge. He wouldn't give him the satisfaction.

"What are you doing here?" Aurelius grumbled.

"I . . . I thought you should hear it from me," said Calix, his eyes averted. "I intend to ask Teigra to marry me."

The words hit him like a punch to the throat.

The prince shuffled in the silence that followed. "Anyway. I just . . . I just thought you should know."

"So that is that, is it? Throw that at me and now you're off?"

His brow hung heavy. "Do you blame me, Aurelius? Once I learned what you wanted from me?"

"Oh, please. You *knew* I had an ulterior motive. A young, gay noble arrives in the city and immediately tries to bed you. Don't tell me the strategos can't see tactics when they're at play. You knew something was up and you didn't care. You entertained my advances. You wanted to see where it was going. You wanted *me*."

Calix's posture grew resolute. "Maybe I did. Maybe . . . part of me still does. But just because I was weak then doesn't mean I have to remain so. I'm doing what is best for my polity. And that is all that matters."

Calix departed.

Aurelius watched him walk into the silent agora—the stalls wrapped closed in old fabric. Every instinct screamed to just let him leave. To deny him the privilege of seeing him vulnerable. To keep himself locked away, tight and safe, just like all those little stalls.

But as much as he tried to ignore it, each footstep was like a spear to his heart. His breath strained. His chest thundered.

Calix was leaving, never to return. And if he said nothing, this would be the end!

Good riddance! I don't need him! I don't need anyone!

(But he saw me.)

His fingernails dug into his elbows. He had watched countless men leave, and he had felt nothing. But now . . . in this moment . . .

Let him go!

(But he saw me!)

Tears welled in his eyes as Calix faded into shadows.

(BUT HE SAW ME!)

Aurelius ran, catching up and taking the prince by the arm. "Nihal," he panted. "His name is Nihal." Calix gave him a confused look. "Back at the Wax Crack, you asked who hurt me. His name is Nihal."

Calix's expression softened. "Go on."

Aurelius breathed deeply. He had never told the story to anyone. Not even Teigra knew all the details.

"Our families were close. Him being the son of the high priestess of Mesti, me being the eldest son of the archon, it was obvious we would be friends. And from the moment we met, we were inseparable. We could never stand to be out of each other's space. Until we both hit twelve, and our wrestling became a little more *animated*."

"Who realized first?"

"I was the first to kiss him. I didn't even think about it, about how badly I could have messed everything up. But he returned it—scared but hungry. And that was how things stayed. He wanted it as much as I did. But his fucking family, all their crap about tempering beastly urges and the reason of the goddess? It fucked him up, Calix. It fucked him up *bad*. In the years that followed, he'd come and go. Say yes and then cry afterward. Promise we would never do it again, then turn up drunk at my door, begging to be with me."

"What happened?"

"*I* happened. At fifteen, I told him . . . I told him that I loved him, all right. I told him that I would go public for him! That I would renounce my birthright! That I would run away and give it all up to be with him!"

Tears flowed down Aurelius's cheeks.

"And do you know what happened? I didn't get a love story, Calix. I didn't get a kiss on a flower-filled balcony! He ran to his parents and told them all about me. About *us*. He said that I'd corrupted him for all those years. He said he didn't know what he'd been doing. And I was kicked out of the family home. I was turned out onto the street. I was ostracized in public. I was disinherited. At fifteen I became the beast who corrupted the priest. I got all the fucking punishment without any of the fucking reward!"

Aurelius wiped the tears away aggressively, resentful of their presence.

"So you want to know the truth? Yes, this started as me trying to seduce you for my end. And that was all it was. Because that is all *I* am, Calix. I am *not* a good person. I use people. I take advantage of them. I cause scandal and sorrow. Because I know what happens when you open yourself up. When you let someone in. But now . . ."

His hands were clenched so tightly his forearms shook—in frustration at himself, at Calix, at *everything*.

"All of the moves were laid out. If you wouldn't be seduced, then you would be *blackmailed*. I would share your secrets. I would ruin you without a second's thought!"

He could barely breathe.

"But I didn't! And I don't know what that means, Calix. Because I don't do this, all right! Whatever *this* is. But what I do know is that when I see you walking away from me, I just can't bear it. The thought of never seeing you again makes me want to fall down and scream. It makes me want to smash every stall here to pieces and set them alight. Why? *Why?* What the fuck is wrong with me?"

He gripped Calix's tunic, burying his head against his huge chest. The tears cascaded now, drenching the prince's fine fabric. "What the fuck is wrong with me?"

Calix's arms surrounded him, strong and warm, pulling him in like he meant something. He didn't know how long he stayed there, sobbing out the frustration of the last few months. Of the last six fucking years.

When his tears at last settled, Calix rested his head on Aurelius's own, running fingers down his back. "His name was Terim," he said, his voice soft as the sea breeze. "My . . . first. He was one of the first fighters I recruited after I'd been made a captain. He was such a little pain in the ass. Always causing trouble and mischief and making the job our Brotherhood faced that much harder. But as we started our patrols of Greater Ardora, we grew closer. Much closer."

Calix's caress was light.

"One night when he and I were alone on patrol, he just jumped on top of me, pinning me down. He knew what he wanted. He knew what *I* wanted, even if I didn't. It was . . . it was *wonderful*. He was wonderful. And once we started, we didn't stop. Ardor save me, we almost got caught so many times—going out on little expeditions to gather firewood, only to return an hour late and with half the expected load."

"What happened?" Aurelius asked, peeking out from a tear-soaked gap.

"*Sama* happened," he whispered. "We were to sneak in and take the enemy camps. All of us. The entire Brotherhood of Ardora. They would all be hit at once. Every outpost, cutting them off from the Rinathi mainland and killing everyone who remained. But . . ."

"There was a great storm?" asked Aurelius.

Calix shuddered as if naked in a winter wind. "It churned the sea into fury. My Brotherhood was lucky. We all made it ashore, taking our outpost under the cover of the snow. *Xiber's* outpost. But the Rinathi managed to raise the alarm before we killed them all—lighting their great warning cauldron, able to burn the hottest blue even amongst the storm. We didn't even bother to extinguish it. All reinforcements were supposed to be dead. But the other Brotherhoods hadn't made it ashore—their boats were wrecked or unable to even approach. And so, instead, every single Rinathi on Sama came for *us*."

"Was that when you consumed the black brave?"

Calix breathed deeply, steadying himself. "Thousands were coming right for us. There was no escape. There was no time! It was like a test from Rina herself. As if she was challenging us to see if we were more worthy than her own soldiers. And the dead war priest's body was right there—the blood barely dried..."

Calix grimaced.

"We'd all heard the stories from childhood, how the Rinathi drink it to give them strength. It was Terim who made the call, cutting out the heart before any of us could protest. Then we stood in a circle—just the four of us, Terim and Zotikos and Glarus and then ... and then..."

Calix's fingernails dug into his back. Aurelius hugged him closer as the heaves began, the big man falling into desperate, gripping sobs.

Aurelius didn't need to hear the rest of the story. The ending was famous—one soldier was found alive the next day, naked and soaked in blood, surrounded by the bodies of over a thousand Rinathi and three of his fallen comrades.

And the question had long been asked: how could one soldier possibly do all that?

But now, Aurelius knew.

In that moment, Calix had awoken as a satyr.

And he had *fed* on his own Brothers.

"They didn't deserve to die like that!" Calix bellowed.

"They would have died anyway," said Aurelius, hugging him as tightly as he could. "You *all* would have died!"

"In battle! In glory! Not as the husks I left behind to have their throats slit. Too empty and broken to even fight back!"

They stayed like that for the longest time. Eventually, the tears stopped, and Calix pulled back from his embrace, leaving a cold empty where the warm had just been.

Calix gripped his own arms tightly, his eyes red. "I know what happens if I let go, Aurelius. That is why I pulled back from society. Last year there was someone ... someone that I almost fed on. And when I look at you, all those feelings come back. I want to *drain you dry*, Aurelius. These urges in my fucking blood are screaming for me to leave you empty! Even now, when the moon is full, it is taking everything in me to resist! I don't want to hurt you! I don't want to feel this way! But I can't stop it!"

The big man bunched his arms together, as if trying to retreat inside his own chest.

"Goddess, I wish . . . I wish I could have had something with Terim. I wish I could have something with *you*. You are so strong. You know that? To be able to live your life and willing to go public at just *fifteen*? To risk it all for the man you loved? But I can't do that! I can *never* allow myself to be that thing again! So if you care for me at all, please, just let me go!"

Calix turned to leave once more.

Every beat in Aurelius's chest yearned to follow him. To just take what he wanted. To put his own desires first.

The forlorn footsteps faded into the sound of the whistling ocean, beating against the fabric gates of the closed stalls.

And he let the prince leave.

65

TEIGRA

THE AGORA BUSTLED WITH MIDMORNING SHOPPERS. LIGHT GLINTED OFF dew-soaked radishes as Teigra hummed a little tune.

It was all going *so well*.

Last night, over a private dinner at Calix's vineyard, they'd discussed when he might propose. The queen had suggested the first day of autumn, in about a month, and offered to make all the arrangements herself.

That seemed like a good suggestion. It would also mean that public sympathy would be at its highest when news of the invasion came.

In the meantime, Calix would ensure the army was primed—getting into the ears of the captains of the various Brotherhoods and Sisterhoods about the threat of a resurgent Rinath; starting chatter in the junior ranks about how it was high time to get their gear bloody, with all the glory and excitement that battle entailed.

And no one was more qualified to drum up that kind of excitement than the Hero of Sama.

Not that he was anticipating much resistance. The way Calix

talked about it, it didn't even seem an inconvenience for the Brotherhoods and Sisterhoods to be supporting Mestibes. Like all the fighters would *want* to see battle. Like it would bring the Reds together and strengthen their hold on the city.

But what she and Calix certainly wouldn't do was *sign* anything. No announcements. No declarations of allegiance. That was important for both of them. This whole arrangement needed to appear like their courtship—it needed to appear *natural*.

This was not just to ensure that Ardora supported Mestibes when war broke out, but also to ensure her family's reputation was preserved. Her falling in love with a handsome prince, and him coming to her aid in a time of need? The senate would accept that, even if they suspected foul play. And with a future queen in their ranks, House Cosmin would be elevated to patrician status as soon as the engagement was declared.

But she still had to ensure that nothing cynical appeared to occur, otherwise all that goodwill, on both sides, would crumble as badly as Jaspar's statue.

There was commotion from the other side of the stalls, over and above the usual din of haggling and animal brays. Something was moving through the press, creating a wave of excitement.

Then, the cause of it all came into view.

It was the *queen*.

And she was walking right toward her.

Teigra gasped. In over two months in Ardora, she'd never seen the queen in the marketplace, or even in this part of town before.

"Teigra! What a pleasant surprise!" she said, laying a kiss on each of her stunned cheeks.

"Your Majesty! How . . . how wonderful to see you again."

The queen took her by the arm and strolled onward, making polite small talk. As if her presence here was the most natural thing in the world.

It *wasn't*. They'd spoken at the dinners and social events she'd attended at the palace in recent weeks. But they'd never been alone like this before.

"The two of you are the talk of the town, you know," said the queen. "There are many who thought that my son would never find happiness again. And to do so with someone from exotic lands? Remarkable. Simply remarkable."

"It is. I am lucky to have him," she said, her mind clicking like summer cicadas.

The queen looked down at her imperiously.

Was Teigra paranoid, or was there a hint of condescension in that look? The way the nostrils flared with her chin held high, forcing Teigra to look up at a sliver of iris?

"But there is much more to the role than the banquets and the balls. It is hard work, joining a ruling family."

"I am no stranger to hard work, Your Majesty."

"Yes, *horses* isn't it?" the queen chuckled. "How quaint. Of course, being the queen of an entire polity is a good deal more complex than running a little stable. I must manage a thousand competing interests. And one must always ensure the love and loyalty of those of importance."

Quaint? Little stables?

Is she ... mocking me?

"I look forward to learning such skills," said Teigra, scowling slightly.

"Ah, but some things can be difficult to learn. And some people are difficult to convince. Even I had doubters during my courtship. I can't imagine how difficult it must be for someone from so *humble* a background."

Mesti!

Is she ... testing me?

Teigra furrowed her brow. None of this made any sense. This whole courtship had been the queen's idea! But now it seemed she was trying to warn her off of it?

Teigra searched her mind. What would Aurelius do? What devious little plan would he concoct if he was in the queen's position?

Then it came to her.

The equation she'd spoken about with Calix—about how he couldn't have courted any of the local girls, as no one would believe that he'd suddenly fallen for them.

That was true.

Or at least, it *had* been.

But now that the public had seen Calix return to the world of romance? If Teigra was replaced, would people really care? Particularly if the new girl had the right name and the right face and the right hair?

Particularly if that girl comes from the right polity, too?

Her blood pressure rose. So that was it? The queen intended to do the same thing that had happened to Ms. Securia, all those years ago? Boot out the Mestibian girl and find a more suitable local? Because Teigra was just that replaceable?

Well, let's see about that!

"Gyges!" said Teigra, releasing the queen's arm. "Your roses look simply *divine* this morning."

"Oh, thanks, Tiggy!" said the giant. "Ardor certainly 'as been kind these last few weeks!"

"How wonderful to hear," she said with an easy smile. "And how have you been since your wedding? It was such a lovely service."

"Oh, it's been wonderful, lass! The whole thing still feels like a dream. But you'd know all about that, wouldn't you?"

The blush came easily to her face—as easily as the names of the dozen other sellers they passed, alongside the details of all their problems and hopes. All their family squabbles about uncooperative children and jealous siblings.

The small details of small people. The kind that the queen couldn't possibly know or care about.

And all the while, the same question came constant: *when, oh when, would the young lovers be betrothed?*

When they reached the end of the row, she returned to the queen's side. "Your Majesty, you must forgive me. I entirely interrupted you."

The woman smiled with her mouth alone. "It was nothing, child. Nothing at all."

66

AURELIUS

My Darling Dagger was a shithole, filled with a ragtag mix of brawlers so rough that even the Brothers wouldn't take them in.

The sort of people who never got hangovers because they never got sober.

The sort of people who didn't remember a face and didn't give a damn about your story.

And Aurelius was one of them now.

He didn't know how many he'd drunk tonight. It didn't even make sense to separate "tonight" from "last night" from "tomorrow."

It was all just time—time counting down until he sucked up his pride, went back to Fabulosa and took the fucking deal, paying whatever price she set.

It was three weeks until the next bronze moon. Three weeks until it would all be over.

He could probably stretch it another week before going back to her. The Black Night Festival would be held then—the big blow-out of the summer season.

One last night of debauchery and freedom . . .

Then he would take the deal. Then he would be the traitor.

Aurelius didn't go to the Beautiful Bunch anymore. He didn't go to the fountain in Green Heart Park. He didn't go to Palaestra Xiphos.

He could still win if he wanted. He knew that.

But he was *choosing* not to.

It was pouring when he staggered out into the mud-squelching street for a piss—the heavy downpours you rarely got back home.

Back in Mestibes, I should say.

It won't be home for much longer . . .

Just as he was wrestling his cock back into his fabric, something grabbed him from the darkness, spinning him around and slamming him against the rancid wall.

"Don't even think about trying to get away," said a nasty little voice by his ribs. A memory rose of a small, sharp-featured woman, one of the two Zosime always hung around with.

"Yeah," came the voice of the bigger one. "The princess is looking to 'ave a little talk."

On cue, Zosime emerged from the squall in full uniform. Rain ran down the length of her helmet—metal tears over dry eyes.

"I will make this brief, Herald. You are aware that my brother and your cousin's courtship is soon to be finalized?"

"Yes," he said, squinting out the driving rain. "But I'm leaving them alone. Congratulations. I'm out of the game."

She glared at him—the kohl-black of her eyes as dark as the puddles underfoot. "Well, I want you *back in* the game."

"What?" he said. He was too drunk for this. His head spun from the wine, from the rain, from the hit against the wall.

"You heard me, *Aurie.*"

"But, why? What would you gain from—"

The two goons slammed him back against the wall.

Zosime smirked. "You know what you need to know. Are you in? Or are you out?"

Ahead of him, the way back to Calix emerged—a sunlit path amidst the gloom. Breaking them up? It would be easy. He could think of a dozen ways right off the top of his head.

And yet . . .

"You hesitate?" said the princess. "I thought it was your mission here? To claim my brother for yourself?"

The rain turned cold on his skin. "I care enough to let him go."

Zosime stared. Droplets plinked against her armor as she searched his face for trickery. There was indecision there. She was, in her own way, as torn about this moment as he was.

After a long time, she placed something into his unresisting hand.

It was a dark stater coin from the Ardoralia.

There was no mistaking it. The coin had the same chip that had been knocked out of the wood when it had pinged off some armor on the path to his prince. It was the very same coin that Aurelius had tossed across the crowd to get Calix's attention in that tragic moment of his wrestling defeat, all those months ago.

It was Aurelius's coin.

Just as it was Calix's coin.

"He has kept it by his bed, Herald. Ever since that day."

Aurelius ran his thumb over the smooth surface, fighting back the swell of tears.

"My brother deserves someone who can make him happy. Someone who can return him to who he was before all of this wretchedness. And I believe you know just how *wretched* this really goes."

Her eyes bore an answer to a question he had long wondered.

She knows what he truly is. Her goons don't. So she won't say it out loud. But she knows the truth.

She knows that Calix is a satyr.

"Why?" he whispered.

"He will never achieve happiness if he commits to this lie. I have laid doubts within my own family—taken all the steps I can to have my mother try to interfere. But it's too far along. It's all moving too fast. The city is now behind this insanity. So for this to work, I need your help."

He stared at her. "You want the throne for yourself?" he said with a bitter laugh.

The thump from her goons came without need of a command. Zosime's eyes were resolute. Her face lacked even a shred of deception. "I want it for him. For *everything* that he is," she hissed.

The coin weighed heavy despite the lightness of the wood. Was Zosime really saying what he thought? Permitting him to pursue Calix? Get Teigra out of the way, and then he could have him? No more interference?

None of this made sense. There were so many questions. And after all, he'd made a promise to Calix: no more games, no more meddling.

The tearful words of their final meeting rang in his ear: *If you care for me at all, please, just let me go!*

"How can I trust you?" he said, thinking back to another time he'd seen Zosime outside a pub. "Last time we made a deal, it was nothing more than mockery."

Her lip curled. "I have *never* made a deal with you before."

"Yes you did! A month ago? Outside the Storming Stallion! You promised—"

The big one slammed him hard once more. The princess glowered. "I don't know what you are trying to start, but I'm not playing. Do we have a deal or not?"

He pushed past the confusion and the haze of wine. His hand closed around the coin.

As much as he tried to let Calix go, the fates were pushing them together. And given a warlord would soon be visiting those very fates to plot the demise of his homeland, who was he to reject his own destiny?

"I'm in."

67

TEIGRA

TEIGRA LEANED INTO THE WARM WATER. THE SCENT OF ROSEMARY AND sweet fig laced the steam.

The Bathhouse of the Crazed Cetus, near the docks and frequented primarily by Ondocian sailors, was almost empty at this time of night—particularly on the female half. It was neither the biggest nor the nearest bathhouse to the embassy, but it was the one she had started using out of necessity.

Her usual routine in Ardora had been to rise early and bathe before breakfast at the Fragrant Forest Bathhouse—the main facility for the merchant classes of Ardora, located in a discreet spot in Green Heart Park, where the towering trees over the brick line made it seem like you were bathing in the middle of a distant woodland, rather than in the center of a bustling city.

That routine, however, had ceased after the Rose Rain Ball.

Having the gaggle of young maidens outside the embassy gate was one thing, but having them all flock around every time she was naked and wet? That was another.

She hadn't told Calix about the walk with the queen. As close as they'd become these last few weeks, she couldn't risk the possibility that he might also realize what his mother had—that he could just ditch her and find a local girl instead.

She was sure he wasn't that calculating, that there was some true connection between them. But she still couldn't risk it. Mestibes was counting on her.

She stayed for longer than usual in the warmth. Back at the embassy, Ms. Securia and Jaspar would be working long into the night. She'd provided some assistance around the edges in preparing for the siege, but they'd not tasked her with anything major.

She was sure that was because the current negotiations required experienced hands, and not because they suspected any ulterior motive in the prince's courtship.

She felt guilty for not helping them in their long hours. But not *too* guilty. After all, she was serving the polity in her own way, wasn't she?

She departed around ten, the cicadas singing in the warm night.

A hidden voice from near the entrance caused her to jump. "You are out awfully late."

Leaning back against the wall, half-lit by starlight, was Aurelius.

Her freshly washed skin prickled. She had barely spoken to him in weeks, though she had often seen him—sitting up on his balcony, drinking endless cups of wine and staring down at them all, like some kind of demented owl.

"Have you been following me, Aurelius?"

"Now, now. Don't make it sound so menacing. I just wanted to talk."

"We live in the same compound. You can talk to me whenever you like."

"We can talk there if you'd rather? I just assumed you wouldn't want prying ears around when discussing your false romance with the prince?"

She hissed and scanned the dark streets. They appeared to be alone. "Keep your voice down! And . . . it isn't like that, all right? We care about each other. He is getting what he needs. And I am doing what I need to do to save—"

"Tiggy, Tiggy, *please!*" he said, with that familiar, boyish smile. "I already know all of that. Calix told me everything."

She narrowed her eyes. "He did?"

"Yes. A week ago he came to tell me that it was over between us."

"And, what? You couldn't convince him, so now you are trying your luck with me?"

"No, cousin. I let him go. He is yours."

She shuffled awkwardly on the spot. "But, what about your mission?"

"The mission was always to save Mestibes, Tiggy. If I could get myself back in everyone's good graces, that was a bonus. But our home was *always* the main concern. And it is clear you have that in hand."

Teigra licked her lips. It couldn't be that easy. "What is this, Aurelius? We don't speak in forever, and now you turn up all sunshine and light?"

"Look, I just came to offer a truce. If you want to do this alone, I understand. After all, I am sure Calix's family aren't playing any games with you."

Games? How does he know about the queen? I haven't told a soul!

"What . . . what have you heard?"

"Heard? Why, nothing, cousin. I just know how those people think. I *am* one of those people, after all." He looked genuinely concerned. "Why? Has something happened?"

The shield of her skepticism cracked a little. He was right about the games. And he did have more experience dealing with people of that class. Maybe he *was* telling the truth?

"I . . . had a meeting with the queen," she said, slowly. "It was strange. It felt like she was testing me? But I'm probably just being paranoid."

"No, you are right to trust your instincts. And Calix mentioned that a proposal would come soon?"

"On the first day of autumn."

Aurelius grimaced. "At some big fancy party, I'm sure? At the palace?"

"Well, yes?"

"And let me guess, the queen also picked that date?"

"Yes, but—"

"And is making all the arrangements?"

"How did you know that?"

"Oh, Tiggy," he said, shaking his head. "It is really quite obvious. They are training you to be their *puppet*."

"What?"

"Well, not literally. But that is how families like that work. They aren't helping to relieve your stresses. They are doing it to exert their control! They are showing how things will be into the future. Get engaged at a time and place they determine? When they say? How they say to do it?"

"I . . . didn't think about that."

"Most wouldn't. But if they get their way now, they will have established the pattern. They will dictate things *forever*. Even when you are queen, you will have a meddling dowager as puppet master."

She felt foolish. It all rang true.

That was what the queen had done, wasn't it? Little tests? Little games? All to assert her dominance? And she had seen it countless times back in Mestibes too—parents and grandparents running over the top of young bachelorettes not strong enough to fight back. Girls joining noble families only to become little more than doormats.

And she had seen it in her own house as well. She had endured the years of subservience. She had endured the rip of cane against skin!

Was that to be her life again? To be a little woman under another tyrannical mother figure?

No! No, I won't allow that!

"So, what do you suggest?" she said.

"This whole relationship? You are playing it a whirlwind?"

"Well . . . yes."

"Then actually make it a whirlwind! Be spontaneous. Take the initiative!"

"But, how?"

"Have Calix propose at the Black Night Festival?"

"But . . . that's just five days away!"

"It is a *whirlwind*, Tiggy! It is supposed to be whirlwindy!"

"Yes, but everyone knows that Calix observes the Sable Moon Sanctum. Withdrawing on that night to pray and reflect."

"Exactly! So what better way to show the complete change you have brought over him—breaking his habit of solitude? People here don't care about that piety stuff. But him coming out of hiding, kneeling before you in the presence of his future subjects? It would be the ultimate confirmation of his love. A moment strong enough to silence the doubters."

"*Doubters*? What have you heard?" A little shiver ran through her. Was that what the queen had meant when she'd said some people were hard to convince?

"Cousin, please, don't worry about idle gossip."

"No, please, tell me!"

"Well," said Aurelius, with a reluctant look. "Some are asking why Calix has not visited the Great Grove."

She bit her tongue accidentally. Of course! How could they have been so stupid? That's what smitten young couples were supposed to do! Ms. Securia had even implied it when they'd walked back from the temple of Vatic. That's why she'd told her the story of her own experiences. She must harbor some doubts, just like all the other citizens did!

"*Exactly*," said Aurelius. "And you can't do that, can you? So why not take the next best option? Do the proposal so quickly, so publicly that you silence the chatter before it becomes a chorus?"

She ran her thumb along her pendant, nodding. "You're right. It's perfect. I'll ask Calix at once. And . . . thank you for this. I know this whole situation must be difficult for you."

"Dearest cousin," he said, taking her by the hands. "All that matters is that Mestibes is safe and that you are happy."

68

AURELIUS

THE RAIN DRUMMED ONTO THE EMBASSY COURTYARD, A SHARD OF lightning in the distance. Aurelius sat on his balcony, feet on the railing, feeling more like himself than he had in weeks.

Teigra had left immediately to visit the prince, no doubt to make the demands he'd convinced her were necessary. The prince would say no, of course. A satyr couldn't wander the streets on the night of the sable moon, not unless he wanted to drink half of his citizens dry.

But the fight they'd have would be the start of their downfall. And from there, it would be easy to pry them apart. Zosime working her magic on Calix and the queen? With Aurelius doing the same with Teigra?

Child's play.

She wouldn't last a week once he started digging up all those insecurities, raising all those risks and dangers that would terrify her into backing down. Then, he could resume what they had started. He would get his military alliance and his prince. Mestibes would still be saved. No one would be any worse off.

He sipped the warm liquor.

If anything, this was a kindness. The girl was so pathetic and needy—just like she'd always been.

Princess Teigra?

Queen Teigra?

The little girl from the stables? Ruling a whole polity?

She would have been eaten alive.

The dark wood of the stater rolled across his fingertips.

Calix had kept it all these months—a brief moment of happiness after a great defeat. He'd kept it because he cared about him. Because he wanted to be different. Because he wanted to live his truth! And this was the way he could do that. By accepting someone who valued him for who he *really* was.

He was about to freshen his cup when hurried footsteps came from the street. Teigra squelched through the gate, the rain so heavy that even the gaggle had departed.

Aurelius almost felt sorry for her as mud splashed all up her stola, just as the tears would surely be splashing down her cheeks.

But she'd been the one who'd wanted to play with power. And now she was going to learn that there were no morals in that game. Now she would learn just how far he would go to win.

Teigra cupped her hands, the sound drowned by a crash in the distance. She repeated it at full volume, again and again, jumping on the spot.

Aurelius dropped his cup.

"He said yes, Aurie!" she screamed against the thunder. "He said *yes!*"

69

TEIGRA

Tonight was the night!

The Black Night Festival was a strange tradition—every Ardoran dressing up once a year as one of the five therians, drinking and dancing and getting intimate in the streets.

Most people dressed as satyrs, of course, competing to have the most dramatic horns, convincing fur and realistic hoofed boots.

But this year many young maidens were going as *eidolons* instead. All because of her. All because of their romance.

Teigra slipped the fabric over her skin. The costume of the therian of Mesti was less dramatic than the satyr's, phoenix's, siren's, or gorgon's would surely be. It was made of a black stola, all the way to the floor and covered in little blue and purple glass beads.

The overall effect did resemble the ghostly stardust described in the codices.

The costume was Ms. Securia's, from back when she was around Teigra's age. The beads had come from her family's glassworks, but the costume itself was barely worn.

Only the one time, Ms. Securia had said a few hours ago, before heading off to the Temple of Mesti to observe the Sable Moon Sanctum.

Teigra considered herself in the mirror, wondering whether this was the costume Ms. Securia had worn to the Great Grove, so confident in herself, when she had plucked the cursed rose.

She'd been wrong about her. When she'd first arrived, she'd thought her a monster—just another bitter disciplinarian. Just like *Mother*.

But she was more than that.

She was someone who'd risked it all for love and had to bear the solitude of that risk. Someone who'd been rejected for where she came from, but still served her polity loyally. Someone who didn't care if others thought it old-fashioned to spend the sable moon in commune with the goddess. She was a strong figure, with strong morals, who was difficult to get close to.

Just like Calix.

Just like her future husband.

Just like the future *king of Ardora*.

And from this night, she would be his *princess*.

And one day, his *queen* . . .

She laughed at the thought of such grand titles being applied to *her*.

Princess Teigra?

Queen Teigra?

She smiled from deep within herself, taking the pendant and laying the twist of pegasus hair among the beads at her chest. It wasn't correct for the look, but she felt naked without it.

It isn't the way either of us imagined it, Da. But it looks like we made it.

She struck a pose at the top of the stairs. She felt a little self-conscious, but she'd been assured by everyone in the agora that restraint was *not* the style of the evening.

She wasn't surprised to see that Aurelius was not wearing a matching eidolon costume. Blending in and paying tribute to Mestibes? For Aurelius? That would never do.

Instead, he wore an obscenely short green-blue tunic, a gold belt, and a long cloak over the top, covered with blue-indigo feathers. The cloak was cut down the middle, all the way up to his shoulder blades and tied around each bare biceps. It wasn't quite as literal as she might have expected, but the inspiration was clear.

He was a siren: the therian of Ondo. A beast of trickery and deception and allure.

"Well, don't you look the part, darling!" he said, sweeping his "wings" with a *thwump*.

Darling? She couldn't remember when he'd last called her that.

"As do you! Although dressing as a beast that lures men to their ruin through dark temptations?"

"A little on the nose?"

"For this party, it might be perfect!" The sounds of the street were already filtering in, laughter and songs and dancing. "Shall we wait by the gate?"

"That may appear a little too keen?"

He was right. Besides, the water clock showed it was still a way before ten—the hour that Calix was to pick her up.

"No Jaspar?" Aurelius asked.

"He says he needs to keep working."

Things were fine between her and Jaspar now, though the minotaur had been unable to hide the sadness on his face when she'd told him the big news of what this night held.

Aurelius plucked a jug from the table. "Well, never mind that. Fancy a little something to take the nerves away?"

"Isn't that breaking one of the rules of the evening? No drinking indoors? No private parties? Everyone has to be out on the streets, mingling as one?"

"I hardly think a Sisterhood is going to burst in over *one* little drink."

"They might. You remember what happened the last time I drank?"

"Last time you managed to bag a prince. I hardly think the grape holds bad omens for you."

She politely refused, and they sat and chatted instead—about their reflections on the polity, about the people they'd both met. It wasn't quite like old times. So much had changed in just a few months that it might *never* be like old times again. But still, it was wonderful to have him back. And as he told stories of the bars she'd not yet visited, she realized how much she'd missed the simple pleasure of his company.

The minutes passed.

First ten o'clock.

Then ten fifteen.

Then ten thirty!

Aurelius tried to comfort her—telling her that the streets were packed, and Calix was probably having a hard time getting through. After all, he hadn't attended one of these in years, so he'd probably forgotten just how busy it got!

But despite his best efforts, the lump in her throat grew.

"Maybe . . ." she said, as the clock dripped toward eleven. "Maybe *one* cup wouldn't hurt."

70

AURELIUS

AURELIUS POURED HIS COUSIN'S FIFTH CUP OF WINE AS THE CLOCK neared midnight.

It was all going perfectly!

He'd spent the last few days wracked with nerves about whether Calix would somehow show up. The prince had spent so many years restraining himself and keeping his instincts at bay, that he feared Calix might just be foolish enough to test his control on the darkest of nights.

What had possessed him to agree to this plan? Some stubborn-headed desire to prove that he controlled the beast? After they had dredged up the horrors of how he became a satyr, was this some misguided attempt to prove that he was a better man than the one who'd left his men to die in Sama?

Whatever Calix's hopes, they had clearly failed. Instead of arriving on a white steed to the cheers of his future subjects, Teigra was descending into fits of deeper anguish.

"Come now, darling. No tears," he said in a soft voice.

"I didn't even like him like that, Aurie!" she said through sobs. "It was just a deal. And he *still* rejected me! Even men I'm only agreeing to marry for a deal don't want me!"

"Why don't we head to bed? What would your *mother* think, seeing you like this?"

Teigra swayed to attention. "That . . . that *bitch*? Yeah, go to bed. Cause that's what little *Tiggy* would do, isn't it? The good lil girl who does whatever she's told. Who smiles and bows and scrapes and never gets a single word of thanks for it!" She gestured with her cup, sending a spray of wine across the table. "But would *you* go to bed, Aurie? Huh? Would *you* go up and cry yourself to sleep?"

"Fuck no!" he said, rising to her energy. "I'd teach them all a lesson!"

"Damn right you would!" she barked, guzzling the last of her wine and dropping the cup. "Jaspar!" The minotaur sprinted out, stumbling in shock at the swaying, ruby-lipped girl. "Hitch the carriage! We're visiting the prince!"

The minotaur didn't dare disobey. And as they clattered down the road, pushing through enormous throngs of revelers, Teigra barked out commands of *faster, faster!*

Aurelius had never seen her like this before. She was possessed. She was delirious.

Perfect!

Before the carriage had even skidded to a stop outside Calix's vineyard, Teigra was out the door, pounding on the villa in a clatter of glass beads.

"Open up!" she yelled. "How could you do this to me?"

"Maybe we should be a little quieter?" said Jaspar with a grimace, looking around the dark hills. "He might not even be here."

"Aspro is here!" she said, waving an arm toward the cloud-white stallion in the nearby stable. "The bastard is here! I know it!"

Louder the expletives came. Until, eventually, the banging softened and the calls became more sorrowful.

Then, Teigra collapsed.

Aurelius came to her, and she gripped at him, sobbing out all of that remnant anger. Somewhere, deep beneath his own wine-soaked breath, a call of pain echoed.

He ignored it.

This is what had to happen. It was the only way.

"Let's go, Aurie," she sniffed at last. "There's nothing for us here."

"No," he said, through clenched teeth. "You go back to the embassy. I have some things to take care of."

"What . . . what will you do?" she slurred, stumbling back into the carriage.

Aurelius cracked his knuckles. "No one hurts my cousin like this! Ever!"

"Oh, Aurie. I'm so sorry I was mean to you. I shouldn't have . . . I shouldn't have . . ."

He took her hand through the carriage window. She was still shaking with emotion. "I forgive you, darling. Now you get out of here. I don't want you to have to see this."

She nodded and slumped back.

"Be careful with her," he said to Jaspar, loud enough that Teigra would hear it.

The mid envoy nodded. With a crack of the reins, they were off, rattling away down the road.

And Jaspar *would* take care of her. He was far more suitable for Teigra than a prince. In a few days, once the pain had eased, she would realize that. With luck, she would settle into a simpler life. A more *suitable* life.

Yes. It is better this way.

Aurelius was left with the quiet of the night, not just from the lack of moon, but from a blanket of clouds that gave the whole evening a muted gray undertone.

The villa lay before him, even darker than the night.

And inside would be Calix.

Would he be transformed? Shacked to some wall or locked away in some room? Or would he be there in meditation, desperately trying to stop the change from happening, still hoping that he might be able to get into town and fulfill his promise to Teigra?

How much control does he really have over himself?

Aurelius didn't know the answer to that. But he *wanted* to.

He was still for a long moment, remembering the promise he had made to leave Calix alone.

But beneath all that pain was the denial. And Zosime was right: Calix was a good man. He deserved to live his truth. He deserved to be happy.

Aurelius shuddered in anticipation.

And he deserves to feed!

71

TEIGRA

THE CARRIAGE GROUND TO A HALT ON THE CITY OUTSKIRTS, THE STREETS so thick with costumed revelers now that there was no chance of getting back through.

Jaspar muffled something about turning around and trying another gate. But the comforting warmth of the drink was starting to drift, being replaced by an awful emptiness.

And just outside the window was the opposite of that emptiness. The pressing crowd. The wild dancing. The flowing wine.

That is where I should be...

"Wait!" said Jaspar.

But it was too late. She was already out in the press—young women in various stages of undress, with wreathes of flowers and close-curled goat horns on their temples. Men wearing nothing but leather loincloths, if that, alongside a smattering of sea-green feathers of sirens or the glistening snakeskin of gorgons.

She melted into them, the beat of the drums smacking her lungs. A beautiful woman with hair hanging past her bare breasts offered Teigra a mug, which she guzzled without shame and replaced with another.

No sooner had she downed that, gasping for air, than her arm was taken and spun into a swirl of dance. Another arm came—a middle-aged woman with a riotous cackle, then an old man barely keeping up with the pace. Arm after arm, face after face, passing her off, swirling her deeper into the sweet embrace of the party.

And in that moment, she wished it to consume her. To make sure she never had to think about Calix again.

"Teigra, stop!" came a shrill voice, pulling her from the fray. Jaspar swung across her vision with the residual momentum of the dance.

"Let me go!" she said, trying to break free.

He gripped her by the wrist as she reached for another cup, held aloft by a dancing young man. "Come on, Teigra. This isn't like you! Let me take you home!"

His big eyes bored into her—so hopeful, so expectant, so caring. And in his words, still lingering, she heard something more pathetic than anything else she'd done this evening.

This isn't like you . . .

"Well, maybe this *should* be like me, Jaspar. Maybe this is who I'm meant to be," she said, pulling her hands free and sinking back into the fray.

The music filled her. The movement and the people were all she could feel. For eons she swirled and drank and laughed, never wanting it to end.

Then, across the haze, a familiar voice spun her around.

"Well, well! If it isn't Ms. Cosmin!"

72

AURELIUS

AURELIUS CREPT THROUGH THE DARK HOUSE, EVERY NEW ROOM CAUSING his breath to catch, expecting to see Calix appear in the dull shreds that filtered through glassless windows.

No, not *Calix*. The *satyr*—the beast that Calix spent his life trying to trap away. The only being in all the world that truly scared the prince.

The only thing, perhaps, apart from Aurelius.

The front door had been locked tight, but it was quick work to find the right tool—a double-headed farm implement from the stables, caked with black soil, which Aurelius still carried in his clenched fist.

He'd ignored the braying of the stallion, just as he ignored the voices that warned him off this venture.

Calix cannot live like this. He deserves to be free!

The main rooms bore no reward but blackened silence. Eventually, at the back of the kitchen, the hearth still warm with coals, he came upon a set of narrow stairs, so far inside the house that there was just the faintest hint of a door at their base, tinted murky red by the fading fire.

With cautious steps, he descended.

He paused at the bottom, tracing his hands over the rough wood, adorned with a strange carving—a circle with a small star at its center, itself surrounded by a three-headed twist of coil.

The door was held by a fist-sized lock.

Locked from the outside? Is this your work, Zosime?

As his fingertips grazed the cold metal, he felt something strange —like the buzzing of bees and the scent of spring. And he knew with a certainty he couldn't describe that Calix was behind the door.

He experienced a moment of final indecision.

But he had come too far. He had given too much.

And he *had to* free him.

It took three swings of metal against metal from the farm tool before the lock tumbled down.

The door creaked open.

And Aurelius gasped.

Out of the earthen walls and floor of the basement grew a garden of the most vibrant colors he had ever seen. Green vines and an array of flowers crept to the vaulted brick arches of the cellar, lit by thousands of luminescent mushrooms, glowing a soft, calming teal beneath the foliage. The ground was blanketed in the lushest grass he had ever seen, coming up to shin height and swaying gently, despite the lack of breeze. The air was rich with perfume from the dozens of flowers—an enticing mix that made his skin tingle.

And sitting in the middle of all this magnificence was the *satyr*.

The face was the same as before, albeit a little more primal—the beard fuller, the cheeks and jaw and brow bones a little more defined. Thick horns curled from his temples, up past his crown in twisted daggers. Black hair fell onto his chest, resting against the thicker *fur* that covered his muscle—somehow even larger than before. That fur grew to a full, animalistic pelt at his hips, stretching down the rest of his body.

A knowing smile came across the creature's face, at once familiar, yet deeply different.

The satyr stood, rising on cloven hooves.

But Aurelius only noticed those for a moment.

Because his gaze was drawn between the beast's legs.

It was the most impressive cock he had ever seen—long and thick, even when flaccid.

The satyr stretched its arms in a luxuriant, languid way, utterly unashamed of his nakedness. "Oh, *Your Excellency*," he cooed, the voice slightly higher and significantly more playful than Calix's smoky tones. "I thought you would *never* come."

"C . . . Calix?"

The surprise he felt was unexpected. He'd known this was what he would find. Of course he had. And yet, seeing the creature there, in the flesh, brought the reality of it all home.

Therians existed.

Satyrs existed.

And Calix was one of them.

That creature *was Calix*.

"In a manner of speaking," said the satyr prince, yawning. There was something utterly at ease in his movements—like every muscle was freed of tension. "And there is no need to avert your eyes, Aurie. I know this is what you came for. And make no mistake, it *will* be yours." The creature gave a lazy flick of his hands and vines crawled across the door, blocking the exit. "So take your time. Believe me. We have all night."

As if on command, he looked back at the creature's cock, drawn to it, yearning for it.

He gulped at the size.

It was so close. So impressive. And it was his. All *his*! He could have it any time he wanted. For as long as he wanted it!

His head filled with thoughts of getting on his knees and servicing the great manhood. The desire slid over him like finest silk. To bend over and beg the creature to take him in his arms and dominate him and—

"You . . . you can't control me," said Aurelius, his skin shuddering

376

hot and prickly at the strange sensations in his mind, the strange thoughts that were at once his own and yet not.

The satyr stepped through the swaying grass. He stopped when they were face to face, running a finger delicately under Aurelius's chin.

That small contact was like fire.

"Dear Aurelius, you've been under my spell since before you even arrived in this garden. There are no jagged edges to my power here, no peaks and troughs like this fool usually suffers. In this form, I can bend your passion, bring it up and down so delicately, and with such delicious domination, that you will never even know it is happening."

With another wave of the satyr's hands, a new image came to Aurelius. The air filled with the smell of steam. Suddenly he was back in the bathhouse, with Calix standing over him, fully human, pinning him back in the corner of the pool. Both of them were completely naked. Calix bore a look of savage intimidation. The warm water brushed Aurelius's aching cock, as hard and yearning as it had been on that day.

A voice far in the distance, and yet everywhere at once, trilled— sticky and hot. *Poor thing. You have been teased for too long. I can feel the desire in you. All that lust. All that yearning? You deserve to get what you've craved.*

Without stepping back, the human prince raised one hand over his head. The cluster of impossibly toned muscles around his water-glinting ribs stretched out. He didn't move his other hand from beside him.

It was the position that started a wrestling match. A competition of wills and strength.

"Have you known battle, Your Excellency?" said the man before him, just as he had on that afternoon, the first day he had arrived in Ardora.

"No," he whispered.

The visage of the man shimmered with steam and sweat. "Do you wish to?"

His features swirled in the mist, at once the prince, and then the beast, and then both at once.

Part of Aurelius was scared—more scared than he'd ever been. That part wanted the creature to step away, to give him space, to just let him breathe!

But another part of him wanted the creature to step closer, to crush him, to make him feel even smaller, even more vulnerable, even less in control.

After a long moment, Aurelius reached up and took the man's hand, double the size of his.

He had barely interlaced their fingers before he was spun around, his whole body consumed by hard, furry flesh. There was a mass of muscle behind him. And against his ass, slippery from the buttery warmth, was the prince's cock.

It was as hard as granite. As huge as a horse.

One of Calix's big hands reached around and pushed on his smooth chest, drawing a whimper from Aurelius's pink lips. The rough fingers continued their path down his stomach, all the way to his groin, splaying his fingers as he did so, until the big man was gripping around and under the base of his sex, without actually touching it.

With his other hand, he pulled Aurelius's head around to face him.

Their lips were just inches apart now.

His breath was sweet as rosewater.

"Is this what you came for?" Calix growled, like the distant rumble of thunder. "Is *this* what you wanted?"

"Yes!"

The water of the bath, the room, all of it melted away until all he could feel was Calix's touch, and the great slab of meat grinding against his ass. He pushed back against it, desperate to have the hot spear plunge into him, to feel its thickness stretch him out.

He moved, standing on tiptoes until he felt the pressure grow against his tight ring.

He wanted it.

He needed it.

He had to have it!

But before he could accept the invasion, Calix maneuvered himself out of sync, laughing at his grunts of frustration.

Aurelius tried again, and again after that, but each time, Calix withheld his liberation.

"Do you want me?" said the voice beside his ear. At long last, the cock didn't slip out of reach but pressed against his entrance. "Do you want *this*?"

"Yes!" Aurelius screamed, grabbing the arm around his chest with one hand, and at the big, firm ass behind him with the other.

One moment, his grip held hot skin; the next it held handfuls of thick fur.

And in that moment, he didn't give a damn which was real. Because they *both* were. And he wanted both. Prince and beast. Monster and man.

Tears of frustration streamed down his face. The urgency was unbearable. His body screamed for release: to be taken and consumed, controlled and commanded.

Then, slowly as the change of seasons, the cock slid into him, opening him up without resistance.

Incomprehensible whimpers fell from his mouth as he was invaded, inch by inch, until it squeezed against his prostate, causing his whole body to shake uncontrollably.

Calix paused at that, throbbing hard, causing his shakes to grow even stronger.

Yesss! hissed the prince soundlessly, the voice an ever-present rumble in Aurelius's core. *You need this more than anything you've ever needed before!*

Aurelius's shaking hand gripped harder at Calix's forearm, fighting the cruel delay.

Screams of relief filled the air as the remaining inches slammed into him, all at once, flexing and throbbing, owning him, possessing him.

"And you . . . you want it too?" Aurelius whispered, barely able to focus, grinding his ass back, driving animal grunts from by his ear.

He turned his head, seeing the human face of the prince, feeling the hot breath against his chin as the thrusts drew groan after groan. With what little strength he had left, he brought his hand up and ran it along the prince's face—through his beard, along the soft skin, up into his human hair.

"But this is not you," Aurelius said, almost delirious with pleasure. "Not who you are in this moment."

The prince paused.

But . . . this is how you wish me to be.

"No . . ." said Aurelius, breathlessly, going faint with yearning. "Feel for the truth of that."

The prince closed his eyes. When he again opened them, his face was washed with confusion.

You yearn for me? You yearn for . . . all of me?

Aurelius nodded. "Be with me, Calix. Please."

With the shatter of silver, the illusions faded. Gone was the bathhouse and the steam, returned instead to the garden. Aurelius's costume was ripped across the grass, although he couldn't recall it being removed.

And on the face overhead, gone too was the visage of humanity, replaced with the heavier brow, the bestial horns. And in his eyes, fleeting as a passing cloud, was the smallest flicker of doubt.

Aurelius reached up, the huge cock having lost none of its rigidity inside his ass, still driving him insane with lust.

He pressed his mouth against the prince's.

Take me, Calix, he thought, the silent words screaming louder than any he could ever speak. *Take whatever you need. Whatever you crave. But I want you. All of you. Everything that you are. Everything that you hide. Give me everything!*

The beast returned his kiss, a new drive within him. Their hot tongues circled each other.

All playfulness was gone. Calix drew back his hips, pulling out almost all of his cock, then slamming it all back in one hard thrust. Aurelius's own cock drooled with every smack, sending him into higher and higher raptures.

The world blurred until all he felt was their union. It could have been hours or days or weeks. He didn't care. The lust and urgency and *passion* were all he felt, their mouths feasting on each other.

And it wasn't just Aurelius who felt it, either. His own body was also driving heavier grunts from Calix, each thrust bringing his prince closer to ecstasy.

When the pleasure finally became too much to bear, Aurelius grabbed his dick, harder than it had ever been. It took just a few flicks before his orgasm roared out, jets of cum bursting in great, racking shakes.

Then his whole body went *cold*.

The ecstasy drained from him—running from his skin into the prince's.

Then came another spike of heat, only to be drawn cold once more.

Each cycle drained him deeper, leaving his insides empty. One second he was hit with euphoria, only to fade to an even deeper loss. Again and again, faster and faster, so frequent and so devastating that each cycle rolled into the next. From deep inside, Aurelius *felt* it happening, like cloth tearing, each strand of fabric clinging to prevent it.

His lust.

His desire.

His joy.

His exuberance.

His confidence.

All of it was torn from him.

The night crept closer, surrounding him in void, until he was lit by nothing but the golden eyes of the man he loved.

And he didn't fucking care.

Because in that moment, their mouths still hot around each other, the prince still gripping him close, he didn't give a fuck what Calix took from him.

Because right now, they were *one*.

Because right now, they were *everything*.

I love you, Calix, he thought.

And as the darkness wrapped around him like a blanket of frost, there came the voice. Not of the beast, but of the man, crackling through his skin with the echo of ages.

I love you too, Aurelius.

With a contented sigh, he let the black envelop him, fading away into soft, freezing nothingness.

73

TEIGRA

It was Fabulosa.

She looked exactly like a siren. Not like she was *dressed* as one—as the half-dozen other Ondocians now staring over top their golden goblets did—but how the real thing must surely look.

Her costume was made of material so sheer and fitted and matching so completely to her skin tone, that it looked like she was naked from the stomach up, all across her breasts and face and arms. A different, feather-lined fabric concealed from just above where her *passage of pleasure* began all the way down her legs, with an elaborate set of beautiful, ornate wings fixed on her back. Closer inspection showed that both the feathered and nonfeathered cloth was cut to just barely cover her intimate places.

"My dear, how rapturous to see you," she said. "Please meet some darling friends of mine from Glintcrown. One of the outer islands, you know. But don't hold *that* against them! They produce more gold and silver there than anywhere else in Dynosia. They've come down just for the evening."

"Well, we heard such wonderful things about the party," said a well-fed man in far too small a costume. "And we thought we should have a go before this war kicks off!"

"Teigra, this is Satrap—" She stopped. "My dear, whatever is the matter?"

Suddenly, the noise and sounds which had been so comforting just moments ago felt *wrong*. The clap of cups toasting, the roar of laughter, the smell of wine—wine, everywhere *wine*! The crowd pressed against her chest. Voices came from a distance, dizzy and dazed.

Suddenly, the streets went by in a blur, until, with a distant pop, even that noise filtered away.

When the spinning finally stopped, she was inside the Ondocian embassy—lit by heavy candlelight. Fabulosa was leading her gently by the arm.

"How..."

"You fainted, my dear. Passing out in the street? It seems you really are becoming a local!"

"I'm sorry," she said, feeling utterly pathetic, trying her best to control her stumbling, wine-twisted steps. "What about your friends?"

Fabulosa flicked a hand, causing the wings on her back to twitch. "Oh, don't worry about *them*. They have been writing for months about wanting to see the real Ardora. I am quite sure it will find them."

"Thank you," she said as they walked up a grand staircase. "Your... your costume looks very nice."

"How kind. Yes, one does have to splash out for these occasions." With another swish, Fabulosa opened the door to what must surely have been her bedroom. It was a palace of pink silks and gold, plush cushions and curios from places she couldn't name. "Yours is also a good first attempt at an eidolon. A little *overcovered* for the occasion. But no doubt once you are taken into the royal fold, these things will start to come a bit more naturally!"

Teigra sat in stony silence on the edge of the bed.

"Ah," said the high envoy. "And where is your prince, little tiger? On a night such as this, you should be embracing the debauchery together."

"We're through," Teigra spat.

Fabulosa sat beside her. "What a great shame. The prince is beautiful. Many women would want him."

"Well, they can have him! And his beauty as well. He's nothing but a heartless thug."

"Ah, a lady of refinement? Not interested in looks alone, but character? So, you and Mr. Accola are free to continue your little dalliance, then? Don't look surprised, Teigra. Any fool could spot the connection. He is certainly a creature of superior character to the prince?"

"You've . . . been watching me?"

"Often, my dear," she said with a grin that made Teigra's pulse quicken. "But let us not change the subject. Mr. Accola? He has been good to you?"

She thought of the boy who had shown her nothing but kindness since she had first been appointed. The man she'd just rejected in front of the whole crowd.

"Yes," Teigra said in a heavy voice. "Much kinder than I deserve."

"And that is what nice girls yearn for, is it not? A loving husband? A companion without serious vice? A good father? And a rather strong minotaur to make sure that fatherhood takes place."

"I . . . I already said he was kind!"

Fabulosa closed the distance between them—not put off by Teigra's defensive tone but seeming to relish it. "I didn't ask whether he was kind, Teigra. I asked whether you *yearned* for him."

She turned away. "What difference does it make?"

Fabulosa pressed a finger against Teigra's chin, drawing her gaze back. "What we tolerate and what we *yearn for* makes all the difference in the world."

Fabulosa leaned in, her decadent perfume enticing with sweet apple and lily. With a soft but knowing touch, she took Teigra's unresisting hands and ran them up her torso, across the soft, bare skin of the costume cutouts, all the way up to the curves below her full, womanly breasts.

A shudder went through Teigra, accompanied by a pain she couldn't explain that the woman had stopped at the fabric's edge, rather than continuing to the secret skin beneath.

"What is it that you *yearn for*, Teigra?"

"I . . . I want to reconcile with Calix," she stammered, her stomach heavy and twisted. "So I can save my . . . so I can help my . . ."

With a slow movement, Fabulosa guided Teigra's hands under the fabric, across her naked breasts.

Teigra shook from deep within—at once wanting to pull her hands away, and yet never wanting them to leave.

The woman's skin was warm and yielding.

Teigra's shaking fingertips traced the edges of Fabulosa's nipples, hard and immediate, drawing a high groan from the powerful woman that warmed her very being, making her own nipples stand desperate.

Teigra felt she was going mad! It was wrong. It was bestial. It was sinful. And it wasn't what she wanted. It wasn't what she desired! It wasn't what she *yearned* for!

Then why does her skin feel so wonderful against my touch?

Then why aren't I stopping?

Some strange desire within her wished to be closer to Fabulosa, to remove their clothing and feel the hot press of skin against skin. To be known intimately by a master, showing her the paths and pleasures unknown.

In this moment, warm from the wine and the room and the high envoy's unashamed touch, she wanted it more than anything she'd ever wanted.

And yet, from the edge of memory, the rest of the night swept by.

Of what she and Calix had agreed to.

Of *why* they had started their courtship in the first place.

And of what was at stake for both of them if they didn't make it happen.

Teigra pulled her hands back, giving Fabulosa a sorrowful look. Her fingers felt cold and alone in their absence from her the silken skin.

Teigra sighed, resisting the intense urge to undo her withdrawal.

"I . . . I have to go."

74

AURELIUS

THE BARE EARTH WAS COLD AGAINST HIS CHEEK.

The first thing he noticed was the smell. The powdery stink of mold choked his senses.

He opened his eyes, gritty and dry, to see the cause.

Across the walls and floor of the garden lay limp strands of death, covered in cancerous patches of mildew. The air was so thick with rot that he could see the spores floating, lit by a thin light through the basement door.

Calix...?

He tried to speak, but his throat ached like a hammer had been taken to it. As he pushed himself up, he felt utterly shattered—a dull weight hanging from every limb, every fingertip, every strand of hair, making even the smallest movements near impossible.

It didn't hurt. Not exactly. It was just all so incredibly *difficult*. So difficult that it would have been easier to lay back against the damp earth and return to sleep. To join the kinship of rot and let his body flake away.

With all the effort he could muster, he resisted, grabbing the torn shreds of his once-glittering costume, now slimy with decay, and wrapped them into something approximating an outfit.

The house stumbled past, lit by a cold, overcast gloom. The rooms were empty. The coals in the hearth were absent any heat.

He found Calix outside, standing atop the hill, staring over the vineyard and the bay beyond.

Aurelius could sense the morning was cold, and yet he couldn't *feel* it. He could hardly feel *anything*.

"Don't!" Calix growled as he staggered toward him, his voice carrying an intensity he hadn't heard before.

"Calix . . ." he squeaked, the single word taking the strength of an oration.

The prince's face was visible now—an expression of sneering contempt. "How could you, Aurelius? After *everything* I told you?"

He tried to speak, but the words wouldn't come.

The prince shook his head. Teeth gritted, he tossed a scroll to the ground in front of him. "Your reward!" he spat. "The only thing you've ever really wanted from me."

The words on the parchment unfurled before him. It was a letter to the archon of Mestibes, proposing the negotiation of a formal military alliance—with abundant clarity that Aurelius had been the mastermind.

And at the bottom, above the barely set wax, was a line of text that stopped his heart.

This offer is conditional on the herald of Mestibes leaving Ardora, never to return.

Somewhere in the pit of his being came the ghostly sensation of sorrow. But no tears came. It was just the shadow of sadness, not the real thing.

"I don't want this," he whispered.

"Well I do!" screamed Calix, his voice echoing through the vines. Tears welled in his eyes. "I told you that I wouldn't become that thing again! I begged you! For five years I had never . . . I kept myself from . . ."

"Please, just let me—"

"No!" said the prince, turning away. "Just leave, Aurelius. Leave now and *never* return!"

Calix's shoulders shook. The sound of his sobbing consumed the gray hills.

Aurelius stood on the spot for what felt like a generation.

Then, at last, he did as the prince asked.

75

AURELIUS

Aurelius stood in the doorway of Securia's office. She looked up with ready-made fire, her face saying exactly how he must have looked.

"Yes, *Herald*?"

He placed the scroll in front of her, gripping the bookshelves to stop himself collapsing. "The prince agreed."

It was barely a complete sentence, but it was all he could manage. Standing was difficult. Breathing was difficult. If it hadn't been for the local he'd flagged down in the vineyards, prepared to take the promise of gold in future for a ride now, he'd surely be passed out on the outskirts of town.

She didn't look at the parchment, either not doubting the validity of the statement, or not caring. Instead, she just scowled, lips pursed and a faint shake of her head.

"How *pleased* you must be, Herald. Your long mission here finally at an end?"

"Seems so."

"If you are expecting congratulations, Mr. Savair, then you have failed to heed any of my warnings. You have disgraced Mesti. And you will pay the punishment for this treason. You and your wicked mother!"

"Tell... the senate," he managed. Each word was like a fork across his throat.

She looked genuinely shocked. "You want the *senate* to support this blasphemy?"

"You think they won't?" he muttered, gripping harder at the wood of the bookshelf, his head spinning. "That this will end House Savair?"

"I do not *think* this. I *know* it."

"Then tell them," he croaked. "Everything you've seen. Then ask what they'd have you do."

She stared at him for long while. Finally, she plucked a fresh piece of parchment and started writing.

He stumbled out of the building, certain the letter would be sent before nightfall. Then, it would be a matter of days before the response would come. A week at most. They wouldn't wait. Xiber would be at Vaticily by now. There wasn't any time left *to* wait.

A voice called as he reached his doorway.

It was Teigra.

Her face was full of focus. Before he could speak she launched into a monologue about her plans for getting Calix back, about how it wasn't over yet and she could still save the polity.

Her words drifted by like leaves on an autumn wind. From somewhere in the broken recesses of his soul came the smallest pang of guilt.

The look in her eyes.

The desire to make things better.

And it was all so pointless.

"We fucked," he whispered, barely able to get the words out.

The silence between them filled the entire courtyard.

There was so much to tell her. So much she deserved to know. But right now, he couldn't bring himself to even think it. He had no temper for tears. No space for sorrow.

"I got the deal. Mestibes is saved."

He stepped into his building and clicked the door closed. Each step up the stairs drained him beyond empty.

He hit the bed like a plummeting stone, wanting nothing but to lay there, unmoving, until eternity collapsed around him.

76

AURELIUS

It took six days for the response to come—six long days of emptiness.

He didn't leave his bed in all that time, feeling no desire to eat, drinking from a half-filled water jug by his bed only when the scratch in his throat became too prominent to sleep through.

On the fourth day, that too ran dry, the rough clay as drained and empty as he. He didn't despair when that happened, nor from the undercurrents of hunger that crept in with each passing hour. If anything, they were welcome visitors. Some sign amongst the pervasive numb that he was still alive.

Those survival pangs seemed to be the only thing he *could* feel anymore. Neither the warmth of the sun nor the cooler turn of the night seemed to touch him.

Late one evening a storm passed by, with errant droplets drifting in through the window. He'd felt those slow drips down his face only as registration of reality—without any true sensation.

It was just like the memories that haunted him through the days and nights. Odd, factual little mockeries, stirring nothing inside him beyond the dull truth of what he had lost.

There came the disgusted face of Securia at the news of his deal. The disbelief from Teigra at his admission. And above all, the face of Calix—with his look of abject hatred.

Of all the memories, that one came closest to stirring some faraway ghost of sadness. His expression had been so raw. So devastated. The utter betrayal, deep to his very soul. Deeper than any armor could protect.

And in a moment of crystal clarity, Aurelius knew that he'd succeeded in his mission.

Calix had truly loved him.

And I betrayed that. I knew Calix was doing everything he could to keep his beast at bay. And I couldn't help myself. I wanted him to feed from me. Because I wanted to possess some gift, some trinket, that no one else has of him.

On the fifth day, a tear finally fell—a warm scratch along a dead cheek.

Well, you got your trinket, Aurie. All Mestibes is probably singing your name. And all it took was ruining the one person who actually fucking cared about you. The one person who actually fucking saw you for who you really are.

He awoke on the morning of the sixth day to the sound of the messenger centaur arriving. His sensations had largely returned by then. That hollow feeling had narrowed, replaced once again by emotions he didn't want. Sorrow and despair. Loss and loneliness. They came back like pins and needles to his heart, until he yearned for the brutal blank of nothingness to return.

Once the messenger had departed, he dragged himself up and staggered into the main house, steering by the kitchen to consume half a jug of water and stuff his mouth with bread.

It wasn't just that the thirst and hunger had become unbearable, he also wanted to give the high envoy time to process the letter.

Around the kitchen were overstocked piles of ingredients, as though there was someone else in the house who had barely eaten for the last few days.

When he found Ms. Securia at her desk she was shaking, the formal letter in her clenched hands, with another scroll unopened by her elbow.

She didn't look up at his arrival, and he didn't draw attention to himself. He didn't need to force the news from her. He'd known what the senate's response would be before she had written.

Despite all that she had put him through, he still felt sorry for her. She was a good person, underneath it all. Oh, she wasn't *nice*. But from all he'd seen, she was *good*. And like so many good people, she put her faith in morals and institutions—in gods and ideals. She believed that loyalty and righteousness would win in the end.

And though she often talked of Mesti, she had been away from *Mestibes* itself for too long to know it anymore. After all this time, the city was more idea and ideal to her than a reality.

Whereas Aurelius had seen the dark hearts of the men and women of the senate up close. And despite their self-proclaimed superiority, they were just *people*. Just normal people in positions of power, hungry for more and scared of losing what they had. They might want it for themselves, or for their family, or to make sure that the "wrong people" didn't get it, but their whole lives revolved around the acquisition and maintenance of that power.

And as much as they might crap on about their superior civilization and culture, when it came down to it, they were just as petty and transactional and scared of dying as any Ondocian trader.

Of course the senate had accepted the military alliance.

How could they not?

It was Ms. Securia who retreated to her bedroom after that. He gave her that space, just as she had him, before he eventually found himself knocking at her bedroom a few days later.

When no answer came, he creaked the door open.

Her room was dark, the curtains drawn. But there was the faint outline of her in the humble bed, facing away.

"May I guess what they said?" he said from the doorway.

Her voice was hoarse. "To gloat at my foolishness?"

"To reinvigorate my cynicism."

She rolled over, assessing him, before rolling back. "As you wish."

He sat on the end of her bed, running his fingers gently over the coarse wool of her blanket. "I assume they said that while they would never *seek* such a deal, and while they thought the circumstances that led to the offer were gravely insulting to the goddess, if such a deal was now being offered, it would be deeply offensive to turn it down. And so, with the greatest of reluctance and supreme reverence to Mesti, they have instructed you to accept the offer and negotiate terms for a military alliance with the royal family."

Ms. Securia's silence confirmed both the content of the letter and her own expectation. She really had thought they would say no—that the senate would choose their principles and their piety over their power and their privilege.

It was heartbreaking.

"Will you follow their orders?" he asked.

"Are you worried about losing your precious glory?"

"That wasn't why I asked."

It was partly true. In the hours that had passed, he'd allowed himself to think about the victory awaiting him back home. After all, Calix never wanted to see him again, and there was no point holding on to ghosts up here. Their polity was saved. He would be greeted as a hero. His position as future archon would be guaranteed.

Perhaps he could even try to restart something with Nihal? Maybe it wasn't too late to force something from the ashes of that inferno.

However, he did also genuinely feel for her quandary, and wondered how she would handle it.

She said nothing for a long while, before eventually whispering a single word. "Yes."

He placed a hand on her shoulder and made to depart.

"Your Excellency?" she said, bringing him to a stop in the doorway. "That clause in the prince's letter, that you leave Ardora, and not return?"

"Yes," he said, the reality setting in, cold and stiff.

"That is unreasonable, and runs counter to the broader intent of the agreement. We could seek to have that removed, should you so wish?"

He gave her a faint smile. "I think the prince would be most insistent on that matter. Besides, it is better for everyone that I leave."

"Even though you love him?"

It was Aurelius's turn to give himself away through silence.

Was it just a guess? A part of him wanted to lie on instinct.

But really . . . what difference did it make? In a few days, he would be gone, back home to soak up the adulation of a grateful city. And the prince would be nothing but a fading memory. Just one of the many other men that he had bedded.

"How did you know?"

"You don't live in the land of passion for this long without being able to see such things."

Aurelius sighed. "Yes, then. It is better for everyone that I leave. Even though I love him."

"I would have thought you beyond such self-sacrifice? No intentions to make a big romantic gesture? Run in and steal his heart?"

"Go to the Great Grove and pluck a rose, you mean?"

"It is the done thing in these parts."

"I think . . . I think we have taken quite enough from each other, Ramuna. The roses of Ardor will live on in my memory. Not in my hands."

After a moment of hesitation, she shooed him out the door and shut it. When she came out a few minutes later, she was fully dressed.

She led him down to her office, closing the door behind them and kneeling by the lower shelves. After a bit of rummaging, she revealed a small leather bag from behind a run of codices. With great care, she withdrew the contents.

Aurelius gave a tiny laugh. He didn't think her the sort.

It was an eternal rose, made entirely of a richly colored glass, with a brooch pin attached to the back.

The workmanship was remarkable, equal to the best he had seen in Mestibes. It was so real, so lifelike, that it looked less like a work of art, and more like a genuine rose had been encased within glass. He didn't insult her by asking where it came from—it was obviously from the Securia glassworks, no doubt a parting gift from her family when she'd first been appointed.

"It is beautiful, Ramuna," he said. The sunlight illuminated a gash where one of the thorns had snapped off. Effort had been made to smooth the surface, but it couldn't hide the damage. "Shame it is broken."

"With something this fine, you cannot guarantee it will never break."

"Then why do it? Why spend so much care making something that will just shatter in the end."

She ran her finger along the smooth stem. "My grandfather used to say that only a fool predicted how a piece would turn out before it was put to flame. You could look at the materials, see imperfections in the sand, or weakness in the color, and swear that it might shatter at first contact with the kiln. Other pieces would be made from the finest materials, and the whole workshop would swear that they would survive unscathed. And he was always surprised at how wrong he could be."

"There must have been many breakages?"

"More than you could imagine."

Aurelius's mouth went dry. "How . . . how did he find the will to keep going?"

She looked out the window. "He told me that if he was afraid of trying, he never would have made anything."

Ms. Securia held the flower out to him. "Take it, Your Excellency."

His eyes bulged. "I can't accept this, Ramuna. This is your heirloom."

A look of sadness swept her face. "It is a memento of a different time. A memory . . . I have clung onto for far too long."

He looked into her eyes, still red from grief. Perhaps this was her own realization? The man who must surely have made this—Safin Securia, her grandfather and one of the finest craftsmen in Mestibes's history—was long gone. And gone, perhaps too, alongside his whole generation, was the piety and morality that she remembered from her youth.

Maybe this was what she needed to leave that past behind? What she needed in order to accept Mestibes for what it truly was?

"Thank you," he said, pinning the delicate thing deep into the curled layers of the toga by his shoulder. It still was far from his preferred garment, but after so many days feeling nothing, there was something strangely comforting about the weight of the heavy wool. "Will you be all right?"

"I have no choice not to be."

"Well, hopefully the *other* scroll gave you better news."

She gave him a quizzical look.

"The other scroll?" he continued. "I'm sorry, but I passed by your office after the messenger came. There were two letters delivered, weren't there?"

Ms. Securia's face grew heavy. "She hasn't told you . . ."

"What? Who?"

"The censor of the senate has concluded that your cousin was working to the archon's interests, rather than the senate's. That she assisted you in acquiring your alliance."

His heart stopped.

His letter! His damn fucking letter to the censor! With everything that had happened, he'd completely forgotten all about it!

"Well, surely that doesn't matter anymore, does it?" he said with a hopeful laugh. "Now that the senate have agreed to negotiate the deal, that is all just old news."

Ms. Securia looked at him gravely. "Your Excellency, I am sure the common folk of Mestibes are all now singing the praise of House

Savair—so loudly in fact, that the senate had no choice but to hum along. But there has still been a grave insult to Mesti. A total betrayal of the goddess. And war is still coming. This alliance will combat it, but not stop battle from bloodying our lands. The favor of Mesti will still be paramount—more paramount than it as ever been."

And someone must pay a price for that, came the unspoken words in his ears. *Someone must be sacrificed to appease the goddess.*

He gave a mirthless laugh as his skin prickled with frost. "Let me guess, they've delayed House Cosmin's attempt to become patricians?"

"No, Your Excellency. It appears that the censor set your aunt an ultimatum. Given your cousin's youth, Senator Beeta Cosmin could either take the family's punishment herself and be removed from the senate, or her daughter would be dragged back to Mestibes and forced to bear whatever penalty the senate deemed fit."

Oh, shit . . .

Aurelius's stomach twisted. He didn't need to see the letter. He knew Beeta Cosmin far too well.

Teigra was taking the fall.

77

TEIGRA

She filled the bag in a daze, taking care to align the edges of her stolas perfectly.

It had been three days since she'd received the scroll.

At first, she'd expected it to be an apology from Calix, or some fanciful letter from Fabulosa. Instead, it had been from Mestibes, cosigned by the censor of the senate on the left and Mother on the right, informing her that she was charged with treason, and must now return to Mestibes to face her punishment.

Treason . . .

Punishment . . .

That could include any number of horrible things—being stripped of her position, or banishment to one of the mid or low polities, or possibly even *death*, although she found some comfort that this particular punishment had not been carried out in Mestibes for decades.

Or, if the senate so chose, she could suffer something even worse —having her name stricken from the records of citizenry, no longer to be known as Teigra Cosmin, but as Teigra *Enklimitas*.

Criminal.

Traitor.

At first, the news had cut her so deeply, breaking her so completely, that she thought she might never breathe again. But then, as the hours passed into days, circumstance stretched into some kind of distant madness.

Under normal circumstances, she'd be driven home immediately to face her punishment. But Ms. Securia was doing the bare minimum on the negotiations, leaving Jaspar too busy to drive her back.

And so, she was left to wait, as the very contract she was being *blamed for* was being negotiated by her superiors.

It was all so absurd.

It was all so *unreal.*

On several occasions, Aurelius attempted to speak to her through the door. She ignored him, not wanting to think about the celebration he would receive on his return. Not wanting to think about *anything.*

Because thinking about anything made it all feel real.

And as the long hours passed, she was taken by the darkest of thoughts: *Why not just run away?*

She knew enough now to remake herself in one of the smaller farming towns in Greater Ardora. It would be the ultimate disgrace to her family name. But at least she could keep the name she had fought for all these years. At least she might never know for certain that they had taken if from her.

Eventually, time beat her to the decision. On the fourth morning, Jaspar knocked mournfully and told her that the negotiations had been finalized, the agreement reached in record time. Ms. Securia would remain to attend a signing ceremony this very evening on behalf of the senate and the archon, freeing Jaspar to drive her back.

Ardora would send a Sisterhood to Vaticily immediately, to shadow Xiber on her pathway down the holy mountain—assessing whether she received favorable news from the god of fate. In the meantime, the other Brothers and Sisters would make their preparations. And if the forward party determined Xiber was making ready to invade, then thousands of troops would be sent south to join them. All to protect Mestibes.

Mestibes . . . Where she'd be arriving a criminal.

Alongside Aurelius. Who'd be hailed a hero.

All for doing the *exact* same thing.

She left her room in a numb, soundless fog. It was only when she stood in the courtyard, the funeral carriage to the rest of her life before her, that it all came welling up.

Everything she had been when she came. Everything she had done since she arrived. It all flooded through, bursting the dams of her unfeeling.

She had been so scared when she'd first arrived here. So young. So *foolish*.

That girl deserved the punishment that was coming.

But *she* didn't.

She was better now! She was stronger now! She had done things in the last few months that she'd never thought herself capable of.

"Tiggy, please," said Aurelius, opening the carriage door. "Let's not have any of that."

"How am I supposed to act, Aurelius?" she sniffed. "I'm returning as a traitor! Everything I worked for? Everything I fought for? Gone!"

"Darling, you know I won't let that happen. Right now, House Savair is more popular than the whole senate combined. Once we get home, I will make sure they reverse this stupid decision. I will publicly shame them for scapegoating you. The people will be behind me. These charges will be dropped and your family will get the reward you have long fought for. I give you my word on that."

Aurelius started to enter the carriage. But Teigra didn't move.

"Why does the senate think I helped you, Aurelius?"

His face was blank. "Well, if we are being fair, darling, you did!"

"Only at *first*. Before I understood the stakes. Then I stopped. I was loyal to the senate. All this time, it appeared I was obeying their instructions. The only people who knew any different were you and me!"

He gave a weary sigh. "Tiggy, you are being silly. Come on. You know how long this journey is."

Her fists curled. "Teigra! My name is *Teigra*! Not *Tiggy*. Not *dear*. Not *darling*! Teigra!" The withheld tears streamed down her face now. "And I know it was *you*, Aurelius. There's no one else it could have been. Ms. Securia was supporting me—I know it wasn't her! It was *you*! So just be honest for once in your miserable life and admit it!"

Aurelius looked at her for a long time, before finally dropping his bags and stepping back out.

His face turned rock-solid, betraying no hint of remorse. "Fine, you want to know the truth, *Teigra*? Yes, I told them. And it wasn't even an accident, either. I wrote a letter to the archon, but I had Jaspar send it to the censor instead."

Jaspar looked down from the driver's seat in horror.

"Why?" she said, his honesty cutting deep.

"Oh, don't act so innocent, *dear*. Don't act like you don't know what game you were playing, *darling*. What did you expect? That I would roll over and take your interference? Of course I took the opportunity to cut you down. And I took it again when Zosime asked for my help breaking you up."

"*Zosime* did this?"

"Yes," he said with a condescending tut. "Really! Someone like you, acting for such selfish reason? You should have taken better steps to protect yourself."

"*Selfish reasons?* Everything I did, I did for *Mestibes*!"

Aurelius looked her over. A bitter smile crept on his face. "You've gotten good. Maybe I missed it happening. Because if I didn't know better, I'd say you actually believed that shit."

"I would have done it, Aurie," she gasped. "Does that mean nothing to you? I would have given my entire life to a fiction. All to save our homeland."

"And what an awful fiction it would have been. All that luxury? All that power? All those opportunities to show up the bitches back home who thought you were nothing?"

"To a man I didn't love! To a man who could never love me back."

"To a man that would have given you everything you wanted!"

"No, I—"

"*Shut up!*" he barked, baring his teeth. "You may have picked up a step, *Tiggy*, but I am a fucking master! If you gave a shit about Mestibes, you would have let me get on with my mission. You knew what I was doing. You knew my plans. And I had it all under control. Mestibes would have been saved just fine without your interference. Just like it has been now! But you stepped in and tried to fuck it all up!"

She turned, stung by his sudden anger.

"Don't look away!" he hissed. "Don't you *dare* look away! You want to play this game? You want me to tell the truth for *once in my miserable life?* Well, I just did. So at least have the guts to admit your own part! That you didn't just do this for Mestibes, but to secure your family's position! To secure your father's fucking legacy! Deny it, Tiggy! Come on! Deny it, and let's see how good you've really become!"

She shook her head. It wasn't true! She was just trying to save innocent lives, not improve her own position.

"You could have warned me, Aurelius."

He grunted. "I warned you every day we grew up together. I warned you with every man I fucked and discarded. With every bitch I betrayed and ruined. You saw the carnage. You heard the tales. You knew *exactly* what happened to those who got in my way!"

"Yes," she said softly. "I just never thought you'd do it to *me*."

Aurelius shook his head and picked up his bags. "For the gods' sakes. Do you want to live your whole life as a victim? The woman who was playing me? I'll admit it, she gave me a real run. She pushed me. She made me lift my game. And do you know what, *that woman* sure as fuck wouldn't march back home to accept some bullshit punishment."

Stick to the path, kiddo. Even if it terrifies you.

The refrain pounded in her head, mocking her failures. Mocking each and every way that she'd destroyed the path to patrician status carefully laid down by her father.

She put her hands over her face. "If I return, there is still some hope for my family. Punishment will be served. But if I run, then the Cosmin name will be disgraced forever! I already took everything from him! I can't take his legacy as well!"

Aurelius looked at her with pity. "For fuck's sake, Tiggy. *You* are his legacy! Not his *surname* or his *reputation!*"

The words hit hard, stopping her tears and breath in one staggering moment. "I ... I ..."

"Teigra, will you stop thinking about the storm and start thinking about the *man*! Will you stop punishing yourself and think about what he would have wanted for you! Exile or execution? Is that how you intend to honor his memory? Do you think for one single fucking second that this is the future that *Andrin Cosmin* would wish for you?"

"I ... But ..."

"Stop simpering and decide, Teigra! Right now! Either get in this carriage and accept the fate your mother and her precious senate have waiting for you. Or be the woman your father knew you could be and *run!*"

Teigra's hands shook as she stepped to the carriage door. As she looked into the cabin beyond, her head swam with memories. Among the roiling black of that nightmare day, among the screams and tears, came the voice she longed to hear again.

And for the first time in years, it came without the baggage of blood and pain. It came as light as the breeze atop a steed. As golden as fresh hay. As pure and warm as the fifteen years before that moment.

And as her father's face and voice embraced her once again, Teigra tried to imagine him standing in the crowd as she was tried for her crimes. She tried to imagine him telling her that she should accept her punishment for the good of House Cosmin. She tried to imagine him saying that she should suffer and be shamed and be sentenced.

And no matter what she did, not matter how hard she tried, the image would not form.

With a sudden intake of breath, Teigra grabbed the door. Then, with all her force, she slammed it shut.

And she ran.

78

AURELIUS

HE BANGED AGAINST THE CARRIAGE WALL AS THEY GROUND TO *ANOTHER* halt.

Progress out of the city was abysmal. Despite it barely being midday, several roads were already closed for the evening's ceremony. While trying to get past the palace itself, where the big announcement would take place, the carriage slowed to a few yards every other minute.

Rumors were whispered under every breath from street level— some informed, some fanciful. The consensus was that a fight was brewing, with most agreeing it was a damn good thing.

Finally a chance to show what a real army can do.

Finally a chance to get out of the barracks and fight, just like ma' always talked about.

Finally a chance to get some blood on our swords and some birds on our cocks!

Aurelius gave a bitter little laugh at the ribald talk. Ardora wasn't going to war for *Mestibes*. That was just an afterthought. These were soldiers who hadn't had the chance to *soldier* for five years. They wanted to put their skills to the test. They were doing it for the glory, for the fame, for the love of the fight, for the chance to finish of Rinath once and for all.

But not for *Mestibes*.

Aurelius didn't care about that. It made no difference why they fought, as long as they turned up.

Soon the voices from the crowd turned.

"I heard the proposal will be right here! Tonight!"

"Sod your rumors. I heard they're so in love they're gonna march to the Great Grove any minute!"

"You think so? Oh, how romantic!"

"Well, did you see her out at the festival? I got to dance with her! I always thought those Mestibians were so stuck up, but she was downing drink and dancing with the best of them!"

Aurelius clenched his teeth as the carriage finally got back under way.

Bitch! Even gone, she is still all these people talk about!

He pulled the glass brooch that Securia had given him from his shoulder, holding the symbol of holy love carefully.

They could never go to the Great Grove for each other! Touching a rose would turn Calix into a fucking imago—a permanent therian! Something that she doesn't even know about! Something he would never have trusted her with. And for her? She couldn't do it, either! Because she doesn't love him! Not the way he deserves to be loved!

The realization hit him like a punch to the stomach. He jerked his head back as the carriage bumped around, flicking the curtains open to reveal the Temple of Ardora, the Fields of Life, rushing past.

There were so many things that Teigra and Calix could do that he couldn't. He couldn't be intimate with the prince in public. He couldn't get married to him. He couldn't take the throne beside him.

But there was one thing Aurelius *could* do that Teigra couldn't.

He clipped the brooch back and banged on the wall behind Jaspar's head. "Stop! Stop this instant!"

There was a whinny as the carriage slid to a halt and he jumped out. "Just wait there!"

"No!" said Jaspar, stamping his hoof from the driver's position.

Aurelius stopped midstep. "What did you say?"

"I said *no*! I am not your servant. You used me, Herald. You had me send a letter to the senate that put Teigra in that position. And now she's gone! So get in the carriage right now, or so help me, I will leave here without you!"

"You would ride back to Mestibes with an empty carriage?"

"Yes, I would! And I will tell everyone in the city that you're *dead* and that they should move on and praise someone else! Because good luck trying to get back to Mestibes after the ceremony, when every steed is commandeered, and every boat is full of supplies."

Jaspar was furious. He wasn't bluffing.

Visions of Mestibes came to Aurelius. The mood was high. All the citizens were waiting for someone to cheer for their salvation. And they were perfectly poised to scream his name.

But, like all crowds, they would only wait for so long. If he didn't arrive soon, someone else would gladly take the credit. Perhaps Benedict would find some way to solidify his own position. Perhaps his mother would claim it was all her idea. Then the war would start, and the focus would shift. By the time he finally came back, no one would care that it had been his effort that saved them all.

That meant he had to get home *now* to consolidate his power. Everything he had worked for? Everything he had fought for? Six years of sweat and suffering? If he didn't get into that carriage right now it would all crumble!

And yet . . .

If he didn't run to the Grove this second, he would always wonder what would have happened . . .

In the end, the decision was easy.

He reached up and grabbed the carriage door.

And with all his force, he slammed it shut.

79

TEIGRA

T<small>EIGRA</small> <small>SPRINTED THROUGH THE STREETS, PUSHING BY THE CROWDS</small> that were already assembling near the palace. The throng didn't distract her, nor did their calls of recognition. Because there was only one person she was looking for. The only one who could make all of this madness disappear.

Fabulosa.

Jaspar? Aurelius? She'd known them for longer. She had spent far more time with both of them. And yet, none of them *knew* her like Fabulosa seemed to. None of them had seen her as clearly as the high envoy had—deep down, to the core of her being.

And right now, that was what she needed. She needed to be held by a stable force. She needed to be touched by a knowing hand. She needed to be seen by eyes that saw what no one else seemed to.

Teigra searched for what felt like hours, visiting familiar places and old haunts, longing to find the one person who would look at her broken life and *laugh*—not out of spite, not out of pity, but because she knew that another life could be bought and built on the rubble.

Just when she thought she might never find her, she spotted the beautiful glimmer across the agora. Flowing pink fabric fluttered in the sea breeze. Her hair was held back with golden pins, encrusted with sapphires. It was the sort of showy opulence that no one else in Ardora could pull off.

Teigra gave a relieved sigh as she approached the group of shopkeepers huddled around the high envoy.

"Called off, I'm afraid," said Fabulosa. "It appears this *Teigra* was nothing more than a spy sent from Mestibes."

Teigra stopped dead.

No . . .

"What?" said Gyges. "But I've seen them together! They're in love. I 'eard they're even planning on making a big show of it this evening?"

Teigra put her hand over her mouth as Fabulosa trilled her little laugh. "Oh, I am afraid not. Well, you didn't hear it from me of course, but my sources say that she tricked His Highness into her arms and probably her bed as well. Preyed on all his weaknesses. All in a sordid attempt to get this military alliance with Ardora."

"Is *that* what the ceremony tonight is for! Nera, are you 'earing this?" said Gyges to Nera Baros, a gray-haired honey trader that Teigra had negotiated a hundred-vase order with just one month ago. "Turns out that girl was just using the prince! Just like she was using poor Jaspar—you remember? Flirting and such, but never following through!"

"Oh, I knew it! Didn't I say so. I told you she was just using them both. Them Mestibians are all the same! With their fancy words and thinking they're better than us!"

"I know exactly what you mean," said Fabulosa. "And the nerve. When they were the ones who stopped the rest of us from finishing off the Rinathi when we had the chance. Now they come down here, trying to trick your own darling children into *dying* for them?"

"Shame!" chorused the voices.

Fabulosa tucked an errant hair behind her ear. "Of course, it is your business whether you wish to honor your contracts with Mestibes. Although, I don't think anyone would blame you if you wished to consider . . . *other options?* At double gold, of course. To cover your inconvenience."

Fabulosa tossed a pouch onto the street in an explosion of glint.

Every gathered shopkeeper turned to face Gyges. The centimane paused long, then nodded. The shopkeepers set at the coin like wolves over a fallen deer, first grabbing for the money, then thrusting forward their parchments—all the contracts that Ms. Securia and Jaspar had negotiated to keep the city from starving during a siege.

With a flick of a golden pen, Fabulosa carried out her capital punishment, signing overtop the documents, cutting out Mestibes and inking in Ondocis.

Swish.

Swish.

Swish.

Each swipe was a cut to Teigra's throat. This couldn't be happening. Not her . . . Gods above! Of all the people!

Not her!

The fire that had sustained her these last few hours was extinguished entirely, a cold pail of water sizzling over now darkened coals.

Everything was gone.

All her hopes.

All her dreams.

And the one person she thought might be different . . .

Fabulosa turned like the world was moving at quarter speed. There was no remorse in her eyes, no apology on her lips. Instead, her first reaction on realizing that she'd been overheard was to *smile.*

"Well, well. Look who we have here!"

Teigra didn't have a chance to respond over the screams and curses—led first by the powerful and influential Gyges, then followed closely behind by the other stallholders. And through it all was the face of Fabulosa, who walked right up to her with that same, nasty little smile.

She leaned in as she passed. "No hard feelings, dear. It's just business, after all."

The pain came from nowhere.

The smack knocked her to the ground, dazing her into a world of stars. Dragging herself to all fours, she looked over at the apple, half disintegrated on the ground beside her.

"*Scum!*" said Sara Arit, the apple seller, grabbing another fist-sized fruit and lining up her next shot. "You got some nerve showing your face here!"

On cue, the rest of the barrage came—oranges and pears, olives and nuts, smashing over her in wet smacks and awful scrapes.

Teigra picked herself up from the mud, slipping on the food underfoot, and ran.

Just when she thought she was away, the other apple smacked right into the back of her head, sending her crashing into a table of yogurt, the thick goo pouring over her hair and face.

Tears streaming, she dragged herself up again, scooping the muck from her eyes and sprinting through the crowd, past shoppers and horses and stalls. It wasn't until she finally reached the docks, alongside the long row of ships, that she realized no one was chasing her.

She could barely breathe. Everything felt distant.

Failing to fight back tears, she kneeled before the salty water, doing her best to remove the worst of the filth. Her hair was stuck fast to her head. Her clothing was a mess of stains and congealed stickiness.

She kept rinsing long after the last of the goat's milk slime had washed away. The now cloudy water below reflected the pathetic, broken body of the girl who had failed everything and everyone.

For there wasn't anyone left in all the world now that cared for her.

She had no one.

Not a single person.

After a long time, she set to walking. There was no direction. She didn't have anywhere to go. She knew this with a heaviness that would have brought her to tears, if she had any left to cry.

She didn't have a home anymore.

She didn't have a family.

She was alone. Completely and totally alone.

And it was all her own fault—for trusting people, for believing in them. Aurelius? Calix? Fabulosa? Securia? She was a fool for thinking they wouldn't betray her, one after the other.

As she neared the final few boats on the dock, something caught her eye. Up on the last ship in the line, smaller and sleeker than the big cargo boats, was a figure.

It was *the* figure!

The one who had done this.

The one who had ruined everything!

Princess Zosime walked up the gangplank, dressed in inconspicuous clothing, flanked by two people of such varying height they could only be Pikra and Elexis. Each of them was leading a pegasus, with a fourth steed loaded with heavy saddlebags.

She ducked behind a crate as Pikra kicked away the wooden gangplank and the hulking body of Elexis cranked the winch of the anchor.

Pegasi? Saddlebags? They are the Sisters that are going to head off Xiber!

Teigra pulled the still-wet hair from her eyes.

Are you a delicate little flower, Teigra? Or are you a rose with fucking thorns?

She knew there was probably still time to make things right. She could find a ride back to Mestibes. She could still serve her punishment for her family.

Or . . . she could show the princess what she was really made of!

She'd been wrong to blame herself. Teigra hadn't ruined everything; *Zosime* had! It was *her* plan that had destroyed Teigra's relationship with Calix! And now she was just going to leave? Sail to distant shores? Not caring about what she'd done?

Zosime shared a laugh with a sailor on the bow of the ship, who was thumbing the long whip that would spur the team of shackled hippocamps into action.

No! thought Teigra, jogging toward the edge of the water. *No! She isn't going to get away with it!*

The leather flail arced through the sky, sending a snap all along the dock. The ship jerked forward, picking up speed fast. Teigra ran alongside it, finding pace she didn't know she had. Pace she'd *forgotten* that she had.

Sailors ducked out of her way as she reached full stride, leaping over crates and spinning around livestock pens, eyeing the anchor at the back of the boat, too far to reach from here.

Up ahead, the ship line ended.

The open bay beckoned beyond.

There was no time left!

She won't get away with this!

Teigra hit the edge of the dock and jumped, sailing out into nothing. She caught the anchor full in her hands, not giving a damn about the cuts.

With all of her residual rage, she dragged herself up, collapsing onto the deck.

80

AURELIUS

Jaspar kept his word. The last Aurelius heard was the sound of the carriage heading south at pace. But that too faded into blur as he ran past the sparse faces in the parklands, through thickets of trees, thicker, *thicker*, until he arrived, panting, at the edge of what had to be the Great Grove.

Dappled sunlight passed through the mighty oak overhead, down onto the field of swaying green buds. It was silent here, with not a single soul around. Just him and the certainty in the pit of his being.

The certainty that he *could* do this.

You just knew. That's what they said. If your love was true, then you didn't need to dwell on it. You didn't need to weigh up the risks.

You just *knew*.

The army of green soldiers stood to attention before him.

And with a slow exhale. He blinked out a single rapturous tear.

Across the sway, one rose glinted without light. It beckoned without call.

And he knew.

With a certainty he had never felt before, he just fucking knew.

He ran along the paths through the field and came to the beacon.

Without hesitation, he reached down, his fingertips just inches from the thorns that would prove his love.

"Wait!" bellowed a voice from behind him.

It was Calix.

"Stop!" said the prince, skidding to a halt at the edge of the field, his full military uniform flapping with the effort. He glared at the roses in horror, like it was a nest of snapping vipers. For him they basically were. "You can't do that!"

"Yes, I can!" Aurelius called back. "I love you, Calix. I know I fucked up. Maybe this whole thing is just some crazy fuck up. But I love you! And I need to show you what I feel!"

"Not like this!"

Aurelius stood, taking in the man who he cared about more than any other. His own voice broke. "Then tell me. Can you see it? Is there a rose that calls to you? A rose you don't even need to look at twice to know that it is the one? Can you see it, just like you see me?"

The prince's jaw clenched, his face in agony.

"Tell me you don't, Calix. Tell me that all you see is a field of identical fucking flowers. Tell me that, and I will walk away and never return!"

Calix raised a slow, shaking hand, and pointed into the field—right at the rose that Aurelius was standing over. "I see it, Aurelius," he said, tears falling. "But you still can't do this! Not for me!"

The tears flowed down Aurelius's own cheeks now—tears of relief, tears of overwhelmed joy.

Calix saw it.

Calix loved him still.

"You can't pick one," Aurelius said. "I know what it would do to you. Because I know what you are. I know what you are better than any other person in this whole fucking city. I have seen parts of you, experienced parts of you, that no one else has. That no one else *would*. Things that other people would run from. But I am not running, Calix! Because I don't care what you are. I am here! For you. For us. And you can't do this, but *I can!*"

"No!" Calix yelled, reaching out from twenty yards away in a desperate attempt to stop him. "You can't do that either, Aurelius. For god's sake! Don't you understand?"

"What are you saying, Calix?"

"Why you are the way you are? Why you are so different from other Mestibians? Why you have urges you struggle to control?"

Aurelius wiped the tears from his jawline. "What are you talking about?"

"You're a therian, Aurie!" he screamed. "You're a fucking *siren*!"

81

TEIGRA

THE SEA WIND SNAPPED THROUGH HER STAINED STOLA AS THE GALLEY sped past the twin headlands of the bay, out into the sea beyond.

Wood groaned beneath her stomach—flat on the deck, which rocked and swayed, rocked and swayed. The sun glinted as vertical crystal against the water, which took up more and more of her view as they traveled away from the safety of land.

Teigra lay amongst a pile of seafaring tools at the back of the long ship—thick coils of scratchy rope, evil-hooked harpoons in racks, and huge fishing nets, caked in dried salt down to their bronze weights—the metal no doubt a form of worship for those who lived in service to the god of the oceans.

She'd been in that pile for half an hour now, holding herself low. Fighting off the stomach-twisting dizziness and the creeping sense of shame.

What was I thinking?

She'd never been on a boat before—apart from the tiny fishing ones that sailed a few dozen yards out from Mestibes's jagged shoreline, and only then to help with exercises for the hippocamps. She barely even knew how to swim. And now? Now she was heading out into a world of water, surrounded by people who sure as Dimethan didn't want her there.

She was lucky that none of the half-dozen sailors had ventured in her direction. The tales of what Ondocians did to stowaways was legendary. If you were lucky, they turned you into their plaything until the next port, then they tossed you out into an alien city to fend for yourself.

And that was on a *normal* merchant vessel. But this?

She pushed her face against the rough wood as a spray slapped up from the side.

A team of Sisters hiding on a normal-looking boat, on a secret mission to follow Xiber down from Vaticily? The whole thing set up so as few people as possible know the truth? If they find me . . . I probably won't live long enough to end up back on land.

As the spray got heavier and the sun grew brighter, Teigra looked regretfully toward the shore, now distant stretches of white and pale green, made blurry by a haze of salt.

She shook her head in silent frustration. Jumping into the boat was madness. But there was no going back now. She'd come here to confront Zosime. And that was what she was going to do.

All through the rest of the hot day she studied the movements of the crew across the deck. There was the driver up front steering the team of thrashing hippocamps, with the rest of the sailors tending to the supplementary sails at midships. Behind them, halfway between the mast and her, was a hatch down to the lower deck.

On occasions, she tried to convince herself to just duck below deck, screaming the princess's name. That would mean she'd completed her job—she could say she'd confronted her. And then, it would ensure her inevitable capture, rather than just waiting in dread.

But she resisted, convincing herself that it was better to wait. Convincing herself that she could do this *properly*.

After all, she'd proven that with Calix. Even though it hadn't worked out, she'd proven herself more cunning than she thought.

What she really needed was to find some way of catching Zosime alone. And to do that, she had to wait, and she had to learn.

And so she did.

She waited all day among the ropes, hour after thirsty hour under a baking sun, her clothing and face soaked in drying crust. The ship bore north all through the day, past an even wider headland that she faintly recalled as being near Gonimos—the mid polity that held the five-yearly, Dynosia-wide sporting spectacle of the Paliad Games.

Then they were out in the sea proper, continuing north before turning east. She drew a map in her mind. They were intending to navigate around Ardora and get to the woods of Vaticily from the Antimos Gulf.

When night at last fell, the tension of waiting and the thirst in her throat forced her into action. She had the cover of darkness now, the deck emptied, save one sailor on watch at the stern, facing the opposite direction.

There were no more excuses.

She rose when the nearly full moon was high overhead, on limbs aching from inactivity, trying hard to keep her balance as the evening breeze rocked the ship. Each step made the deck groan beneath her, causing her heart to stutter. But she forced herself on and reached the hatch.

Below deck was a medley of guttural snores and the stink of sweat. It was dark, but time soon brought clarity to the gloom.

Between the stairs and the front of the boat were the living quarters of the sailors, such as they were—occupied hammocks hung over low tables and the rubbish of life at sea. They rocked with the sway of the swell.

As her eyes grew even more accustomed, she spotted the cabin at the far end, right below where the whip-man would have stood.

That was where the Sisters would be. But sneaking past the sailors? To a room where Zosime would surely be with Pikra and Elexis? No. That seemed like a stupid move.

Behind her, rows of amphorae were stacked from wall to ceiling in the main cargo hold, stuffed with hay at their bases, such that they barely moved as the ship rocked. The only gap between them was a narrow path that led to some pitch-black pen at the very back of the ship.

Though there were no windows to provide any light, she caught the familiar, comforting smell.

Horses.

And an idea crept over her.

Pegasi stocked for transport needed to have their legs massaged and wings manipulated at least once a day. And she doubted that one of these Sisters, so reliant on their steeds at the best of times—and somehow possessing the only pegasi she had seen in all of Ardora— would allow a *sailor* to do that job.

Maybe she could get Zosime alone there, during the day, while all the sailors were up on deck? As long as the other two didn't join her? Surely even those three would want *some* time apart?

Yes. That might just work.

With a plan in place, she tiptoed just far enough into the sailors' quarters to find a waterskin to drain and a chunk of stale bread to force down her salt-stung throat.

Then, tiredness from the long day creeping in, she found one of the few gaps between amphorae, moving the straw just enough that she could squeeze in and cover herself.

And to the gentle sound of clacking clay, surrounded by a cocoon of dry grass, she drifted to sleep.

82

AURELIUS

Aurelius froze, his fingertip a hair's width from the thorn. Calix just stared, letting the words hang in the sweet air.

Siren?

Aurelius looked back to the flower.

With a sudden realization, he yanked his hand away, tucking it deep into the folds of his toga. "That is one of the five divine chrysalides! The things that turn therians into . . . into . . ."

"*Exactly,*" said Calix. "So will you please walk very, *very* carefully out of the Grove, before you end up as a monster!"

With steps more cautious than any he'd ever taken, darting his head around to make sure there was no stray thorn lurking underfoot, he high-stepped out of the field and joined Calix.

Only then, panting from the sudden shock, did he process the words.

"You can't be serious. A *siren*?"

"Yes."

"Big blue feathers?"

"Yes. Not now, admittedly. But that is what is inside you."

Aurelius looked at his hands. They appeared just as they always had. His skin, his fingers, his arms, and after an internal self-check, his body and his mind? All of it felt *exactly* the same.

And yet, as surprising as it was, as shocking and impossible as it was, it somehow felt . . . *right*.

It was like that first time he'd kissed Hal. A sparkling moment when all the accrued questions of his childhood—why he didn't want to kiss girls or throw rocks at them like all the other boys did—were instantly answered.

Why was he so different from everyone else in Mestibes? Why had he always held affection for Ondocis and their ostentatious culture? Why did nothing thrill him more than making little deals and tricking little people?

Because I am a fucking siren!

"So all of my desires . . . ?"

"Oh, you mean your desire for money and power and attention and one-upmanship? For unique curios and experiences that no one else has held?"

"Yes. Are they all because I am a siren?"

Calix nodded, before giving the smallest of smiles. "Well, I am sure *some* of that is just you being an impulsive, impossible little brat. But mostly, yes, I think that is from being a siren. Just as my own youth as a dormant satyr was very *indulgent*."

"But . . . what does that mean?"

"Well, you are in the dormant stage. If you avoid the five chrysalides, it shouldn't mean anything. You could live your whole life just as you are."

Aurelius looked back into the field. "And if I had touched one of them?"

A darkness descended over the prince. "Then you would become like me. You would move to the metamorph stage—activating your powers and all the curses that come alongside it. All your darkest desires, all your deepest impulses, they would grow from simple yearning to an unquenchable thirst. You could also transform yourself. And as a metamorph, one night a month, you would be forced to transform, even if you didn't want to."

Teenage tutelage crept forth. "Sirens are tricksters? If I transformed, I would draw people to me with the ability to grant their darkest wishes?"

"And extract from them the heaviest of concessions," said Calix knowingly, before adding a shrug. There was something different about him. Like he carried a little of the satyr's ease. "Or so I believe."

"Believe? You don't know?"

Calix shrugged again. "Remember what I said? We don't get a tutor."

"But you *are* a therian."

"So are *you*. And we don't all meet up for drinks, Aurelius! Plus, I've never met a siren before."

"And yet, you somehow *knew* that I was one?" said Aurelius, narrowing his eyes.

Calix gave him a guilty glance. "Look, I only found that out for certain when I ... when we ..."

"When you *fed* on me?"

Calix grimaced. "There was this force within you, like a glowing blue seed, waiting to sprout. It's probably why you're still standing here, rather than just being a husk. But ... even before that, I knew there was *something* different about you. From the moment we first locked eyes, back in your Pentheon. I had never met anyone who so instantly shattered my barriers. That first time I saw you I ..."

"Go on," said Aurelius with a raise of his eyebrow.

Calix blushed a deep red. "Well ... I got so hard I thought my dick would break in two. It took all my strength not to drag you into a dark corner and fuck your brains out."

Aurelius chuckled. "At least you weren't standing around your family at the time!"

"And after that, at the bathhouse, and then at the Wax Crack and finally when you came to my ..." His voice drifted, the levity turning mournful. He suddenly looked like he might burst into tears.

"Goddess, I'm so sorry for what I did to you, Aurelius. Are you alright? Did I hurt you?"

"I survived," he said, soothingly. "But what about you? How did you feel? To finally feed after so long?"

A curious look contorted across Calix. At first, it seemed like he was trying to hold something back, before the excitement burst forth. "Ardora forgive me, it was *amazing*! I know I shouldn't like it. I know I shouldn't want to feel this way. But the last five years have been like having the sun touch your skin and not feeling any warmth. But in the last few days, I've felt it all again! I've finally felt *alive* again!"

Aurelius thought back to his days of recovery. It had been truly awful. And yet, he felt no resentment toward Calix's joy. Because *he* had caused that joy. It was his passion that was now shimmering in the prince. It was him who had let Calix finally feel something again.

Eventually, that happy moment faded, as the inevitable question hung in the air.

"So, what do we do now?" said Aurelius.

83

TEIGRA

ON THE DAY THAT FOLLOWED, IT BECAME CLEAR THAT THE OCCUPANTS of the ship were living two different lives. Zosime and her colleagues were in the far cabin, keeping away from the rest of the crew—having food delivered to them, and only coming out to stretch their legs or occasionally head above deck for fresh air.

When their cabin door was shut, the sailors muttered and milled by the stairway, just a few feet from her hiding spot, unaware of Teigra's presence.

"Can't believe they're making us take the long way around to Ondocis, just to drop off a couple of *girls* along the way."

"Yeah. We could've done the whole trip in three days, in these winds. Now it's gonna take almost a week to get there and back."

Another voice came from halfway up the stairs. "Oi! You've been paid good coin to keep your lips sealed about our other passengers!"

"Yeah, yeah. Who's going to overhear? We're a hundred miles from another soul."

"And I just can't believe the Ardorans up and assisted the Mestibians like that. Hope they drove a hard deal."

"What difference is it to you? War'll be a boon for all of us.

Soldiers need transport. Supplies need moving. And 'bout time we had some cargo that don't shatter or spoil!"

As the day drifted on, the angle of the sun said they were continuing to head east. It was the next day, about midday, when they shifted southerly. From her rough calculations, that meant just one more day before they reached the river pathways that led to Vaticily. With another day to get to the foot of the mountain, the Sisterhood would reach Vaticily on the night of the bronze moon, precisely when Xiber would commune with Vatic.

Just one more day on the boat, maybe not even that, depending on where they were landing! And then, the Sisters would be gone. And there had been no chance to get Zosime alone. So far, the three soldiers had all tended to their steeds together.

Teigra wondered what she'd do if she had no opportunity to confront the princess before then. Would she disembark alongside the Sisters? Sneakily try to follow them on foot through unfamiliar forests—without supplies or steed? Surrounded by wolves and drakons and gorgons, just like Ms. Securia had described? Or would she just remain hidden and creep ashore wherever the boat eventually moored, never confronting the woman for her wickedness, and never likely to see her again?

As it happened, she needn't have worried.

"Game of tali, Cap?" said Elexis, the three of them heading below deck around midafternoon.

"Hardly! Haven't you both had your fill of my coin? I swear, Pik, you must be loading the knuckles."

"Oh common," said Elexis. "What've you got better to do? Going to fondle your stallion again?"

"Honestly, Captain, you treat that thing like a child. We all know how rare they are, but soon they'll have more chance to stretch than they could ever want!"

"Oh just leave 'er, Pik. It makes up for not 'aving a man in 'er life! Got to be putting them fingers to use somewhere!"

"Now, now! We can't all be as versed as you, El," said Zosime with a wink. "Two you got at the Black Night Festival, wasn't it?"

"Three, thank you *very* much."

"Poor bastards never even stood a chance!" said Pikra.

Teigra peeked from the hay as the trio parted—the two junior Sisters heading toward the cabin, with Zosime entering the hold.

Her heart thundered. She'd never get a better chance than this.

Those nerves were joined by an apprehensive little voice.

Leave it. They haven't found you yet. Just hide and disembark at the next city.

But her jaw set firm against that idea. She'd come this far. This was the woman who'd ruined everything. She had to do it!

Teigra pushed out from the hay pile, stepping into the barely lit hold on stiff legs.

Princess Zosime was kneeling by her pegasus, massaging its thighs while humming some little song. The powerful woman seemed totally oblivious to her presence.

Whatever happened, that was one victory at least. The trained scout, the trained tracker, outwitted by her.

"Well, Princess," she said. "Fancy seeing *you* here."

84

AURELIUS

CALIX TOOK AURELIUS IN WITH A MIX OF UNCERTAINTY AND SADNESS. "Next? I don't know. Will . . . you be leaving?"

"You *did* command me to. But . . . I could always stay. If you wanted?"

Calix blanched. "I don't know. I don't want to become that *thing* again, Aurelius. You knew how important it was to me, and you still forced me."

Aurelius's first instinct was to deflect. Of course he had done that. He was a *siren*! It was in his nature—a nature he was only now just understanding.

But that feeling was tempered by the memory of the cold morning after the night of primal heat. Of how utterly betrayed Calix had been.

He took the man's hand, his palm dwarfed. "I'm sorry. I should have listened to you. I won't put you in that position again. I promise."

Calix's hand closed around his, his touch tentative. "How can I believe that?"

"Because I understand now. For the first time in my life, I finally understand. And now that I know what I really am, I can work to control myself. *You* can show me how."

Calix looked to him as he had at the docks, like a scared cat who'd been kicked one too many times.

Aurelius squeezed the big hand. "I came here, didn't I?"

"Yes, you did," he whispered, returning the faint squeeze.

And if you asked me to do it, right now, knowing everything I now know, I would still pluck the rose.

"Please Calix, I almost lost you. I am not going to do anything to risk that again."

Calix stepped away. "No, it won't work. In times of peace, maybe we could make something happen. I do want to try. But we are about to start a war! I am the strategos. I will be away! Commanding my troops!"

Aurelius's heart dropped. Amongst all that had happened, he hadn't thought about that. But of course Calix would be gone. All Dynosia was about to change, wasn't it?

"Exactly," said Calix. "What would we do? Try to carry out an affair under the nose of thousands of troops, with all of them watching my every move?"

"You were a soldier before?" said Aurelius, desperately. "You must have had your own affairs back then? With Terim?"

His face darkened. "That was different. He was also in uniform. Tasks had to be done. Reconnaissance. Guard duty. Chopping wood and hunting for food. There were reasons you could disappear for hours with another soldier. But I am not some captain anymore, I am the *strategos*. And I won't be with three other men, but with *thousands*. I'll be in the big tent, in the middle of the camp. I'll be the one giving the orders. How am I supposed to hide you? Keep you in a barrel of wine all day and drag you out at night?"

"There are worse ways to live?"

"I am serious, Aurie."

Aurelius's mind whirred. "What if . . . what if you didn't have to hide me?"

Calix glared. "You know I can't do that. I'm not like you."

"No, I mean, you are going to war in a foreign land. In *my* foreign land. On the back of a deal that we created together?"

"And?"

"So . . . what if you took me on as your *advisor*? An allied aristocrat, in their own homeland? Someone to help you plan and strategize? Someone who knows the terrain? That wouldn't look out of place, would it?"

Calix was still. "War isn't a joke. We don't employ proxenos, foreign advisors, just for show."

"But I wouldn't be there just for show! I know every power player and every noble in every mid and low polity in Greater Mestibes. They all sit in our senate—it's one of the ways they keep the territory united. Sure, those small leaders, the prefects, aren't that powerful in Mestibes proper, but in their own little patches they are basically kings. Aren't they exactly the people we'll need to be working with? To get intelligence and prepare tactics and . . . I don't know, to convince people to hold lines and assist with defense when they think they're all about to be killed?"

"Yes," said Calix, cautiously. "Yes, they are."

"Well, I could help with that!"

Calix shook his head. "We can't be contemplating this. Can we?"

"Why not? Is it crazier than anything else we've done?"

"War wouldn't be like anything you've experienced, Aurelius. It's mud and saddle rash and running out of food and watching people die. It's *not* a good place to be."

"If I were beside you, that wouldn't matter."

The prince's demeanor turned serious. "My soldiers come first. They will want to be in the battle, but I still hold their lives in my hands. Where I send them. The tactics I employ. I will not betray that. If this got in the way . . ."

Aurelius patted his hand. "I promise that if we try it and it doesn't work then we can figure something else out. I can go away if I must— wait until after the war is over. But at least let us *try*."

Calix looked at him for the longest time, at once scowling then giving a faint smile, turning away and looking back.

Aurelius's pulse pounded, wondering whether it would be enough—after all he had put Calix through, would he be able to forgive that betrayal? Even now, he could still send him away, ask that the agreement be fulfilled and that he leave Ardora forever.

At last, just when his heart couldn't take anymore, Calix released his hand, only to extend it once again, this time for a shake. "Proxenos Savair, I welcome you to the Brotherhood of Ardora. May you serve with passion and loyalty."

Aurelius took the hand, the grip firm.

He felt like he would cry.

Then, looking into his honey-colored eyes to make sure it was agreeable, Aurelius embraced him.

He didn't dare kiss him. Not yet. Not after the forgiveness he had shown. Instead, he nuzzled his head into the man's neck, having to stand on tiptoes to do it, with his thick beard against his forehead.

Calix smelled of clean fabric and rosemary. His big arms surrounded him, wrapping him in an ocean of safety.

"I love you, Calix," he whispered, no longer able to hold the tears back.

"I love you, too, Aurelius," whispered the prince, running a big hand through his hair, trailing down his slender back, down toward his perky—

There was a twitch by his stomach. Calix pushed him away, holding him at arm's length. The soldier's face blushed as red as his cloak.

The bulge beneath the prince's uniform jutted the skirting strips of studded leather. It was the same bulge that soon jutted out from his own clothing, remembering the big beast that had consumed him a week earlier. He yearned to touch it, to taste it, to feel it again.

With all his willpower, he resisted. "We should take things slow," said Aurelius, with a chuckle.

"Yes," said Calix, looking directly into the afternoon sun. With a blinking grimace, the bulge finally went away. "And we should get moving. The strategos and his new proxenos shouldn't miss the signing of the agreement they helped forge."

"No," said Aurelius, turning up his nose and doing his best military march. "One must ensure that one's new subjects see one at the helm, mustn't . . . one?"

"They aren't your subjects, Aurie. You won't be issuing any orders."

"Oh, come on! Just a few here and there?" Aurelius said, giving him a playful shove. "And honestly, how do you hide that thing?"

"It was even worse when I was your age. I had to wear two loincloths, and he'd still stick out at the worst possible times."

"Sounds like you were quite the bull."

"You have no idea. You wouldn't have been able to handle me."

Aurelius gave him a little wink, running his tongue along his lips. "Oh, I think I've shown that I can handle you just fine, my prince."

"Stop!" pleaded Calix, the tent growing anew. "Why would you say something like that?"

"Control yourself, Strategos!" said Aurelius, dragging him by the elbow. "We can't miss the big ceremony!"

85

TEIGRA

Z<small>OSIME TURNED SHARPLY</small>.

If Teigra had been expecting a scream or call for backup or any other concession to the fact that the princess had been outwitted, she was to be disappointed. That single moment was all she got.

Instead, Zosime gave a patronizing laugh. "I *knew* you were hiding there," she said, looking from beneath her long locks of raven hair. "Why do you think I came here alone? Consider it a small kindness to let you out of that pathetic hiding spot."

Teigra pursed her lips. That was a lie. It had to be! Someone like her? On a mission like this? She wouldn't let her just hang around for two days without intervening.

"Why did you do it?" she hissed. "Why did you sabotage Calix and I?"

Zosime rolled her eyes. "Stop being so dramatic. It doesn't suit you."

Teigra clenched her teeth to stop herself from screaming. "Dramatic? You ruined my life!"

"And what *life* did I ruin? Some concocted plan of my mother's? Some insult to Ardora, created for cynical reasons?"

"Calix and I both knew what we were doing. Mestibes would be saved and Ardora would get the story they longed for!"

"You think *you* are what my polity longed for?" Zosime scoffed. "You think you could have sat your bony ass atop the throne of Ardora and served as our symbol of fertility and earthly toil?"

Old stings burned hot, coming in language blunter than she'd ever heard as a child. But rather than shame or that familiar embarrassment, she burned now with rage. Rage joined by the advice from Ms. Securia—that in Ardora, you had to give as good as you got!

"And you think *that* would've made him happy? Some big-titted cow? Are you too stupid to know that your brother is *gay*!"

Zosime shook her head. "Ardor save me. I thought you Mestibians were supposed to be the smart ones. You think I don't know that Calix is gay? And he isn't gay, *actually*. He likes both men and women but only feels romantic attraction toward men. What? Surprised? *I* realized his desires before he did. If it was up to me, he'd have found a man that makes his heart melt and gone public with it—damn the consequence! Ardora would come around to a display of true passion like that. Played right, he could be his honest self and still take the throne."

The wind was knocked from Teigra. Calix had told her as much on the balcony of the Rose Rain Ball, hadn't he? But in her rage, it had slipped her mind. "Then ... why?"

"Are you really that thick? I didn't tear you down in the hopes my brother would find someone more *attractive*. I did it in the hopes he would find someone more *inspired*." Zosime clicked her tongue. "Your cousin may be a manipulative son of a bitch, but at least he *burns* with something. At least he has a fucking soul. At least he takes each day by the scruff of the neck and shakes it into submission. But not *you*." The word was said with utter disgust. "Not *you*."

"How ... how can you be so cruel?" she stammered.

"Just look at yourself. You think you would have survived the coronet of oak? You would have been eaten alive, *Tiggy*. By my mother. By the Greens who dream of their own lineage. By the same ones who spoke fealty to my father when he was poisoned, but privately started jockeying. By the citizens who'd have turned against you as reliably as winter follows fall. How do you think it would have gone when you recoiled from the blows you weren't strong enough to take?"

Teigra turned away, willing the tears not to come.

Zosime stepped forward. "Really, what was the hope in coming here? That you would *shock* me? That you would convince me that I'd made some awful mistake? I saved my future king from a loveless life with a damp, dead fish!" Zosime leaned right in close, till her lips were by Teigra's ear. "And I saved my polity from the indignity of a pathetic, weak-willed, feeble queen!"

"I am not pathetic!"

Zosime smirked. "Then hit me."

"What?"

"You heard! Hit me, *Low Envoy*. You called me out and I've just further insulted you. Just like I did at Palaestra Xiphos. A queen of Ardora would never tolerate such indignity. Even my hoplites wouldn't take this. If I'd said these things to Elexis or Pikra, I'd have been knocked on my ass—damn my rank or my bloodline. And yet, here you stand, with your angry little face and your clenched-up rage. You want me to think you aren't pathetic? Then *hit me!*"

Part of Teigra recoiled. It thought back to all the blows she'd endured at the hands of Mother. All the duties she'd undertaken on others' behalfs, without ever fighting back or receiving a word of thanks. That part of her knew that Zosime was right. What could be more pathetic than her? What could be more weak-willed and undeserving of respect than *her*?

And yet, another part—newer and hungrier—vibrated with fury. She had made the plans with Calix when no one else had supported her. She'd run from the certainty of lifelong punishment, all to take a chance on a new life. And she'd come *here*! She'd snuck aboard a boat, she'd hidden for two days, and she'd confronted Zosime!

439

That pathetic girl? That weak-willed girl? She wouldn't have done that!

And just as Zosime once again clicked her tongue in disgust, it happened.

Teigra punched her.

The blow was sweet. The strike was strong from years of stable labor. Zosime stumbled to the floor. And as she looked up, blood pouring from her nose, the surprise that Teigra had craved when she'd first emerged finally washed across the princess's face.

Who's pathetic now, bitch?

The shock didn't last. The princess kipped up, somehow graceful despite a face smeared crimson. She grabbed Teigra by her sweat-ridden fabric and slammed her back against the hull.

Teigra braced for the punch in return.

Before it could land, there came a sickening scream from above deck.

86

AURELIUS

They returned to the palace on foot, Calix having sent his stallion away with a slap on the rump, saying he would find his way back to the villa. There would be no point in trying to enter on horseback anyway—it would have been impossible to squeeze through.

He had been part of several crowds since arriving in Ardora, and each had brought a different impression. There had been the casual atmosphere of the Ardoralia; the noble decadence of the Wax Crack; and the mad enthusiasm of the Black Night Festival, glimpsed from the speeding carriage. But as they approached the courtyard beyond the palace walls, the signing ceremony brought back an impression he'd only felt once before, while standing in the crowd at the Gipedo Thanatou of Kastro Machiton.

Soldiers. Hundreds and thousands of trained killers.

Oh, there were also myriad giants and farmers further back in the crowd. But they weren't his focus.

Aurelius gulped. Only now did he appreciate Calix's reluctance to take him on as an advisor. Seeing them like this, with their shining weapons and strong stares, he'd been a fool to think they could keep a relationship hidden.

Calix carried himself with apparent calm, as Brothers and Sisters saluted their general, only to eye Aurelius suspiciously. The sharp lines of their helmets made their faces even darker, suggesting how quickly that curiosity might turn to contempt.

If they knew what we are, would they even offer us a chance to walk away? Or would they gut us where we stand?

"We don't have to do this," he whispered, half hoping Calix would concur. "We could always duck somewhere quiet for now, and you can introduce me more slowly?"

Calix set his jaw. "No, Aurelius. You were prepared to go to the Grove for me. Now it is my turn."

"But, what if they suspect? I don't want you getting into trouble on my behalf."

"Don't you? There must be first time for everything."

"I'm serious!"

"So am I," he whispered through the corner of his mouth. "Trust me, it'll look worse if we creep around. No one here will question two men slapping asses and spending all their time together, as long as they're relaxed about it. But the second you start acting nervous, questions emerge."

"Yes, but—"

"Don't worry. I can do this for you. For *us*."

He sighed. "Thank you."

He did his best to follow the advice and relax as they moved into the courtyard proper, where a wooden platform had been erected in the middle. That stage was already surrounded by people, and lit on each side by a large brazier, crackling in the dusk air.

The two of them weaved deeper into the crowd, with more senior captains, both men and women, coming up to gossip with Calix about upcoming strategy. The prince warmly embraced them all, including one large, older woman in a hugely plumed helmet, taking frequent swigs on an amphora and appearing barely able to stand from the drink.

Though most seemed curious about his presence, Aurelius slipped into the comfortable role of a cultured Mestibian idiot, all artsy and passive, who now needed the big strong fighters of Ardora to sweep in and save them from their past foolishness.

It worked a charm, as he knew it would. Sometimes it was good to shock a potential rival. Other times it was better to hew completely to expectation—for as long as someone could slot you into a ready-made groove, then you melted into the background of their prejudice.

In less than half an hour, he went from a virtual unknown to just another part of the furniture.

Son of their ruler, you know. Going to help us navigate those poor defenseless little towns down south.

Horn trumpets swept the night, reverberating back from the steadfast stone. First to the stage was the king, climbing the wooden stairs without any apparent pain, buoyed by the great wave of affection from the crowd.

Then, from the very back of the press, moving slowly, came Ms. Securia. She was dressed in the cleanest, whitest stola he had ever seen, trimmed with a brilliant yellow. She clearly wasn't happy to be there. But still, she'd turned up, which counted for something.

She spotted Aurelius from across the crowd and made her way over. "Your Excellency," she said, looking from him to the prince. "I thought you had departed?"

"I decided he could stay a little longer," said Calix, with surprising warmth.

That warmth must surely have been for the new journey the two of them were starting together, and the remnant glow of his recent feeding, rather than for *her*. He couldn't recall Securia having met with Calix since Aurelius arrived. Although, now that he thought about it, she must have known him for decades?

"You aren't nervous?" Aurelius said. "Half the polity must be here."

She took his hand, and for a moment he became lost in her eyes —as if they were the only thing in the entire world. There was such resolution there. Such focus. And yet, such pain as well.

She deserves this. All the credit, all of the glory, all of the fame and reputation. She has earned it all.

"No, Your Excellency," she said, blinking him free. "I think I will be just fine."

Aurelius cocked his eyebrow once she'd left, shocked at his thoughts. Not wanting the credit? Allowing someone else to have the glory? That wasn't like him at all.

But it was true, wasn't it?

He didn't need anything else, as long as he had Calix.

He nestled a little closer to the big man, feeling the press and pressure of thousands of bodies around him.

It was strange. He never normally felt nervous in a crowd, but suddenly, his heart was racing at their mere presence. His throat felt tight, his mouth dry. And he was very glad it would be Ms. Securia giving the speech, rather than him.

Must . . . must be all the swords . . .

By contrast, Securia positively bounded onto the stage, throwing her arms up to receive the cheers. She blew kisses and bowed, pointing to a few people and waving.

I never imagined her as someone who rose to the energy of a crowd! But she probably knows most of them, doesn't she?

Securia and the king alternated speeches. As their uplifting words on camaraderie and duty and passion brought the crowd to repeated cheers, Aurelius's mind wandered, able to think properly for the first time since the grand revelation that he was a *therian*.

"What is it?" asked Calix, off his furrowed brow.

"I just realized. If I'm like you, that means my family must have done something to upset Ondo?"

"Your *father*, you mean?" said Calix with a little smile.

"Oh, shit," said Aurelius through clenched teeth. "I hadn't even thought about that."

"Believe me, it'll probably never feel normal," he said with a chuckle. "And on upsetting him? Yes, your mother must have done something."

"But I can't think of anything. And it would have to be something really massive for Ondo to take notice."

"Not necessarily."

"Oh really, wise sage? You never actually told me what House Viralis did to anger Ardor?"

The prince stared up at his father, his eyes narrowing. To Aurelius's shock, Calix's next words didn't come in Dynosian, but in *Voresoma*, a language he didn't know the man could even understand, let along speak. It was somewhat hesitant, clearly from lack of use, and laced with the strange infiltration of his Ardoran accent, but it was still comprehensible. "My father was seeing two women in the year before I was born. One of good breeding and socially powerful, but who he certainly didn't love. The other was a much less typical choice, who brought light to his days."

"And he chose the one he didn't love?" said Aurelius, also in the ancient language.

Calix nodded.

"Why?"

"Class? Power? Arrangements between the right families? Patriotism? But the main reason was that the noblewoman was already pregnant with me. And that was the sin. Keeping a child out of calculus, rather than affection." The prince sighed. "I might be the only one of our kind that created *myself*."

Aurelius rubbed his pinkie against Calix's, hidden by the mass all around them. Calix returned the gesture.

"It isn't your fault," said Aurelius. "You weren't even born yet. And besides, I can't believe that something so small would be enough for Ardor to punish your family? If that were the case, half the people here would be therians."

"We are born to ruling families. The Five probably hold us to a higher standard than regular people."

As the king spoke, a final piece clicked into place. Aurelius chuckled. "So *that* is what she meant."

"Hmmm?"

"A few months back, Zosime proposed that I seek the military agreement through her, not you. I thought she was trying to take your spot in the succession, though I now realize she was just messing with me to protect you. But she hinted that there was some scandal related to your birth. I finally know what she meant now."

Aurelius laughed. Calix didn't return it. "*Zosime* said that?"

"Yes. Why?"

Calix looked around. There was something desperate in his movements. In his face was a look of *panic.*

"What? Calix, tell me!"

Calix spoke in Dynosian once more, clearly too shaken to use a second language. "Zosime doesn't know *anything* about my father's past!" he hissed. "The whole thing was hushed up, even from our own family. The only reason I know about it is because . . ."

On the stage, Securia's face flushed with the same panic as Calix. She snapped to her feet, pointing emphatically.

Pointing right at *the two of them.*

The high envoy dove to the deck.

Then came the roar.

There was an almighty explosion of smoke, billowing from the stage. It moved so fast it sent people tumbling over each other with clanks of armor and smacks of flesh.

Aurelius dragged himself up from the pile of fallen fighters. Calix was nowhere to be seen—not on the ground, nor in the panicked press.

A bloodcurdling scream snapped him back to the stage. Amongst the roil of smoke was something that turned his blood to ice.

Standing in the center of the wooden platform, looming over the crowd, was *himself.*

"A gift!" the thing screamed, using his own voice, drawing all eyes upon it. "A gift from the herald of Mestibes!"

The figure held something aloft, smoke curling around it.

Aurelius's stomach turned.

It was the severed head of Selkus III, King of Ardora.

87

TEIGRA

Zosime dropped Teigra and ran up the stairs, joined by Elexis and Pikra from the other direction. The screams from above were piercing, punctuated only by the sound of horrific slashes and wet gurgling.

Teigra followed, poking her head slowly through the stairway portal.

She jumped as dead eyes glared right back at her. It was one of the sailors. His body was mangled, a pool of blood and organs laying in a disgusting heap beside him.

She spotted the cause. Her skin crawled.

Harpies.

They were just like those that had attacked her and Jaspar and Aurelius all those months ago. But this time, rather than three, there were *a dozen* of them—ripping and tearing and swooping everywhere she looked. Their hideous faces screeched, skeletal wings and bony bodies, blood-drenched from fang-filled mouths all down to their sagging breasts.

Other bodies were strewn across the deck. It had been only a matter of seconds, but there wasn't a single sailor left alive.

The three Sisters stood as one in the center of the ship. Pikra dodged lightly as one swooped, sending a dagger flying after it, piercing it right in the head and sending it crashing down into the blue waters that surrounded them. Elexis didn't even dodge, grabbing one out of midair and stamping on its razor claws. The harpy's eyes bulged as it tried to escape. With a sickening sound, the big woman reached down and snapped its neck.

And next to them both, a vision of dancing death, was Zosime.

She moved with malicious grace, her sword deflecting and slicing, her boots skipping as the beasts hit nothing but empty air. When one at last connected, grabbing her sword arm in its awful talons, she flicked her trapped hand, sending her blade arcing behind her and catching it effortlessly in her free hand, before plunging the steel right into its heart.

In short order, the numbers were even.

One of the remaining harpies flew up and sat atop the sails, hissing. One swooped down to the front of the ship, accompanied by the frightened bray of hippocamps. And the largest one, its feathers a darker shade of brown, came to rest on the railing at the very back, right where Teigra had hidden on her first day onboard.

Without a word, the Sisters ran to their targets. Pikra jumped onto the mast, scaling the ropes effortlessly. Elexis took the fallen driver's whip and propped herself over the edge, sending sharp cracks into the late afternoon air. And Zosime sprinted to the back.

Just as before, the princess was magnificent, like she could predict the beast's every movement. But this one was older and more cunning than the others, feinting its wings, moving in one direction then swiping in another.

As the fight went on, the sound of Zosime's strikes became less sweet. The beast attacked faster and faster. The princess moved at impossible speeds, blocking and deflecting, her eyes darting to keep up.

Then, the creature connected.

Teigra gripped the stairs hard.

The harpy's claws caught both of Zosime's wrists, sending her sword clanking across the deck.

The princess was defenseless—both arms pinned! Her compatriots were too far to reach! The beast was poised to strike!

For Teigra, the moment seemed to stretch forever. Half of her wanted to run back below deck; the other half screamed that she had to help.

But why should she? Zosime was the one who'd ruined everything. Was this not fitting? Was this not what she deserved?

The indecision didn't last. She couldn't let someone die. Not even her.

The big harpy hissed at Teigra's sprinting arrival, but she ignored it, grabbing the bronze-weighted nets from a few feet away and throwing them.

The blind toss wasn't perfect, but enough of the rope tangled the creature's wings to leave it thrashing around, like a fish out of water.

She didn't wait, she didn't dare. Her eyes half closed, she grabbed one of the harpoons from the rack and thrust it out.

It was a messy hit, missing the creature's chest and cutting a few inches below its shoulder. Still, with a spurt of rank blood, it stumbled over. Before it could rise, she pulled the harpoon up and struck again, this time directly into its stomach.

The harpy screeched right into Teigra's face as blood and stomach contents spewed onto the deck. The smell—rotting flesh and bile—was disgusting, but Teigra didn't stop. Again and again, she stabbed. Chunks of flesh stuck to the hook of the blade with each manic thrust.

At last, the harpy slumped back, a red-splattered lattice as its funeral blanket.

Zosime rose and grabbed her sword, incomprehension on her face.

"I . . . I did it," Teigra breathed, feeling as if she could cry. "I saved you."

"Yes, you did," said Zosime, in shock.

The moment was broken by a sneering voice from behind. "What the fuck are *you* doing on our ship?"

88

AURELIUS

THE KING'S DEAD FACE WAS A STATUE OF AGONY—HIS EYES ROLLED back, his mouth slack, his tongue hanging limp in the curling smoke. It was a brutal contrast to the wickedly grinning figure on the podium —with *his . . . its . . . my . . .* fingers threaded tightly through the gray hair, now streaked red with lost life.

It was like looking into a hideous, ruby-smeared mirror.

What the fuck is happening!?

From somewhere within the mass came an almighty roar. The sentinel shock of the crowd was shattered, turning now to fury, as soldiers drew their weapons, clambering over each other to be the first to the podium—to avenge, to kill, to *slaughter*. They bellowed for their king. They bellowed for their polity. From all sides they came, like frenzied ants up a wooden mound, their steel clattering in the smoky firelight.

From atop the podium, the beast that somehow bore his face seemed unfazed by its imminent demise. It turned upon Aurelius a lazy glare. Its grin seemed to grow even greater at the sight of his shock. And just as the blades were about to slice it to pieces, it gave him a wink.

Then it vanished into starlight.

The soldiers clattered into each other. When they got back to their feet, they held nothing but fistfuls of smoke and, eventually, in the arms of the big man who had started the charge, the mournful, decapitated corpse of their former ruler.

Then, it happened.

There was a change around him. The smoke seemed to thin. And then he was aware of a shift in the crowd. Before, he had just been one among many. But now eyes were turning to him.

And those eyes were full of fury.

"No . . ." he said, holding up his hands in realization. "That wasn't me! I was standing right here the whole time! You all saw it."

He hunted for Calix as the crowd pressed in. He hadn't done anything wrong! This couldn't be happening!

Directly behind him was an older man who appeared slower on the uptake.

Aurelius's breath quickened. He shouldn't *run*! Running would declare him guilty. But the moment for decision was just a few seconds.

The crowd pressed closer.

Stay or go.

Run or explain.

He had to decide!

He stole a quick glance at the oncoming fighters. The look in their eyes was frenzied madness. There would be no explaining.

He barged into the old man, knocking him to the ground with an awful crunch.

I'm sorry! I'm sorry!

Like a rabbit through brush, he darted, keeping his head low, ducking toward anyone who still looked confused. He smacked his head again and again, bringing swirls to his vision.

He didn't know where he was going.

He didn't care!

Snippets of the palace wall disappeared, telling him that he'd somehow found his way out into the city beyond, still heavy with the press of people.

"Stop him!" came a bellow from behind. "He murdered the king!"

On cue, what few gaps remained narrowed. Hands tore at his clothing and fingernails slashed across his face. He tried to keep going, but his movement slowed. He struggled to maintain what little momentum he had.

And then, in one awful moment, there were no gaps left. All that remained was the crush of anger and the stench of sweat.

Blows rained down upon him, all happening so quickly and from so many angles that he couldn't tell them apart. He tried to shield his face. He could barely breathe!

Suddenly, there was a rumble beneath his hands, the ground shaking. Then came a whipping sound, and the crack of bodies being flung.

The mass flew away, bringing clear air.

The dozen people who'd been kicking him were now being held back by fast-growing grape vines—turning from succulent green into the gnarly brown whips of winter dormancy.

Calix?

Up ahead, more vines exploded from the ground along a little side street, knocking people back and pinning them to walls.

He returned his pace, pain shooting across him. The vines burst from the roads ahead, guiding his path, twisting and turning, left and right, all the while people were knocked out of his way.

When he thought his lungs could take no more, he was grabbed around the waist, bringing him to a spinning stop. He threw an elbow back at whatever was grabbing him, but it landed hard against a thick shoulder.

It was Calix.

He was on one knee, his other hand to the ground—from where the path of vines was extending. The prince picked him up and staggered away, ducking into some private courtyard and collapsing at the base of an olive tree.

"Where were you!" Aurelius said as he gathered his bearings. "I was—"

Calix's face was pale and drenched in sweat. He gasped for air.

"The vines!" Aurelius said. "You made the vines even though you aren't in satyr form! And we are just a few days from a bronze moon!"

Calix bore a look of relief mixed with an awful pallor.

"Gods, you're exhausted. Just stay a moment. You have to rest."

"No!" he wheezed, dragging himself back to shaky feet. "We have to go after her!"

"Her? Her *who*?"

Calix's eyes were more wrathful than Aurelius had ever seen them. "We have to get *Ramuna Securia*!"

89

TEIGRA

"WELL, WELL, WELL. IF IT ISN'T THE PRINCE'S SPURNED LITTLE LOVER!" said Pikra. She pulled at Teigra's sweat-soaked fabric with an exaggerated upturn of her sharp nose. "One minute she is walking the agora with the queen—practically trying on the coronet for size —and now, she is stuck on a boat with the rest of us. Oh, how the mighty have fallen!"

"Now, now, Pik," said Elexis. "Leave the girl be. Can't you see she saved the captain!"

"Yes, she did," said Zosime—to Teigra's surprise, who'd expected her to deny it.

"And look, she's a natural!" said Elexis. "Still clutching 'er weapon, ready for the next attack."

Teigra was indeed still gripping the harpoon, blood and chunks of flesh coating her fingers. But it was more from shock than anything else, and certainly not a battle tactic.

Pikra gave her a long glare. "Oh, yes. Yes, that *must* be it. An *utter natural*. And so then, *your naturalness*, I am sure you have a good explanation for how you ended up on our ship?"

Whatever battle bond that'd formed vanished in an instant. Now,

Teigra was back where she'd started—a stowaway staring into the suspicious eyes of three soldiers who could cut her dead in an instant.

"I . . . I . . ." she stammered.

Zosime stepped forward. "She's with me."

Pikra looked as shocked as Teigra felt. "With *you*?"

"Of course. I've been cultivating her as a recruit for weeks now. And as a final test, I set her a challenge to get onto the ship and remain hidden without either of you noticing."

Elexis looked hurt. "You never told us about a fourth Sister, Cap!"

"No," said Zosime, pointedly. "Because I thought you'd both spot her right away!"

Pikra rolled her eyes. "Oh, come on. How were we supposed to know she was onboard? We thought we were just relaxing before the big mission."

"And you think Xiber will give us a big scream and a wave before sending an arrow through our chests?"

"Yes, yes. Message received. But why would we need *her*?"

"When was the last time you left Ardora? Ever been to Mestibes? Apart from the Emphanisi Springs?"

"She's got you there, Pik!"

"Granted, but—"

"Enough of this," said Zosime, glaring at Pikra. "Clear this deck before any more of them come. That's an order, *Hoplite Trypono*."

When the two Sisters had trudged away, Zosime reached out her hand. "I owe you my life."

In her eyes, Teigra could see that this was no idle statement.

Teigra wiped the blood from her own hand and took Zosime's sheepishly, the lingering rush of battle still pounding in her blood. The princess's hand was warm and surprisingly soft. "I just did what anyone else would've done."

"No, you didn't. Most civilians would have run below deck and hidden. They certainly wouldn't have rushed out to save someone they hated."

"I don't hate you. Well, I mean, I might have at the time, but—"

A splash caught her attention, and she turned a mortified look to the others. They were tossing body parts from the slain sailors over the side.

"What . . . what are you doing?"

Elexis laughed, tossing a dismembered torso out as if it was weightless. "How many Ondocians 'ave you known, my girl?"

"Enough," she lied.

"Well, then you know that burial at sea is something them folk aspire to. So say a prayer if it'll give you comfort. But we ain't 'aving dead flesh hanging around to attract more of the buggers!"

"Yeah," said Pikra, taking pleasure in her naivety. "And besides, none of them are alive to complain, *southerner*. So why don't you be a good Sister and pitch in?"

She turned to Zosime desperately, but the princess was already tossing a severed leg into the ocean. "Many hands, Initiate Cosmin. Many hands."

Initiate Cosmin?

She's calling me a military recruit!

Teigra gulped at the closest piece of flesh—an arm, severed just below the shoulder, the blood soaking through the fabric. She didn't want to touch it. But Zosime had thrown her a lifeline by lying about her being on a secret mission. And that could still turn in a heartbeat.

She approached the limb, feeling the sudden urge to vomit. The man's uniform was darker than the others.

The driver . . .

Biting her tongue, she took the arm by the palm, touching it in a crab-grip between thumb and middle finger. The flesh had already started to cool, and disgusting as it was, the thought of just throwing it away, as though it wasn't part of a person who'd been living and breathing just a few minutes ago, seemed a wretched thing.

But Elexis was right, wasn't she? The sea? The salt? That was practically prayer to an Ondocian. They wouldn't want to be thrown into the ground or burned in a crematorium.

Teigra thought back to the little Temple of Ondo back near the docks. Of the chalice of salt water. With a great sigh, her skin crawling, she tossed the arm overboard, where it tumbled down into a foam-tipped grave.

"Not a single one survived," said Zosime, running the long, finely twisted whip through her hands. "And I'm guessing neither of you two know how to direct a team of hippocamps?"

"Won't do us no good anyway, Cap! Them 'arpy buggers took out at least two of the team. And all the others snapped their restraints and made off before I could stop them."

"Oh *fantastic*," spat Pikra. "So we are stuck out in the middle of the ocean. We've no sea steeds. The sails are all scratched to shit. And, to top it all off, night is coming."

"I'm afraid so. The steeds could be anywhere by now!"

Teigra shook her head. "No, not a trained team of hippocamps. They are very loyal to their masters, even more than pegasi. They'll have fled to protect themselves, but they shouldn't be far."

Silence followed as all three Sisters stared at her. Zosime gave a faint smile and moved below deck.

"What did I say?" said Teigra.

"Nothing," said Elexis, looking up at the sky.

Pikra leaned in with a malevolent smile. "Congratulations, *Initiate*! The Sisterhood does love a volunteer."

A smack echoed from below deck, followed by a series of whinnies. At once, four pegasi flew out of the hold, circling overhead for a moment before coming gracefully down. Without being called, three went and stood by their masters.

She'd seen them before, but only now did she have the chance to look at them properly.

Pikra's was a skeletal mare, mouse gray, and with wings that seemed scruffy and flea-bitten—a common trait among Messara steeds. And yet, there was a knotted musculature beneath its coat that told her not to approach.

Elexis's was a huge Tobiano stallion, with a glossy coat in

chestnut skewbald, and the most neatly groomed wings she'd ever seen.

And the steed that stood beside Zosime was a majestic thing—a smoke-black stallion, with a lean body and eyes that gave her far more attention than the others. To Teigra's shock, she now realized he was a *thundermane*, a breed of wild horses found only in the Stormkiller Mountains. They were fabled to be near impossible to tame. She'd only ever read descriptions of their distinctive ears, shaped like spear tips, though she'd long dreamed of seeing one in person.

Those three were lightly packed, with four-horn saddles and scabbards for weapons. This was in sharp contrast to the *fourth*, which carried great bags all the way down to its strong knees.

Teigra's eyes bulged. For a moment, she was back in familiar stables.

It was a Zante mare, with hair of blood bay and wings that glinted gold in the light. It wasn't Astrapi, her faithful friend, but it could easily have been a sturdier cousin. It gave her a curious look through kindly eyes, as well as the gentlest flutter of her wings.

"Here," said Zosime, handing her the reins. "You can ride Varas."

"Ride? Ride where?" she said, staring at the straps but not taking them. "And come to think of it, why do you even have pegasi! I haven't seen another one the whole time I've been in Ardora."

"Oh," said Elexis, looking excited to tell the story. "So, a few years back we were doing a job for this big shot in Mavelix, and the journey took us to the Emphanisi Springs—"

"Shhh," hissed Pikra. "She doesn't need to know about all that, thick skull!"

"Oh, right! The whole deception thing."

"Deception?" said Teigra. "What deception?"

Elexis and Pikra kept their mouths shut.

Zosime stood unmoved, arm still holding out the reins. "We can't just stay on a floating coffin," she said to Teigra. "We have a mission to get to. And the only way to do that is to get the hippocamps back."

Zosime gave the reins a slight shake. There was no speech. No motivational spur. But the implication was clear.

I know damn well that you haven't ridden solo for three years, she seemed to say. *And I know why. But I won't say anything to the others. Instead, I'm giving you a chance to get on this steed and show me how nonpathetic you truly are.*

It was the final test. The final chance to prove herself.

The thought of riding again after so long caused her stomach to drop. After all, the last time she'd done that . . .

But Zosime was right. They had a mission. If they didn't leave now, they might miss Xiber entirely, and then all of Mestibes would be denied the warning of what was coming.

All because of her? All because she was too pathetic to get on a horse?

Are you a delicate little flower, Teigra? Or are you a rose with fucking thorns?

Doing her best to silence old nightmares, she took the reins.

90

AURELIUS

"Securia is an *eidolon*?" hissed Aurelius, as Calix guided him through the streets by hand, having to duck behind shadowy doorways as members of the mob ran by. He had tied the scraps of fabric around himself as best he could, gathering several torn strips into a twist by his heart and closing it with the eternal rose pin—the delicate glass somehow free of further damage.

The pin gifted by the woman who just killed the king . . .

"How many therians are there in this fucking city?" asked Aurelius.

"That I know of? Just us three," said Calix.

"And she knew that you were one too?"

"Yes. After I returned from Sama, she came to me. She got me through those first few months. She taught me about the Sable Moon Sanctum—about keeping the beast at bay. Zosime is the one who locks me away, but Ramuna was the one who kept me in check."

"It seems she failed to heed her own lessons," he muttered, as they moved through the more expensive districts. "And where are we going?"

"*We* aren't going anywhere, Aurelius. I need to get you out of the city."

"We both need to get out of the city."

Calix smoldered. "No. I must face her."

"Calix, I am not leaving."

"I told you, it isn't safe—"

He wagged his finger. "And *I* told you, I am not leaving. So, what are we fighting then? What are her powers?"

Calix seemed for a moment as if he might protest further, but then relented. "I have never seen her in therian form. To my knowledge, she has been resisting her change so long, that she even manages to hold it at bay during the sable moon."

"I didn't know that was possible?"

"Neither did I. I've tried myself, but I can never managed to do it."

Aurelius pulled dusty lectures from the recess of memory. "The therians of Mesti are fueled by jealousy? Not for money or possessions, but for skills and talents, intellect, strength, charm . . ." Realization twinged. "That bitch!"

"What?"

"When she came to talk to us. Her eyes were hypnotic. Afterward, I felt suddenly shy and reserved, which I never do. And she was bounding up and soaking in the crowd! She used her powers and *stole my confidence!*"

"Really?" said Calix, with concern. "How do you feel now?"

He hunted inside himself. "Fine? I suppose? She must have only drained it briefly? Is that even possible?"

Calix's brow furrowed. "She's been a metamorph since her early twenties. Maybe she's learnt a way to just drink what she needs? Rather than draining people dry?"

"Maybe," said Aurelius with a shrug, resisting the urge to ask whether that was something Calix might be able to learn as well. Now was not the time.

"And she also has the power to alter her physical form," said Calix.

"Don't I know it! I got the fright of my life when I saw—"

He remembered too late. Calix's hands gripped tighter and stopped.

Oh... gods...

"I'm so sorry, Calix. Your father . . . he didn't deserve that."

Calix paused only briefly before continuing. His face was hard. "We don't have time for that."

The streets rolled by until they eventually came upon an ominous building.

"What is this?" said Aurelius.

Calix shot him a look. "You *really* don't go in for worship, do you? The Temple of Mesti? Built and maintained by your embassy for the last hundred years?"

"Oh," he said, faintly embarrassed. "And she will be in there?"

"This is where she comes for her Sanctum." Calix placed his hand on the doorknob, his knuckles tensed. "And it's a fitting place for her to receive her punishment."

It was dark inside, lit only by the orange fire of a glass kiln, humming with a low heat that cast long shadows. It smelled powdery —the same powdery smell that had filled the palace grounds during the explosion of smoke.

One shadow slithered up the far wall of scrolls, shaded thin and dark across the face of the goddess, before finally settling upon a kneeling figure.

Aurelius didn't know what sound he had expected. Manic laughter? Some evil soliloquy?

What he hadn't expected was *crying*.

Her voice wavered. "It . . . it couldn't be allowed to happen. Not like that. *Not like that.*"

There was a war between rage and pity on Calix's face. "I know, Ramuna," he said, approaching her slowly. Each footstep was an echoing stroke of a funeral bell. "But I come to deliver your punishment."

"*Punishment?*" she sniffed. "How much more must I endure? I went to the Grove for him! I picked the rose! And it *bloomed*. We loved each other! And rather than a life of bliss, I got *this* as my reward! A lover who betrayed his love. A city that betrayed its goddess. And a goddess who long ago betrayed *me*, no matter how much I gave and I gave and I gave!"

"Stand, Securia," said Calix, looming over her, his voice a low rumble.

The bronze curves of the goddess were washed red with firelight. "Is this your will, Mother? Is this your plan for your own daughter?"

"*Stand*, Securia," repeated Calix, a great tension in his jaw. "I am offering you the mercy of a swift death. But defy me and I *will not* hold back."

With surprising speed, Securia swung around, placing her hands against Calix's cheek. "Don't worry, dear boy. *Neither will I.*"

Calix froze.

And Securia swung.

Rather than some feeble slap, she connected with an almighty punch—the fist structure perfect, the placement sublime, and the force phenomenal.

Calix went flying across the room.

She twinkled in blue and purple stars, the light refracting across motes of dust. "Goddess! The *vitality*. The *strength*. And all of it will be mine. Not in the hand of some miserable boy. But in the hands of someone *worthy*!"

With a glimmer of midnight and the sound of sand falling against marble, she *changed*.

Where she had once stood was now a perfect copy of Calix. She held herself with a confidence and domination that the real prince only had in satyr form. "Don't worry, boy. I will do a much better job on the throne than you would have!"

The fake Calix leaped, but the prince rolled away just in time and lunged back at her. Securia caught him in midair and threw him to the side. She mounted his chest and laid into him with punches, one after the other, the sick sound of wet meat being struck.

Calix was helpless to respond, trying to grab the hands, to shield his face, but all his strength had been stolen.

"It was you!" screamed the fake Calix as the blows rained down. "I would have had him if it weren't for *you!*" She grabbed Calix's head and smacked it back into the floor.

"Get off him," screamed Aurelius, diving onto her back. He writhed, scratching and biting with all his might against the slab of muscle.

The Calix copy grabbed him around the throat and sneered. "Still here, Herald? Well, best you stick around. After all, the people will need someone to *execute!*"

Aurelius was smacked against a slab of upright marble at some kind of sculpture station. He crashed into the floor in an eruption of dust.

The first thing he saw when he opened his dazed eyes, as if by divine fate, was the door.

As he lay there, body aching, he knew she was right. If he stayed, and she took the throne, then she would drag him before the people and execute him.

The fake Calix returned to its beatdown of the real prince. And there was nothing he could do to stop it.

But there was one thing he *could* do.

As he reached out to drag himself up, his hand fell upon cold metal. It was a stonemason's hammer, still covered in the dust of countless projects. He had never wielded one in his life, but he could feel the weight, the *strength* within the tool.

Just like the strength that Securia had stolen from Calix. Just like the strength she was beating out of the man he loved.

Aurelius took another look at the door, closed his grip, and ran.

The smack of metal was sweet against her ribs. In her daze, the bloody hand of the real Calix grabbed his mirror's jaw. There was a moment of stillness, then her false form faded back into the high envoy.

She rolled off Calix. Her gaze was suddenly frenzied.

"You!" she bellowed to the statue of the goddess. "You are the one who did this. You are the one who did all of this! I gave you everything. *Everything!* And you have forsaken me! You made me into this monster! This beast!"

Calix's face was a bloody mess. "Can you stand?" said Aurelius. "We have to get out of here while we can!"

"No," he spluttered, red droplets spat across the floor. He picked up the hammer. "This must end."

She didn't even notice him hobbling over, too consumed with the passion Calix had amplified within her.

He didn't pose or posture. There was no speech. There was no hesitation. When he came within striking distance, he swung hard, metal cracking against her head.

Securia was knocked into the scroll hive, parchments crashing onto the floor. She still had enough of Calix's strength in her, and had taken enough of it from the prince, that the blow didn't kill her, though blood now poured from her own head.

Before she could stand, Calix mounted her chest, just as she had him, with his big legs pinning her arms against the floor.

Her body was tiny between his tree-trunk thighs. And the hammer was raised overhead, poised for the killing blow.

Just before he could, there was another sparkle of stardust. And now, Calix was no longer looking into the eyes of a middle-aged woman.

Now he was looking into the eyes of *Aurelius*.

"Don't hurt me," the figure whimpered. "Not again. Not after what you did last time."

Calix froze—shame sweeping his bloody mask, the streams dripping down onto the lighter skin of the fake Aurelius. It was just long enough for the figure to wriggle free and stagger away.

"Calix!" yelled Aurelius, grabbing him by his enormous arm. "Snap out of it!"

Securia stumbled toward the door, clutching at her head—a thick line of blood falling behind her. Calix gathered himself and followed.

She tried to slam the door closed but the prince smashed it into splinters on its hinge.

Aurelius sprinted after them but was brought to a screaming stop at the broken doorway. Rather than running into a confrontation with Securia, Calix was met by a dozen members of the city mob.

And the high envoy was nowhere to be seen.

"Where did she go?" Calix bellowed, blood spraying on his breath. The crowd pawed him—not in anger as they had to Aurelius, but in mad relief. They were almost as frenzied as Securia had been in front of the statue, all chanting the same thing.

The king is dead!

Long live the king!

He's hurt! Our king is hurt!

Calix fought against their clutches. Aurelius covered his own face and ducked out just long enough to yank Calix away, dragging him a few streets in the opposite direction.

Calix broke free in a dark alley. "Take me back! I can follow her blood. I can find her!"

"And you think you will get through *them* unimpeded? They'll all be like that, all through the city!"

"I have to . . . I have to . . ." His eyes were at once blank and filled with heavy meaning. He slumped against a wall, sliding to the ground. His panting was guttural as everything he had been holding back hit him at once. The blood across his face was so thick he looked like a human rose petal.

"Calix," Aurelius whispered, tearing a strip of his cloth and pressing it against the man's head. "You are the *king*."

Calix's shoulders tensed. Red dripped through his clenched teeth. "Like *fuck* I am!"

91

TEIGRA

Teigra dug her knees into Varas's flank, gripping the reins so hard her knuckles went white. The pegasus's feathers fluttered on the breeze, at once familiar and alien.

It's fine. It's fine, she thought, desperately trying to convince herself.

But it wasn't fine. *None* of this was fine.

Not only was her stomach in her throat with three years of buried terror, she found that she'd lost a good step of her instincts, too. And besides, in the Alogo, the entire pegasus race was short and sharp, taking just a few minutes. That meant they could fly fast and low to the ground, where the paying customers could see them.

She gulped and closed her eyes.

Even the strongest pegasus could only fly for about five minutes, and even that was so taxing to the heavy creatures that it was done sparingly. And though she'd long heard of the flight technique of *gliding*—extending flight time hugely by catching warm, spiraling updrafts that required no additional effort on the steeds—she'd never experienced it herself.

"What are you doing?" asked Zosime, from a dozen feet away.

Teigra forced her eyes open, trying not to look down. "I was just . . . thinking of a plan."

"Really? Because it looked like you were scared of heights."

"What? Of course not. I've done this plenty of times," she lied, sneaking the smallest peek below. Their ship was now so small and distant she could cover it with her thumb.

"What are we looking for?" said Zosime, over the sound of the cool winds that whipped her long hair, glinting like black glass in the warming light.

Teigra shielded her eyes, waiting for the clouds to clear beneath them. "That!" she said, suppressing the twisting feeling in her stomach.

Zosime stared at the distant, gold-tipped waves. "I don't see anything."

"Just there. Can you see the little circles running counter to the swell?

"How the fuck did you spot that?" squinted Zosime, reaching for the whip she had looped onto the saddle.

"We used to take them down to the shoreline for exercise sometimes. They have very distinctive movements in deep water. And you don't need that. The whip isn't to *whip* them into submission. They use it because, at full pace, the animals are completely underwater, so they can't hear commands. The whip is cracked just above the waterline to keep their pace steady and tell them which way to turn."

After a long stare, Zosime restowed the whip and gestured for Teigra to lead.

She'd never rounded up hippocamps before. The ones back home were so well trained that they came at a whistle and a toss of sardines.

The first few swoops toward the swell made her feel physically sick, not just with the long-forgotten plummeting sensation, but with the lingering memory of the last awful dive she'd taken. But after a few attempts, the old instincts filtered back—the way you could position your weight to steer, without needing to yank at the reins; the arcs that conserved energy and maximized the speed of the approach; and the way you had to trust your mount, even if it felt like she might slip from the momentum.

That lesson was the hardest, and she certainly wasn't going to learn it today. With every swoop, her knees gripped hard.

Varas was pure pack horse, sturdy and strong, but without the finesse or near-instant turn of speed that a thoroughbred racer like Astrapi had. But with some trial and error—swooping down and yelling through cupped hands, flying their two steeds so low their hooves dug turquoise grooves into the swell—they managed to get the hippocamps moving, with her and Zosime weaving behind on warm drafts.

"I'm sorry," said Zosime, when they were about halfway back.

"What for?"

"You're not as useless as I thought."

"Then why did you say it? You barely even knew me, but you acted like my existence was an insult?"

Zosime stared at the sunset, touching purple and pink at the edges. "I don't have any contempt for those without the stomach to fight, Teigra. There are plenty of women who attend Palaestra Xiphos or turn up at the Gipedo Thanatou who just don't have the heart for it. Maybe they've been forced into it by their family, convinced of the message that the Brotherhoods and Sisterhoods need strong and willing bodies. Maybe they're ashamed of their lack of ferocity and want to change. But one throw, one bad landing, and they're a sobbing mess. Those women can try all they want, but they'll never be Sister material. It just isn't in their stars."

There was a stab in Teigra's chest. *So that's what Zosime thinks of me?*

"But," continued the princess. "I *do* have contempt for those with the potential to do great things, who are too weak to apply themselves."

"What do you mean? Do you know how hard it was for me to get on this steed? To get on this ship? To run out and save you?"

"*Now*, yes. But I first saw you when you crossed our borders. I saw that Accola boy stunned and your cousin cowering. I saw you leap into action when no one else would, despite having no training and no proper weapons." There was a bitter turn in her face. "And then I saw you *freeze*."

"I . . . I was scared."

"No. Scared I could forgive. You were *indecisive*. I saw you reach for the rope netting. You knew what to do. But you didn't commit. That is what I found pathetic, Teigra. To have the skills, to have the *instinct*, and not use them properly? That's a wretched thing."

They rode on for a while, until Teigra finally broke the silence. "I used the nets today, though."

The harshness in Zosime's stature faded. "Yes, you did."

At last, they arrived back at the ship, rehitching the team of hippocamps and landing on deck.

Zosime appeared in no hurry to join her comrades. "What I said, Teigra? About you joining us on the mission?"

"Don't worry. I know you were just helping me. I'm sure we can stop near some coastal town and I'll just swim ashore. I can't go back to Mestibes anyway."

The fading light cast shadows across the princess's strong cheeks. "It doesn't have to be a lie."

"You mean . . . me? A Sister? Tracking down a warlord?"

"Why not? I wasn't lying to Pikra. None of us have visited the southern lands for more than a few days. We could use someone who knows the territory. The customs. The leaders. And you've shown that you can fight."

"In *desperation*. But I don't know the first thing about actual combat."

"Initiates rarely do."

"Yes, but—"

Zosime raised her hand. "I'm not going to beg you. I'm just

making the offer. If you choose not to, that's your decision. We'll pass by a coastal town, just like you said, and you can swim to shore, starting whatever new life you wish." The princess's eyes glinted like the wave tops. "But I see something in you, Teigra. You're so much more than you think. And there's so much more that you could still be."

Zosime congratulated her again on getting the steeds back.

And then she was alone.

I ... I can't do that. Me? A fighter? A Sister?

The idea was too absurd to even contemplate.

And yet ...

Today she had ridden, overcoming three years of terror. And what did she have waiting in Mestibes, anyway? A mother that would probably pour the hemlock before her sentence had even been given? A city that would never appreciate the sacrifices she'd made?

Almost dizzy with the moment, Teigra dismounted, patting the big girl's neck.

The sun was low on the waterline, casting the sky as a raging fire.

From around her neck, she drew her pendant, heavy in her hands.

It had been passed through seven generations of Cosmins. And for the last three years, she had felt every single member of that lineage weighing against her. Felt the loyalty she needed to earn back. Felt the duty that she had to perform.

Stick to the path, kiddo. Even if it terrifies you.

She gave a little laugh. For so long, she had thought it a promise she'd broken. She'd taken a risk on that awful day, and she'd found herself outside the path. House Cosmin's path. *His* path.

But that wasn't it, was it?

Stick to the path, kiddo. Even if it terrifies you.

Because it wasn't a mantra of compliance. It was a scream of *defiance*!

Father had never followed a conventional path—the one laid out by society and his position in life. He had never failed to dream big and aim for things that everyone else said was impossible. He had never been scared of risk. Of breaking old ways. Of defying tired expectations. He had set his own path. And he had stuck to it. No matter the risks. No matter the costs.

That was what he meant.

That was what he'd always meant.

And now . . . now it was her turn to do the same. To forge her own path and commit to it. No matter how much it terrified her.

She laid a kiss on her fingers and placed it against the heirloom, saying a prayer for the man who was better than she had ever deserved, and to every member of House Cosmin who had worn it before her.

When she returned it to her neck, it suddenly felt a great deal lighter.

Breathing deeply, Teigra approached the trio.

She saluted Zosime. "What are my orders, Captain?"

92

AURELIUS

Aurelius chased after Calix, who had half staggered, half run back to his villa. He reached the open door, struggling for breath, just in time to have Calix steam back out, thrusting something heavy against his chest. He'd arrived several minutes before Aurelius, and had wrapped a rag around his head, staunching the worst of the bleeding.

Aurelius opened the sack of supplies—cooking equipment, old clothing and a goat-skin tent. "What is this?"

Calix strapped his own bag to his steed, a few lines of now-tacky red streaked across its white coat. "We'll ride fast to the border with Ondocis. Then you have to disappear. Vanish into one of the low polities. Head for the islands—that's where I'd go. Change your name. Cut your hair."

"What? Shouldn't I go back to Mestibes? The archon could find a way to fix this! Securia was one of our people after all!"

"And you think your senate will believe your word over her reputation?" Calix shook his head. "I've only been to your city once, but even I know they'll have you tried and hemlocked before you get halfway through your first sentence."

"They . . . they wouldn't do that," he said. "Killing an innocent man? Just to try and preserve the alliance?"

"*Alliance?*" said Calix. "What *alliance?* Mestibes will execute you in the name of its own justice."

"But . . . the war . . . ?"

"Don't you understand, Aurelius? The pact is dead. Ardora is not coming to your aid. Mestibes is going to be invaded and it will get no quarter from us. After what happened tonight, it'll be a miracle if Ardora doesn't switch sides and fight *alongside* Rinath!"

"But you are the king! You could order the Brothers to fight against whoever—"

"Aurelius!" Calix snapped. "We don't have time for this. I have only two options right now! And neither of them involves sending my men to save the city that just killed my father!"

The silence which followed stung.

But he was right. Of course he was right.

It had all happened so fast. Moments ago, they were planning their future together. Working alongside each other, hand in hand, to repel an invasion?

And now he was to disappear? As a criminal? As a *murderer?*

"But I didn't do anything," he whispered, hugging the bag of supplies.

"I know," said Calix, more softly, placing a hand on his shoulder. "But Securia played this perfectly. My father is dead. The military pact is gone. Your family's name will struggle to survive. And she's put me in an impossible situation."

"Your two options?"

He nodded. "I was an architect of this deal, and everyone knows it. I'll be deeply damaged in the eyes of my people. More than I already am. If I stay and take the throne, the only way I could ensure my legacy—my *family's* legacy—would be to go to war against Mestibes."

"You wouldn't!"

"I wouldn't want to, Aurelius. But my family is more important than what I want. And my people have been promised a battle. You saw them. They weren't scared of the coming war. They want their blades to taste blood. They hunger for a fight. And I would have no choice but to give them one."

There was something else in his eyes. Something which hit Aurelius with freezing realization. "And you would have to turn me in, wouldn't you? Just like Securia said she would. So you could prove that there was no collusion."

Calix looked wretched.

"Would you do it?" said Aurelius, a catch in his throat.

Calix's face was a statue of torment. "No," he whispered. "I could never do that."

Aurelius let out a slow sigh of relief. "So . . . what is the other option?"

Calix lashed the final strap of the horse. "I have to find the one person who might be able to avoid that possibility."

Aurelius stared at him for a while before it clicked. "*Zosime*? You would give up your birthright to Zosime?"

"She's known to hate your polity. She wouldn't need to prove anything. She could take lesser steps that I couldn't. Cut off relations. Starve Mestibes of trade. Laugh as Mestibes was invaded. But not actually join the war against you."

"What difference does that make? Either way, Mestibes would be destroyed."

Calix breathed heavily. "A peaceful city, considering itself to be the last bastion of decency and reason in an illogical world? There have been worse moments for heroes to rise, Aurelius. And there have certainly been worse moments for the Five to reward the faith of their flock."

"You can't seriously believe that *Mesti* is going to swoop down and reward the city for not putting up a fight?"

Calix ran his hands along Aurelius's arm. "We both know the power of the gods. And their strange sense of humor. Weirder things are possible."

Aurelius took the hand, holding it tightly. "You would give up your birthright? For me?"

"It isn't just for you. Zosime will be a greater leader than I could ever be." From atop the hill, Calix looked over the dark city beyond. When he next spoke, it was little more than a gravel whisper. Aurelius was shocked to realize that it was a line from a play he knew well: "Creatures of Carnage" by the Mestibian actor and playwright Lyrisi. "What therian should sit upon this throne? What Beast of Bronze this city should endure?"

A pang of sympathy grazed Aurelius's lungs. "But, how do we even find her?"

"She's heading to the foothills of Vaticily. If we hurry, we might be able to catch her. Because from there? God only knows where she might travel."

"But surely she will find out what has happened anyway? The death of a king? She will hear that in a few weeks at most. And then she will return on her own?"

"We can't wait that long. Even a week is dangerous. My mother can keep the nobles at bay for a while. If we can get Zosime on the throne quickly, they'll probably back down. My sister will make sure of that. But the Greens have waited for six generations in the shadows. House Kormos almost launched an attack after Father was poisoned. If the crown lays empty for too long, Kleio and the rest of his brood *will* make their move. And any family who takes the throne will be certain to launch a war against Mestibes—the ultimate consolidation of their new power. The only solution, for both of us, is to find Zosime now!"

"And what about Securia? She could still impersonate you?"

"We'll have to take that risk. She could be anywhere and anyone right now." He again looked over the rolling hills. "Our two families disgraced and much blood still to be shed? Hopefully, she's already gotten what she intended."

Calix mounted his steed and extended a hand. The stallion gave him a stubborn look, and Aurelius returned it.

Fucking horses, he thought, momentarily wondering where Teigra was.

Would she be safe? Despite it all, he hoped so. She was always so much stronger than she realized.

Wherever she is, hopefully she is learning that.

Calix pulled him up and they clicked into a gallop. They avoided the roads, moving swiftly through fields and groves under a blanket of night.

"Do you really think we will find her?" he said, eventually.

"*We* don't find her, Aurelius. I told you. As soon as we cross the border, you're going into hiding."

"Calix. I am obviously coming with you."

"My sister will be following Xiber to the front lines, Aurelius! To the edge of Rinath and beyond! Lands of war and death! It's no place for someone untrained in—"

"Calix, we are doing this together. That is the end of it."

They rode on in silence before Calix finally asked. "You would give up your chance at safety? Travel to the pits of the enemy's territory? Just to be with me?"

"Yes," he said, squeezing the big man's chest, as much in affection as for grip. "And besides, there is Mestibes to think of! What is the life of a single man, even that of the *herald*, in exchange for a whole city?"

Calix turned, raising an eyebrow. "*That,* I don't believe."

"All right, fine. What about the fact I just discovered that I'm a therian? And I'd quite like to learn what that means from an expert?"

Calix snorted and snapped the reins, driving new speed. "More believable."

93

TEIGRA

Four sets of hooves pressed into the beach.

"Well, bugger me," said Elexis, taking it all in.

"Bugger me, indeed," said Zosime.

Ahead, the shore transformed into a tapestry of green and warm colors, as poppies of red and lilac and orange and yellow drifted away, eventually meeting a twisted forest beyond, shaded impossibly dark despite being in full sun. The forest itself stretched higher and higher —up the sheer incline of a mighty mountain, a single fang rising to thunderous clouds above, so dense and black that they hid the summit.

Vaticily.

The polity of fate.

A place filled with all manner of venomous serpents and ferocious predators.

And amongst them all would be the most dangerous predator of all: Xiber Feron. Warlord of Rinath. The woman who would see Mestibes burn.

"Ready, *Initiate*?" said Pikra with a mocking smirk.

Teigra gulped but found some comfort in the steed beneath her.

Three months ago, she would've sworn that she'd never ride again. In three months more, perhaps she'd look back on this moment and laugh that she'd ever been scared.

She stole a look at Zosime, who gave her a little wink. It made Teigra's chest flutter—like the most beautiful statue in the entire land had come alive and noticed her.

The newest Sister glared back at Pikra and returned the smirk. "Yes," said Teigra, cracking Varas's reins, reaching such a gallop that she had to turn and yell behind her. "But the question is, are the rest of you able to keep up with a *real* rider?"

94

AURELIUS

AURELIUS WRIGGLED AGAINST THE GROUND WITH WHAT LITTLE strength he still had.

"I would've thought the strategos's quarters would be more comfortable than this?" he said, the earth pressing against his ribs.

They had ridden as fast and as hard as they could—all through the night and all through the day. But now, as night once again fell and he could barely keep his eyes open, they needed rest. And so too did the damn horse.

Calix had set up the goat-skin tent in some abandoned field well off the road. It was meant for a single occupant, meaning that they needed to sleep together. They had a second tent, but neither of them had the strength or inclination to bother.

"A leader must suffer the same as his troops," said Calix, getting beneath the blanket that separated them from the green. His face was fucked. The bleeding had long since stopped, but the swelling had only just started. On the plus side, he'd said that nothing felt broken. At least, not *too* badly. "Believe me, grass is much better than some of the ground I've slept on."

The king of Ardora settled into the bed, facing away from

Aurelius, so they were back-to-back. Aurelius was sad about that but knew it was for the best.

He was surprised when, after fifteen minutes of stillness, Calix rolled over and put his arm over him. The big man nuzzled into the back of his neck, and Aurelius melted into the safety of his embrace.

The moment was broken when Aurelius felt the now-familiar twitch against his ass, as another tent joined their traveling party.

"This was a mistake," said Calix, his face panicked.

He made to roll away, but Aurelius stopped him, his fingers reaching back and digging into his wide, muscular hips. He desperately wanted to grind back against the bulge. To reach up and taste Calix's mouth. To join together in that wonderful, magical communion, no matter the consequences.

But with the greatest of efforts, and a mournful exhale, he didn't.

"I'm fine to stay like this if you are," he whispered. "I won't do anything. I promise."

Calix was still for long while. "You promise? You'll just ignore it?"

"It is impossible to *ignore*. But I will do my best to *resist*."

After a moment's hesitation, the big arms wrapped around him again.

"I love you, Calix," said Aurelius, as he moved contentedly back into his embrace.

"I love you too, Aurelius," said his king, the arm gripping him a little closer.

Eventually, the throb faded to calm. As did the two of them.

Then, with the leaves rustling above, and the certainty of a long day's ride ahead, they both drifted to sleep.

THE END

CONTINUE THE STORY TODAY

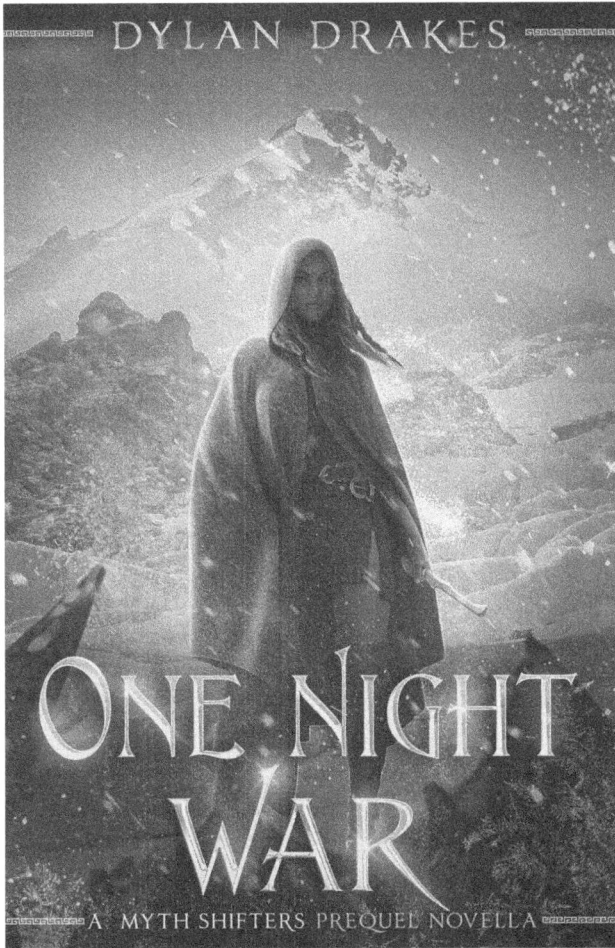

***ONE NIGHT WAR*: A PREQUEL NOVELLA**

~

A HERO RISES. A HERO FALLS.

For seventeen years, Dynosia has been at peace. And now that peace has been shattered. Xiber Feron, the ferocious Rinathi warlord, has invaded our island. Stolen our territory. Killed our people. And they will pay for that hubris.

As Ardor as my witness, I, Captain Calix Viralis, will take back Sama from the invaders. They will pay with their blood and their bones. In song and myth, it will be called the One Night War! The glorious night that we make Rinath scream for mercy!

With my Brothers at my side, my lover in my arms, and my sister, Zosime, lurking in the shadows, there is no way we can lose!

Or so I thought . . .

Set five years before the events of *Our Satyr Prince*, *One Night War* is the heartbreaking story of how Calix and Zosime's lives changed forever.

For Calix, this night is the origin of his therian affliction and the source of the emotional scars that haunt him to this day.

But for Zosime, it is the start of the journey of slaughter and sisterhood that will one day lead her to become a true legend.

LEAVE A REVIEW!

Hello, precious pixies, my name is Dylan Drakes, and I'm the author of *Our Satyr Prince*—which just so happens to be my debut novel! Thank you so much for taking the time to read the world and characters that I've created!

If you enjoyed the story of Aurelius and Teigra, I'd love you to leave a review (even if just a quick star rating). As a new author, it really is the biggest thing you can do to help other pixies find this story, and to help me grow the Myth Shifters world!

Reviews / Ratings can be done on Amazon or Goodreads.

Thank you enormously!

ABOUT THE AUTHOR

Dylan Drakes is a queer fantasy author from sunny Australia.

When not making mythological stories even gayer than they already were, he can be found with a controller in hand, cursing the existence of the Soulslike genre.

His other passion is his YouTube writing series *Genre Monster*, which explores the creative potential of random writing prompts, usually with disastrous results.

He also enjoys eating any and all carbohydrates, acting a total fool on his socials, and snuggling his cavoodle.

www.dylandrakes.com

instagram.com/thedylandrakes
tiktok.com/@thedylandrakes
youtube.com/@thedylandrakes

ACKNOWLEDGMENTS

It feels surreal to write an acknowledgements page to my debut novel. Because this is something I genuinely never thought I would achieve.

When I first came up with the idea for *Our Satyr Prince* (in May 2021), I was at my lowest ebb as a writer. At that time, I was seriously thinking of throwing away the pen and accepting that I just couldn't write a novel.

I have never struggled with story ideas (quite the opposite, I have a dozen a day and want to write them all), but the process of turning those ideas into reality always undid me.

Our Satyr Prince changed everything.

The idea was so immediate and the characters so intoxicating that I committed to making it happen by the end of 2021—no excuses. To do this, I worked on mastering the techniques that were preventing me from making my creativity concrete—plot structures and writing schedules in particular. I woke up at 4 a.m. every single day to squeeze a few hours of writing in before a ten-hour shift. I turned down more social events than I could count.

And it wasn't a struggle—the words flowed and the characters grew and it all just came together.

In November 2021, for the first time ever as a writer, I was able to type "The End" on a novel. It was a 192,000 word goliath, that would later be wrangled down to around 130,000. And it would be another year and a half before I plucked up the courage to release it into the wild, but at long last, I had done it.

I don't mind admitting that I cried that day. Just like I cried the first time I held my completed book in my hand.

The reason was that I finally had something to show people. To let them into my world. To allow them to meet the characters that had shared my dreams for so many nights.

Some writers yearn to be famous, or rich, or both. Neither motivates me. I am a world builder and a storyteller. I have no interest in following "hot trends" or "maximising story beats to enhance KDP page reads" (with zero shade to those that do—I admire the hustle).

What gets me up every morning, dark and cold and tired, is the knowledge that I am creating something that a small group of people might read and love.

Something that might speak to people, often ostracized and on the edge of society, who have never read a story quite like this. That might give them some little moment of escapism, with the full-queer-spectrum cast and rich worldbuilding that they wish they'd had growing up.

So my first acknowledgement goes to you, for reading this book (and reading all the way through the back matter like a fiend!). It is humbling to think that you have now met the world and characters and crazy drama that I created. I am so glad you did, and I can only hope you will stick with me as this series grows!

My second acknowledgment goes to my precious pixies on social media. I cannot fathom the kindness and the generosity that led to thousands of people following me and supporting me and offering me their voice and their energy and their platform—all before they had seen a single word of my writing.

At the beginning of this book, I said that I am only here because of you. And I mean that. Without my precious pixies I would not have had the courage to put myself out here like this. And this novel would have been left as a first draft in a drawer.

I cannot thank you enough for what you have done for me. I hope that we will continue to build our Pixie Party together for years and decades to come!

And my final acknowledgement is to Adam, my husband and a constant source of motivation and support. You were there for me when I thew out that first dumb idea, on a car ride to your mother's house, of "what about smashing together Ancient Greek, werewolf, and vampire mythologies, with sexy satyrs and sirens?" And you were still there for me over two years later, when I finally held the finished book in my hands.

From start to finish. From anguish to achievement.

I am your Aurelius.

And you are my Calix.

DETAILED CONTENT WARNING

Racial and Religious

Prejudicial language against fictional races and nationalities

Prejudicial language, including disparaging and harmful terms, and the practice of "othering," are common throughout the Myth Shifters world. For example, terms like "sea wolves" or "goatfuckers" are used to convey prejudicial views against people from other cultures and communities.

Additionally, prejudice between humans and nonhumans is a plot point in this novel. In particular, the subjugation and implied segregation of the giant population of Ardora is repeatedly referenced.

Queer

Bi-erasure

Calix Viralis, the primary love interest of point-of-view character Aurelius Savair, is a homo-romantic bisexual. Throughout the book, Aurelius fails to engage with the fact that Calix is also attracted to women, and almost universally defaults to assuming Calix is entirely homosexual.

Homophobia

Many societies in the Myth Shifters world are intolerant of nonheterosexual behaviour. Judgment, disparagement and persecution of homosexuality is frequently referenced in this book, and forms a major plot point.

This includes noting that the penalty for homosexual conduct in the polity of Ardora is death.

Mental Health

PTSD / reliving trauma

Although the term "PTSD" is not used in this book, two characters relive and reflect upon past trauma at various points in this story.

Calix Viralis, a former captain of soldiers, is directly responsible for the death of three men under his command, and relives the suffering of the day they died.

Teigra Cosmin, a former pegasus jockey, once participated in a race that resulted in her accidentally killing her father. The trauma this caused is frequently referenced throughout the story.

Sexual Content

Explicit Sex

- In *Chapter 1*, two male characters perform oral sex on each other.
- In *Chapter 5*, sexual intercourse between two male characters is fantasized about.
- In *Chapter 12*, a male character masturbates.
- In *Chapter 28*, sexual intercourse between two male characters is fantasized about.
- In *Chapter 36*, a female character masturbates.
- In *Chapter 39*, a female character masturbates.

- In *Chapter 44*, two female characters engage in sexual touching.
- In *Chapter 50*, two male characters engage in sexual touching.
- In *Chapter 72*, two male characters have sexual intercourse.
- In *Chapter 73*, two female characters engage in sexual touching.

Violence (inc. sexual violence) and Death

Death of a parent

Two characters in this story experience the death of a parent.

- Teigra Cosmin, a former pegasus jockey, once participated in a horse race that resulted in her accidentally killing her father at the age of fifteen. This does not occur within the timeline of this book, but is frequently referenced as a plot point.
- Another character witnesses their father's murder. This is explicitly described at *Chapter 86* and *Chapter 88*, and alluded to in subsequent chapters.

Domestic Violence (nonsexual)

- In *Chapter 9*, a young female character is assaulted by her brother. This event is also explicitly referenced in *Chapter 11* and *Chapter 67*, and alluded to elsewhere.
- The story also notes that this (and similar) family violence has been experienced by this character before.

Gore

- Monster viscera is described in *Chapter 20, Chapter 21, Chapter 87, and Chapter 89.*
- Human decapitation and / or dismemberment is described in *Chapter 86, Chapter 88, and Chapter 89.*

Sexual Harm

A central part of the Myth Shifters world is the existence of "therians"—halfway between a werewolf and a vampire in vibe, but the creature is from Ancient Greek mythology. These creatures "drink" various talents, desires, and abilities from their victims.

In *Chapter 72*, sexual intercourse occurs involving a therian. This sexual act involves the dominant partner "drinking" the passion and strength from the less dominant partner during intercourse, leaving the less dominant partner in a severely debilitated (near-death) state.

The less dominant partner eventually recovers.